A SONG OF WAR

Also Available

A YEAR OF RAVENS:
A NOVEL OF BOUDICA'S REBELLION

by

Ruth Downie

Stephanie Dray

Eliza Knight

Kate Quinn

Victoria Alvear

SJA Turney

Russell Whitfield

with an introduction by

Ben Kane

A SONG OF WAR

A Novel of Troy

Kate Quinn, David Blixt,
Libbie Hawker, Stephanie Thornton,
Victoria Alvear, SJA Turney,
and Russell Whitfield

With an Introduction by Glyn Iliffe

WILLIAM MORROW
An Imprint of HarperCollins*Publishers*

HarperCollins books may be purchased for educational, business, or sales promotional use. For information, please email the Special Markets Department at SPsales@harpercollins.com.

Originally published in ebook format by William Morrow in 2023.

FIRST WILLIAM MORROW PAPERBACK EDITION PUBLISHED 2025.

Designed by Diahann Sturge-Campbell

Library of Congress Cataloging-in-Publication Data has been applied for.

ISBN 978-0-06-331064-3

25 26 27 28 29 LBC 5 4 3 2 1

CONTENTS

CHARACTER LIST

TROJANS

Priam, king of Troy
Hecuba, Priam's wife, queen of Troy
Hector, their eldest son, prince and heir of Troy
Andromache, Hector's wife
Kabriones, Hector's charioteer
Hellenus, second son of Priam, born to a Nubian concubine
Cassandra, twin sister to Hellenus
Paris, Priam's favorite son
Deiphobus, Troilus, Polites, Cebriones, Polydorus, Lycaon: other sons of Priam
Aeneas of Dardania, a royal cousin, supposedly son of Aphrodite
Anchises, Aeneas' father
Creusa, Aeneas' wife
Chryses, a priest of Apollo
Chryseis, Chryses' daughter
Penthesilea, Amazon princess and ally to Troy
Katu, son of a Trojan warrior
Other Trojans: Coroebus of Phrygia, Dryops, Laoganus, Dardanus, Pelias, Iphitus, Tros, Acmon, Misenus, Iapyx

ACHAEANS

Menelaus, king of Sparta
Helen, Menelaus' wife, queen of Sparta, supposedly a daughter of Zeus
Hermione, their daughter
Agamemnon, Menelaus' older brother, king of Mycenae
Clytemnestra, Agamemnon's wife, Helen's sister
Iphigenia, Agamemnon's daughter
Orestes, Agamemnon's son
Talthybius, Achaean herald
Odysseus, king of Ithaca
Penelope, Odysseus' wife, Helen's cousin
Philoctetes, prince of Meliboea
Ajax, prince of Locris
Diomedes, king of Argos
Calchas, Achaean priest
Nestor, king of Pylos
Achilles, prince of Phthia, leader of the Myrmidons, supposedly son of a sea goddess
Briseis of Lesvos, Achilles' captive
Automedon, Achilles' charioteer
Patrocles, prince of Aegina, Achilles' companion and lover
Skara, concubine of Patrocles
Phoenix, captain of Achilles' Myrmidons
Neoptolemus, son of Achilles
Other Achaeans: Leitos of Plataea, Idomeneus of Crete, Antiphos of Trachis, Stichius of Boeotia, Eurypilos

INTRODUCTION

Glyn Iliffe

THE Trojan War is an early milestone on the winding path of Western culture. Hovering on the threshold between mythology and history—nobody can say for certain that it actually happened—it has inspired artists and writers of every kind for over three thousand years, and will do so for thousands more. There's something about those ancient tales of action, intrigue, romance, and treachery that has gripped people from generation to generation, demanding to be told and retold in ever-changing formats for ever-changing audiences. Just as compelling are the characters that move through the stories: Achilles, the sulking superman; Odysseus, the wily wanderer; and Helen, the wayward beauty whose looks inspired a war—to name just a few.

But what's the draw? Why don't these tales dim and lessen, like so many others have done? For me, it's the accessibility of the Trojan War myths. Although the stories come from a culture markedly different from our own, they take events familiar to the human condition and magnify them tenfold. How many fights have broken out over an attractive woman? Who hasn't suffered and railed against their god or gods? How many women have taken revenge on abusive husbands? How many prophets of doom have been ignored or mocked? And who hasn't faced a few obstacles getting home? Not that missing your flight and having to sleep overnight in an airport lounge compares to Odysseus' ten years at sea, but that's the appeal of a good story—it puts somebody else through the grinder so you don't have to go through it yourself. And the Trojan War was a big grinder.

The myths also have a depth not found in many other traditions. Each familiar story is built on lesser-known events, without which the main action would lack meaning. The characters appear and reappear throughout the different stories that form the whole, weaving a tapestry that makes them feel real. And there is a powerful spirituality that dominates everything. The immortal gods and their schemes form an immovable background, which the mortals must either accept or rage against and perish. This spirituality—the contrast between seen and unseen forces, the natural and the supernatural—has more meaning for modern audiences than we might think. Take the popular mythologies of our own age. Would the Star Wars universe be half as appealing without the Force, or Harry Potter nearly as exciting without witchcraft and wizardry?

Just as importantly, the mythology of the Trojan War is not the construct of a single mind. It's like a snowball rolling down a long but gentle slope, growing steadily larger as different eras add their own layers to the original and enrich it with new perspectives. *A Song of War* is the latest addition to that snowball, bringing something new and unique to an old narrative and helping us to see it through fresh eyes. It's the work of a group of very talented and quite different authors—following on previous collections—*A Day of Fire*, about the end of Pompeii, and *A Year of Ravens*, about Boudica's rebellion—who have collaborated to produce a story in seven parts. Each part is a whole in itself and can be enjoyed separately; but it is more rewarding to read them in sequence, following the characters and plot threads as they unify to create a bigger picture.

As the author of a series of novels about Odysseus, I have been fascinated by the approach of each writer in *A Song of War* toward places, events, and characters that I've been familiar with for several years, in the guises in which they appear in my own books. Unlike me, they've chosen to keep the gods out of sight and base their tale in the historical and political—though belief in the supernatural clearly shapes the attitudes and actions of the characters throughout. They have also recast the likes of Hector, Cassandra, Aeneas, and others in new molds, imparting fresh DNA to well-known characters that forces the reader to reevaluate their preconceptions and assumptions about them. This, of course, is essential and natural, or what would be the point of retelling the story? And without such additions and innovations the myth of Troy might not have endured.

Authors of historical fiction also have to take liberties with historical reality, too. Some modern conventions have been adopted in *A Song of War* that weren't used in the Bronze Age, such as measuring time in weeks. It is also worth stressing that mythology and historical fact are uneasy bedfellows. What we know about the Trojan War comes mostly from myth, and the most celebrated source of these myths is Homer, who is renowned for being a mishmash of different eras. Although authors should be historically accurate where possible, they should also be allowed some license. It's fiction, after all, and if the writer is restricted to relating pure facts, then his or her story will quickly become stale. The authors of *A Song of War* have told their own story of Troy, and they have made it original and exciting. I hope you enjoy it as much as I have.

THE FIRST SONG

THE APPLE

by Kate Quinn

Ah, might the gods make you the prize in a mighty contest, and let the victor have you for his couch!
Ovid, the *Heroides*

HELLENUS

SHALL I sing to you of Troy?

Shining Troy, windy Troy, many-towered Troy. The city of gold, gatekeeper of the east, haven of the god-born and the lucky. Aphrodite's sweet breath kissed every breeze that wafted over our gates; Apollo and Poseidon raised our mighty walls; we were ruled by a white-haired king wise as Athena, and defended by the mightiest heroes ever to stride the earth.

That is the story you want—but I am not the singer for that song. I am no hero, and I did not call Troy home, though it was the place of my birth. I hated its every brick and banner. Watching those fabled towers fade beyond the horizon of the sea, as sails bellied and oars splashed, I made a vow.

I will return only to leave again. That I swore as the seabirds cried overhead. One last task in the service of my father, the king, and then I was done. I would return only for my sister, my dark and shadow-haunted twin, and then the two of us would be gone from Troy forever.

That I swore. But instead there would be war, because the gods had other plans.

The gods and a woman named Helen.

MY moods could be as dark as my skin at times—those moods were a curse all Priam's sons shared, except perhaps Paris, who was made of bright copper and sunshine—but I loved the sea, and a voyage in the height of summer lifted even a somber soul like mine. With every oarstroke that pulled our ships away from Troy, my heart lightened. The winds came soft and sweet from the west, blowing us toward Sparta, and I rode the deck easily, savoring the salt wind and the sunshine. I could see my brothers doing the same on their respective ships, Paris, ever more burnished by the sun, and Hector, prowling the deck like a great dark-maned lion. Three princes riding three ships with painted eyes and hulls full of treasure: the song at least had a proper beginning.

"Sparta," Paris mused when we disembarked at the port in Gythio. "Is that the city where the women cut off a breast and grow beards like men?" He grinned. "Sounds like an adventure."

"I doubt you'll see any bearded women here," Hector rumbled.

"At least one single-breasted woman, then?" Paris pleaded. "Just one? You promised me excitement, and royal weddings are so damnably dull!"

"I did not promise you excitement," Hector reproved, but he was grinning, and so was I. Paris' charm was like ambrosia, heady and irresistible, and his never-ending ripple of jokes was a natural antidote to any dark mood. Even mine and Hector's.

"Sparta is the city where kingship comes from queens," a lighter voice laughed behind me. "Menelaus is king, but it comes through his wife. Someone will have to explain how *that* works, if only so I can tell Priam and see him *harrumph.*" Andromache stepped to her husband's side, small and bird-boned and barely up to Hector's vast shoulder. She was dusted all over in freckles like powdered gold, and her sand-colored hair flew everywhere in cheerful disarray. Cheerful disarray was my sister-in-law's usual state, paired with the infectious grin of a happy urchin. Hector, I knew, found it charming. His mother did not. Perhaps that was the reason for Andromache's greater than usual smile as she shook out her salt-streaked skirts without hearing a pained reproof of *You do not look very queenly, dear.* "I don't care if the Spartan queen has a beard as long as she offers me a bath."

"They've heard of baths, haven't they?" Paris grimaced comically. "Dear gods, what have we let ourselves in for?"

Hector gave a laughing warning of "Behave!" and we were off: a rolling array of chariots assembled from the bellies of our ships, followed by a string of donkeys laden with Trojan treasure: gifts for King Menelaus, our host in Sparta, and for the lavish wedding he was hosting for a royal cousin.

"What king is this girl marrying again?" Paris wondered when we halted to water the horses. "King of Ithaca? Who ever heard of Ithaca anyway? Any man with an island of three sand dunes and a few stingrays can call himself a king in these parts."

It was true—none of these little kings in the west could compare with Priam, our father, who considered them no better than pirates. He believed in reminding them of his greatness with lavish gifts at royal weddings, proving just how much gold he could afford to toss away to the pirate rulers of sand dunes and stingrays.

"Aphrodite's tits," Paris exclaimed when at last we reined up before the palace of Menelaus. "Hector, you wouldn't lodge your horses in that shed. Of course, you'd take one look at the palace at Olympus and decide it wasn't good enough for your horses . . ."

"He has you there," I told Hector.

He smiled, then turned serious. "Give Paris a helping hand during our stay if he needs it," my older brother murmured. "His first diplomatic visit—under all that joking, he's very anxious to do our father proud."

"Aren't we all?" I said lightly. To win and keep Priam's approval—that was a burden I'd seen stoop the shoulders of all my brothers. All but me, for I knew I'd never earn it.

Perhaps Hector guessed my thoughts, for he gave a silent squeeze of my shoulder. It was his way—to give comfort without words, to speak affection in a glance, to show fury in stillness. We think of heroes as loud crashing creatures, their reputations and the clatter of their weapons announcing their presence in every movement, but Hector approached everything from spear practice to common conversation with the same calm, reflective ease. His soul was warm, strong bronze to Paris' flashy copper and my own humble tin. And over us all, our father with his core of granite.

Only Paris acted unruffled before that stone gaze. He could make an irreverent face, the one he wore now, and even our father would laugh.

Hector handed Andromache down, and we advanced on the palace gates. Sparta was lovely country—rich hills furred with pines, brush rustling thick with boar and deer to be hunted, streams clear and bubbling—but the king's abode was a poor thing compared to Troy's massive palace atop the citadel. A double porch opened into a small courtyard, pillars of painted plaster rather than stone rising around us as we awaited our host.

Curious slaves and Spartan guards were already gathering, whispering behind their hands as they stared at the donkeys laden with gifts, at our heavy Hittite-styled chariots, at Andromache, who had tamed her hair if not her freckles and stood in full fringed skirts and gold bracelets. Hector bore the weight of eyes calmly, accustomed to being stared at: twenty-six and standing tall as any god, his shoulders massive under armor that alternated gold and bronze with silver and iron and studded with lapis lazuli. Paris, at nineteen, lounged in his blinding white tunic and upcurled shoes, running a hand through his oiled-back curls and returning the stares just as frankly, dropping his eyelid in a wink if any of the starers was pretty. And I braced myself for gaping of a different kind, for though I was the second of Priam's sons and born just after Hector, I was the least of them. And the darkest.

My mother was a Nubian, a princess given to Priam as a concubine to seal a truce with her father—she was dark as a night sky, so they said. I had no memory of her. She died birthing my twin sister and me, and we stood out darkly among Priam's other offspring, much ogled and pointed at. My sister would have garnered stares even had her skin been pale; she had beauty and fire, and to look at her was to see a torch burning to its base. I had nothing special about me; I was merely Hellenus, stockily built, modest in height, and modest in talents, too. I had no beguiling charm like Paris or hero's strength like Hector, no wily brain like Priam or unearthly beauty like my twin. A lesser prince, an ordinary man—that was me. But my face was dark, and so I was accustomed to pointing fingers and barely concealed whispers everywhere I went in Troy. *Does he bleed black?* people would mutter, staring curiously. *Do you think a sun-born spirit sired that one instead of Priam?*

I ignored the whispers, but my sister would whip around and say, "Nothing so gentle as a sun spirit. More like a daemon. Priam *is* the daemon!" just to see the reactions. I tried to hush her in such moods, for our father's displeasure was savage, but sometimes she wouldn't be calmed. She had clung to me weeping when I left her on this voyage, muttering, "Death begets death until only the flies and carrion remain." I'd held her till she calmed, telling myself that when I returned, I would take her with me away from Troy. From Troy, where the commoners stared at us as though we were curiosities, and our family—apart from Hector and Andromache and a few others—hardly considered us part of the palace at all. We were not housed with them; we did not dine with them; our brothers and sisters mostly ignored us. Priam only addressed my sister to harangue her, and he never summoned me unless there was some duty or service he thought I should be grateful to perform—like making up a third envoy to this Spartan wedding. No, few in Troy would miss my sister and me if we were to leave.

Only where would we go? To build any kind of home, I would need a king willing to shelter a pair of Trojan castoffs, and I knew of none who would risk offering a welcoming hand to mine for fear it would displease my father. Though I did notice, standing in the Spartan courtyard, that though my face attracted glances, I was not receiving the kind of open stares that were my lot in Troy.

There was a ripple then, and the doors of the anteroom parted. Our hosts appeared, the king and queen of Sparta, and I thrust aside my musings to examine them. Menelaus proved to be a short and stolidly built man with a crown of red hair that clashed against his purple robe, and a wide, perspiring face. His spear-slim queen towered over him by a head, towered over every man in that courtyard save Paris and Hector. I tilted my head to meet her eyes, Argive Helen, swan-born Helen.

And the gods began to scheme.

ANDROMACHE

THE mere sight of Helen of Sparta would make most women hiss and spit. I chuckled inwardly when I first laid eyes on her, having an immediate flash of what would happen if she stepped among my husband's sisters. Most of them would have narrowed their eyes like cats, claws coming out even as they cooed a welcome. As for my mother-in-law . . .

Well, that was when my chuckle faded. Hector's mother would have looked at Helen and thought, "That is what my son should have."

I didn't envy Sparta's queen her ivory skin, her long throat, or her pale gold hair falling in rose-oiled spirals nearly to her knees. I envied her the poise with which she gazed at our delegation, her perfect stillness as she watched her husband and Hector trade courtesies. She might have been a swan gliding on still water, allowing us to stare at her, knowing it was her right. In short, she was every inch a queen . . . as I was not. I was little and ordinary and rumpled, and moreover I'd always been happy that way; a wren with no desire to be a swan. But then Hector had chosen me a year ago, a freckled minor princess who laughed too much and squirmed restlessly if she was stared at for too long. He had chosen the wren when he really should have picked a swan.

I attracted my own share of looks as Hector brought me forward. "My wife, Andromache," he said in the Achaean language, which we all spoke well enough for the purpose of trade and diplomatic visits, different though it was from our Trojan tongue. King Menelaus' red face turned even redder at the sight of me, and an old man standing at his shoulder harrumphed. I flicked my glance to Hector, wondering if I had a spider in my hair or a seed in my teeth. He continued in the grave flow of courtesies, filling his princely role to his usual perfection, but on his other side, Hellenus' mouth upturned in a smile, reassuring me. By far my favorite of Hector's brothers. Paris was the charming one, but Hellenus was friendlier, a voice of warm, matter-of-fact welcome when I'd first arrived in Troy trussed up in impossible finery and desperate for someone who would talk to me like a mortal woman and not a goddess on a plinth. Hellenus had. I'd been glad to learn he would accompany us on this journey, though I knew Priam had only included him because Hector requested it. Priam did not seem to care much for his second son, though he should have; Hellenus had Hector's capable quietness, though it was the easy calm of an ordinary man, not the ocean-deep calm of a god walking the earth.

God walking the earth—ha! Perhaps I seemed a dazzled little bride to think such things about my husband, but he had that effect on absolutely everyone. I could see King Menelaus in his purple robe, eyeing Hector's lapis-inlaid armor and feeling a touch inadequate.

"My dear," he rumbled to Helen, who had not moved a whit in the entire exchange. "Perhaps you will escort Troy's future queen to the women's quarters."

Troy's future queen. After a year of hearing it, I managed not to laugh incredulously, though it was absurd. I had never been intended for such honor. I might have been born a princess, but my father was one of those kings Paris mocked, who ruled over a few villages and fields of goats. I was born and bred for humble things, for simpler palaces like this one rather than great walled citadels. So how in the name of all the gods had I become the future queen of Troy?

I still didn't know.

Hector gave a mute squeeze to my fingertips as I released his arm, and I followed Sparta's queen through the courtyard to another columned porch guarded by a pair of spearmen. Helen glided rather than walked; I barely reached her shoulder and felt like a scuttling urchin. We passed the guards, and both men gave me the same half-embarrassed, half-hungry looks I'd received in the courtyard.

"You're wondering why they stare." The words came suddenly, and I heard Helen's voice for the first time. Low and cool, perfectly detached, as though she were a goddess commenting without much interest on the affairs of mortals below—and she spoke in our Trojan tongue, very well indeed. "They are all wondering if the prince of Troy's wife is a priestess or a whore."

"*What?*" I stopped.

So did she. Her eyes traveled very slowly down me. Gray eyes, like old ice. "In Sparta, it is more often the priestesses and the whores who bare their breasts and risk tempting men."

I looked down at myself. Skirts layered with fringed kilts, gold bracelets winding about my bare arms, and yes, a snug scarlet bodice displaying my small freckled breasts. "Many respectable women of Troy dress so. But I'll don a shawl before we rejoin the men."

"We will not be rejoining the men." Helen resumed her smooth glide, leading me through an un-columned megaron with painted walls and a smoking hearth open to the sky. "My husband prefers me, and my loom-maidens, to keep to our own company in the women's quarters. For the most part anyway. I suppose I will be out and about a trifle more freely during the wedding festivities."

The king of Sparta sounded like a possessive husband. Though, of course, there were many such men in Troy, too; men who would not allow their wives to mingle in common crowds or public places where eyes might be covetous or tempting. I was fortunate my husband wasn't jealously inclined. The rooms opening up before us were pleasant, if not luxurious like my quarters in Troy, where every palace chamber was stuffed with luxuries from the east—here there were couches piled with fine woolen cushions, looms strung with half-finished weaving, slave women laying out platters of figs and olives—but I couldn't imagine spending *all* my hours here, as Helen apparently did. What on earth did the queen of Sparta do all day?

I asked her that as she gestured to a slave to bring me a basin of rose water. "I do a great deal of weaving," she replied, moving to the largest of the couches, heaped with purple cushions. "I supervise the slaves, and my loom-maidens tell stories and tend their children." A tilt of her head on that long, long neck. "Do the women of Troy do more?"

"I can't speak for all the women of Troy, but I am allowed to come and go in the citadel as I please." I smiled, splashing my hands with rose water as the slave washed and toweled my feet. "I receive Hector's messengers and deputations—I have a seal of my own for such occasions." It hung at my belt, heavy gold carved with Hector's sigil on one side, my own on the other.

Helen regarded it. "Menelaus would not allow me to have a seal."

"My mother-in-law has one, too. Most of the royal women in Troy do."

"Do you indeed?" Thoughtfully, she began to toy with a lock of rose-oiled hair. "How very grand."

"It's not all grandeur. I also help my husband feed and water his horses." My favorite hour of the day: both of us with hay in our hair, moving down the line of horses with wooden pails. Hector cupping his huge hands for the beasts to nuzzle, me telling a string of jokes for the pleasure of seeing that princely face dissolve into a common grin. When we were simply Hector and Andromache, not the future king and queen.

Helen laid a white arm along the couch, scrutinizing me. Hers was not an easy face to read; I had no idea what she was thinking. "I rarely travel," she said at last. "I have never seen my sister since she went to be queen of Mycenae; it would never occur to my husband to bring me on his journeys. But I see your husband saw fit to bring you here to this wedding. Do Trojan women often travel?"

"Some do." I moved to a couch of my own, taking the cup of wine the slave offered. "It's my first delegation. Hector said he would not be without me for even a month."

"An Achaean husband who said that would be called womanish." Another long stare. Helen never seemed to blink or clear her throat or shift her weight; she simply moved from one statue pose to the next. It wasn't *natural*, that stillness. I had no idea what to make of her, to know if I disliked her or not, but she made me want to fidget madly.

A little girl ran up to Helen's couch then, regarding me through strands of bright red hair. "My daughter," Helen said, stroking the hair, which was just like Menelaus'. "Someday she will be queen of Sparta, too. Forty suitors came to this palace to court me; I wonder if Hermione here will have as many."

"Forty? That's something to turn a girl's head."

"Not at all. They came to be king of Sparta, not lover to Helen. They came, they made some pretense that the choice was mine, my father maneuvered the resulting lottery, Menelaus moved into the palace that same night, and it was done. There is very little softness in these Achaean kings. They transact weddings as they transact war."

"Weddings go on for days and days in Troy." I smiled, remembering my own. "I was sent from my home in a huge procession of family and friends, and Hector must have dragged half of Troy to meet us. I was so in awe of him I could scarcely speak." Sometimes I still was.

She tilted her head. "You have not given him his heir yet, I am told."

I put down my wine cup. "No."

"Does he beat you for that?" A gleam in those gray eyes that might have been sympathy. "So many husbands beat their wives purple for failing to provide heirs. How that is supposed to warm our wombs is beyond me, but they still do it."

"Hector would never raise a fist against me. He's the gentlest of men." What a conversation this was—Helen was probing me, but I didn't know what for. "He doesn't wish me to breed yet. He worries I am too small to birth easily." I feared it myself but never admitted as much. My mother-in-law already thought me sadly unsatisfactory; how was I supposed to tell her what happened in my marriage bed and why my belly hadn't swelled yet?

"A considerate husband? Curious. In my experience, the only one husbands consider are themselves."

There was bitterness here, even if I couldn't hear it in that low, cool voice. "Not all men are so selfish."

Helen surprised me by laughing. "Don't you Trojans call our Achaean men little better than pirates? Sea wolves? No, don't blush and stammer; it's true. My sister married a ruthless man. My mother did, too. The forty suitors who vied for my hand were ruthless men, every one; the only way to stop them killing whoever won my hand was to vow them all to a pact to protect the winner should he call upon them. That was a thin rope holding them back; I still wondered if I'd see a bloodbath in the megaron when Menelaus won me."

"Is he a ruthless man?" I asked, thinking of that broad chest, ruddy face, and red hair.

"Yes." Helen's lips curved thinly. "That is all a woman can hope for: a ruthless man with a tiller."

"You are cynical." I kept my voice light. "Women can always hope for more."

A graceful shrug; she clearly did not believe me. She kissed the red head of her little daughter and sent her off again toward the nursemaid. "I am lucky to have my Hermione strong and healthy. I've never managed to carry another child to term, though Menelaus quickens me often enough. Your husband is right about the birthing bed; it's a hard, bloody place."

I tried to imagine marble Helen struggling and screaming to give birth and failed utterly.

"I always hoped I'd lay an egg like my mother, but I wasn't so lucky." Another smile, this one scornful. "Then again, Menelaus is no Zeus."

"An *egg*?" I said blankly.

"You haven't heard the tale? People whisper things of me. My mother was beautiful, so beautiful Zeus visited her in swan form. She laid an egg and bore me: Zeus' mortal-born daughter."

"A *swan*?" I laughed. She did look like a swan, but still, what a tale. "These stories do spring up, don't they? My husband's cousin Aeneas believes himself a son of Aphrodite—he's sure to tell you the tale himself when he arrives here from Dardania. He tells everybody; by now, we all sprint when we see him coming. Do people really believe some story that you're a daughter of Zeus?"

Helen didn't smile. "Who said it was a story?"

The moment hung in the air, uncomfortable. My smile faded. Helen's face was a mask.

The silence fractured as a group of girls blew into the room, giggling over armloads of flowers. Helen rose. "You have yet to meet my cousin, our bride who is to wed the king of Ithaca. Penelope, this is Andromache of Troy . . ."

Even as I came forward to greet the rosy-cheeked bride, I was still wondering about Helen. I still did not know if I liked her or not; if she was a woman who even *could* be liked or disliked. She seemed less a mortal woman than a statue of a goddess, so beautiful men spun tales that she was a daughter of Zeus.

I wondered if she truly thought she was one.

HELLENUS

"WILL we get another look at Queen Helen, do you think?" Paris said to me as we sauntered into the megaron. "I haven't clapped eyes on that long blond filly since the day we arrived, and those are flanks I wouldn't mind inspecting a second time."

"It's a wedding banquet, not a horse market," I retorted, but I couldn't help smiling. Paris had been fearsomely bored over the past ten days as we all waited for the rest of the wedding guests to trickle in. The last guest-king had arrived this morning—Agamemnon of Mycenae, Menelaus' elder brother, coming late to make the point of his importance—and Menelaus had announced that the official welcoming banquet would be hosted this evening. The painted plaster walls were hung with garlands of ivy, slaves carried platters of spiced olives and delicate octopus and roast venison, and more slaves twanged at lutes. I saw no sign yet of Helen, Andromache, or the bride. Apparently the women would not join us until after the feasting.

"We know how to celebrate in Sparta!" Menelaus waved us in with a broad sweep of his arm. "Even in Troy, you'll see nothing more stupendous!"

"Stupendous indeed." Paris grinned at the megaron, made garish by torchlight instead of clean-burning oil lamps, enough of the smoke lingering to sting the eyes despite the hole in the ceiling above the hearth. "Our Trojan goatherds feast every bit as well as this!"

I distracted Menelaus with a hasty gesture to the long dais, "The white-bearded fellow, he's a new arrival from Pylos?" as Hector clamped a brotherly hand around Paris' elbow and rumbled in a nearly soundless whisper, *"Behave yourself."*

"I only meant to joke. It's what I do." But Paris made a repentant face, perhaps aware that Hector was for once not amused, and moved out into the clusters of sea-lords and island kings to turn his charm on them. No one could resist him in such a mood, not even me, and I shook my head in reluctant admiration as I watched my younger brother win them over. He flitted like a butterfly, gold glittering at his fingers and at the hem of his short tunic, as Hector took his place beside Menelaus and I lingered alone with a cup of sweetened wine. Was there a king among these sea-wolves who would offer sanctuary to a prince of Troy seeking a new home? I toyed with the idea, half in jest and half in earnest. White-haired Nestor of Pylos, holding long dissertation over a pair of young warriors stifling yawns . . . Stolid Prince Philoctetes of Meliboea, gray streaks in his hair, said to be a great archer . . . Odysseus of Ithaca, the bridegroom, with his watchful eyes and wicked grin, chatting up our dour cousin Aeneas, who had arrived yesterday from Dardania. I'd known Aeneas all my life, but I wasn't going to apply to him for sanctuary; he was the greatest prig in creation and would undoubtedly say that nothing excused a son's filial duty. Then he would probably tell me all over again how his own father wooed Aphrodite herself, and how many times had I heard *that* old yarn?

"You're another son of Priam, aren't you, boy?" A voice boomed behind me. I bristled as I turned, for I was twenty-six and no one's *boy,* but it was Agamemnon behind me, king of Mycenae and leader among these sea-wolves, if they could be said to have a leader, so I inclined my head in a bow.

"I am, my king."

He waved me up: perhaps thirty-five, not fleshy as kings so often become through indulgence. This one was whipcord lean, a full two hands taller than I, wearing power light and easy as a cloak. He had gold on every finger, and those fingers were callused, still accustomed to spear and tiller. This one was a sea-wolf indeed, a cold, merry-eyed pirate.

He probed a little about my father's eastern alliances—the king of Mycenae was very keen to learn just how many ships Troy had recently sent to the Hittites to aid in their internal wars—but I parried those questions, and he changed course. "Is it true your father has fifty sons?"

"Nineteen from his queen. Myself from a concubine. Who knows how many in the slave quarters." There were no concubines after my mother—Queen Hecuba made certain of that—but Priam had sired children on uncounted slave girls.

"I've a daughter reaching the age to marry." Agamemnon swirled the wine in his cup. "Iphigenia would like that pretty princeling over there, if I brought him home for her."

He nodded toward Paris as though picking out a puppy to bring his daughter on a ribbon, the insult deliberate, but I saw something behind it. "You're fond of your daughter?"

"Guilty!" His grin turned genuine. "A king is supposed to favor his sons, but it's Iphigenia who can turn me round her finger. I want a golden prince like your Paris for her. You take it to your king, dark one. Tell him I'd make it worth his while."

He moved off without farewell, and I passed the rest of the banquet in quiet, fending off the occasional probing question about Troy's tin trade or the levies we would ask next year for passage through our straits to the east. That was the true reason we were here; not to give congratulations at a wedding, but to sow information and gather it in return. Hector did it strongly and straightforwardly, and Paris did it with charm and dazzle. I did it by watching and listening. No one notices the man in the shadows when he blends so well into the dark.

The torches were guttering by the time the banquet was reduced to roasted bones and crumbs. Wine and fruit were brought in, and as I plucked an apple from the bowl, the women were brought in to shouts of welcome, escorted to a dais of their own. I examined the bride, a rosy little thing in layers of scarlet and gold, darting glances at her bridegroom. Then came Andromache, freckled and laughing in sea green; I'd scarce seen her in ten days since she'd kept mostly to the women's quarters with the others. Finally, Helen of Sparta entered in a swirl of loom-maidens. Beautiful in her purple and gold finery, and I could see how men desired her, but I thought her cold. Paris was eyeing her appreciatively, making no effort at all to keep his eyes from roaming over another man's wife even when Menelaus' hand hovered possessively near her shoulder. I busied myself tucking the apple away.

The wedding gifts came in a stream, each lord rising to present his offering to the king of Ithaca and his bride. I saw Paris restraining a snicker at the offerings: jars of wine, lengths of fresh-dyed cloth, silver pins to fasten a tunic—all crudely made to Trojan eyes. Troy came last, and Paris acted as presenter, ushering each new addition to the pile with theatrical flourishes. There were rumbles of admiration at first: Agamemnon looked envious at the boar-tusked helmet, the carved horn, the ship's sail dyed in vivid stripes of crimson and black. Helen looked impressed at the elaborately carved ivory hand mirror, the alabaster cups, the gold brooches and bracelets. A loom was brought out of finest wood inlaid with bronze, and I saw King Odysseus' mouth flatten as he watched his bride run wondering hands over the shuttle. Clear as day, he was ashamed he could not offer his future wife anything so fine.

That was when I saw the smiles among the wedding guests begin to grow tight. The gifts of Troy were an embarrassment. Andromache saw it; up on her dais, I could see her chewing her lip as she looked down into her lap. By the time Hector entered with the last offering—a stallion and mare from our famous Trojan breeding stock, clip-clopping into the megaron on oiled hooves—the feast was choked with taut, angry greed as the sea-wolves stared at the contemptuous pile of wealth. I felt myself flushing and wondered how my wily father had miscalculated so badly.

Or if he had done it on purpose.

Hector didn't often miss such furious crosscurrents, but he missed them now. He'd slipped out before the gift-giving began so he could ready his beloved horses with his own hands; his eyes shone with the pleasure of sharing them as he began to point out their glossy coats and finely modeled heads, their strong legs. Paris stood grinning, but I rose with all the haste I could summon. "My brother can drone on about horses forever," I said with a smile that I hoped would rouse laughs. "But unless you wish to hear sire and dam of each horse back to the nineteenth generation, I suggest our good King Menelaus cut him off and call for wine."

A grudging rumble across the crowd, not entirely amused, and the king of Sparta lumbered to his feet. "We thank Troy for such splendid gifts," he said, and the bridegroom also managed a nod of thanks. "Give all compliments to my fellow king Priam."

It was the best he could manage, equating himself openly as Priam's equal, and I saw Paris' eyes sparkle with amusement, but Hector veered into the wind he now saw was blowing and made a graceful speech before leading out the horses. Pipes and lyres struck up again, a troop of dancing girls rushed in with fringed skirts lifting to show bare legs, and I exhaled as the shouts went up and the wine began to flow. An awkward moment had passed safely. I took an unusually fast gulp of wine and wondered again what my father was up to.

Paris seemed to be aware of the gaffe; he was lounging between Menelaus and Agamemnon, making himself charming and telling some long joke that had them both in fits of laughter despite themselves. "You're a silver-tongued liar, boy," Agamemnon managed to say, and Paris shook his head.

"On Aphrodite's perfect tits, I tell the truth."

"Who here's seen Aphrodite's tits?" That was a brute of a fellow named Ajax, a prince of Locris whose humor didn't rise above the tits-and-farts variety even when he was sober, and he was now falling-down drunk. I could see Queen Helen eyeing his vast slumping form with distaste.

"I've seen Aphrodite's tits, and I tell you, they're perfection." Paris grinned. "You want to hear the story?" A roar went up as the men sensed a tall tale. I couldn't help grinning as I saw my cousin Aeneas stalk out of the megaron with a face of stone outrage. I suppose no son likes to hear about his mother's tits.

"There was a glittering golden apple destined to belong only to the most beautiful goddess of all"—Paris plucked a barely ripe apple from a horn bowl, tossing it high—"and of course, all the goddesses of Olympus wanted it for their own!" He went on, describing the squabbling goddesses and poor henpecked Zeus, who could hardly be blamed for looking to a mortal man to take the punishment of deciding such a thing. "Who wants to get between *mortal* women when they're quarreling, eh?" My half brother had them all in the palm of his hand, and I reflected that perhaps my father had been shrewd to send him on this delegation, not just playing favorites. Paris had a subtlety and a wit neither Hector nor I could match when he chose to exert it.

"I hesitated to make my choice!" Paris was winding the tale up now, still tossing his apple high above one hand. "Flashing-eyed Athena, regal Hera—I trembled at their beauty! But Aphrodite dropped her gown on the grass, and great lords, I fell to my feet at the sight of those tits. For those tits, she won the golden apple, and she gave me my prize in return: the only woman in the world as beautiful as she!"

"Then she played you false," Menelaus chortled, red-faced with so much laughing. "For Aphrodite's only equal is my wife!"

"Indeed," said Paris.

Not everyone stopped laughing. Most of the megaron's occupants were drunk by then, too wine soaked for subtlety. Menelaus himself had missed the moment, too busy swallowing his wine and thumping the table for more. But I saw Agamemnon's wolf face sharpen, and so did the clever-eyed bridegroom's. For Paris had fixed his eyes boldly on the Spartan queen and ceased tossing his apple. With a smile, he offered it to her.

Queen Helen might as well have been marble. I searched those gray eyes for dislike or offense, but I could read no expression at all. I scrambled for words to cover the uneasy joke, and Hector rose as though to do the same, but Andromache beat us both to it. She plucked the apple from Paris' outstretched hand, laughing that merry laugh of hers like a bubbling stream. "You must save this for your daughter!" she exclaimed to Helen. "For if my brother-in-law is to have the loveliest woman in the world, then he must wait until Hermione is old enough to match her mother."

Clever Andromache. This was why I admired my brother's wife. She was not the queen his mother wanted for him; she was not regal or beautiful or stately, but she was *quick*. "Paris," I grinned, slapping his arm, "you sly one, angling for our host's daughter! Does our father know you aim for a Spartan bride?"

The moment passed. By the time I looked at Helen, she was shaking her head a little, taking the apple with contemptuous amusement at the outlandish compliments of drunken young guests.

I drank the rest of my wine in a gulp.

ANDROMACHE

"PROMISE me you will scold him till his ears burn."

Hellenus looked at me over his shoulder, and I saw the gleam of his teeth in the shadows. He didn't need to ask me who I meant, though it had been hours since Paris' little joke, and we'd both presided over those hours watching Hector brood, Paris swan on unfazed, and the rest of the wedding guests drink themselves into a stupor. The banquet was at last done; the warriors had stumbled off to their own quarters or collapsed in the megaron to sleep off their wine, and Queen Helen had retired with the bride and the loom-maidens. I'd lingered behind in the courtyard beside the guards and smelled the familiar scent of cinnamon that meant my favorite brother-in-law was nearby—the scent with which he oiled his rough hair into its warrior plaits. I wasn't surprised he had lingered in the shadows tonight. Hellenus was often the watcher; there wasn't much those thoughtful dark eyes missed.

"Hector has dragged Paris off to the stables under the pretext of seeing the wedding-gift horses settled," Hellenus said as I wandered to his side, voice soft and amused. "He is probably delivering a stern lecture by now."

"Good. We all adore Paris, but he's such a *child* sometimes."

"Says the maiden of seventeen."

"You know what I mean." At seventeen, I had an enormous place to fill; duties to learn, standards to live up to. Paris at nineteen could play on as a golden young prince forever—or until the gods brought some hard duty to his door.

I leaned against the wall beside Hellenus, the layered kilts over my skirt brushing his knee, my gold rings and fringes and bracelets chiming in the dark. "You're stacked in gold tonight," he observed. "I thought it made you feel weighed down."

"I'm trying to be a touch more like Queen Helen," I sighed. "Regal and queenly."

"You don't need to be like her."

"Yes, I do. Though part of me thinks she might be mad as a maenad. There's something not right about her."

"Was she offended by Paris' little joke?"

"I have no idea. She's about as easy to read as a statue. I suppose you're madly in love with her? Most of the men here are."

"I don't fancy bedding statues." Hellenus produced a small rosy apple with a flourish.

I took it with a crow of delight. "My favorite!"

"I managed to save it for you before that ape Ajax vomited into the fruit bowl."

We traded grins, and I sank my teeth into the apple with relish. I could relax my guard with Hellenus as I could with no one else, be the untidy cheerful girl I still felt I was rather than the young queen-to-be. Hector would not have chided me either for munching an apple like a child, he'd have been charmed—but I wanted my husband to be proud of me, not just charmed by me. He deserved a wife to be proud of.

In the faint moonlight, I saw the dark shape of Hector's shoulders coming across the courtyard from the direction of the stables and hastily set the half-eaten apple aside. "Is Paris suitably chastened?" Hellenus called.

"He meant no harm. He only intended to flatter the queen, he said. I told him to think before he flattered. It's his first diplomatic visit; he has much to learn." Hector reached his big hand through the darkness, and I felt the heat of him burning me as our fingers linked.

I had spent ten days and nights in the women's quarters, keeping the queen of Sparta company, and my own blood flared in response. I think even Hellenus felt the heat through the dark because he rose with a wry, "Good night, Brother."

Hector was not demonstrative in his public affections; it would not have been dignified in a prince. He did not touch more than my hand as he led me to his chamber, even though the palace was dark and there was no one to watch. But as soon as the doors closed, his mouth closed on mine, and he crushed me back against the wall, big hands winding through my hair. "I have missed you," he breathed as my jeweled diadem slid to the floor.

"I've missed you," I murmured back against his lips, and we never made it to the bed. He lifted me up in those strong arms, pinning me between the wall and his broad chest, pushing my heavy skirts out of the way as my limbs clung around him. We drank each other down, openmouthed and lingering, moving together in the dark, until the end when he pulled sharply away before he could spend himself inside me.

He had done that since our very first night together. In our bridal bed high in one of Troy's vaulted towers, my wedding flowers crushed and fragrant on the floor, I had lain against him in the fading glow of my tentative new pleasure, suddenly terrified I had somehow displeased my husband of one day. Hector had raised himself on one elbow, curving his huge hand around my face and answering my unasked question simple and direct: "My mother has borne nineteen living sons, and I've seen it age her before her time. And you're a tiny thing, Andromache. I won't risk you in childbed too soon."

"But you need heirs," I'd managed to say. To be a fit mate for a prince, I must be a mother to his sons. I'd known of no husband—none—who put his wife's health above such a concern.

But Hector only smiled, his hand moving over my hair as he'd stroke the mane of a nervous mare. "I have almost twenty brothers. Heirs can wait."

And even now I was relieved that he continued to spare me, even as the relief made me guilty. I was seventeen and still small, and part of me did not feel fit to be a mother of kings.

Hector laughed now as he set me on my feet. "Making love against a wall and not in a bed! Ten days among the Achaeans and I've turned barbarian."

"Maybe they'll think better of you for it?" I suggested, finally shedding my crumpled skirts.

"Perhaps. They already think me womanish for doting so on my wife."

I laughed, too, and soon we lay curled together in bed. "There's hardly room for the two of us," Hector complained.

"Soon we'll be back in Troy. Our tower bed, open to the moon." His hand slowed as it moved across my shoulder, and though I kept up my flow of chatter, he gradually fell silent.

With dread, I saw him frowning toward the ceiling. *Not again*, I thought. *Not again!*

I put my palm to his close-bearded cheek and turned his face toward me. "What ails you?"

"I hate to be so far from home," he said, simple and direct, as always. "Take me outside the Scaean Gate, and I grow chilled in spirit."

"We return to Troy soon," I cajoled.

A brief smile. "Yes." But his eyes were dark and restless, moving over the ceiling as if looking for Troy's towers, and I felt a familiar clutch of worry. It was not only homesickness that could move Hector to such moods—it could be the death of a new colt, the lightning displeasure of his father, the bad omen of an eagle passing over Troy's walls, or sometimes no reason that I could see. All I knew was that there were nights I woke to find my husband sitting sleepless on the edge of our bed, hands clasped between his knees as he stared into some nameless anxiety. "Worry likes to sit on my shoulder at times," he said now, making light of it, but sometimes it was days before these moods of formless sadness took themselves away.

You should be brave, I thought. *Go into the darkness with him and drag him out.* But I had no idea how to do such a thing, so I fell back on old habits and became playful, pinching his arm. "Shall I make you smile?"

His hand squeezed mine, but he made no answer, continuing to stare up at the ceiling.

"I think all these Achaean kings we saw tonight aren't sea-pirates, they're wild beasts. Can't you see old Nestor of Pylos as a molting eagle, thinking himself so high and wise? And Ajax as a great ox, lumbering about with his head hanging. Odysseus is clearly a fox, that wicked grin of his . . ." I chattered on, imitating the wedding guests mercilessly, feeling my heart sink as Hector continued to stare at the ceiling. Sometimes my funny chatter worked, winning a reluctant smile as he began to shake away the storm clouds. But sometimes it did not, and tonight was a night when all my jokes won only a deep sigh as he rolled over and took me in his arms. "You dear, funny thing," he murmured, wrapping me tight against his chest, and I could hear the love in his voice. An emotion as broad and uncomplicated as a calm sea, but I did not understand it.

I am not fit to be the future queen of Troy, I thought as he slid into sleep. *I am not fit to be the mother of your sons. I cannot even banish the clouds when you are sad. Why do you love me at all?*

HELLENUS

CONSIDERING that a wedding is an occasion for joyful celebration, it is astounding how few of the festivities are friendly—at least where kings gather as guests. Perhaps if it were a gathering of goatherds, the competition of foot races and spear throwing would have been good-natured. Perhaps a cluster of smiths would have risen from the wrestling bouts laughing when they were bested. And had it been lowly spearmen trooping out for a lion hunt, perhaps there would not have been dark looks when the man who brought down the lion with a single spear thrust was the same man to win the foot races, the wrestling matches, and the spear throws. After another ten days of competitions, contests, and other displays of skill, I had some advice for my elder brother.

"Sprain something today," I told Hector bluntly, coming to his quarters, where he was rubbing down his great bow for the afternoon archery match. "Let someone else take the victory wreath for once."

One of Hector's rare smiles—even rarer here in Sparta, where I'd frequently seen him brooding over the past few days. "These are games of skill," he said mildly. "If I win, don't I honor the gods? Isn't that the purpose, to attract the gods' favor to the wedding?"

He was teasing, I knew. "Honor our father instead by coming home with your skin intact. Win the archery bout today on top of all your other victories, and one of these sea-wolves will likely plant a wheel-spike in your back."

Hector studied me. "I think you rather like these sea-wolves, Hellenus."

"Barbarians," I scoffed.

"Barbarians who do not stare at you quite as much as our citizens at home."

I glanced up. He held my eyes. I shrugged.

He folded his great arms across his chest. "I know it is not easy for you in Troy." Quietly. "It is not your face that sets you aside, truly. It is our father. I wish he valued you as highly as he does his sons from his queen."

I looked down, checking his bowstring for soundness.

"Never doubt that I value you, Hellenus. Things . . . will change."

"How?" I asked. "You cannot make our people cease staring, and you cannot make me anything but the son of a concubine."

"But men can be punished for not treating a prince of Troy with the honor and respect he deserves. I regret that our father does not see you as a true prince of Troy and that others take their cue from him. But our father will not always be king."

It was the closest he would come to saying someday Priam would die, and then things would be done Hector's way. I wondered for a moment what that world would look like for me, for my sister: a world with Hector as king. A world where I was welcomed into the family that excluded me unless it wanted something and shunned my sister altogether.

But our father had lived more than fifty years and looked hale enough to last fifty more. I could not wait that long for a new world, not if I had to spend those years watching—

"We'll be late to join the rest of the archers," I said before I could conjure up images of what exactly I did not want to see.

"Then we'll be late." Hector took the bow and laid it aside. "I believe I sprained my ankle running after that lion yesterday.

Give me your arm to lean on, and we'll go cheer for Paris. He's a better archer than me anyway."

The training ground at the Spartan palace was large, well-sanded, stocked with weapons both wooden and bronze. For the wedding festivities, the pillars and posts had been draped with ivy and ribbons, and seats had been set along the highest wall so the women could watch, Andromache and Helen flanking the bride. The archers were already jostling and shoving, challenging each other in edged, friendly voices, comparing their bows. Odysseus flashed a strange double-curved bow while old white-bearded Nestor of Pylos held forth on the superiority of Cretan bows. "In my day," he trumpeted, latching on to my arm, "there was none of this double-curve nonsense and none of these ibex monstrosities, either. Wood and sinew was good enough for any king . . ." I let him batten my ears for a while, jaw tightening in an effort not to yawn, and finally slid away before I fell dead of boredom. I saw Andromache's shoulders shake up on her high perch. She always could see through my polite masks.

The targets were set out, and the men jostled into line. Shafts flew. King Menelaus went red as his hair to be eliminated in the first round, as were a dozen others who all retired loudly saying that a bow was no warrior's weapon anyway. "Give me a spear, and you will see blood like rain," Menelaus grumped, settling into his ornate chair beside Helen, and I wondered why I thought she despised him because her face never moved.

I lasted another round, but I was no Apollo with a bow. It all came quickly down to two: Paris, laughing and playing to the crowd, and Philoctetes, the sturdy middle-aged prince of Meliboea, with Odysseus and his fox grin a distant third.

Philoctetes took aim at a target hardly bigger than a pomegranate, and Paris tossed jeers from the side, trying to throw off his concentration. "Getting tired, Prince? I see that old arm starting to shake!" But Philoctetes' shaft flew sweet and true.

"We'll see who's getting tired," he growled as he made way for Paris. Philoctetes was older than many of the sea-lords here, perhaps thirty-five with a gray-shot beard and an archer's callused fingers. "You've got so much oil in that hair, boy, I'm surprised you can lift your head to see the target."

Paris was quick, loose, careless—he shot as though he'd barely looked at the target, though he split it down the center. "I can plant a shaft wherever I want it, old man. And I know where *you* want it." With that he turned and flipped the other man's tunic with the tip of his bow, giving everyone a flash of Philoctetes' buttocks. "That's where you'd really like my shaft, eh? Pity you're too old to be anyone's mattress anymore."

Philoctetes' broad face darkened in sudden fury. I'd seen him at banquets with a handsome young spearman of perhaps sixteen; it was common enough: an older warrior showing a beardless youth the ways of the bed and the world. To imply it went the other way around, a bearded warrior playing the woman's role for a youth . . .

For once, I was not remotely charmed by Paris' wit. I wanted to choke him with his bowstring.

"Please," he continued to Philoctetes, grinning. "Take your shot."

I thought for a moment the graying prince would put his arrow between Paris' eyes. Hector, I could see, was trading words with Agamemnon along the far wall; he could not have heard the insults under the rise of hoots and claps going up from the watchers. I could have stepped forward, but I stayed where I was. I had already pulled Paris and his incautious tongue from trouble during the first banquet. It occurred to me that perhaps what my charming half brother needed was the drubbing Philoctetes clearly had in mind.

But he ruled himself and turned his bow to the target, and after that the shots came fast and thick. The shouts and jests among the watchers faded away under that fierce concentration, both princes deadly determined to win as the targets grew smaller. Philoctetes wore a face like wood, and Paris' mockery redoubled as he swaggered and bowed to the watching women after every shot. Andromache looked exasperated. Queen Helen was leaning forward, gray eyes narrowed.

I didn't know how long it could continue before it went to bloodshed, but the king of Ithaca put an end to it. "Let us change the game before you're shooting at targets no bigger than splinters," he called at last. "A simple shot, but with this double-curved bow of mine. Put an arrow through a row of axe rings."

"That's too easy," Philoctetes objected. "When we both make it, who wins?"

Odysseus grinned. "You'll see."

He set up the shot, and compared to the targets they had hit, it *was* easy: a shaft through a straight line of axe-handle rings. "To the victor," Odysseus said, handing his unstrung bow off to Paris.

My brother bent the bow, trying to re-string it, but it writhed in his hands. He could not fit the string over the horn tip, no matter how he flexed the shaft. "What kind of trick is this?" he said, trying to laugh it off, but I could see anger glint in his gaze. Above all things, Paris hated to look the fool.

"There's a special way to string a double-curved bow." Odysseus grinned. "Do you know it?"

"No, damn you, I don't!"

"Well," the bridegroom said. "That's a pity."

Philoctetes tried his hand, but with no more success: the bow wriggled like a snake, refusing to be strung. He flung it to the ground in disgust, and in one movement Odysseus gathered his weapon, flexed it under one knee, and between hands and legs bent it to its double-curve and strung it. He whipped an arrow through the axe rings, and took his bow as the shaft stood quivering in the post behind. "I win."

"That's a low cheat." Paris' cheeks flushed, and I found myself perversely enjoying the sight of him jolted out of his charm. "No better than one might expect from a pirate."

"A pirate who has just won the prize for his bride," Odysseus said, not offended in the slightest, and bounding up to the high dais, he claimed the gold bracelet that had been set as prize and slid it with a kiss over his future wife's hand. A ripple of mingled laughter and disapproval went over the watching warriors, but the laughter won out. No one liked a trickster, but even less did the watching kings like the pretty prince of Troy, so applause drowned out those like white-bearded Nestor who huffed, "In my day such tricks were seen as shameful."

Philoctetes took it graciously, clapping Odysseus' shoulder when he rejoined the men, saying, "Well shot, m'lord king." But Paris collected his own ibex bow aside with an oath, shaking off Hector's placating hand on his arm and heading for his own quarters. The low, cool voice of Queen Helen stopped him.

"Son of Priam," she said from her dais, brilliant in yellow skirts and beaten gold bracelets. "Well shot."

He looked over his gleaming shoulder and approached the dais. "Hardly, my queen. I hate to lose."

"Do you?" Her lips had a double curve like Odysseus' bow. "I would not know how that felt. I have never had the luxury of winning."

"Oh, my lady, I think you have won much today."

A quick exchange, almost lost in the noise of warriors already bored with the overlong archery display and now clamoring at King Menelaus for a deer hunt. I doubted many noticed the silence that fell between my brother and Sparta's queen for an instant. Paris stood with his shoulders thrown back, looking her over with the kind of deliberate crude appraisal he might have used to size up a shepherd's daughter. I thought Helen would dismiss him with her cold scorn, but she held him in her gaze an instant, and for the first time I saw those ice-gray eyes kindle into brilliance.

Just an instant. Paris bowed, Helen flicked her fingers, and he was shouldering back toward his quarters, Hector in pursuit and no doubt lining up another stern brotherly warning. I looked at Queen Helen, immobile and bored on her dais with Andromache, and unease crawled in my stomach.

I wondered if I had imagined it.

Well, even if I had not, what of it? A harmless flirtation at a wedding—it is what weddings are for. Revelry and love are in the air; you bed your host's servant girls and perhaps get misty-eyed over one of his prettier daughters or concubines, and then on the voyage home any rosy regrets sigh away on a sea breeze. Aphrodite worked too hard at a wedding, busying herself with bride and bridegroom, to plant her darts deep in any of the guests. Paris desired Queen Helen, but so did most of the men here. They did not act on it, nor would he.

My charming younger brother was, for all his fecklessness, too clever to be such a fool.

ANDROMACHE

"TELL me of your brother-in-law," Helen said the following afternoon.

"Hellenus?" I prepared to bristle, knowing how people liked to stare at my husband's half-Nubian brother, but Helen shook her head.

"Paris," she said, and her ice-colored eyes had a speculative gleam.

I paused, wondering how to answer. It was a more raucous day than usual in the women's quarters, as our morning had been enlivened by the arrival of some strange wedding guests: a pair of Cimmerian princesses in an entourage of black-clad guards, almond-eyed, olive-skinned girls with jingling headdresses of silver discs and spears at their sides, grandly announcing in their thick accents that, as a dynasty descended from Zeus, they came to offer gifts for the cousin of Zeus-born Helen. I hid my urge to laugh in a convenient coughing fit, but Helen greeted the Cimmerians graciously and invited them back to her quarters to join the weaving. "Amazons," the derisive whisper had gone through the Achaean kings, eyeing the princesses hungrily. "They cut one breast off at womanhood and train with spears like warriors!" I saw no evidence either princess had cut a breast off—what imaginations men have!—but they certainly seemed better fit for weapons than weaving. The elder princess was poking dubiously at her loom and trying to look like she knew what a shuttle was, but the younger—Penthesilea, a girl of perhaps sixteen—had given up altogether and was chasing Helen's red-haired daughter all over the courtyard, yelling strange war cries.

"Your brother-in-law Paris," Helen said again, passing her shuttle through the threads of her loom. "I heard he was not raised in Troy."

"No, he was born under an ill omen. Our priest of Apollo said he might bring down Troy someday, so it was advised he be put out to perish as an infant." I grimaced. "Priam thought to have him killed, but his queen begged mercy, so Paris was sent to foster with shepherds."

"Obviously, hc did not stay in a shepherd's hut."

"At fourteen, he made his way to Troy. It was Hellenus' twin sister who recognized him for who he was." I neglected to say Paris had been on the point of being slain as an intruder in the temple of Zeus. Paris owed his half-Nubian sister a great deal for being so sharp-eyed, but he seemed to take his luck entirely for granted. "He had such charm, even as a boy—once he was recognized, my father-in-law relented and welcomed him back as prince."

"Mmm," Helen said.

I eyed her, stringing my own loom without much skill. "Why do you ask?"

I knew perfectly well why she asked. I'd seen the gleam in her eye as she looked at Paris after yesterday's archery display. He'd stood straight and handsome as a young Apollo, golden in the sunlight. The attention between them did not really disquiet me; all women admired Paris—but I should let her know her gaze had been noticed. Some husbands did not want even their wives' eyes wandering, and red-haired King Menelaus was clearly of a jealous temper.

"Prince Paris is pretty," Helen said, her directness surprising me. "I wondered if there was anything behind such a pretty face."

"Sometimes I wonder," I said just as frankly. "He's Priam's favorite, and he can joke his way out of anything, but he's too fond of stirring up trouble." Someday he'd stir up a mess his charm couldn't get him out of, and then he'd have the surprise of his life. Yesterday I wondered if Prince Philoctetes might be the one to finally teach Paris a lesson. Part of me wished he had. For someone so eager to earn his father's approval on his first diplomatic voyage, Paris was behaving recklessly.

"Does Priam plan a bride for Paris?" Helen asked. "My husband has some idea of betrothing him to our Hermione." Helen's eyes traveled to her red-haired daughter, who gripped a stick and was squaring off with young Penthesilea. The Cimmerian girl's laugh was a raucous shout, but her callused hands were patient as she corrected the little girl's grip. "Not so tight, little one, don't strangle your spear!"

"Paris is not betrothed. Though Agamemnon has also proposed his daughter Iphigenia as a bride." Maybe I'd mistaken the gleam in Helen's eyes as she looked at Paris—perhaps it was as a son-in-law that she evaluated him.

"Paris would not make Hermione a bad husband, I think," Helen said. "If he would keep her his sole wife and not wed Agamemnon's daughter, too, as a rival for her. Do the princes of Troy take concubines?"

I again had the sense that Helen was probing and gave my shuttle a yank. "It is not usual for Trojans to take concubines, no."

"Your Priam did, if he fathered that dark one."

"And my father-in-law found it was not worth the strife in his palace."

Helen lifted pale brows, inviting gossip, but I held my tongue. I did not trust her enough for confidences, and Hector had told me in confidence of his mother's rage when Hellenus' Nubian mother joined the palace. "When she died, my father swore there would be no more concubines," my husband had said. "Only slaves who were no threat to a queen."

Will there be slaves in your bed? I'd wanted to ask Hector, but I did not. Of course there would be. I would simply have to look the other way, as all wives did.

But Hector had read my mind. "There will be no slaves and no concubines for me, Andromache. Even the slave girls give my mother offense, much as she hides it. I will not see you hurt the same way."

I sighed. I was the luckiest of women; I knew that. But if my husband continued to spare me childbearing, his mother was going to start hinting he take another wife to bear him sons. How was I supposed to tell her I wasn't barren, and tell him I was fit to give him sons, when neither would believe me?

If you have no children, you'll be easier to set aside. The thought whispered, a leaden, poisonous dread. *You aren't fit in any other way for your position—when Hector's passion cools, you'll be replaced by someone dignified and fertile and suitable.*

No. I pushed that thought away, not for the first time. My husband would never have taken me to wife with such a thing in mind. But I wondered if that was why Priam had let him wed me, unsuitable as I was. *Let him plow the girl and grow tired of her; she's easily replaced.* My father-in-law could easily plan such a thing. Even perhaps suggest to Hector that I be spared childbirth for a while to ensure his grandsons came from a better broodmare than me?

Helen was gazing at me, curious. I gave a bright, meaningless smile, holding up my shuttle. "See what a tangle I've made! I should take lessons from your cousin Penelope here." The bride stood at Helen's other side, hands flying twice as fast as either of us as she worked at her own weaving. "My, how quickly you work."

The girl nodded. I'd grown to like her very well in these past weeks: a bright-eyed, rosy little thing of fifteen with a sharp wit under her quiet demeanor. "I'm making my betrothed a cloak," she explained. "Striped in the colors of Ithaca."

"You have a tight hand and a good eye." Helen looked over the nearly finished cloak. "Such care! I never saw the point in becoming an expert at the loom when one has slaves to do the household weaving."

I wondered if that was a barb at her cousin, who would be queen of a much poorer household than this, but Penelope only grinned.

"It's to a woman's advantage to weave well, not just for her husband's convenience. Weaving keeps a woman looking busy but leaves her mind free to scheme with no one the wiser."

"You already intend to scheme against your husband, then?"

Another of Helen's cynical laughs. "And here I thought you were quite content with your bridegroom."

"Oh, I am. I shall scheme *for* him, if he ever needs it. Men may not know it, but they need wives with fast wits as well as good weaving hands and wide childbearing hips."

"Clever girl," Helen approved. "I hope my daughter grows up as clever someday."

We all looked at little Hermione, who was begging for a turn with Penthesilea's spear. The Cimmerian girl was demonstrating the proper throw, her shoulders lean-muscled like a warrior's, loose trousers showing under her skirts. "Put your hips into it as well as your arm, and it will fly like an eagle!"

Unexpectedly, Helen looked envious. "When I was a child, I was allowed to wrestle with my brothers in the training yard and even train with their arms . . . I wish I had never given it up."

I could not imagine Helen sweating and covered in training-yard sand any more than I could imagine her in a birthing bed or lying under Menelaus. I was trying to frame a response when young Penthesilea approached her elder sister with a quick whisper and then came to Helen in a careless light-footed swagger. "I'm no good for a loom," she said in her abrupt, thickly accented voice. "I'm going to join the men at the training ground and show them how an Amazon throws a spear."

"They do not compliment you when they call you an Amazon," Helen observed.

A grin from Penthesilea, crinkling her almond eyes. "Then they will be even more shamed when I beat them. Though I may not beat your prince," she added judiciously, looking at me. "He is *very* good."

I stifled a smile. Helen looked speculative. "Perhaps I might accompany you. It has been a long time since I entered a training ground to participate and not merely watch. My husband would not be pleased if I joined the men, but perhaps we might try spears at a private target . . ."

Penthesilea laughed carelessly. "You'll roughen your hands, my queen." She bowed and was gone in a jingle of silver disks. Her elder sister trailed after her, looking exasperated, and I looked up to see a flare in the Spartan queen's gray eyes.

"Helen?" I said, using her name for the first time.

Her gaze slid down to me, blank as a wall. Why did I think that flash had been fury? She clearly felt nothing at all beyond her remote amusement, her distant cynicism. If that was the price of goddess-like beauty, I was glad I had none.

"Tell me more of Paris," she said, returning to her loom. I shrugged and told her of his first audience with Priam when he'd been accepted back as a prince of Troy, feeling no danger from her curiosity about my handsomest brother-in-law. Paris liked hot-blooded women, not marble statues.

"Are you so certain?" Hellenus asked me late the following evening as we lingered in the courtyard under a half-moon, waiting outside the megaron for Hector to finish listening out young Diomedes of Argos in some bit of bombast about someday bagging a lion for a cloak. "I saw how Paris looked at our Spartan queen after the archery was done. He wants her."

"He wants everything in skirts," I said tartly.

"True enough." My brother-in-law leaned against the broad pillar, tracing the bright plaster with one finger. Painted horses pranced in a frozen parade—even in paint, the horses were small and scrubby, not like our proud Trojan stock. Hellenus must have been thinking of the horses, too, because he said, "Hector offered to train one of King Menelaus' colts tomorrow."

"Perhaps working with the horses will lighten his mood. The

stables always cheer him." I peered at Hellenus through the dark, worry rushing back to the pit of my stomach. "He's been brooding since we left Troy."

"All the sons of Priam are victim to such moods, Andromache. The bane of our house."

"What do I do?" I heard myself ask because I felt sometimes like Persephone married to Hades: a goddess of spring finding herself linked to a somber lord of shadows. I said some of this to Hellenus, twisting the fringe of my layered kilts between my fingers, and he listened with quiet attention. "A girl who only knows how to pluck flowers and laugh isn't a match for a dark-mooded lord," I said, trying to make light of it.

"Perhaps Hades wanted Persephone *because* she was a creature of flowers and laughter."

"Perhaps he should have chosen a mate who could face the dark as well as he and left Persephone to her flowers and her silly jokes so she could be claimed by an ordinary man." I looked up at my brother-in-law, suddenly curious. "Who jokes you out of dark moods when they descend?" I didn't think his poor, troubled twin sister could be much use there.

The brief gleam of his teeth as he smiled. "Ah, but my moods don't pass! So I don't need to do a thing."

I bit my lip. "Hellenus—"

"No pity, Andromache. Please."

What to say? I didn't know, only that I had no skill to cheer my husband *or* his brother. A queen like my mother-in-law, like Helen, would know what words put fire into a man's heart in dark moments. All I could do was muster a scolding tone and take Hellenus to task. "Your plait is coming loose."

"Fix it for me?"

He turned, and I neatly retied the leather lace that fastened the end of his tight warrior's braid. I smelled cinnamon again, the oil with which he plaited his hair. "I always liked that scent of yours. Paris prefers oil of lotus."

"Paris smells like an Anatolian whorehouse."

I laughed. "Why cinnamon for you?"

"The slaves say my mother always wore it—something she brought from her homeland. It's the only thing I know about her."

"She would have been proud to see the man you grew to be."

"Would she? I'm no great warrior or seer or diplomat, after all. Quite ordinary."

He turned back as I finished with his plait, and I linked my hand through his arm. We stood silently, waiting for Hector, and I thought of all those swaggering would-be heroes who filled the megaron every night with their tall tales and their boasts. My quiet brother-in-law in all his ordinariness was worth more than all of them put together.

HELLENUS

A storm of hooves and sand. A colt's black mane tossing. Hector standing perfectly still, holding out a hand.

It was something rare, watching my brother with an unbroken colt. He used no whip, just a little grain, a few soft words, and an ocean of patience. Even the raucous sea-kings had quieted, watching from the edge of the training yard.

Andromache had a seat on the dais beside Helen, as usual—and between them sat Paris, which worried me. He'd bounded up ostensibly to offer his sister-in-law a dish of grapes, but then he'd lingered, lounging as he told the Spartan queen some low-voiced story. I saw her listen; I saw her look. *Harmless*, I told myself.

Andromache was not worried, after all, and King Menelaus frowned now and then but did not appear more than usually watchful over his wife's actions.

I would be happy when this wedding was over. The ceremony would take place tomorrow; a day or two later we could surely take our leave.

The colt danced skittishly away from Hector. He advanced a step, murmuring, intent.

I glanced at the dais again and saw Helen descending, making her way through the throng. The warriors looked at her sideways, muttering as she passed, taller than any of them and self-possessed as a goddess. To my surprise, she made her way to my side where I leaned against the pillar.

"Prince Hellenus," she said in that level voice that never seemed to rise and fall in mortal cadences. "I have spoken to all my husband's guests these past weeks except you. If we do not trade some friendly words, I shall think you are avoiding me."

"On the contrary, my queen." I made a small bow. "I did not think myself worthy of your company."

She gave me her faint smile. Her eyes were lined in black, making them enormous, and her rose-oiled pale gold hair spiraled to brush the backs of her green-skirted knees. She could dizzy a man's senses, but she had no effect on me whatsoever.

Her smile grew a touch more amused, as though she had read my mind. "How interesting you Trojan princes are."

"I thought you only interested in one of us, Lady," I dared to say.

"Paris? On the contrary, he's the dullest of you. If the prettiest."

I wished Paris could hear her calm dismissal. He'd be crushed. "I thought he had found favor in your eyes, my queen."

"He wants my favor, certainly. But all men do." It was said not as boast but blunt fact. "All men, that is, except you and Prince

Hector. It is so rare that I look into a man's eyes and see complete indifference. No wonder I find you both interesting."

I did not know how to answer her directness. "Of course I find you very lovely, Queen Helen—"

"Don't bore me. I hear so much flattery."

"As you wish." I decided to match her bluntness. "May I say I am relieved to hear your opinion of my younger brother is not so warm as I had thought?"

"Your older brother is the one I could have viewed very warmly indeed." She nodded down at Hector, who had lured the colt into nibbling warily from his palm. "Heir to Troy, a great warrior, perhaps the only man in this pack of pirates who could call himself a hero. But he has eyes for no one but that cheerful little wife of his. I confess I don't see the appeal; she's a coltish, freckled thing with nothing queenly at all about her, but only the men pricked very deeply by Eros' arrows remain as unaffected by me as Prince Hector is."

With a flash of anger, I glanced at Andromache, leaning on her folded arms and smiling down at the training ground. "You will not speak ill of my sister-in-law, Lady."

"No indeed." Helen looked amused. "Freckled little thing or not, Aphrodite has blessed her. The day Andromache came to Troy, I think two arrows sped from Eros' bow. One landed there"—another nod to Hector—"and one landed here."

She tapped me over the heart and then glided away, leaving me dry-mouthed and furious. *You bitch,* I thought, *you swan-necked, spiteful bitch.*

Sharp-eyed bitch. She saw what no one saw, even my own family.

I looked up at Andromache again, pushing a lock of hair back behind her ear as she gazed, entranced, down at Hector, and felt the familiar desperate pang. What a thing it is to love your brother and desire his wife.

It was not supposed to be this way, I thought bleakly for perhaps the thousandth time. Andromache had never been intended for Hector at all. When Priam decided his heir needed a wife, a dozen nobly born girls of Troy and various neighboring kingdoms had been invited to our lavish summer festival to be quietly appraised. Everyone wagered on Chryseis, daughter of the high priest of Apollo: a lush-hipped beauty as regal as Hera, royalty on her mother's side, pedigree perfect in every way. And as Troy's eyes fastened on Chryseis, mine drifted to the minor daughter of a minor neighboring king, a girl with sparkling eyes and an unabashed laugh like a sunlit stream. Not even a contender in the running to be Hector's wife, no beauty or riches to her name—except that she lifted my heart every time I saw her and never once gaped at my dark face.

I will offer for her, I'd thought in a rush of painful hope. *When Hector announces his choice of wife, I will ask for the princess Andromache.* No one would object; Priam had no interest in me or my marriage and wouldn't think of forbidding me, nor would Andromache's father object. For a princess from a kingdom so small they kept goats in the megaron, a prince of Troy was a catch, even if he was born of a concubine. So while all eyes had watched Hector and Chryseis, I befriended Andromache, heart in my throat, dreaming of the gold strands I'd wind about her throat on our wedding day, dreaming of the small palace we could inhabit together, the life we could carve in Troy, which had never felt like home to me. Such a small dream, really: an ordinary man who had never felt like a prince, living an ordinary life with the smiling girl who said she never felt like a princess.

And then Hector had looked past regal Chryseis and her prince-bearing hips and chose Andromache.

A ripple of applause spread over the watching crowd. The skittish colt stood calm at my brother's side as he slipped a rope over its willing head. Andromache blew him a kiss from the dais, and again—as it did every day I watched them—my heart broke.

FOR me it passed in a haze. The bride was escorted from the women's quarters, rosy and blushing, a wreath of wildflowers crowning the fine veil that had been one of Troy's gifts, escorted by that bitch Helen in purple on one side and Andromache on her left—and when I saw Andromache in her layered skirts, small breasts bared in a tight lapis-colored bodice, I reached for the nearest jug of wine. I didn't often seek Dionysus' oblivion, but today it had its appeal.

The rites invoking Aphrodite and Hera, Artemis and Potnia. The sacrifice, a brushed and beribboned horse going to its knees under the priest's knife. Bride and bridegroom joining hands under a shower of ribald jokes. The wedding feast as the sun sank, many of the warriors already drunk as they fell on the dishes of roast venison and boar, the fruits and cheeses and honeyed cakes. The king of Ithaca and his new queen sat in splendor on the dais, sharing a long-stemmed wine cup. Hector, Menelaus, and Agamemnon conferred over a *krater* of wine, Paris made eyes at Helen and she ignored him, the Cimmerian princess Penthesilea was laughing with Andromache, who had tipped her head back to drop grapes one by one between her own lips. Her hair was the color of glistening sand on a dawn beach.

I drank.

Music, lutes and pipes and lyres. The women took to the floor to dance. Queen Helen remained on her dais, but the bride joined hands with Andromache and the Cimmerian girls and all the Spartan loom-maidens, their skirts opening like a circle of bright flowers. The watching warriors whooped and clapped, and I was glad of their crude company. I had all the excuse in the world to stare at the women, no one knowing I looked only at one.

"You look far too haunted for a wedding celebration, my friend!" A cheerful voice sounded behind me, and I turned to see the bridegroom in his gold-embroidered finery. I'd not exchanged many words with Odysseus these past weeks: a stocky man a year or two older than I, black-haired, with a smile of cheerful wickedness. "More wine?"

I took the cup he offered and drank deep. "Congratulations upon your bride."

"Thank you." He turned to look at the radiant young Penelope, dipping and twirling among the women. "All the kings in this hall vied once for the shiniest bauble in the box"—a nod up to Queen Helen—"but I believe I've made off tonight with the one whose gleam runs deep and true."

I grunted agreement, watching a shining jewel of my own as she laughed and spun. "I wish you happiness and many sons when you bring your wife back to Ithaca."

"I would be honored to have you as a guest in my home someday, friend. Do your travels ever take you to my seas?"

To little islands with nothing but stingrays and sand dunes? I thought ungraciously, but I stamped on my sourness. "I have never traveled so far west as Ithaca, no. Is it beautiful?"

Odysseus' smile widened. "Ithaca may not have Troy's wealth, but my island is rich with charms of its own. Do you know the light is different there? As if Apollo smiles on my hills with special affection. The wine-dark sea comes directly to the land, as if it cannot bear to be separated from it by sand. My people might be called rustic, but you would always know us as peaceful friends, ready to share a meal of fresh cheese on our sunlit hills. A simple life, but rich."

What would it be like to love a place so much? I wondered, half-mesmerized by his voice, still watching Andromache's whirling skirts. When I thought of splendid tall-towered Troy, all I felt was dull resignation.

Odysseus turned to look at me. "My island is good for a poet's soul, as I imagine yours might be. You are welcome as my guest any time you wish a rest from your glittering court."

No one in this hall had been half so ingratiating to me since I arrived. I slanted a brow at Odysseus. "Why are you wooing me, lord king? If you have some petition for my father, put it to my brothers. Paris is my father's favorite and Hector his heir—I assure you, few in Troy hear my voice."

Odysseus laughed. "Was I wooing, sir? I was merely extending hospitality. But now you must take me up on my invitation, if only so that one day I may visit you in turn and learn the charms of your city."

I swirled my wine in my cup. "I doubt your island would welcome me as a guest. Herders and fishermen tend to look on those like me and my twin sister as foreign oddities." And even if oddities were admired, as my sister's beauty was always admired, they were not often trusted by insular peasant folk.

"On the contrary, we have many traders from Nubia and Aegyptos, who come for our dried fish and goat cheese. The kings of these southern lands, they tell me, consider our goods a delicacy. The sight of both you and your sister would raise little comment in my kingdom."

"I doubt that. She has a troubled soul, thinks she dreams of the future. She tends to cause worried mutters wherever she goes."

"I would still welcome you both. Consider it, my friend—I have a feeling our paths will cross again." Odysseus clapped me on the back and moved off to greet my cousin Aeneas, with whom he seemed to have struck up an unlikely friendship. The king of Ithaca could make even dour Aeneas smile.

Ithaca.

A poor place, no doubt, for all the honeyed praise I'd just heard. And yet I found myself musing about a sunlit island where breezes came gently off the sea rather than blowing fierce and northerly like Troy's winds. Since the day I had lost Andromache to my brother, I had begun to dream of leaving Troy . . . But to go where? I'd known I would need a king willing to welcome a Trojan cast-off, a hand outstretched to offer me sanctuary. Was Odysseus the man I was looking for?

Foolish dreams, I scoffed at myself, but in my wine haze I was suddenly imagining a modest house on a grassy hill overlooking the ocean, a table where dried fish and goat cheese could be eaten in peace, a place where my poor twin could find the silence to heal her wounded soul. And why should I not dream of it? Was I truly going to spend the rest of my days in Troy serving a father who barely acknowledged my existence and my nights burning for a woman I could not have?

No. I watched Andromache at Hector's side on the dais and thought again, *No.* I would return to Troy to collect my twin, and then we would stake our futures elsewhere.

Night wore on, noisier and more raucous. The enormous ox-like Ajax had passed out at the foot of the dais. Old Nestor was droning about how wine had been much better brewed in *his* day. Bride and groom were escorted to their borrowed bridal chamber in a shower of rose petals and obscene jokes. The women retired to their own quarters, and the warriors trooped back to the megaron to fall on the wine and the slave girls. Leonine Diomedes was rutting a girl in a corner, and bearded Philoctetes was kissing his handsome young spearman. A pair of Agamemnon's fighters brawled drunkenly near the fire. Hector would retire soon, I knew; he had no great taste for wild revelry. Paris had already disappeared, doubtless with a dancing girl or two.

I was in no mood for revelry, either. I took a jar of wine to the courtyard and sat drinking, listening to the sounds of drunken singing and raucous cheers, and I was almost on the point of sleep when I saw a shadow slipping from the women's quarters.

Queen Helen. Surely there was no other woman so tall. She glided noiselessly against the wall, dark-cloaked—it was only merest chance I'd spotted her in the darkness. There was a set of bathing quarters just off the courtyard, very close to the women's rooms. I watched Sparta's queen slip inside.

A bath at this hour? I discarded my wine jar and rose, a little unsteady but curious. Stealing to the entrance, I heard noises. The rustle of cloth, the sound of panting, a stifled groan.

I risked a glance inside.

A single guttering lamp lit the scene: Helen of Sparta leaning against the painted frieze, her head thrown back, her pale gold hair loosed from its jeweled band and uncoiling wild as a Fury's. Her purple robe pooled at her feet, and a man's head was buried between her pale breasts. Her marble calm, her goddess-like reserve, had utterly gone. Her lips parted in a snarl that looked more like hatred than passion as her fingers snaked through her lover's hair, yanking him up so their mouths nailed together. He dragged her long thigh around his hip as their lips clashed violently, and against the lamplight I saw Paris' perfect profile.

It could only have lasted an instant, the moment I stood there with my eye to the crack of the door watching my brother rut between the thighs of another man's wife—but that instant lasted a year. In that endless moment, I hated him. He desired another man's wife, and what did he do? He reached out and took her, as he reached out and took everything else he wanted, and his reward was to be the golden prince, everyone's favorite, forever forgiven. I desired another man's wife, and what was my reward for holding myself back honorably? Heartache and loneliness inside a family who found me worthless.

Part of me wanted to haul Paris out of that chamber and beat him unconscious. But I didn't trust myself, once I started hitting my brother, not to kill him. I backed away noiselessly, no longer wine-fuddled, and went to the chamber assigned for Hector. But I found only Andromache.

"Hellenus," she said sleepily, waving me inside. She had clearly retired to wait for Hector, still dressed in her layered kilts and lapis-colored bodice, but with her hair falling free and her feet bare. Her eyes were heavy-lidded, drowsy with more wine than she usually drank—but they sprang open wide as I told her in a few terse sentences what I had just seen.

"That idiot," she said in blank astonishment. "Paris and *Queen Helen*?"

"Yes. And if King Menelaus gets wind of it, he'd be within his rights to run Paris through."

"Maybe we should let him." Andromache sighed. "Paris. How could he?"

"Because if he sees a ripe apple on a tree, he plucks it and sinks his teeth in without a thought for who the tree belongs to," I said, and the envy was bitter in my mouth. "Tell Hector when he returns. We cannot keep this from him." I couldn't stomach waiting any longer; I wanted my bed and my envious dreams.

"Hector will . . ." Andromache trailed off, her eyes growing miserable. "Hellenus, he will be so wretched. If Paris shatters something, it's Hector who will have to pick up the pieces, even if the edges cut him to the bone."

"We can get out of this with no one the wiser. Tell Hector to find Paris and pack him off at dawn to Gythio, where our ships are moored. Give whatever excuse he likes; Paris leaves now as the rest of us make our formal farewells and follow in a few days. No one will know but the four of us."

"And Helen. What was she thinking?"

"I don't know." I could have sworn that yesterday Sparta's queen had no more desire for Paris than for a tarnished bracelet. And yet her face in the bathing room had been all savage, passionate intent. Perhaps she *was* a daughter of Zeus—beyond the power of mortal man to comprehend.

Andromache sank down on the edge of the bed, twisting the fringe of her layered kilts again. "Hector won't sleep tonight once he knows," she said softly. "He'll sit brooding, no matter how I try to help. And I will have to be brave and tell him all will be well, no matter what I truly think."

I sat beside her and put an arm about her, smelling the oil of iris in her hair and the wine she'd drunk that evening. She let her head fall against my shoulder, and I felt her breath hitch. My breath hitched, too. Sweet Zeus, how hard it was to have her so close. Wanting to tighten my arm around her—

"I weary of trying so hard," she whispered. "It is so *lonely*, Hellenus."

"I know," I said, stroking her hair, and in a moment's cool clarity I saw how it could happen. I could hold her in my brotherly arms till she was comforted; I could wait until she lifted her face and then kiss the tip of her nose to make her smile, and then while she was smiling, I could kiss her mouth—and her lips would yield. Her lips would yield and so would the rest of her, coming pliant and soft into my arms, which could then stop being brotherly and lay her back on the bed. And Andromache, I thought, would let me. Because she was lonely and tipsy and far from home, hurting from worry and aching for comfort, and she had always found me so comforting. Because I was her friend; because I was an easier man than my brooding, godlike brother. Because she *trusted* me. She trusted me, and I could have her if I wanted. Here on my brother's bed, her hair coiled around my hand and her small freckled breasts against my chest.

I was so bitterly tempted. For an instant, it did not matter that Andromache would hate herself afterward, that Hector could walk in at any moment and throttle me as his eyes widened with betrayal. I didn't care. I wanted to be like Paris, to reach out and pluck the apple, take what I wanted so much, all the consequences in the world be damned.

Andromache lifted her head, raised her face toward mine. I pulled in a breath thick with choked desire, and I kissed her—kissed her smooth forehead just at the line of her loose hair. I gave myself that. "Good night," I said, rising fast and clumsily, turning away from her because she looked puzzled and a little guilty, as though she'd sensed something of my inner turmoil. "Tell Hector when he returns—" and I fled to my lonely bed.

ANDROMACHE

I had no idea what Hector said to Paris, but my foolish brother-in-law was gone by noon the following day. He left quickly in his chariot, unseen by me and certainly unseen by our hosts, while Hector made uncomfortable excuses. "We have received news our ships may have been attacked in Gythio where we left them moored. Forgive my brother for leaving so hastily to get word."

King Menelaus only shrugged his heavy shoulders, seeming to suspect nothing, and I breathed easier. Paris' exit caused little comment when all the guests were preparing for departure: two days after the wedding, Odysseus left with his Penelope, whose cheeks I kissed as I wished her happiness in her new home, and then there was a flood of guests departing Sparta's gates. Menelaus himself was planning to leave Sparta with his brother, Agamemnon, for lion hunting in Mycenae and seemed impatient to see the last of us all.

"We'll be home soon," I told Hector, hoping to see a smile, but Paris' foolishness had sunk him as deep in gloom as I'd feared. It was Hellenus who made the arrangements for our departure, and three days after the wedding, we were making our formal farewells to red-haired Menelaus and rattling away in our chariots, the pack donkeys trotting behind considerably less burdened than when they'd arrived.

I dreaded seeing Helen at our departure, for I was no liar and didn't think I'd be able to hide my contempt for what she'd done. A queen soiling her marriage bed—I could not conceive of such a thing. And to take such a risk for Paris? I thought Helen had better taste than that; certainly, I'd thought she had more wits. For someone who thought she'd hatched from Zeus' egg, she'd behaved like a peahen, and had I laid eyes on her, I didn't really think I'd be able to stop myself from telling her so. But the Spartan queen had taken to her bed after the wedding, claiming illness and commanding utter solitude, and I hadn't seen her since. "Perhaps Paris tired her out," I told Hector tartly, and for that he *did* smile, just a little.

I rejoiced as we drove away from Sparta, leading our entourage through the wooded hills along the wheel-rutted road. The horses seemed to dance, tossing their manes in the summer wind, and I could see Hector's black mood lightening almost by the hour, lifting under the simple pleasures of sunlight and sweet air and leather reins in his hands. He had a charioteer for battle but otherwise drove himself, balancing steady as a tower and needing only the lightest touch to turn the horses. He smiled down at me, and my heart contracted with love—and a touch of shame. Perhaps it had only been the wine, but the night Hellenus brought the news of Paris' betrayal and I'd contemplated my husband's certain gloom, I'd had the tiny, furtive wish that I could have married an ordinary man and not this grave and complicated one who needed so much from me.

Perhaps Hellenus had read my mind, as he so often seemed to. He had been avoiding me ever since.

Well, I would leave such shameful thoughts firmly behind in Sparta with the rest of the unpleasantness. "Home to Troy," I said, squeezing Hector's arm. "Before you know it, your little brother Polites will be clamoring to know what you brought him from Sparta, and your mother will be bringing out your favorite wine, and all your horses will have their heads over the fence looking for you."

"And I'll talk to Father about building more ships this winter," Hector decided. "With most of our fleet going to aid the Hittites, it would be foolish to have nothing more than the three we sailed here and a few fishing boats . . ." He talked keels and sails all the way to Gythio, happy and active again, and soon our three ships were visible, beached high and dry, guarded by sentries, the wide ocean lapping softly behind.

Paris had made camp when he arrived a few days ago and had clearly unloaded a good many supplies from the ships to pamper himself. Woven tapestries had been thrown down to cushion the sand; two stools of gilded wood stood together with a bowl of fruit; a bed frame of stretched hide was piled with furs. Paris himself was lounging with a lyre and a cup of wine; he discarded both as we stepped down from our chariots. "Welcome," he said cheekily as I stood shaking the dust from my skirts and Hector passed his reins to a guard. "We've been waiting an age!"

"We?" I raised my eyebrows frostily, not inclined to forgive him yet. "Did you pick up some shepherd's daughter on the way home?"

"Not precisely," Paris grinned and waved up to the stern of the beached ship, where a tall figure had just risen. I looked at her in a wave of horror, barely hearing the surge of whispers around me from the staring slaves and guards, and I realized that the trouble Paris had caused was not over yet. It had only just begun.

"Hector," Helen of Sparta said calmly, twining her arms about Paris' neck as he lifted her down to the sand. "Andromache, Hellenus. How I look forward to seeing Troy."

HELLENUS

HECTOR stood frozen with shock, but Andromache and I moved as one. As she came forward in a flare of skirts and delivered a ringing backhand slap across Helen's cheek, I advanced on my younger brother and drove my fist into his handsome, grinning face.

He went down, tumbling into the sand. I flung myself on him, rage roaring in my ears, hammering him like a sheet of copper on a smith's anvil. I wanted to pound his pretty profile into ruined oblivion. More, I wanted to kill him, wrap my hands about his throat and crush it to pulp. I had killed men before in spear raids and skirmishes, and though I never enjoyed the taking of lives, I could have slaughtered my brother on that beach and washed my hands in his blood without a qualm.

It was Hector who hauled me off Paris, lifting me up and flinging me back as though I weighed no more than a child. He had Andromache by the arm as well, pulling her back from Helen, and a moment later shoved her into my arms. "Both of you, back," he snapped, planting himself between the two of us and the guilty pair. I could feel Andromache trembling in my arms, staring at Helen. Menelaus' queen stood immobile, mouth curving in her mysterious smile, scarlet mark standing clear across her cheek. Paris rose, wiping blood from a split lip and a split eyebrow, one eye swelling shut—but he was still smiling.

"What the *fuck* have you done?" I spat.

"Got myself a wife," he said, and again I wanted to kill him.

I turned to Hector instead, still gazing numbly back and forth between Paris and Helen. "Strap that bitch into a chariot and send her back to Sparta. Menelaus has gone to Mycenae; we might be able to return her before he realizes she's gone."

"The slaves will know by now." Helen's voice was amused. "I claimed I was too ill to eat more than the figs and wine already in my chamber and threatened beatings to any who opened my door, but by now *someone* will have tiptoed in to see. A message is doubtless on its way to Menelaus as we speak."

I ignored her, still speaking to Hector, my pulse hammering. "Give her back along with her weight in gold, then. He might not ask for Paris' head on a spike." Though frankly I would have considered giving it to him.

"She's not going anywhere except home to Troy as my wife," Paris said. "And I assure you, our father will welcome her with open arms."

"You have *dishonored* him," Andromache cried. "You have dishonored us all—stealing another man's *queen*—"

"No one stole me," Helen said, still calm. "I came willingly."

Hector stared at her a long moment. "Stay here with my wife, Queen Helen," he ordered at last in a whisper like a roll of soft thunder. "Paris, Hellenus. Come."

I released Andromache, who crossed her arms and glowered at Menelaus' errant wife. Hector turned and made for the shadow of the next beached ship, which might afford us some privacy from our gaping entourage. Paris sauntered after, and I fell in behind him, my hands bruised and aching from hitting him. My ears roared dully. *What have you done?* The mindless thought circled. *What have you done?*

"My, my." Paris grinned as the three of us came to a halt beside the ship. "Am I to be scolded now?"

Hector's massive hand shot out and gripped him by the throat.

"Will you joke your way out of our father's displeasure, too? When he realizes you may have provoked war with Sparta?"

"You're an ox-brain, Brother. What do you think our father wants?" Paris shook Hector's hand off, flippancy finally falling away. "You had your own instructions for our Spartan visit, and I had mine. You think our father cares about placating these pirate kings with gold and gifts? They're little better than sea-rats, forever nibbling at our territories in raiding season and complaining our tariffs on the strait are too high. They need to be taught a lesson. Father sent you to keep the surface civil, but he trusted me to look for opportunities."

"Opportunities for what?" I spat.

"Trouble, war. Who cares? Any chance to bloody their noses."

Hector shook his head stubbornly. "Father would have told me."

"You're too much the honorable dealer for subterfuge. Father trusted *me* to keep my eyes open, any way I could see to spark trouble, and I did."

I thought of how his usual sunny humor had acquired an unaccustomed rude edge during our visit. His insults, his arrogance.

"Helen was ripe to fall on her back, anyone could see that," Paris continued. "It was the easiest thing in the world. All I had to do was fuck her till her eyes crossed, and she was ready to run away. The bitch is so wet for me she'll do anything. She even brought a chunk of Menelaus' treasury with her when I suggested it. I bring her and her Spartan gold home, and those Achaeans will follow—Menelaus got his throne through her, and even if he didn't, he'd be a laughingstock if he let his prize cunt run away with half his treasury. He'll come, and he'll bring that sharp-eyed brother of his, Agamemnon, and we'll bloody their noses on our own turf, outside our own gates. Not at sea, where they're strongest; on land, where *we're* strongest, where we can fall behind walls a god couldn't breach, and they'll have nowhere to fall but

Hades. We'll send them home like whipped puppies, and then they'll be happy to pay doubled rates for using our strait."

Hector and I stared at him, dumbfounded.

"Troy needs money, if you haven't noticed. We had to send our fleet to help fight the Hittite rebellion; how soon are we going to get those ships back trading and turning a profit? And the Hittites won't be near as quick with their tin shipments as they used to be, not with all the fighting roiling Hattusa. The Achaean sea-rats can keep our coffers full; they just need a lesson first." Paris spread his arms. "And I taught it to them. Not noble Hector, me. Father will be proud."

He had a hard, feverish gleam in his eye. This was not about lust *or* money, I realized. *I am not the only son of Priam to feel myself lacking a place in Troy.* Paris had joined our family late after his indifferent fostering among goatherds, a prince discarded because of a prophecy of ill-luck and only taken back because my sister had recognized him for who he was. He'd only regained a toehold in the palace due to his charm and his eagerness to please. Paris, I thought, would have provoked war with the whole world if it meant keeping our father's careless favor.

What have you done? I thought again, but to my distant father instead. Pulling strings across the sea, making us all dance to his tune . . .

"I suggest we set sail," Paris said. "Father will be eager to greet his new daughter-in-law."

"You should never have—" Hector began, but I seized his arm, holding him as Paris stalked off.

"Leave him be," I said. "He's not so much at fault here as our father. Priam gave the orders."

"I would not have followed such orders!"

"You have never lacked our father's approval. Paris has, and he'd kill to keep it." For the first time, I felt lucky that Priam had never extended his affection to me. Never having felt the smallest ray of that paternal sunshine, the craving for its warmth could never drive me to desperate acts, as it had Paris.

"What do we do now?" Hector whispered. My heroic brother, for once utterly at a loss. And I had no answer.

ANDROMACHE

"I do hope you won't slap me again," Helen said coolly as the men stormed away to their whispered argument. "I would hate to greet my new family with a bruised face."

I stared at her as if she were a hydra. She had discarded her purple robes and dressed in layered kilts and a blood-red bodice baring her white breasts. She glittered with gold: a diadem dropping long strands to her shoulders, heavy earrings, bracelets climbing her arms, rings at each finger. She wore a king's fortune in gold—Menelaus' fortune, I realized, as I watched her pluck an apple from the bowl. "It wasn't enough to cuckold your husband? You had to rob him blind as well?"

"My gold, not his. I had every right to take it with me." Helen sat on one of the gilt stools and stretched herself under the sun like a lazy cat, sinking her neat white teeth into the apple.

I stood frozen where I was as she sat there calmly eating. I had been so happy leaving Sparta and its clouds behind. Now this, another broken mess for Hector to sweep up with bleeding hands. "I hope Menelaus wrings your swan neck when Hector drops you at his feet, you faithless bitch."

"Hector won't be dropping me anywhere." Helen regarded me with her ice-colored eyes. "Paris and his father want war, and I'm far too convenient an excuse."

"Did Paris *tell* you that?"

"No. He tells me he loves me." A smile of fond contempt. "He thinks I haven't figured the rest out for myself. Not too bright, that one. Ah, well, he's the material I have to work with."

"You're—you're wrong," I managed to say. "Priam will never accept you in Troy."

"I doubt that. He likes war, and he likes beautiful women, and I am both. I will flirt with him slightly, and I have a feeling he will chuck me under the chin and give me a palace." She took another dainty bite of apple, swallowed with satisfaction. "Troy . . . after all you've told me, I feel sure I will like it."

War. I saw Achaean ships thronged with pirate kings; I saw Hector in his lapis-decorated breastplate; I saw death. "Why did you *do* this?" I cried. "You are a queen; you live in a palace; you have a beautiful daughter and a chest full of gold and slaves to wait on your every whim. You don't love Paris—you don't even like him—so *why*?"

"Oh, you sheltered child." Helen shook her head. "What do you know, you pampered girl with your prince who adores you and spares you childbirth and gives you a seal so you can walk the world independent of his shadow? What do you know of being a prize? I have been a prize all my life, passed from one sea-wolf to the next. I was captured at eleven by a hero who called himself Theseus who could hardly wait to push himself between my thighs and make himself king; I spent a month weeping in his bed before my father reclaimed me with never a kind word for my pain. *That* is the fate my beauty won me. At thirteen, I looked at that pack of petty killers who came to court me—the same men who thronged to watch Penelope marry—and the best I could do among them was Menelaus, who beats me because I have never given him a son and is too jealous to let me walk alone outside the women's quarters. I am a *queen,* yes, but what has that brought me? If Menelaus ever falls in battle, I will go to the man who defeats him, to be raped and beaten again if I fail to please. If Menelaus lives to grow old, I will sit in the women's quarters weaving until I am so ancient and ugly no one wishes to ravage me anymore, watching my daughter go to a husband's bed at thirteen to be raped and beaten and passed from man to man in her turn, a prize just like me. That is my fate, Andromache. But I reject it."

She uncoiled like a snake, tossing the half-eaten apple aside and rising to her full height. The marble statue had come to life; her eyes were fires full of bitter, bottomless hatred, and she hissed like a Fury.

"I am a daughter of Zeus. I was meant for more than to be a prize between squabbling killers. I want what you have: a husband who does not black my eyes or force me to bear a child every year, a seal of my own so I can receive petitioners and give council in my own right, wide streets where I am free to walk and bare my breasts and do anything, *anything*, but sit at a loom. Your pretty prince Paris is as pliable as clay; it was easy to make him dance to my tune. He will bring me honor and freedom and respect, and I will have him and Troy at my feet."

"What of your daughter?" I lashed out. "Your Hermione. Can you abandon her as easily as the rest?"

Pain streaked across Helen's face like a shot of lightning, but she did not flinch. "I could not bring her with me without being noticed, but I will have her back. Priam will barter for her, whether as a victory prize for defeating Menelaus' warriors or in negotiation in return for my Spartan gold. Priam will barter for her if I have to become *his* wife instead of Paris'. I will have her back, whether or not it means war."

"What of those who would have to fight such a war for you?" I whispered.

She shrugged. "If Menelaus brings an army to your shores, it is his own decision. Men wage battles with no regard to the advice of women. If he decides to go to war in my name, it is not my fault." A mirthless smile. "Besides, some might say mortal men *should* fight for a daughter of Zeus."

"My husband will be first on the field! If he falls—"

"I hope he does not. I like him, and in truth, Andromache, I like you. But I will not sacrifice the remainder of my wretched life for your convenience. I saw this chance come to my door, and there is no amount of liking in the world that would make me pass it by."

"What if it all comes down?" I cried. "My husband, my family, *Troy*! What if it all falls because of you? What then?"

I was not seeing the future. I was no seer catching glimpses of what the Fates had in store. I was only afraid, speaking my fears in the hope that they would never come to pass.

"Then we will all be prizes again, all of us women, and go to the bed of whatever man drags us off by the hair." Helen's face was like flint. "But I will have tasted some measure first of freedom."

In a blood-colored sunset, we set sail: three ships gliding east toward windy Troy. Helen and Paris took the foremost ship, Hector and Hellenus and I the rearmost, already keeping our eyes trained for pursuit. "I will not rest easy until we are behind the Scaean Gate again," Hector said.

I thought it would be considerably longer than that before my husband rested easy. He sat still as a statue on the narrow bed that was our small share of privacy on board, his huge hands dangling helpless between his knees.

"My father did not trust me," he said, "and now he courts disaster."

"Perhaps not," I cajoled. "Perhaps we can make Priam see sense, send her back."

"Perhaps." Hector sounded listless. I felt the old clutch of panic, wondering how to pull him from the black grip of such hopelessness. I wanted to perch on his knee, turn my talk to lighter things, chatter and joke as I always did—but this was no time for chatter and jokes. My husband needed more from me than cheer and distraction.

I took his face between my hands and made him meet my eyes, steadily drinking in his silent misery. "My love, you will do what must be done." My voice started to tremble, but I forced it to remain steady. "If there is war, you will fight it. If there is death, you will face it. If there is dishonor, you will bear it. You can do nothing less, and you know it."

He gazed back at me. This time I was the one to stroke his hair as though he were a frightened horse.

"You will bear whatever the Fates bring," I said quietly. "You must. And so will I."

"That is a bitter thing, Andromache."

Yes, but I was done avoiding bitter things. Helen had called me a sheltered child, and perhaps I was. No more. "Whatever comes, I will be at your side." I pulled Hector down to our marriage bed, murmuring my love for him, murmuring my faith in him, and he held me so hard I could barely breathe. We fell into each other, desperately seeking comfort in warmth—but this time I was seeking something more. When he tried to pull away at the end as he always did, I whispered, "No."

"Andromache—"

"No," I said again, pulling him closer till the final shudder racked him and he filled me. I was not too weak, too unsuitable to bear his sons. Not anymore.

No more, I thought, cradling my husband as he slid into sleep, as the waves lapped the hull outside and the moon rose. There would be no more laughing off my duties, no more unburdening my troubles to Hellenus, who made me long uncomfortably for a more ordinary life. I would shoulder my duties and my troubles uncomplainingly, and Hector's, too.

I was ready. I had to be. I was Hector's wife, the future queen of Troy.

HELLENUS

SHALL I sing to you of Troy? Shining Troy, windy Troy, many-towered Troy. We made our way toward it, day by day across a calm sea.

I will return only to leave again. That I had vowed the day we sailed for Sparta, as the seabirds cried overhead and the sails bellied with a west wind. Now I wondered if Odysseus would still welcome me when I turned up on his shore with my sister, or if Trojan princes would be welcome nowhere in the Achaean lands after Paris had stolen an Achaean queen.

I didn't care. Troy was bound for strife, and I would not waste my remaining years trying to mend the senseless chaos my father had courted. I would risk a journey to Ithaca and stake all on Odysseus' welcome holding true.

The decision made, I was strangely calm, passing my days at the prow watching the ship sailing ahead, where Helen and Paris no doubt enjoyed their false idyll. I thought Andromache might join me in my vigil, sitting down with her ready smile and her feet swinging like an urchin's—but Andromache had drawn away from me on this voyage. Her small freckled face had a new gravity, turning always toward Hector with quiet attention. I wondered if my cheerful, sunny girl was gone for good . . . but she had never been mine. I was just an ordinary man, after all, and she would be a queen.

Hector was the one to join me, strong arms folded across his chest, broad bracelets glinting. There was no matching glint in his eye as he watched Paris and Helen's ship ahead. "It may not mean war," he said without preamble.

"No," I acknowledged.

"But if war comes, I will need you at my side, Hellenus."

I blinked, surprised. "I am not the strongest spearman among our brothers."

"Brothers." Hector spat the word. "What good are any of them? Deiphobus is a fool, Troilus a young hot-head, Polites a child, and Paris is more likely to spend himself between his new wife's legs than in battle. As for the others—" he cut himself off. "Of my many brothers, there is not one I value so highly as you."

"Hector . . ."

He gripped my shoulder, voice coming low and harsh. "Promise that you will fight at my side if war comes."

My pulse skipped. *No,* I thought, *no, do not make me stay.* "Hector, you do not need me. Our cousin Aeneas would be your willing right hand. A far better warrior than I—"

"But you are my brother," Hector said simply.

Such simple words, and yet they made my heart both lift and sink.

"There is something else I ask of you." His grip tightened on my shoulder. "If I fall in battle, you must protect Andromache."

I stood there, shaking, watching my dream of Ithaca fade away in the face of his pleading. There would be no island home, no new beginning for my sister and me. I had dreamed of escape, but the gods had other plans.

"Promise me," Hector pleaded. "Swear that if I fall, you will take Andromache for your own and keep her safe. Swear it."

I wondered if Aphrodite was laughing at me up on Olympus. How the goddess of love had played with my future: if I ever held the girl I loved, it would be over the corpse of the brother I revered. "I swear it," I said hoarsely. "I swear it now by all the gods, and when back in Troy, I will swear it on the sacred Palladion at the temple of Athena. I will fight at your side whatever comes, and should you fall, I will keep Andromache safe."

A single fierce nod and Hector's hand fell away from my shoulder. We stood gazing over the endless sea, and after a time, my bitter heart eased a little. I still could not call Troy home, but I now had purpose there: a brother to serve, a woman to protect. Modest aims compared to the desire of most warriors for glory and gold, but I am a modest man.

A cry went up from our sharp-eyed man at the tiller. Hector and I shaded our eyes, searching the horizon. Suddenly, I was longing for Troy, if only because I would see my twin again. My other half, who had muttered of death the day I left for Sparta. *I hope you are wrong, Cassandra,* I thought. *Most dearly do I hope that.*

The cry went up again, and on the distant, glittering horizon, I saw it.

Troy.

THE SECOND SONG

THE PROPHECY

by Stephanie Thornton

Oh, oh! Agony, agony!
Again the awful pains of prophecy Are on
me, maddening as they fall . . .
Aeschylus, *Agamemnon*

CASSANDRA

THEY called me mad because I uttered truths no one wished to hear.

When they refused to listen, I screamed the warnings, yet they only jeered and hurled jagged epithets at me.

Palsied slack-wit.

Empty fly-skull.

I thought perhaps if I whispered, they would quiet and listen, but I was mistaken.

So very, very mistaken.

Only once did anyone heed my visions, when I recognized handsome young Paris as my erstwhile brother, fostered to a shepherd after it was prophesied that he would cause Troy's downfall. How I wished I could go back and undo that moment, let my twin, Hellenus, and my half brothers believe Paris a temple intruder and bash his head into Zeus' altar. Then I might have danced like a maenad in the pool of his lifeblood upon the tiles. For I knew now that the prophecy still stalked Paris like a black shadow and that his journey to Sparta would somehow set its wheels into motion.

It had been years since the nightmares had plagued me, since a different day in a different god's temple, but they started afresh the night after fourteen-year-old Paris rejoined our family from his exile. More than two months ago, he'd departed for Sparta with our Trojan entourage, and my nighttime terrors had redoubled. Only Hellenus could banish the dark terrors with his songs and stories from our childhood. Still, there always lurked the horrors only I could see.

Why, oh why, could only I see them?

"Paris is dangerous," I'd warned Hellenus, shuddering violently despite his arm around my shoulders. "Nothing good will come of this mission to Sparta."

"He is young and untried," Hellenus had admitted. "Perhaps our father might command him to remain behind."

"Please ask," I'd begged my brother after my pleas to Father fell on deaf ears. "Tell him what I've seen if you must. Anything to keep him from going."

But Father had refused to keep Paris in Troy, had instead encouraged him to travel to Sparta to learn his greater responsibilities as a prince of the realm, especially now, as Troy sought fresh forms of profit in the wake of the internal wars ravaging our Hittite neighbors. Paris had even boasted that our father had set him to a special task, although he remained tight-lipped about its details. And Hellenus had gone as well, taking all my solace with him. I'd watched their ships sink into the dark horizon and then retreated into a roaring silence, defenseless and alone.

I might die in my room, and no one would notice until my corpse began to stink and rot.

Those were dark weeks of nightmares and such an aching loneliness that I thought I *would* die. But today the sun finally came out again.

There were no portents or careening hawks overhead, no dreams or hidden messages in fire smoke to tell me that my twin had returned after being months away in Sparta. Still, I knew he was coming home, and my heart fairly sang in my chest at the thought of embracing him again.

"A sister always knows," I mused in a voice rusty from disuse. Only today did I dare speak again, knowing that soon my words would no longer be wasted on deaf ears. I'd dressed in my best finery by the dim light of a single oil lamp, a flowing black skirt embroidered with a gold geometric border and a soft fringed kilt pinned with a golden snake brooch that matched the serpent girdle coiled around my waist. Between my breasts was the small terra-cotta vial I always carried, its contents a secret reminder of my strength. Thick golden bangles covered my wrists so I looked like a pampered princess, save for my bare feet, which no one could see.

Now all that remained was to wait. And hope.

Idly, I scratched the bony chin of my tomcat. Fairly decrepit now, he had been a beloved gift from Hellenus when we were both scarcely older than children, just after the incident in the temple of Apollo. My scrawny mouser loved to catch birds and nibble on all manner of insects, provided they'd been appropriately dispatched first.

Except ants. He hated ants.

A conveniently fat fly had somehow gotten in and landed on a wall fresco, this one depicting my father on Troy's limestone ramparts, his hand raised in salute. The insect skittered up my father's shoulder and stopped on his head. There was a sudden thwack, and my unfortunate victim fell to the tiled floor, slain by a gold-and-pearl flyswatter.

"Pesky little nit." I plucked the fly from the ground, marveling for a moment at its iridescent wings and stunning cacophony of colors on its hard shell. As a young girl, I'd collected insects until Queen Hecuba loftily informed me that the hobby wasn't fit for a child of my father's blood. The queen might have reluctantly claimed Hellenus and me after my birth killed our true mother, but that didn't mean she harbored soft feelings for either of us. Thus, into the midden heap went all my moths and butterflies, my beetles and ladybirds. I'd watched in morbid fascination for days as maggots slowly consumed their fragile forms.

"Our hold on this life is tenuous," I said, turning the dead fly in the lamplight so I might further admire its colors. "Would that we all met such quick deaths." My dreams last night had been filled with slow agonies, filled with both old and new faces and fresh scenes of carnage and fire.

I was a true seer, and the terrible clarity of these new terrors told me they were no mere dreams. I willed myself now to be calm despite the claws closing around my throat at the remembrance. There was no war right now, only a brother to welcome home.

I dropped the fly as an offering before my cat. "Enjoy," I said. Like a true feline, he ignored me entirely, content to recline on his woven cushion. "Perhaps I'll get a dog," I taunted him, but still he didn't answer. "Some beast that can be bothered to acknowledge my existence."

The heavy door behind me creaked open to let in a flood of morning sunshine, and my attendant poked her head inside. "Princess Cassandra," she said, stepping fully into the chamber and sniffing in disdain. "Were you speaking to someone?"

"The cat."

She arched an eyebrow. Perhaps speaking to cats was frowned upon, especially when one hasn't spoken to another human in weeks. Honestly, I much preferred the company of animals to people. Especially this bent-backed woman with her sour smell and face puckered like a rotting peach. She might bring me my meals every day, but that didn't mean I had to like her, especially as I knew she reported my every sneeze to Father. "Your brother and his entourage have returned from Sparta."

"I'm well aware," I said. "They arrived after the seventh hour."

She scowled, at my rudeness or the way I'd done my hair or just because she didn't care for anything about me. I noticed then that her customary tray with its normal spread of crusty bread, goat cheese, and olives was missing. My heart leaped at what that might mean.

"Am I to attend the royal entourage?" I asked, hoping against hope that I might be allowed to welcome home my brothers.

"Hellenus requested your presence, and King Priam has relented, *if* you can promise to behave in a civilized manner this time."

"Of course," I said, cringing inwardly at the memory of my begging Father not to send Paris to Sparta. That had not ended well.

"Your father sent me to escort you to the citadel," she said, gesturing outside with a pale arm. I swept past her without another word onto Troy's battlements and into the glorious sunshine.

The sun . . .

Apollo's light, but how I loved the sun. I closed my eyes and relished its warmth on my skin, like the warmth of Hellenus' smile.

Then I opened my eyes and drank deep the sight of the city around me. Its inhabitants reviled me, but there was no denying that Troy was the most breathtaking city on earth, a glittering crown perched atop the world. Not only were we beautiful, but strong, too, for the gods who'd forged the city knew that the rest of the world would slaver like feral dogs to claim our riches. The towering limestone outer walls built by Poseidon and Apollo encircled the city like a warrior's sword arm, and defensive towers peered beyond those walls to shield the inner courtyards and colonnaded halls. This was a city where we god-born walked in safety and prosperity—and after the terrors I'd seen in the night, those walls were more comforting than any dram of poppy milk. Those walls would protect us all, so long as they were never breached.

The gleaming royal citadel was perched atop Troy's highest hill, adorned with colonnades and palaces of hewn stone to house fifty bedchambers for all of my father's sons, plus twelve more for his daughters.

Only I was kept apart, ostracized to the lower reaches of the citadel. Yet I refused to let the long fingers of loneliness curl around my heart today.

From here, I looked down upon the many gardens and expansive stables, for Troy was famous for its horse tamers and the beasts they raised to pull our chariots. My oldest half brother Prince Hector's penchant for the beasts had earned him the title Tamer of Horses within our family. The smell of manure was barely palpable, for no foul scent would dare defile our city. Beyond that were the wool-gatherers, their sheep freshly shorn for the summer and their clouds of white gold spread out to dry in tiled courtyards. Men worked to bind and stretch the shorn wool between two trees, like clumsy spiders. In the most far-flung district, smiths labored at fiery forges to mix precious tin and copper into the bronze that was the lifeblood of our trade with the Achaean sea-kings. So many little lives lived by so many little people.

To the west of the city lay its sprawling golden beach, the fickle River Scamander with its hot and cold springs that drained into the boundless waste of the wine-dark sea. Today a far-off pod of dolphins frolicked in the waves, and playful winds tossed the briny air, whipping my dark curls about my face.

I ran in the opposite direction to the uppermost heights of the citadel, ignoring the harpy attendant screeching behind me. I could taste my freedom.

I loathed crowds—I loathed people in general—so the crush of humanity that now packed the citadel from the lower city almost brought me to my knees after so many weeks alone. Of course, I should have known that every noble, foreign dignitary, and shepherd in Troy would have noted the return of our ships and followed the entourage back to the palace in the hopes of ogling any trade goods and hearing the gossip from far-off Sparta. Whereas I'd envisioned a warm family gathering—warm meaning my family would tolerate my presence—it seemed that the entire city had packed itself onto the rocky plateau of the citadel.

I wanted to scream or turn and bolt, but the knowledge that Hellenus was somewhere in the horde of people made me press on.

My tarrying had caused me to be one of the last to arrive, yet still the rest of the perfumed courtiers gave me a wide berth, pulling their hems close. Perhaps on a different day I'd have spit in their faces, for the blisters of their insults had not yet turned to calluses, but today I would restrain myself. I glanced to where my father stood on the raised dais in regalia that would have rivaled that of Zeus himself: a tall man, gray-bearded but strongly built despite his half-century of years, his eyes, piercing as blades, that narrowed when his gaze fell on me.

I bowed my head in submission. I would be on my best behavior, even if it killed me.

The entire royal family was assembled for this spectacle, all the way down to my young half brother Prince Polites. It was a simple matter to locate my twin, for Hellenus stood stocky and dark amongst my fairer skinned half brothers, his warrior's braid secured with a simple strip of goat hide. My heart leaped, and I called out to him, waving my arms frantically. Against all odds, he saw me, and a grin cleft his dark face.

I could breathe easier then, feeling as if everything was right in the world. That illusion was shattered when I looked to see which brother stood beside Hellenus.

Paris laughed at something someone had said while he adjusted his ibex bow and the quiver of arrows slung on his back. I'd hoped against hope that a mighty albatross would pluck Paris from the deck of his ship and drop him screaming into the dark depths of a monster's maw. Instead, he appeared more hale and hearty than when he'd left, with an extra swagger in his step as he broke off whispering with our father to take his official place behind Hector. Still, I thought I detected a hint of healing injuries on his face, a yellow shadow around his eye and a cut around his eyebrow, as if he'd been in a fight at the end of the wedding festivities. Not for the first time—and certainly not the last—I rued the fact that it was my vision that had saved the miserable pissant in the Temple of Zeus.

I wended my way to the far side of the dais to join the women beneath a woven canopy, past Queen Hecuba in her luxurious layered kilts and golden laurel crown, to settle in an open chair next to Hector's wife, Andromache. She was a sunny-natured girl, a few years younger than I, with a small freckled face and a pair of dancing eyes that had made my eldest brother grin like a fool on their marriage day.

That was no mean feat, for Hector was anything but a fool.

Like her husband, Andromache erred on the side of being kind to me. Still, I knew that I unsettled her, although I went out of my way not to.

"You look lovely today, Cassandra," she said to me. "Black suits you."

"Thank you." I struggled to find something more to say, but the crush of people and all their clanging voices pressed hard against me, like sharp red triangles of sound at my temples. I closed my eyes and beat a rapid tattoo with my foot.

Why, oh why, couldn't I just run to my brother, drag him out of the city onto the plains and into the clean air to escape this mess of humanity? I felt a gentle pressure on my leg and flinched, but it was only Andromache's dainty hand.

"More than two months away from Troy." She looked drawn and grave, I noticed, lacking her usual cheerful energy. Perhaps the voyage home had been difficult. "You must be glad Hellenus is home after so long an absence."

I nodded and willed my foot to cease twitching. "More than you know."

"I have some idea." A smile, but a somber one for Andromache. "I could never have been separated from Hector for so long. He needs me terribly."

One didn't have to be a seer to prophesize that Andromache would one day have a baby perched on those slender hips of hers. That would bring the cheer back to her smiles. I smiled, too, for Hector and Andromache were kind. And there was no denying they'd make lovely babies. Still, I caught the way Hellenus' eyes strayed to Andromache every so often, like the tides toward a full moon.

Oh, Hellenus . . .

Father raised his hands for quiet then, and the crowd settled. That was better, without all the nattering of so many mouths like bleating lambs.

"My sons, kinsmen, and fellow Trojans!" my father called out, his voice deep and sonorous. "We are here today to celebrate the safe return of your Trojan princes from a successful expedition to the bleak and distant lands of Sparta!"

The assembly cheered and clapped. "Did you bring back any spoils?" The question came from a prosperous merchant who had lost a ship to a raid last year. "Those Achaean sea-dogs deserve it after their foul attacks last spring!"

The taller spectators craned their necks for a glimpse of any glittering luxuries my brothers might have procured along the way. After all, the Achaeans were little better than pirates, raiding our coasts during fair winds. It seemed only just that our men might have returned the favor. But the dais was empty of any gold or sacks of rubies, slaves, or livestock.

Instead, Hector stepped alongside our father. "This was no mission of retribution. Sadly, we had no time to relieve the Achaeans of any of their valuables."

Perhaps no one else noticed it, but Hector's fingers rapped a steady beat against his thigh. He was lying.

But why?

A quick glance at the rest of the assemblage showed several of them to be on edge. Even Hellenus seemed tense, a vein in his neck throbbing. Only Paris and my father seemed at ease.

Paris stepped in front of Hector then, though his slender frame scarcely blocked our eldest brother. "In Sparta, we witnessed the wedding of Odysseus of Ithaca to Penelope. Her father is a champion runner, you know, and was reluctant to part with his favorite daughter, and so he proclaimed a contest! No man would have her save he who could beat her father in a foot race. Along came Odysseus . . ."

I scowled to realize that the crowd was leaning forward, drawn to Paris' sweet story like mindless honeybees to nectar. He did know how to weave a tale, hands flying to illustrate his words. I refused to be charmed, leaning back in my seat with arms folded across my chest, willing this to be over before we were all old enough to be in our graves.

"He bested Penelope's sire by tricking him into calling for a drinking game the night before. The poor man did his best to keep up with young Odysseus, but he could scarcely stand, much less sprint the next morning. Odysseus wasn't impervious to the wine, either; both were violently ill at the finish line!"

The crowd laughed, although I noticed Father's frown. Paris was foolish to believe he'd appreciate the tale of a king being bested by such simple trickery.

Paris continued, "Sadly, the Spartans are a shabby people, lacking all the polish and splendor of Troy, and many of their Achaean compatriots are even meaner folk. There was only a scrubby mare to sacrifice for the wedding feast and drab wildflowers to adorn the young bride. However, there was one glorious jewel there, rarer even than those that adorn my mother's crown."

The crowd swiveled to look at Queen Hecuba's laurel diadem with its riot of gold rings and amber flowers. She gave an indulgent smile, and Paris continued.

"It would have been an affront to the gods to leave such a jewel in the hands of those Achaean swineherds," Paris said. "So do you know what we did?"

Polites' little hand shot up. His face shone with the simple joy of a child who lived in a world far happier than the rest of us. "Did you bring it back?"

Paris laughed and jogged down the dais, ruffling his brother's hair so he beamed with pleasure. Why was I the only one who saw Paris for the weasel he was?

"We did indeed, little brother." He stood his full height and threw back his shoulders. "Or rather, I did."

Hector might have been Hellenus' twin in that moment instead of me, so identical were their clenched jaws and narrowed eyes. They didn't approve of what was about to happen, but I still didn't understand why.

"By the grace of all the gods," Paris said, "I have brought to Troy the finest, most beautiful woman in the world. Aphrodite cannot walk among us mere mortals, but if she could, she would look like Queen Helen of Sparta. My Helen," Paris continued. "Once of Sparta and now of Troy."

"*Your* Helen?" Hecuba asked. "If I'm not mistaken, Helen of Sparta is wife to King Menelaus."

"You're almost correct," Paris said, preening like a damned cockerel. "She *was* married to him."

"Then Menelaus is dead?"

Paris shook his head. "Menelaus is very much alive, although he may wish for his death after losing so lovely a pearl. Helen now belongs to me."

He spread one arm wide in an expansive gesture. There was a collective intake of breath as a veiled woman moved from behind Father's throne. I recognized his hand in this turn of events. For all that my father appeared the benevolent shepherd to his flock, I knew his darker side. I didn't understand what he was orchestrating here, only that it didn't bode well for any of us.

The woman moved like quicksilver, tall and graceful, bells tinkling at her wrists and ankles. Every man assembled—the old, infirm, and those with the first fuzz of manhood on their upper lips—watched her with hungry eyes while the women muttered darkly. Cloth of gold embroidered with apple blossoms rippled over well-placed curves with her every move. My breath caught, and I clutched Andromache's hand next to me so hard she gasped.

The foreign woman lifted her golden veil in a slow movement. My veins filled with ice water as I recognized her chiseled cheekbones and lush lips like rose petals, her honeycomb of pale golden curls and skin smoother than fresh cream. The gleam in her icy eyes as she took Paris' outstretched hand.

Hers was the face from my nightmares.

Once again I felt the scorch of flames, their fiery arms clawing at Troy's towers to devour the helpless souls within while enemy spearmen poured into the city. And atop the walls, cackling over the inferno, a golden fiend.

The woman before me was the flesh-and-blood version of the daemon that lurked in my nightscapes. I knew with certainty that this was no mere dream, but a prophecy now set in motion by Paris and this woman. I recalled his boasts of possessing a special task in Sparta; Father's broad smile now confirmed that it was he who maneuvered the pieces on this board.

But why? Why bring war to Troy?

For the usual reasons, you empty-headed simpleton. Every king craves riches and power. Your father more than most.

Hector was addressing our father in low tones, clearly arguing Helen's welcome, though out of respect he kept his voice low. *Listen to him, you mad fools!*

The voice clanged in my head like a warning gong, but Father was waving Hector off, and the crowd was roaring, shouting in their haste to congratulate Paris.

I quailed only a moment, brushing with my fingertips the vial tucked into my bodice to fortify me. Then I lunged from my chair before Andromache or Hecuba or even the gods could stop me.

"Send her back!" I screamed, launching myself at Helen's face. I had no weapon, but I would destroy the beauty that had entranced Paris and entrapped us all. My fingers tore at her golden veil and my nails found purchase in the soft skin of her cheek. Helen screeched in pain, startled out of her marble poise as she tried to defend herself with bare arms, but I was possessed by the wrath of a thousand vengeful gods. My fists came away with handfuls of her beautiful golden hair, and still I attacked, even as I heard Hellenus yell my name. "She will destroy us all!" I screeched.

Rough hands clamped down on my arms and dragged me back, yet I fought against them, my bare feet kicking in vain and my claws tearing at air. Paris ran to protect Helen, who fell back panting and quivering on the dais. Despite the damage I'd done to her face and hair, she was still lovelier than a goddess. "She will bring the Achaeans to our shores like a nest of hornets," I screamed, spitting at her. "Send her back!"

"Get away, Mouth of Evil!" Paris shouted, shoving me away from them so I fell to the ground.

"Restrain her," my father said, and at first I hoped he spoke of Helen until rope scratched at my wrists. I fought like a woman possessed then, spitting like a hydra and clawing like a chimera until I was tightly bound and thrown over Hector's shoulder. I saw guardsmen holding Hellenus back from coming to my rescue and knew I had lost.

"Cease struggling, and it will go easier for you," Hector said in my ear. There was no way I could best him with physical force, yet I refused to fall silent as I'd done so often in the past.

"Send her back, Father, or you shall be the last Trojan king to sit upon that throne!" I shrieked. "Women, begin weaving burial shrouds, for your husbands and sons will soon be carrion for the crows!"

That was when they gagged me.

By the time Hector deposited me in my chambers, I was sobbing uncontrollably, spent and exhausted from the futility of the fight.

"You do this to yourself, Cassandra," Hector said, looking down on me from his great height as he gently removed my gag. "Rest now, and perhaps tomorrow will be kinder."

He was wrong. There would be no kind tomorrows, only sorrows the like of which singers would recite for years to come.

"Cassandra!" My twin's voice, calling me as he burst through the doorway in Hector's wake, and suddenly I was enveloped in his strong arms. No matter what happened, Hellenus would protect me.

"Are you all right?" he asked, and I nodded into his shoulder.

"Silly girl," he muttered. "You know better than to challenge our father."

I ignored my twin as Hector paused in the doorway. "Hector," I said, my voice barely a croak. He turned to look back at me, his features blackened in the shadows from the sun behind him. I shuddered then with another dark premonition of Hector, somewhat older but irretrievably lost to us.

Like so many others would be if the war I saw came to pass.

"Hector," I said, this time more urgently as the mania that had possessed me began to clear. My hands were still bound, and I struggled to sit. "Why did you let Paris take her? Why?"

My eldest half brother's lips were tight set. "What's done can no longer be undone."

"There will be war," I said, sliding off the bed to fall to my knees before him, like a supplicant before an altar. "Please, Hector—"

But he only held up the massive hands I'd seen calm countless frightened horses. "I have done my best. Father has made his decision. Helen stays."

The distaste was writ clear on his face as he beckoned to Hellenus, and I caught Hector's whisper of "touched by the gods" as he glanced at me. Then his expression softened to a melancholy frown, and he closed the door behind him.

I slumped to the floor then, staring at my chamber's walls. Last night, after I'd woken shrieking from the visions, I had dared not return to sleep and had instead set myself to painting the images on my walls. It was a habit I often resorted to when nightmares clawed my skull, for in drawing the nightmares, I might draw them *out* of me. I stared at the newest images: the ships, the towers, the men.

Troy.

I touched the old scars at my wrists, finding comfort in their hard edges despite the fresh wetness seeping from last night's cuts, newly opened when Hector trussed me up like a sacrificial lamb. I would add to the marks tonight, for seeing Helen had brought the rest of the dreamscapes into perfect clarity. The blood and flames, the rage and the grief.

This morning I'd thought our walls would keep us safe. Little did I know the enemy had already slithered inside.

I glanced down at my palms, my heart lightening to see the glint of gold there.

A single strand of blond hair. Helen's hair.

My heart leaped, and I coiled the treasure around my thumb for safekeeping.

"Helen must return to Sparta," I said.

"We tried to send her back when we first discovered her," Hellenus said, a dejected slump to his broad shoulders, although not so broad as Hector's. "Hector even demanded it, but Paris claimed he had Father's blessing to nettle the Achaeans."

"He's not nettling them," I said, picking at my knuckle, relishing the hairline crack of blood that emerged. "He's jamming a stick into their hive. And we shall all pay the price when they come after us." I gestured to the macabre paintings along my walls. "I've seen it."

Hellenus stood and frowned at the image of the temple of Athena on fire with the goddess' statue toppled to the ground, a great hulking Achaean hovering over a crumpled woman while a Trojan soldier stood helpless in the shadows outside. Next to it was a wall of a thousand ships—I'd counted—bearing all manner of strange sigils, a vision I couldn't shake from my mind, try as I might. Near it was my first painting—now faded, even though the memory of that night was still blade-sharp in my mind—the temple of Apollo with two figures in the shadowy forecourt.

Nothing good ever came to be in the house of a god. I'd learned that at the first blush of maidenhood, after I'd taken my vows as a priestess of Apollo. I'd gone to Father in a fit of sobbing but had received the opposite of the help and solace I'd expected. I'd thought of ending it all that night, but my twin had found me at dawn where Father had locked me away—for my own good, he'd claimed—the knife in my trembling hand and the stark ribbon of blood curling down my wrist. That was the first time I'd felt pain's cleansing release, the same I now craved.

"No, Cassandra," Hellenus had said, taking the knife from me. "Whatever it is, it isn't worth this."

Perhaps not, but it had seemed a small price to pay for a father's lost love and a god's displeasure. Still, I'd allowed Hellenus to tuck the blade into his own belt and sing me to sleep.

Now Hellenus knelt beside me and set to work removing the ropes that bound my wrists. I squirmed to keep him from seeing my mangled wrists, for not even Hellenus would understand the bone-deep need to purge myself.

I moved too late, for he grasped my wrist and turned it over as the ropes fell to the floor. "What have you done?" he whispered.

I forced myself not to yank my hands back. "After you left—when I told everyone it had been a mistake to send Paris to Sparta, Father locked me up."

"Like last time."

I nodded. But it had been worse this time, for I'd been entirely alone. For months.

"I'm so sorry I wasn't here." Hellenus pressed a kiss to my forehead, further comforting me with his familiar scent of cinnamon oil. I blinked back rare tears as he released me. I could hear the questions in his mind as he looked around my room, at the paintings of ships and fire I'd painted with my own blood. He lifted his eyes and stared up at the rafters.

"Oh, Cassandra," he murmured.

Don't let him see, you fool. He'll hate you if he sees everything.

I jumped up, tried to cover his eyes, but he only gaped. Never before had I let it go so far.

I hated the way his eyes changed then, filled with pity and something else. Revulsion, perhaps?

I wanted to die then. I wanted to be better, different, not to see the things I'd seen and know the things I knew.

I flinched as he flung open the door and bellowed at a passing slave to bring baskets to remove all the rubbish from my room.

Not my room. My cell.

A pyramid-shaped chamber on the ramparts where Father had locked me the night of Apollo's temple, complete with the sour-faced attendant who reported my every utterance to him. Eventually, I had been allowed out—this time I wondered if I would be so lucky. After my attack on Helen, I predicted it would be a long, long time before I felt the sun on my face again. If ever.

The tiny cell felt even smaller as several slaves packed inside to do Hellenus' bidding.

"Do we remove those, too?" one asked, making the sign against evil as she lifted her chin toward the rafters. All manner of animal skulls hung from roughly hewn ropes, gifts my cat had brought me, sneaking in when my attendant delivered food or deigned to empty my night bucket. There were tiny mice, birds, and bats, and even a slender snake—Apollo's mouthpiece—with its desiccated skin still clinging to its bones. That one I'd tied the highest to keep it from whispering foul prophecies in my ears while I slept. It worked some nights, others—like last night—not at all.

All were painted with charcoal and blood, meant to keep away the daemons I saw in my visions.

"I want this room fit for Priam's daughter by nightfall!" Hellenus commanded the slaves.

Soon the detritus of the last few months was swept away: plates of moldy bread, fouled bandages and filthy clothing, and so much more that I'd forgotten about and failed to notice. It looked worse illuminated by the light from the door—easier to ignore it all in the perpetual gloom of my windowless cell. I would miss the bones of my silent friends, but only two treasures had to be safe from the slaves' pillaging: the terra-cotta vial in my bodice and—

"No!" I yelled as one slave moved to sweep away a set of yellowing bones atop a small cushion. I whisked away the precious skull and clutched it jealously to my chest, careful not to disturb the tiny bits of dried skin and fur that still remained. "Not my cat!"

"Your cat?" Hellenus stared at me in horror. "Tell me that's not the one I gave you?"

I shrugged, not knowing how Hellenus wanted me to answer. "He died after you left for Sparta, and I couldn't bear to part with him." Not even when his body had bloated with putrefying gas and the ants had covered him. I'd killed so many that my fingers had been black for days, and I had finally stripped away his rotting flesh myself to keep the insects off him. "He's the only one who listens to me when you're not around."

Hellenus just stared at me. "What am I going to do with you, Cassandra?" he finally asked.

I took offense at that and bared my teeth at the slave woman as I replaced my cat—or what was left of him—on his cushion. I'd bite off her fingers before I'd let her touch him. "You could listen to me, for a start," I said to my brother.

Hellenus sighed and ran a hand over his tightly plaited hair. "There's nothing that can be done, at least not right now. The entire court was congratulating Paris on his cuckolding of Menelaus when I left to chase after you. All of Troy sees Helen's presence as a victory won, nothing more."

"Until the Achaeans come calling with their warships. There will be war, Hellenus."

"I've seen the Achaean forces. They may build fine ships, but they're provincial compared to the might of Troy."

"Farmers with pitchforks can still set their neighbor's fields ablaze."

"Hector and I expect they'll send a delegation to ask for Helen's return before it comes to war." He reached out to clasp my hand.

"You could leave, Cassandra. Leave here and go somewhere quiet where no one can hurt you again."

I shook my head. "Father will never make the mistake of letting me loose again."

"I'll reason with him, ask for your release. I won't go without you." Hellenus' eyes suddenly shuttered. "I can't leave, especially not if it comes to war. I promised Hector I would fight by his side. He relies on me—"

"So does Andromache. That's the real chain holding you here." Hellenus opened his mouth to protest, but I stopped him with a raised hand. "Don't worry; I doubt anyone else can see how you look at her."

Hellenus flushed and ducked his head. "I can't leave them," he muttered.

"Then neither can I, especially considering it was my misfortune to recognize Paris and unleash all this upon us." I clutched Hellenus' hand tight. "When the Achaeans come, swear to me that you'll find a way to send that bitch Helen back."

"I'll do what I can," Hellenus promised. "I only hope it's enough."

It would have to be. Elsewise, my nightmares would break free from my dreamscape to embroil us all.

I didn't pray because I no longer trusted the gods, but in that moment, I made a vow more sacred than the one I'd once sworn on Apollo's stone-cold altar. All my life I had seen what others could not and despaired when they refused to heed the truth. This time I would make them listen. *This* would be the nightmare prophecy that never came true.

And looking about my scrubbed and shining chamber, I had a sudden faith that I could do it.

TROY accepted Helen as a jewel meant to enhance the city's beauty.

I listened in horror from my cell as heralds shouted her praise and the city cheered while she was paraded about in a celebration to set fire to the heavens. Singers wrote new songs claiming that her coming had brought glory to our city, but I knew she would make those same flames fall from the heavens to earth.

It was only a matter of time unless something was done to stop this madness.

All this while I was kept under lock and key.

Me, the only sane one in the entire kingdom, reviled as a madwoman while the rest of the city seized with pleasure akin to a Dionysian debauch. I shook my head grimly to hear my family made such fools and imagined how they would hang their heads when I rescued them from their own folly. A tiny flare of hope deep in my chest believed that in doing so, I might finally win their love and acceptance.

It might have been days or weeks since my attack on Helen when I was woken from a deep and blissfully dreamless sleep by the scrape of the heavy bolt being removed from the other side of the door. It wasn't time for my next meal, at least not judging from the full tray of food that lay untouched by my lone oil lamp. I yelped and scrambled out of the way as the door swung open, blinking at the sudden light.

"See that we're not disturbed," Father ordered before the door closed behind him. He strode past me to my only chair, and I scuttled away from his upturned boots, pulling my knees to my chest from force of habit.

"You have disappointed me yet again, Cassandra," he said after he'd finished arranging his tunic, looking down his nose at me. His beard and nails were freshly trimmed, whereas my hair was a tangle, and I'd yet to wash the blood from my wrists. "Your brother came to ask for your release, but I had to tell him that's not possible."

"It is," I said, stumbling closer. "I promise—"

He held up a hand, his gold lion ring gleaming dully in the weak light. "It is not, not when you rage against my decisions even from within these walls. This rabble-rousing of yours must stop, Cassandra. It *will* stop, or I swear before Zeus you'll never see anything outside your cell again."

My cell, which he had used to lock me away after the temple of Apollo, to protect me from myself and my own lack of virtue, he'd said. I'd gone to him hysterical, seeking solace from the father who I thought would protect me, but I'd been betrayed.

Just as I was betrayed now.

"I speak the truth," I said, heart hammering in my ears as I faced the man who had created but never valued me. "You know not what you do, inviting this war with the Achaeans."

"Foolish girl," he said, eyes flashing as he rose. "I know exactly what I do."

But I was no fool. I'd had much time to think in the darkness between Hellenus' visits, to ponder why my father didn't send Helen back on the first ship to Mycenae with enough gold to placate Menelaus for so egregious a crime.

Power. Always power.

"You seek to steal more glory for yourself while Hattusa is distracted by civil war. You think to strangle the tin trade with the Achaeans and squeeze ever more taxes from them for harboring their ships in Troy after they lose this fight." I knew I was right from the way my father's eyes narrowed. "Your desires are transparent to me, as is the future."

"The future is never clear," he temporized, and my heart lifted. At least he was arguing with me—if he could argue, he could be convinced. "You defile your own tongue to say otherwise."

"I have seen it," I said, gesturing to the sketches of charcoal and blood on my walls. "You will lose all if you let this war come to pass."

For a moment, I thought I saw doubt in his eyes, but then he blinked, and it was gone. "Helen will go back if she proves to be more trouble than she's worth, beauty and Paris be damned. I never risk all, for I'm no fool," he said. "Yet you risk all in your defiance. These four walls will be your prison until you speak a prophecy in Troy's favor against the Achaeans."

"I won't do that." I pushed down the panic that threatened. "You cannot mold prophecy to your whim. I'll not lie for you."

"Then you'll remain in here to tame your tongue and mend your mind." He rapped once on the door, and it groaned open—how I longed to shove past him and break into the sweet sunshine, if only for a moment. "Remember, one favorable prophecy and the world is yours again."

I forced myself not to fall screaming to my knees as the bar came down on the other side, locking me in darkness once again.

If only Helen would come and visit you, then you could slit her lovely throat.

The voice was no longer a comfort, proof I wasn't alone in the dark. It taunted me instead, proof of my broken mind.

I *must* succeed in saving Troy from its own folly. For in doing so, it was the only way I would save myself.

HELEN never came, only my attendant and Hellenus when he managed to bribe the woman with trinkets of gold. I kept my cat's fragile skull belted about my waist but refrained from speaking to it, my father's mandate echoing in my mind. Hellenus brought me a new patchwork kitten to keep me company—although he'd made me swear that none of her bones would ever end up decorating my rafters. Each time the door opened, my new cat brought me all manner of dead birds and mice from her forays outside. How I envied her every time she slipped in smelling of sun and sea breezes. I used a filched knife to cut open her macabre gifts and spill their entrails by the light of my lamp. The slaves thought me mad, but I worked in deadly earnest; the entrails gave me the opportunity to augur as I'd learned in the temple of Apollo.

For my city and my family. Though most of them reviled me, I refused to allow my blunder to let Paris and Helen wreak havoc on all of them.

On Hector and Andromache and little Polites.

On Hellenus.

I would save them. I would save them *all.*

Paris and Helen were rash, foul creatures who deserved to writhe in the flames of Tartarus for eternity, but I could bide my time, at least until the ships arrived. So I was on my best behavior in the weeks that followed Father's visit, even as summer darkened toward autumn and my patience was pulled tauter than a bowstring ready to snap.

There would soon be a time when I would no longer be quiet and demure. Until then, I would be my father's most perfect daughter.

In the meantime, I asked Hellenus to procure a few items for me to replace those taken from my room. I'd been at work with the chisel and thin sheet of lead for ages, but it was finally complete. I wound the strand of Helen's golden hair around the rolled metal.

The delicate tablet was inscribed with daemon words unintelligible to the eyes of mere mortals, taught to me by an Achaean slave girl who knew darker ways to commune with the gods.

"I curse Helen of Sparta," I chanted over the tablet. "I curse her mind and her memory and her face. May her liver be rotten and spotted, her tongue gnarled and twisted. May this curse hasten her to her grave or back from whence she came."

With that, I stabbed the flimsy metal and its strand of golden hair through with iron nails.

And I braced myself to do what I swore I wouldn't do.

I lied.

I sent word to my attendant that I'd dreamed of Troy, our glorious city still standing while the Achaeans withdrew their ships from our beaches. I *had* glimpsed this in a dream, but it was only a fragment of some larger, bleaker story. But as my cell doors swung open and I stepped into the sunshine for the first time in months, I told myself the lie didn't matter.

I'd made it over the first obstacle. I could do this.

In the first moment of forgotten freedom, I felt like a drowning woman brought to the ocean's surface for air. I ignored the guards at my side with their spears and daggers and instead closed my eyes, briefly letting my fingers touch the vial tucked into my bodice. In my own head, I could make everything fade away and focus on the play of the sea air on my cheeks and the feel of the warm stones beneath my bare feet. Perhaps people stared at me, but I was accustomed to their glares. My dark face would always garner attention, as did my twin's, and I received twice the number of gapes he did as I was not just dark but mad. But today I didn't care about the stares. I was free.

My attendant had dressed me in a fresh skirt today, my customary black but emblazoned with golden suns at the hem. I'd embroidered the skirt myself after my girlhood incident in Apollo's temple, enjoying the fact that I could kick the symbol of that treacherous god each time I took a step. But today it was a different deity that I sought.

Guards escorted me to Athena's grand temple at Troy's highest point, stone lions guarding her outer entrance, the inner shrine flooded with light from high windows. The goddess' altar lay heaped with flowers, and a meager fire burned in the brazier, its smoke rising in a sullen crown. A great statue of Athena towered, yet it was the small figure of the Palladion that was the most sacred object in Troy. It stared at me from its small niche with wooden eyes, the goddess holding tight to her lance in one hand and distaff in the other. The wooden Palladion was a gift from Athena, fallen to earth at the founding of Troy, and so long as it remained within our walls, Troy was impervious. It was because of this that I offered Helen's curse tablet to Athena alongside a vial of my own blood, collected drop by drop since I'd been confined to my room.

"A maiden's blood," I whispered, overturning the blood into Athena's sacred fire, where it hissed and fizzled. "I have no drink offerings to pour for you, or firstling lambs to lay upon your altar, but I beg you to hear my plea. Help me find a way to return Helen to the foul backwater from whence she came."

If the great goddess heard me, she didn't answer. But from the way a sudden shaft of sunlight fell upon the Palladion and made the stars painted on her cloak suddenly glimmer, I believed she accepted my offering.

"I don't think I've seen you so at peace since we played *morra* here as children."

I startled and knocked the vial and tablet into the fire so my brother couldn't see them. I hated to hide anything from Hellenus, but my brother was far too upstanding to understand something as sordid as a curse, especially one paired with a blood offering. "A game I always won."

Hellenus bumped his shoulder against mine. "Because you cheated." He walked around as if inspecting my clean hair and finely woven skirt. "I see you've left that skull in your chambers."

"Or so you think." I pulled back the hem of my fringed kilt to reveal the cat skull at my hip.

My brother blew out an exasperated puff of air but didn't

comment. We left the temple side by side, and I watched a sleek black vulture soar lazily overhead, scanning the plains and beaches for an easy meal. Finding none, it flapped its wings and flew away.

Death, death, go away . . .

"Never to return another day," I murmured, transfixed by its movement. Was it a sign? My hopes rose further.

"What's that?" Hellenus asked.

"Nothing." I smiled.

He studied me, then gestured over the expanse of rooftops toward the horizon, where two ships approached. "I came to find you," he said. "The Achaeans are here."

Gooseflesh rippled down my arms as I peered at the foreign ships with their striped black sails, half fearing to see the waters swarmed with Achaean vessels as I did in my visions. The vibrant sun dog overhead might have been a good omen, but I'd learned not to trust Apollo. "There are only two ships, so they bring an offer of reconciliation. This may be the final opportunity to preserve peace," I said.

"Father said you'd had a positive vision—"

"I lied," I said, unable to meet Hellenus' eyes. "It was the only way he'd release me. If we fail . . ."

Yet I knew we could *not* fail.

"It's not our decision," Hellenus said. "It's Father's responsibility to set our course."

"Then we must make him set the right one."

"Tell me again of all you've seen. I'll try to convince Father."

I recounted the various sordid scenes commonplace in any war. Save the newest, one that had left me clawing at an unknown attacker and crying out for Hellenus as I'd woken. Gods, but I hoped that was a false vision. I didn't say more, for we had an unexpected visitor. "Greetings, Andromache."

I saw Hellenus' pulse thrum a quick beat in his throat before he turned around to greet our brother's small, bird-boned wife. "Good day, Andromache," he echoed.

"A happy morning to both of you," she replied. "King Priam requests your presence in the megaron," she said to my brother. Her gaze went to the foreign ships, growing taller on the horizon, and a line appeared between her straight brows. If there was anyone else in this city not utterly delighted by Helen's presence, it was Andromache—since her return from Sparta, my sister-in-law had been more solemn-eyed than the laughing lighthearted girl who departed our shores. I wondered if she shared my disquiet about the future—she was the future queen of Troy, after all, and watching those ships approach our shores, she looked it. "It's the Achaeans, isn't it?" she asked, unsmiling. "Have they finally come for Helen?"

"Without a doubt," Hellenus answered.

Andromache bit her lower lip. "Is there a chance King Priam will relent and send her back?"

"Not if he's found a way for Troy to profit from a war against the Achaeans," I answered.

"War?" Andromache blinked. "You still believe it will come to that?"

"I will stop it from happening." But her attention had already shifted.

"Hector will lead our forces in any fight that comes," she said. "So we will win." Conviction brought a flush to her cheeks. It was easy to see why Hellenus loved her. "I must summon the rest of your brothers for the king," she said, and we watched her go.

"I'll bring the goat cream with honey you like tonight," Hellenus said to me, but I could tell his mind was elsewhere, lingering on freckled cheeks and a pair of solemn eyes. I put a hand on his arm but didn't mention his heartache again. There were more important matters at hand than my brother pining for a married woman, feelings I knew him too honorable to act upon.

"Help me stop Father's mad plan," I said instead. "Together we can do this. Together we can do anything."

"Looking at you now, I believe it," my brother said. He touched my oiled curls with a smile. "You seem happier than I've seen you in a long time."

Not happier, perhaps, but filled with purpose. I would avert this war and heal myself in the process, and then Hellenus and I could leave Troy, start a new life filled with sunshine and laughter.

We discussed the bones of my plan as the sun climbed high and the Achaean ships approached, their oars working in perfect unison like giant dragonfly wings. The ships were black, their keels tarred and their prows stained a vibrant hue to match the sky. The oars raced to build momentum, then held themselves aloft as the hulls rammed onto the beach. Hellenus departed then, but I stared down at the ships, fascinated.

They seemed like children's discarded playthings in the shadows of our walls, their palsied sails flapping weakly in the breeze. I squinted to see a short man with a beard and thick shock of black hair standing at the bow of the first ship. Even from this distance, I could see him lift his eyes toward the citadel ramparts to where I stood. I knew then how a warrior must feel before a battle, facing off across a broad field from his enemy.

For we *were* enemies; there was no denying that. So, too, were Paris and Helen, and perhaps even my father. Troy was beset upon by all sides and from within.

Although the surveying Achaean couldn't see me, I dropped my chin in respect of his mission. He was a peacekeeper, and so was I.

May the gods aid us both today.

A flurry of movement down on the beach caught my attention. Rather than jump into the shallow surf, the black-haired Achaean threw a round shield onto the sands. He leaped with the grace of a wild cat onto the metal disc, as if he dared not sully his feet with Troy's sands.

I watched in confusion as, from the ship, a man in a striped tunic raised his arm, then jumped feet first onto our shores. Only then did the black-bearded man retrieve his shield and lead the way to our city's colossal main gate, more man-locusts leaping from the ships to follow him.

The riddle tickled at the edges of my mind, but I dared tarry no longer. It would take time for the Achaeans to make their way through the lower city to the citadel, but I could linger no longer to witness their approach, not while the men of my family plotted below. Yet I couldn't very well saunter into my father's megaron when my two guards had explicit orders to keep that from happening.

Why must everything in life be so difficult?

I walked in silence along the ramparts, my guards trailing like cursed shadows. I didn't stop until I'd reached the gardens. I lingered near the kitchen herbs in their giant terra-cotta pots, plucking new leaves and tasting fragrant rosemary and basil, thyme and marjoram. Near the gardener's shed was the customary pot of sand taken from the same beach the Achaeans had just landed upon, used to mix with soil for the coriander and other plants.

"Curses!" I exclaimed, suddenly kneeling down near the pot. "This wretched sandal strap has finally gone and broken."

The guards were imbeciles, for I was always barefooted as the day I was born. I wiggled my exposed toes at them and gave a nervous giggle, relishing the looks of consternation.

Ah yes, I was a mad one, wasn't I?

I bent as if to fix my imaginary sandal, waiting for the most opportune time as my guards drew closer.

One, two . . .

I exhaled, making as if to brush off my black skirt.

Three.

I grabbed two fistfuls of sand as I straightened, then whirled and threw them in perfect unison.

Straight into the eyes of my guard dogs.

They howled, their orders suddenly forgotten. I didn't waste time, my feet flying over the cobbles as if they were glowing embers. I raced down all manner of back corridors to ensure that the guards didn't find me.

Sometimes the gods favor us. Today was one of those rare moments, a sign that they wanted me to succeed.

I skidded to a halt outside my father's grand hall, for the contingent of Achaeans had already arrived. A fire burned in the great hearth where entire goats would turn on spits tonight and the room would fill with the tang of meaty offerings to the gods, but for now the only scent was that of cloying wood smoke.

Smoke and fire.

I fought away a heavy crash of panic as I slipped along the back walls, refusing to allow the now-familiar vision to gain hold over me. My mouth filled with the taste of copper coins from biting the inside of my cheeks until I could breathe again. A quick survey proved that no one had noticed me, although my sand-blinded guards were now pushing their way through the crowd in search of a barefoot princess. I ducked my head and pushed farther into the hall.

A quick glance revealed that this was no normal assembly, for the panoply of Troy's showy women were absent. Including Helen.

This was a council of men. A council of war.

"We must succeed," I whispered, stroking the top of my cat's skull for reassurance. He only stared at me with dead and hollow eyes.

I stumbled a step, for suddenly everyone seemed to stare at me with the same eyes, as if I were surrounded in a room of rotting corpses and sun-bleached skeletons. A scream built in my throat, but I swallowed it raw and willed myself to keep walking.

Gradually, the bodies around me returned to living, breathing men.

But not for long. They'll make lovely carrion for the crows.

The black-bearded Achaean stood on the bottom step of my father's dais, one hand holding the round shield he'd leaped onto earlier and the other clasped behind his back in the relaxed posture of a man before his equal. A cluster of other men stood with him, including the soldier in the striped tunic who had followed him onto the beach, a hulking Achaean larger than an ox, and a flame-haired one that could only be Menelaus. Had this been a normal greeting among kings, my father might have been alone on the dais. Instead, his armada of able-bodied sons flanked him.

Yet all was not as it seemed, for both my father and Hellenus were narrow-eyed. So Hellenus had done his best. Perhaps he had been successful, and if not, there was still my part to play.

"Greetings to Menelaus of Mycenae, Odysseus of Ithaca, and Ajax of Locris," Priam said, nodding in turn for Red Hair, Black Beard, and the Ox, and making a great show of leaning back on his throne as if bored.

Helen's husband and Odysseus of Ithaca. The ox Ajax I discarded; he was only here to intimidate, but my eyes lingered on the black-haired bridegroom who had tricked Penelope's father into parting with her. That one bore watching.

Father accepted a rock crystal *rhyton* from a slave and took a long draft of watered wine, as if the Achaeans had interrupted his leisure. "My sons tell me you wish to see me as a matter of urgency."

Menelaus moved to speak, but Odysseus stopped him with a hand on his forearm. "King Priam, you rule over many rich vassal cities," he said with a gallant sweep of his hand. His voice was a slow drawl. "My King Agamemnon is also a great king, one with a most fervent desire for peace between our peoples."

"Is that so?" My father laughed. "Did he tell that to the Trojan villages he raided last summer? I think not."

"And did you tell your sons of your wish for war before they availed themselves of my wife?" Menelaus demanded.

"Your wife chose to leave you," my father said. "She has found a new home here in Troy."

I wanted to howl and scream at my father, for he had heard me in my cell and felt my same doubts, yet he persisted in this folly.

"Your sons violated their guest-rights at my wedding," Odysseus said calmly to my father. "That's no small crime in the eyes of the gods." The king of Ithaca frowned at my eldest brother. "Condoning the kidnapping of Helen of Sparta was beneath you, Hector."

Divide and conquer. That was Odysseus' strategy with my father and his sons, but it would fail. Nothing could turn Hector into a betrayer.

"Helen was not kidnapped," Paris said from his place on the dais. Still, the coward stood half-hidden behind the shield of Hector's shoulder. "She came of her own free will, escaping a husband too much a worm to hold her."

"That worm could kill you with his bare hands," Menelaus snarled, opening and closing his fists for emphasis.

Once again Odysseus stepped in as peacekeeper. "Menelaus has his brother's full support. Agamemnon is not a man to trifle with."

"Neither am I," my father said. He rose from his throne in a leonine movement.

Odysseus bowed his head, switching to a fresh tactic. "Troy has held hostage the precious tin we need for our bronze forges and demanded outrageous taxes from us for years now, but we never guessed that your taxes included other men's wives. We are sent here to negotiate for the return of Menelaus' queen. What are your terms?"

"We have no terms."

My father's pronouncement was like the heavy roll of a war drum. I wanted to rail at him, but all was not lost . . .

The megaron erupted into a cacophony of shouts and jeers. It didn't take an oracle to know that they would bluster and boast, and Odysseus would leave without having accomplished his mission.

Thus, I covered my ears and skirted my way along the room, but not before I'd caught Hellenus' attention. He nodded his acknowledgment. Then I slipped unnoticed from the megaron and took up a post in the corridor where the thwarted Achaeans would have to pass on their retreat. I didn't have long to wait. Menelaus stormed from the megaron first, his face mottled purple with anger. I let him go, for there would be no reasoning with that one. Odysseus soon followed, although I silently cursed as two men fell into step behind him, the ox-like Ajax and the striped tunic I'd seen jump from his ship earlier.

"Odysseus," I called out. He startled, and his hand went to the dagger hilt tucked into his belt while the oblivious Menelaus disappeared around a corner. Odysseus' confusion only deepened when he saw no assassin lurking in the shadows, but a mere woman.

I'd have played the part of assassin if I thought it would solve this labyrinth of a mess, but these Achaeans were like the heads of a hydra. Cut one off and more would follow. Unfortunately, that was what my father had just done.

"I am Cassandra, the most beloved daughter of King Priam." I almost choked on the half lie. "Leave your men and please follow me." Hellenus had not yet detached himself, but I dared not waste this opportunity. I beckoned for Odysseus to follow me, ducking into an airy, columned anteroom used for ritual animal sacrifices. Storage chests built into the floor beneath wide windows held sacred *faience* figurines of gods and goddesses. Terra-cotta jars painted with seashells and my father's double-axe motif lined the walls, filled to the brim with precious wines and oils. Hellenus and I had played here as children; he knew to follow me here from our earlier discussion.

"I'll admit I've enjoyed a clandestine meeting with a pretty girl more than once," Odysseus said as he joined me at one of the windows. He hadn't entirely followed my directions; the Ox lurked at the doorway. "But I must admit this is most unusual, Princess Cassandra."

"Thank you for indulging me," I said. "It appears that you and I share similar goals. Might you spare a moment for a little game?"

Ajax crossed his arms over his barrel chest, his eyes black stains of pitch. "We don't have time for games, girl."

My skin prickled at the sound of his voice, like a jagged blade against a whetstone. I liked this one not at all, especially not the way his eyes scoured me. Suddenly, luring Odysseus here without Hellenus seemed foolhardy.

Odysseus scratched his short black beard, looking at his companion. "You know me not at all, Ajax, if you think I've no time for games. There is *always* time for games." He gestured for the man to wait outside, giving me room to breathe. "What manner of game do you have in mind, Princess Cassandra? I fear you and your Trojans enjoy only the dangerous kind."

This one was no fool.

"I ask only that you allow us to set aside our differences so I might ask you a question, and you answer. Then you ask, and I answer. We swear only to tell the truth."

"And the winner is decided . . . ?"

"When the other can no longer answer without lying. Are you up for the challenge?"

"It would be my honor to play with the likes of Priam's favorite daughter."

I almost snorted with laughter, for I'd already broken the rules by claiming my father's love. I could look forward to my cell becoming my tomb if Father ever found out what I'd done here. "Why did you jump upon your shield when you landed on our shores?"

Odysseus blinked. I had caught him unawares.

Better and better.

"An oracle prophesized that the first Achaean to land on Troy's shores would die," he answered. "I thought it better to be safe than sorry."

I chuckled at that. "I assume your friend in the striped tunic hadn't heard the prophecy."

Odysseus gave a devious grin. "You would be correct in that assumption. Your turn, daughter of Priam. Can your father be persuaded to return Helen of Sparta?"

"You've wasted a question, Odysseus of Ithaca, for my father made that answer readily apparent," I said. "Although if it were up to me, I'd serve you her head on a golden platter."

Odysseus chortled at that. "I've always thought that woman more trouble than she was worth."

"Then we're agreed on something. Can Menelaus be persuaded to let Helen go? Perhaps if Father were to buy him off?"

"Is he willing to do that?"

I shrugged. "Answer the question."

"It's not likely. Especially with . . ."

"With what?"

"It's not your turn," he said with a sly grin. "Is your city prepared for war?"

"Our walls have never been breached." I dodged the question, for Troy thought herself invincible. "What did you mean, Menelaus isn't likely to let Helen go?"

Odysseus hesitated, and I knew he was contemplating ending the game. "Menelaus' brother, Agamemnon, looks for an excuse to wage war against Troy. Your brother has just delivered the perfect opportunity."

"*Half* brother," I corrected Odysseus out of habit.

Agamemnon, king of Mycenae. That was the second time I'd heard that name today, and it didn't bode well.

I strummed my fingers on the window ledge but stopped when Odysseus watched the movement. I doubted whether the scars on my wrists or my battered knuckles escaped his notice.

Too late.

"Those are terrible scars for a gently born princess to bear. Where did you get them?"

I might have ended the game there, but my scars weren't worth the lie.

"By my own hand," I said.

"So you're tormented by daemons." It was a statement, not a question. I wondered what Hellenus had mentioned of me while he was in Sparta.

"We all fight our own daemons." Mine just happened to be louder than others. "My father also craves war. You believe Agamemnon is willing to walk into his trap and find himself a client state of Troy once he loses?"

"You assume Troy will win," Odysseus said with a sly smile. "Agamemnon will be happy to avenge his brother's honor if it means he can steal Troy's riches for himself. The question is, who will win this war?"

"Do you think I'd play games with you if I knew the answer to that question?"

"No, I suppose not. Are there any holes in your city's defenses?"

"It's not your turn," I said.

He waggled a finger at me. "You asked if I thought you'd play games with me. I answered."

I wrinkled my nose. This Odysseus was more slippery than a saltwater eel, yet I had to admit that I'd have liked him very much had he not been a cursed Achaean.

"Are there any holes in Troy's defenses?" he asked. "Chinks in your city's armor?"

I sighed. "None I'm aware of. Not that I'd have told you if I did know."

He waggled his eyebrows at me. "I had to try."

I laughed, sad that this game was almost finished, for there was little left to learn. "How long do you believe this war will last?"

"So there will be a war."

No. I will die trying. "Answer."

He shrugged. "Your reputation as an augur precedes you, Lady, for your brother spoke of you at my wedding. I fear this fight, if it comes to these shores, will last long enough for the bards to sing about us for years to come."

"That's a long time to be away from your new bride," I said, raising an eyebrow. "Shouldn't you go home to fair Penelope and persuade Agamemnon that these walls aren't worth assaulting?" I saw that the thought of his wife swayed him, but the hulking Ajax reentered then, his patience finally run out.

"Enough of this game, Odysseus," he said, running his pitch-black eyes over me. My skin crawled. "The mealymouthed Trojans won't give Helen back, but it occurs to me that this daughter of Priam's would make a fine substitute."

Odysseus held up a hand. "We are not thieves, Ajax. And Princess Cassandra has done us no harm."

"Doesn't matter." Ajax moved to close the distance between us.

I forced myself not to shudder, but bile rose in my throat anyway. This was one Achaean I would rejoice to see slaughtered should our peoples clash on the battlefield.

"Don't take another step," said a voice behind Ajax.

"Hello, Brother," I said to Hellenus as he stepped around Ajax's huge shoulder. "You missed all the fun. Odysseus and his friends were just leaving."

"It was my pleasure to while away the time with you," Odysseus said to me, bowing. "I do hope you're able to change your father's mind before the tides change and we must carry his words back to Menelaus' brother."

It was a threat and a promise. I didn't answer, only watched the Achaeans march away. It wasn't until the echo of their sandals faded that I allowed myself to slump against the wall, spent and exhausted—but hopeful.

"What did you think you were doing, letting yourself be cornered by *them*?" Hellenus grabbed my arm when I didn't answer.

"I don't care if meeting with the Achaeans was dangerous," I said, shrugging him off. "Odysseus listened to me. He'll speak reason to Agamemnon, keep him from declaring war on Troy."

"Do you truly believe Agamemnon will listen?"

"He must. Because if war comes, we *will* lose. There is no escaping death's gate if the Achaeans come again. But they will not. I will stop it."

My brother only gathered me into his arms. "Hush," he said, stroking my hair. "You can't know that."

He doesn't believe you. He thinks you cursed by the gods, just like Hector and the rest of them.

I shoved him away. "You don't believe I can avert the Fates, do you? You think me mad." I glowered at him, wrapping my arms around myself at the sudden chill. "You have to believe me, Hellenus, or I'll lose myself . . ."

While the snickers of laughter and snide comments from others had always stung, Hellenus' love and belief in me kept their insults from piercing my heart. I grasped the window ledge, for this would be a mortal wound if Hellenus no longer believed me.

"Of course I believe you," Hellenus said, but I wasn't entirely sure I believed *him*. He tucked my hand around his arm and led me out of the anteroom. "And you are right—much can change. Perhaps Apollo grants you visions of what may be, not what *will* be."

Yet none of my visions had been wrong, not since Apollo's priest had cursed me.

A terrible idea blossomed, but I pushed it to the back of my mind. Hellenus himself would lock me in my room if he knew what I planned. In fact, I might lock myself away.

"Promise me you'll stay behind the walls if the time does come," I begged him. I could survive much, but I'd never survive witnessing my twin cut down by the Achaeans, his lifeblood watering the plains along the Scamander.

"You know I can't promise that," Hellenus said. "All of us will fight if it comes to war: Hector, Paris, Deiphobus, all the family. Father has spoken of calling Aeneas from Dardania and the rest of our cousins."

My father would gladly send his family to die for his foolishness. Yet I would spend my life on my knees making sacrifices to all the gods to keep them safe.

Except Paris. He could go hang himself.

"Aeneas won't fight," I mused, thinking of our dour cousin. He was the only sheep in the family blacker than me—his uppity religious views made everyone go running whenever they saw him. "He wouldn't think a war like this godly."

"He doesn't." Hellenus smiled. "He's already sent our father a foul-tempered letter condemning Paris' behavior and predicting godly retribution if Helen is not returned to Sparta. You can imagine Father's rage."

"I always knew Aeneas was clever. He'll probably outlive us all." I wondered if my cousin felt as I did, like all the advice in the world was nothing more than futile shouting into a winter storm. I'd screamed until my throat bled. I wondered then if I might enlist Aeneas as an ally, for he was one of the few to speak out against Helen's presence in Troy.

"You know, Father didn't just talk of war and the Achaeans today," Hellenus said. Something in his tone had changed, and my ears pricked in warning. "In fact, he spoke of you before Menelaus' and Odysseus' arrival."

"Lovely," I said, my voice flat. "Does he plan to redecorate my cell? Perhaps shackle me to my bed each night?" Hellenus shook his head, his dark eyes clouding, and I wondered why Father didn't see his worth. He wasn't dazzlingly handsome like Paris or an extraordinary spearman like Hector, but he was kind and dependable, his advice sound, his arm strong, his temper calm. He might not please our father, but he'd make some woman a happy bride one day.

"No, he spoke of your betrothal. If war comes, he will promise you as a prize to the greatest warrior outside our family."

I laughed then, great gut-wrenching guffaws that no princess should have uttered, as I clutched my ribs. Hellenus waited patiently for me to finish, his eyebrows raised in silent amusement.

"Ha," I finally managed to say, wiping the tears from my eyes. "My hand in marriage would be a punishment, not a prize. Father missed his chance ages ago. Now I'm old and cursed, so no man this side of the Aegean will have anything to do with me."

"If you're old, then I must be ancient," Hellenus said, for he'd emerged first from our mother's womb, before I'd killed her. "Surely, we're neither of us too old for a marriage bed."

As if age was the biggest hurdle a potential suitor of mine would have to jump.

I thought of Andromache then. She and all the other wives of Troy should steal as much happiness with their husbands as they could in the months before the sea lanes opened again and the ships came.

But I refused to dwell on that. The ships would *not* come. I'd seen to that today.

I clasped my twin's hand so we might walk along the sunny ramparts before I returned to my cell. I'd impressed myself by ducking my guards this long, but all good things must come to an end.

"Don't fret, Brother," I said, kissing him on the cheek. "I shall not marry, for no man could ever compare to you."

"You deserve a good man at your side," Hellenus continued. "One with a more adequate sword arm than mine."

"I have all the champion I need in you," I said, pressing a finger to his lips when he made to protest. "Yet I shall not fight Father if he decides to give me away as if I were a trinket."

"Meek obedience? From you?"

I laughed again. "Probably not. I'll merely make my new husband so heartily sorry that he'll send me right back." Hellenus and I shared a chuckle, then walked on in silence until we reached my cell. Although my punishment was officially over, my attendant had informed me that this would now be my permanent residence, although my door was no longer barred and I could travel inside the citadel with a chaperone. Still more reminders that I wasn't to be trusted.

That same attendant waited outside, arms crossed before her broad chest and wearing a scowl that might have made Zeus piss himself. I only gave her a honeyed smile as I released my brother. "Go well, Hellenus."

"I'm sorry I couldn't persuade Father today," he said. "Truly, I am."

"It doesn't matter. I had better luck with the Achaeans." In fact, I had high hopes. Hellenus gave a brief smile and let me go. I slipped back into my cell, giving my attendant a snide curtsy before closing the door myself.

I stayed in my room, pacing like a fox whose next meal was just out of reach until the night owls hooted outside, the terra-cotta vial tucked safely in my bodice. Finally, I gathered my courage. The Achaeans might be gone, but I would do *everything* in my power to save Troy.

I might have chosen some other night to bring my plan to fruition, but I'd never been one to suffer patiently. There was no yelling this time. I only rapped a relentless staccato beat on the door in the way I knew irked my attendant.

I allowed myself a smile of satisfaction when the door groaned open.

"What is it?" she asked.

"I require that you chaperone me to the temple of Apollo. Now."

"It's the middle of the night."

"I wasn't aware that the gods accepted sacrifices only after dawn. My punishment is over, and I can go where I please. Escorted, of course."

My attendant may well have been sucking lemons for the face she gave me, but she stepped aside and let me pass, no doubt cursing me to the gates of Hades and back. The sickle moon shone brightly, and the Archer pulled his starry bow taught overhead. Everything seemed to me a blade or weapon now, but soon I would rectify that. Apollo's temple was nestled against the southern walls of the palace so it might catch the most of the sun's rays during daytime, and that was where I went now.

I'd not been to the sun god's abode in many years, nor had I ever planned to go there again. My heart battered against my ribs—the last time I'd walked this path, I'd been running away, hysterical. Panic threatened to overwhelm me, but I touched the lump in my bodice for reassurance. One step at a time.

I could do this.

The exterior of the temple shone dully in the weak moonlight, illuminating the pediment's carvings of the god's four horses pulling his sun chariot. I purified my trembling hands in lukewarm water from sacred urns in the forecourt before gesturing for my attendant to remain behind. "I won't be long," I said without waiting for a response. With my back to her, I removed the vial from its hiding place in my bodice and clutched it tight in my palm.

My footsteps echoed eerily off the tiles of the columned portico until I stood before the marble statue of the God of the Silver Bow, his mighty hands clasping a laurel and a round *phiale*, the symbols of his oracle. Remainders of the day's offerings lay heaped at his feet: piles of laurel leaves, golden honeycombs, and bottles of olive oil. The god seemed to be laughing down at me, as if he knew what thoughts churned in my fractured mind. I wondered if Apollo favored the god-born Trojans or the sea-wolf Achaeans most among his worshippers.

Long ago, as an acolyte in this very temple, I had placed on the altar the loin of a sheep and the chine of a tusked boar before offering them to the sacred fire. Now the god's house reeked of death and dripping blood, a stench like the breath of a tomb. This time I stood before the sacrificial fire empty-handed, for I'd already made the sacrifice of my sanity on the sun god's altar.

If I succeeded in changing Troy's fate, perhaps he would give it back.

I waited, knowing that my presence wouldn't go unnoticed

for long. I was right, for soon a foul and familiar terror arrived to greet me.

"Cassandra," the high priest said, his lone eye blinking as he passed the line of trim bronze *kouros* statues sculpted in Apollo's image. Their male nakedness made me shudder, a stark contrast to the balding, middle-aged filth standing before me. "What makes you think you can trespass against the most august of gods?" he asked. His good eye was the color of newly threshed wheat, but his other was a withered and puckered hole, its empty socket attesting to the bleakness of his soul.

Chryses, High Priest of Apollo, was a powerful man, but I refused to cower before him.

"I am the daughter of Priam and can go where I please."

We both knew that wasn't true, for my father had locked me in my cell after I'd first come here. He'd claimed it was for my protection, but not until he'd made it clear that he blamed me for what this priest had tried to do to me. I'd been only a frightened young girl. Locking me away had only broken me further.

Yet I hadn't come here to relive the past.

"War stalks Troy like a starving vulture," I said simply. "I intend to avert it."

The priest laughed then, his single eye bulging. "You think Apollo listens to you? Your hubris alone would lay this city low—"

"You owe me." I stepped closer, my eyes narrowing in the way that made most mortals recoil. "I served the god of light with faith and dignity, but you robbed me of that. Now you'll pray to Apollo that his plague arrows will smite Helen and Paris and avert the tidal wave of war that threatens to crash upon all of us. If you won't do it to save the city, you'll at least do it to save your daughter. A father's heart must beat in there somewhere—do you want your Chryseis to become a war prize to the Achaeans if they overrun this city?"

Chryses didn't cower as I'd hoped, only stepped closer so I could smell the smoky tang of sacrifice that had always clung to him. The gorge rose in my throat, but I swallowed it down.

"I never collected on what you owed me," he said.

I had to force myself not to bolt. "You will not come upon me sleeping this time, priest. Tell me, though, for I've often wondered: Did Chryseis hear you accost me? Has she learned what sort of vile serpent she has for a father?"

"You're the vile one, Cassandra," he said, taking another step. "Why else have you been plagued with such a miserable life while I reap the blessings of the gods?"

"Take one more step and I'll gouge out your remaining eye. My guard waits outside. If I scream, not even Apollo will protect you this time."

Liar. It's no wonder no one believes you.

"Not now," I whispered with a twitch. The priest's gaze flicked to the temple forecourt even as daemons whispered in both our ears.

"Leave," he finally said. "You have nothing that could make me strike a bargain with you."

"No?" I sneered, removing the precious object from my bodice. "Not even this?"

I knocked the wax seal from the terra-cotta vial and withdrew his desiccated eye from the honey I'd used to preserve it, a thin ribbon of connected tissue still attached. His eye had been the first in my collection of bones and oddities after I'd plucked it from the priest's face in the hooked-thumb gouge Hellenus had once taught me. Chryses had come upon me sleeping after the completion of my temple duties and thought to force his attentions upon me. He'd lost half his sight for his troubles.

It was the scene that visited me often in my nightmares, waking to find him hovering over me, yanking up my skirt and promising that glorious Apollo wished me to sacrifice my purity to him. When I'd fought and finally stood with his slimy eye in my palm, the priest had shrieked and thrashed on the ground. I'd preserved my virtue, but he had damned me as I'd run away.

I curse you with the gift of prophecy, he'd screamed. *You shall writhe with visions of the future, and none shall believe a word that falls from your lips.*

To see the future and never be believed, that was my burden. It was a load that had broken me, especially after my father had muzzled me in my dark chamber.

Chryses had lost an eye, and in the days that followed, I'd lost my sanity.

But I would win it back. I *would* be believed this time, and I *would* save Troy.

"Begone, foul witch," Chryses said as I replaced the precious eye in the vial, shaking his hands as if I were some sort of filth he could sweep away. "Apollo cried cataracts of tears to see his temple defiled by so wretched a woman."

It wouldn't have mattered if I'd brought a sacrifice of twelve yearling heifers that had yet to feel the goad; this corrupted priest and the god he served would never lift a finger to help me. So be it. I would do this alone, and his agony when I thwarted his curse would be my reward.

"Get out," Chryses thundered. "Get out and never return. The altars of all the gods will be forever cold to all your sacrifices."

I ran from him to the battlements, where the beach and ships lay to the west, and the olive groves and scattered temples stretched in all other directions. My fingers still sticky with the befouled honey, I tore at my hair and scratched my face as if in mourning, trying to rend the doubt from my soul, but it did no good.

The familiar voice clanged in my head all the way back to my cell, laughing and chanting all the while.

You will fall. Your city will fall. It will burn, burn, burn.

I denied it with all my soul, screaming myself into oblivion that night. But no one heard. Or if they did, no one cared.

After all, I'm nothing but a madwoman.

I had an unexpected visitor the following morning.

"I don't care if King Priam hasn't given prior approval," came the voice arguing with my attendant on the other side of the door. "I'm cousin to the royal family and the son of Ishara, although you probably demean her with the name Aphrodite."

"Princess Cassandra is too wild for visitors—"

"I daresay I can handle a young woman."

I smiled to hear the voice of my cousin Aeneas, harsher than iron and typically raised in lectures about piety and duty to the gods. Scrambling to my feet, I looked down at my crumpled clothing in dismay. I'd fallen asleep on the cold flagstones of my cell last night, and my dark hair was in wild disarray. I glanced around my cell, wondering how I might position myself to seem whole and healed to my cousin, but I lacked the usual props of a woman's loom or distaff. I settled for lighting a fresh oil lamp to chase away the gloom and sitting on the edge of my narrow bed, smoothing my skirt.

The door groaned open, and Aeneas entered, grim-faced and somber, as he usually appeared before our family. He was dark-haired and intense-eyed, as handsome as Paris, but unlike Paris, he did not seek to charm and ingratiate. "Cassandra," he said and winced as my attendant slammed the door behind him. "It is so good to see you."

I couldn't help it; I threw myself into his arms before he knew what was happening. Of all my family—perhaps even including Hellenus—Aeneas alone understood the magnitude of the crime

Paris had committed when he stole Helen away. Aeneas' piety also meant he understood that Troy couldn't duck the wrath of the gods forever.

"I'm glad you came." I released Aeneas and stole a glance at his startled expression. So much for appearing healed then, for what sort of woman acted in such a manner? My fingers twitched, and I managed a nervous laugh. "After all, I so rarely have visitors."

"I would have come sooner," Aeneas said, looking up and spreading his arms as if measuring the breadth of my meager cell. "I tried to visit shortly after hearing of Paris' folly, but Priam was adamant I not come to Troy until I could gather my Dardanian warriors to bring with me."

"You've brought warriors?"

He gave a single nod. "In case the Achaeans do come. I felt it my duty." He tilted his head to one side. "Have you been mistreated?"

"How could I possibly be mistreated?" A trill of laughter. "My father has seen fit to provide me with the protection of these walls and an attendant to see to my every need."

Aeneas saw through the veil of my words. "I'm sorry, Cassandra. Truly, I am. If there's anything I can do—I am disgusted with our family's conduct, with Paris and Priam. With all of Troy, actually."

"I know," I said. "None of this will end well, not if the Achaean fleet arrives at our shores."

Aeneas cocked his head. "Have you seen it?"

I crossed my arms in front of me as if to ward off some terrible chill. "I've seen much, Aeneas. And none of it good."

He came and clasped my hands in his own, then led me to a chair. "Tell me."

I did then, unburdening myself as I'd only ever done with

Hellenus, yet I told Aeneas even more than I had my twin. I told him everything: the arrival of a thousand ships and years of bloody battles, the never-ending pyres for the dead and the flames that devoured the city.

"I've done much to avert all this," I said. "I won't rest until I've done everything in my power to save us."

"And what if it's not enough?"

I shook my head hard. "It has to be. I alone can overcome the faults of our family to keep my visions from becoming reality."

Aeneas rubbed my hands; I hadn't realized how cold they'd become. "You're not alone, Cassandra. I believe you, and I'll do everything in my power to save Troy."

I touched his face, the stubble on his cheeks sharp against my palm. "If anyone can overcome the hubris of man and the pride of the warrior, it's you."

Aeneas gave a sad smile. "Is that a prophecy, Cousin? I fear not, for I am as guilty of hubris as any Trojan."

I answered his smile. "Perhaps."

We chatted about nothings until I knew Aeneas lingered only for my sake. Finally, I rose and rapped on the door. "Be well, Aeneas," I said. "You can best help me by casting your prayers to your divine mother and the rest of the Olympians."

Aeneas winced. "Only if you promise not to refer to our gods by that dreadful Achaean term."

"I promise," I chuckled. "Pray that what I've done is enough. Pray that Troy is safe."

"I will." Aeneas pressed his forehead to mine. "You have my word."

I spent the rest of the day in quiet contemplation, feeling calmer than I had in a long time. Perhaps Aeneas' visit had been a sign of the gods' favor. Perhaps they smiled on me—and Troy.

If so, I prayed they'd guide me in the days and weeks to come. For I had one more wild, desperate plan to ensure Troy's safety.

Then, and only then, might I rest.

WINTER had passed, spring had come, and soon the sea lanes would be calm enough for ships. Word had flown to Troy on the tongues of news-bearing travelers that the Achaeans were building more and more vessels, hoping to enlarge their pirate fleet to something truly vast.

I would know soon enough whether that was the fleet of my nightmares, and if so, whether they would truly be moved to sail on the winds of war.

I touched the jagged shard of pottery with my thumb and inhaled sharply as it pierced the soft flesh of my thumb. My nails had been bitten to the quick in recent nights, and Hellenus had forbidden knives of any kind on my meal trays after he'd seen the state of my wrists. Yet he hadn't forbidden jars of my favorite date wine from Aegyptos, and my attendant hadn't noticed the missing shard after I'd dropped and shattered the most recent amphora. The sharpened terra-cotta had felt foreign on my wrists tonight, less comforting than the cold metal of a blade, but I'd made do. It had been months since I'd had a proper night of sleep, for the new terrors had made even Hellenus rear back in horror when I'd told him of my visions in garbled and halting words.

I saw not only the war now, but glimpses of its terrible outcome.

An empty beach, the detritus of war scattered in the sands.

A mother gone mad, barking like a dog over the corpses of her children.

A wise and weary soldier, tossed about on Poseidon's waves for years on end.

A conqueror murdered by his loved ones.

New cities founded from the ruins of old.

I'd tried so hard to save this foolish city of mine. I'd ranted and raved, negotiated and begged both gods and men. Was it all for naught?

Let Troy fall. Escape and let this cursed cesspit crumble to the ground, remembered only in the tales of blind singers meant to warn children of the crime of hubris.

These were the words that woke me each night, taunting and teasing me. But I would not let Troy fall, that I knew with a dark certainty. I was intended to save her—and if that meant the hubris was mine, then may the gods strike me in her place.

Morning, clad in a robe of pale saffron, had suffused light over the earth. The great black doors of the Scaean Gate would soon be swinging open to expel the fishermen and farmers to the bounty of the sea and their fields for the day. I tucked the shard of terra-cotta into the fold of my kilt and wrapped a black veil over my unkempt hair before picking up the woven basket. The terra-cotta vial was back in its rightful place in my bodice, reminding me to be brave. Hellenus waited outside for me. Over the winter, he'd vouchsafed for my behavior with Father, so I was allowed to leave the city in a rare respite. He took the basket from me, and we walked silently down the narrow steps of the citadel while the inner city stretched and woke around us. I was struck by Troy's beauty in that moment, at the way the sun broke through the marbled clouds to gleam off her limestone towers and light the purple anemones that spilled through the cracks of the steps. Even the market was lovely, silent and empty of the fishmongers and peddlers who would soon arrive to set out their wares. Hellenus and I gathered our cloaks nearer and continued past the bleary-eyed wives waiting at the wells and the dogs that looked up lazily from the doorways they'd protected during the night. The guards at the Scaean Gate stood at attention in front of its colossal red pillars as we passed, the shadows from the walls casting them in semidarkness.

"Prince Hellenus," one said, and I smiled at the respect in their voices. My brother commanded more respect than he knew, whereas I . . . I was glad that his presence shielded me from their spittle and insults today.

I breathed easier once we were outside the city. Despite the many oak trees, the winds were fierce without the walls for protection, and the waves of the sea looked like a herd of wild horses galloping just beneath the surface. Our waters were bereft of ships; our own fleet had still not returned from the Hittite troubles, and Father—hearing the news of an Achaean fleet being built, just as I had—decided our few remaining vessels should be taken for safekeeping to Aeneas' holdings in Dardania rather than be outnumbered in our own bay.

Perhaps my father was finally seeing sense. I prayed it wasn't too little, too late.

"Are you sure you want to do this?" Hellenus asked.

I nodded, and we continued in silence past a weather-beaten wild fig tree to the two fair springs that fed the river Scamander. At this early hour, only a few women beat linens against the stone washing troughs, but soon the banks would swell with their idle gossip. The gods toyed with these waters, for steam rose from the first spring like smoke from a burning fire, yet the second felt colder than ice when I dipped a toe in its waters. It was on the muddy banks of the latter that I finally untied the rope at my waist and held my cat's skull for the final time. I kissed his smooth forehead, then released him into the river. He tumbled in the waters, and I blinked back tears until he disappeared from view.

I set him free because I didn't need him now. Letting him go was proof to me—and Hellenus—that I was truly healed.

"I'm proud of you," Hellenus said when I straightened. That

was all I needed to bolster myself, to keep from splashing into the freezing waters to retrieve the skull that had become a part of myself over these past months. Hellenus and I walked in silence back to Troy, the winds scourging us until we were through the gates. Now my city anticipated a possible Achaean attack as though preparing for a spring banquet. Slaves sang while they worked to fill enormous storage jars packed along the citadel, and fiery sparks flew like laughter from forges in the bronze-smiths night and day. Men played like children as they sparred with wooden swords and shields.

Including my brothers as I sought them out in their wing of the palace. All save Hector acted as if this were all a game, hoping the Achaeans would arrive as soon as the sea lanes opened.

"I must speak to Hector about the city's defenses," Hellenus said. "Will you be all right?"

"Of course," I said, feigning a sunny smile.

"Are you sure?"

"They'll pay no more attention to me than they would a stray dog." Hellenus squeezed my hand, then ducked into Hector's chambers, leaving me free to follow my own path.

"I'll challenge mighty Agamemnon to fight me for Helen! I'll present his head to King Priam and use his carcass as target practice for my poison arrows!" Paris yelled as he pulled taut the string of his mighty ibex bow, sixteen palms long, its horns tipped with gold. I'd seen him fumble with a spear and shield like a greenling, but there was no denying he was deadly with a bow. His long fingers brushed his face, releasing the bowstring to hurl an arrow at the target dangling from an elm tree. It skewered the bag of sand with a dull thud that made me cringe as sand sprayed everywhere.

A spray of blood.

Mangled bones.

A skull caved in, the brains inside a ruined and quivering mess.

I grabbed Paris' arm and whirled him around. "You tempt the gods with your boasts," I snarled. "Beware, or they'll strike you down for your arrogance."

"Go away, lunatic," he said, shaking me off and holding out his bow as if in challenge. "No one wants to hear your latest mumblings. You yourself foretold of Troy's continued greatness in the face of the Achaeans. Father said so, had heralds proclaim it throughout the city."

"I lied," I said, then screamed the words. "I lied!"

Paris only laughed, and the rest of my half brothers joined in. I knew how I must look to them, barefoot and wild-haired, my skin ashy and eyes sunken from lack of sleep. "Did you hear that, Brothers?" Paris called. "Our sister isn't only moon-brained, she's a liar, too!" He leaned in close so only I could hear. "And I swear on my dying breath that no one will ever again believe a word from that foul mouth of yours."

You shall writhe with visions of the future, and none shall believe a word that falls from your lips.

I wanted to die then, but I forced myself to stand and take his abuse even as the priest's curse and Paris' laughter rang in my ears.

Let them laugh, for then Paris turned his back to me.

On my dying breath . . .

I lunged and leaped onto his back with the shard of jagged terra-cotta suddenly pressed against the jutting apple of his neck. The warmth of his lifeblood pulsed there, and I had the sudden urge to bite down against it, to tear at his skin with my teeth. I'd hoped Helen would be here today, but Paris would suffice as my victim. "If Menelaus does bring his warriors to our shore, all he will find is your corpse." My final scheme in my determination to save Troy: if the Achaeans did wing their way across the sea to our gates, they would be met and satisfied with Paris' corpse, which they could feed to the dogs for all I cared. If honor was satisfied, surely they would return home.

I raked the terra-cotta against his neck just as I was torn from his back, and the fragment went skittering from my hand. I knew instantly that I'd failed, for there was no gush of warm blood on my hands before I crashed to the hard-packed sand of the courtyard, squinting up into the sun to see my assailant.

Helen.

She stood between Paris and me, her heaving breasts commanding the gazes of every male assembled. She might have been a wrathful Aphrodite with the way the sunlight played in her hair and set ablaze the gold discs hanging from her ears. A full contingent of Father's guards surrounded her, so not even Hermes himself might have spirited her away or harmed a hair on her head. Perhaps she *was* a daughter of Zeus if he'd shielded her from my curse tablet. "Shall I fetch one of your venom arrows, Paris?" she called to my brother, her icy eyes never leaving me. "Or perhaps the yew berry? It seems a livelier target practice might be in order."

"Get away from me," I said, but she only crouched over me, a lioness toying with its prey.

"How dare you try to ruin all I've worked so hard for?" she murmured.

I'd have spit viper venom into her face in that moment if I could have. Instead, I scrambled away, tripping again as my feet tangled in the folds of my skirt, my eyes frantically searching for the terra-cotta shard. Helen saw it first and picked it up, pressing it to her full lips to give it a kiss.

"You have such a pretty neck," she said before her gaze dropped to my wrists. "Perhaps you should add a necklace to match the bracelets that you've made for yourself."

"Move away, Helen," Paris said, and she obeyed, although I caught the flash of contempt in her eyes before she bowed her head to her husband. If Paris thought he held sway over her heart or commanded her obedience, then he was more a fool than I'd thought. My half brother nocked an arrow fletched with owl feathers and aimed it straight at my heart. "Perhaps it's time to silence this harpy once and for all."

I refused to cower, only spat at his feet.

"Lower your bow, Paris," came Hellenus' beloved voice. "Only cowards threaten women."

"She tried to kill me!" Paris protested, the arrow still poised.

"Never in all the tales of old have I heard of a man who slew his own sister and became a hero," Hector said. "And we shall need all the heroes we can muster in the days to come."

My brothers stood united, both of them with daggers drawn. Yet Paris still didn't move.

"Do it," I whispered to him, for the thought came like a whirlwind that it was my death that would save Troy. My murder would silence the voices and end the dreams that tormented me every night. Hellenus would avenge my death by slaying Paris, and then Helen would be sent back to Menelaus. My miserable, unhappy life in exchange for that of my family's.

Your ungrateful family, who locks you in a cell and wishes you'd never been born.

If that was the price, I'd pay it. I stifled a sob, which Paris mistook as a gurgle of fear. He smiled and exhaled, readied to loose the arrow.

"Put down your bow," Hellenus repeated to Paris. "Or I shall slay you myself."

Paris let go. I closed my eyes, prepared for the pain and the ensuing blackness. Instead, I felt only the whoosh of the arrow over my head, heard its twang as it embedded itself in the tree behind me.

"Stay away from us, Sister," he warned. "Or next time you'll find that arrow buried between your eyes."

I didn't struggle when Hellenus lifted and shielded me in a retreat from the onslaught of angry shouts as Hector sought to silence them all with reason.

I lay in my twin's arms in a curious, shattered serenity. I had done everything in my power. There was nothing more I could offer the Fates for my city's survival.

FEET pounded past my walls like a hail of giants fallen to earth, but I could see nothing, only feel the reverberations through the ancient stones of the citadel and hear the shouts outside. Despite the iron shackles that now adorned my wrists day and night, I pounded on the thick door, crying for someone—anyone—to release me.

In vain.

I slumped against the wall and closed my eyes against the onslaught of the scenes I'd painted with my own lifeblood.

Ships.

Horses.

Fire.

Murder.

I'd searched in vain for messages in tiny coils of mouse intestines—gifts from my new cat—to confirm that I'd averted this terrible war, but they refused to share their secrets. I'd taken to braiding the entrails while humming hopeful songs from my childhood until Hellenus had them taken away. Instead, the nightmares intensified so that I cried out every night. I had tried so hard to keep from slipping back into my old habits, but on the worst nights, it was impossible to resist. I told myself it would purge my mind to paint, and so I slashed my own wrists, staring at the crimson welts that blossomed there before I started painting. I told myself that the nightmares were false and that I *had* succeeded.

But now this . . .

Only when the melee outside had died down and I'd given up hope did my door finally groan open.

"Hellenus—" I started, then promptly swallowed the greeting. For it wasn't Hellenus who had come to set me free, but Aeneas. He was in full armor, his helmet sporting the tall sea-colored plumes he always wore in honor of Aphrodite, who had been born from the ocean, and looked more dour than usual. My heart climbed into my throat.

"The Achaean fleet has arrived," he said. "We have known for some time that they were becalmed at Aulis. But it seems they placated the gods and obtained a fair wind, for their sails now crowd the horizon."

Dear gods, no . . .

I was already tugging him along by the hand. "How many ships?"

The eastern side of the citadel was empty, for all of Troy seemed to have poured itself to the west to witness the arrival of the Achaeans. "Many."

Many ships carrying scores of men greedy for glory, ready to devour Troy like black flies on a pail of milk.

Yet I gasped as I approached the walls.

Aeneas was wrong. It wasn't *many* ships.

It was a thousand.

The thousand ships from my visions.

Their approaching white sails polluted the dark sea like flotsam after a storm, carving a wake of silence through the watching crowd just as their prows carved a path through the waves. All manner of sigils decorated the sails: great horned bulls and tentacled octopi, double-headed axes and open-armed goddesses. This was an invading force such as the world had never seen, yet our great Scaean Gate wasn't locked tight as it should have been, but was flung open to disgorge our Trojan warriors onto the plains.

"Death Gates," I whispered, for it was from those gates that our spearmen would leave and enter Hades' cold embrace. "All hail to you."

I shuddered to feel the dark shadow of madness fall over me at the sight of all those ships, the same that I'd seen so many times in my nightmares.

No. No, this couldn't happen, not after I'd schemed so hard, sacrificed so much. I pulled hard at my own hair to keep me anchored to this moment, for perhaps not all hope was lost. There was still a chance that Menelaus and Agamemnon would fall to Hector's spear, and the Achaeans would flee as quickly as they had come. I calmed then, for surely it would happen like that, and Troy would be saved.

"What's happening?" I asked, suddenly realizing that Aeneas had delivered me to the crowd of royal women. He'd disappeared, likely to harangue my father against incurring the gods' wrath.

Most of the women, including Hecuba, edged away from me. Only one emerged from the crush to move closer.

"Our warriors have gone to welcome the invaders," Helen said with a sly smile. Her words were maggots in my ears that refused to be dislodged.

"You're the invader," I whispered, locking my gaze on the fleet of ships, yet Helen only *tsked* under her breath.

"And I thought you'd be grateful for my invitation to join us."

"Your invitation?" I asked. The full weight of my stare must have been disconcerting, for her gaze flickered. Yet to her credit, she didn't back down.

"Of course," she said. "I asked Priam if you might attend, and he capitulated like a little lamb."

I saw the renewed gleam in her eyes and knew she reveled in this, the war that she had caused and these men who bowed to her whims. It seemed that Father had found a kindred spirit in his lust for power.

"You will rue this day," I said to her. "Your scheming will destroy us."

She gave an elegant shrug. "Perhaps. Regardless, the world will never forget the name Helen of Troy. Look there," she said, lifting a languid arm. She pointed not at the skirmish below, but to the greatest in the flotilla of ships with a sail emblazoned with a lion emblem and unblinking golden eyes painted upon its prow. "Agamemnon's sail."

I felt a sudden coil of dread, a premonition of some great evil to follow, but refused to indulge it. Not here, not now.

But if not here and now, then when? Or are you afraid to see what waits for you, cowardly Cassandra?

"Where Agamemnon goes, Menelaus will follow," I said loud enough to try to drown out the voice battering my mind. "Do you not fear the return of your true husband?"

"Menelaus is no husband of mine," she said. "He cowers in the shadows of great men. Hector will likely dispatch him the moment he steps onto the beach."

"It's your fault they came. You crooked your little finger, and they all came running—"

She tilted her chin. "Men will do what they will. I refuse to shoulder the blame for their greed."

I'd have killed her with my bare hands this time had it not been for the contingent of guards surrounding her and the shackles at my wrists. I could barely grind out the words through my fury. "If it were up to me, I'd have you locked in a cell with only Paris' severed head for company."

Helen wrinkled her nose. "Yes, I've heard of your penchant for decorating with skulls. No wonder they call you a madwoman."

All winter, I had clung to my dream of sanity, my defense of my city—and it was Helen's careless words and the sight of those ships that broke me. I *was* a madwoman, and my city was doomed.

You've failed, you miserable, worthless worm.

You thought you could thwart the Fates, but you were wrong. So very, very wrong.

You will fall. Your city will fall. It will burn, burn, burn.

So many voices clanging in my head, drowning out my very thoughts. There would be no escaping them now, no keeping the voices at bay once Helen had unleashed the daemons of war upon our city.

I shrieked and collapsed there on the rampart, clawing at my hair and face, raging against Helen and the gods, and howling for my brother and for my city. And for myself.

I was truly alone now, save for the voices that would only grow louder with each passing day. But I would not shield my eyes from the sight of my visions made true, no matter how I wished to.

I owed Troy that.

I dragged myself to the edge of the rampart and keened with despair as the first Achaean ships beached themselves. Soon Troy's beautiful plains would be overrun with soldiers, our wildflowers trampled underfoot and our waters choked with their piss and filth.

"Our men march today through the Scaean Gate to usher our enemies to the gates of Hades," Hecuba said assuredly to her women, and I wondered if my father had planted the words in her mouth. Regardless, many of the women gathered near twittered their approval like brainless hens. The war had only just begun, and I alone knew we had already lost. And all I could do was watch, weakened and despairing.

There was hardly a sea-wolf who had not answered Agamemnon's call—they swarmed the beach like the locusts I'd dreamed of. With a heavy heart, I saw the striped sails of Ithaca that meant wily Odysseus was here. Odysseus, who had tricked me into believing I had a chance at persuading him to avert this war. Odysseus had done Agamemnon another good service, I'd later learn, in luring the Achaeans' finest warrior to the cause: young Achilles of Phthia, whose mother had tried to hide him dressed as a girl when the summons arrived. But Achilles, too, had come; Hecuba's twittering women pointed out his Myrmidons' banner. A bitter whisper of prophecy told me Agamemnon would rue the day that banner joined his, but I could only let the visions come and wash away like black waves. Already they were dragging me under. For now, I could only watch the coming carnage below. There would be no rest for the Achaeans today, no opportunity to entrench before they faced our forces, men eager for their names to be sung about through the ages. Beneath us, Hector bellowed orders and the Trojans took their places. Next to me, Andromache stiffened.

"Hector will not die this day," I heard myself say. "I swear it."

She gave me a wan smile, freckles standing out stark against her pale face. "Yet this is only the first of what I fear will be many battles."

I might have said more, but I was too busy scanning the rest of the soldiers for Hellenus. I clutched hard at the irons of my shackles when I found him not far from Hector.

Both readied their spears as the first Achaeans streamed onto the beach, but then Hector yelled a command, and the archers took their positions, kneeling with Paris and his ibex bow, men who preferred not to see the eyes of those they slew. "Your paramour pales in comparison to his mighty brothers," I said to Helen.

"He does," she agreed coolly. I could never prick her as she pricked me. How I hated her.

The first Achaeans finally came within range. Hector dropped his arm, and the archers released their rain of death. The grisly onslaught screamed through the air, and the Achaeans shouted, raising their shields. From such a distance, many of the arrows missed their mark, but a few drove into the meat and bone of exposed arms and legs.

Our foot soldiers continued to hug the wall while the archers reloaded, releasing a second hail of death-hissing arrows into the enemy ranks. The Achaeans moved into tighter formation, but they were too few against too many.

For now.

Our men sensed their advantage and charged with raised shields and spears. It didn't escape me that Paris remained behind, safe with his archers, while Hector and Hellenus and Aeneas ran at the front. We'd later learn that Hector's hungry blade claimed the first Achaean life, that of Odysseus' companion in the striped tunic who had been the first to touch Troy's sands during the peace mission last summer. He had led forty ships from Phylace to Troy, and all for naught.

Yet another prophecy fulfilled.

I reached for the reassurance of my cat's skull, then remembered that I had released him into the Scamander. I bit the knuckle of my forefinger to keep from crying out, tasting blood before I felt it dripping down my lips.

Some of the women cheered for our men while others turned white at this first encounter with death. There was nothing we could do but watch until the skirmish faded. Our men pushed the Achaeans back, then returned behind the walls as the bulk of the Achaeans remained on their ships. This had been a warning to them, one that they would never heed while Troy's riches still beckoned.

And Troy would not heed my warnings, not as the entire city

cheered on our victorious men. Some industrious soul located baskets of rose petals, and soon the air was festooned with the smell of the delicate flowers.

Yet no one save me seemed to notice those same petals trampled underfoot. Or the way the tang of Achaean blood on the blades of our victorious warriors overpowered the floral fragrance.

It was an agony to look at Troy's towers and know that one day I would watch them fall. There was no escaping our fate now, only vain delay.

The arrows of my words had flown too wide, and now the yoke of war was nailed firmly upon our necks. With tears in my eyes, I uttered a final word to the corpse of the city that had borne and sheltered me.

"Farewell," I whispered to Troy. And welcomed my madness with open arms.

MINE was not the face that launched a thousand ships, but the gods cursed me all the same, just as they'd cursed Helen of Sparta as being a viler creature than Scylla and Charybdis combined.

Her face with its high cheekbones and full lips was lauded by singers and harpists. I, too, was beautiful, heralded by all who visited my father's court as the loveliest of King Priam's daughters. But that was where the similarities ended.

Helen's exquisite fairness, like the first heady bloom of a peony on the longest day of summer, hid a soul as black and thorn-filled as Hades' heart, while my dark complexion and even darker words cast me out as a pariah from the rest of my golden family.

Her name meant *Shining One*, yet she sought only to bring death and destruction to our shores. My name—Cassandra—meant *Winnower of Men*, yet no man could hear my truths over the deafening sound of his own hubris.

I'd seen my own death—and worse—in my dream visions, my face not much older than it was now. Whereas Helen . . .

The justice of the gods is never meted out in equal portions.

Would that Helen's mother had possessed the good sense to truss her infant daughter into a burlap sack weighted with rocks and throw her into the sea, or that her divine father, Zeus, had drowned his daughter on her way to Troy's fair shores. Instead, the golden temptress found her way to our city, where she intended to wreak havoc.

I'd done everything in my power to stop her, but I'd failed.

Now our fate rested in the hands of our warriors and our walls.

I knew neither would save us.

And so on the day that ships arrived, with the briny sea breeze whipping at my unfettered hair and the solid walls of Troy beneath my feet, I stood in the wreckage of my sanity and keened.

My song was a funeral dirge to make even Hades shudder, for myself, my family, and my city.

Our end had begun.

THE THIRD SONG

THE SACRIFICE

by Russell Whitfield

The death of honor, rolled in dust and blood, Slain for a woman's sin, a false wife's shame!
Aeschylus, *Agamemnon*

AGAMEMNON

THE pennants hung limp, bereft of wind to stir them. The smoke from the hecatombs was a funeral pall hanging thick over this obscenity, filling the throats and watering the eyes of the eager scum who watched.

Agamemnon was glad of it because tears ran unchecked down his face. Tears of sorrow mingled with impotent rage. He looked at Calchas, the priest and harbinger of this dread oracle, and his grip tightened on the dagger. A quick rush, a thrust, and he could open the fat bastard's guts and leave him mewling out his last breaths in the mire of his own blood and shit.

There was a murmur from the assembled troops as they saw his daughter. His Iphigenia.

She won't feel it, Agamemnon told himself. Thank the gods, she won't feel the pain. She was so sluggish from the draft of poppy milk she could hardly stand—her eyes impossibly black as two women supported her, leading her toward the altar. He could not bring himself to look at his wife. Clytemnestra's hatred for him was tangible, a palpable thing he could feel deep in his soul. She could not know that his hatred for himself paled hers into insignificance.

His soul.

Agamemnon could feel the fire of shame and self-loathing burning it away with each step Iphigenia took toward the altar, leaving him with nothing inside.

It was not as though this was all about acquiescence to the gods, though everyone would say that it was. The truth was that the assembled Achaean kings, princes, and warriors hungered not to appease the Olympians, nor even to bring Helen of Sparta home. It was all for the gold that King Priam held in Troy. Lust and greed covered with the rank veneer of religion. The gods demanded sacrifice for some imagined offense that he—the high king, ruler of Mycenae—

had caused the goddess Artemis. So spoke Calchas, and the kings and princes agreed. The gods would be appeased, would send a fair wind to the Achaean fleet becalmed at Aulis—but only if a sacrifice was made.

That sacrifice was to be his beloved daughter.

What kind of god asked of a man that he take the life of his own child so that a fleet might sail?

Calchas' whining voice invoked them now, Apollo and Artemis, Zeus and Athena, and all the other bastards that inhabited that lofty palace on Olympus, playing their games with the lives of men, guiltless and unfeeling in their immortality.

Agamemnon hated them, too. Hated all of them—soldiers and princes, priests and gods. There was nothing left to him but hate. Perhaps he should plunge the dagger into his own throat now and end it.

But what then? They would still kill Iphigenia, and probably Clytemnestra and little Orestes, too, of that Agamemnon had no doubt. They had an "honor guard" anyway—led by huge Ajax of Locris; the threat was implicit. Back out, and they die. But the truth—the hated truth—was that he, Agamemnon, was the only one who had the strength to hold this band of fractious, petty, and dishonorable reavers, who had the gall to call themselves kings, together. If he fell, then the war at Troy would be forgotten as they fell on each other, contesting for the right to be high king in his stead.

The irony was not lost to him. Wherever the dagger struck, it would result in war. Wherever the dagger fell . . .

The slave women laid his daughter out before him on the altar, her golden hair spilling out around her head, her eyes looking up at him, pupils so huge, evidence of the poppy he'd insisted they give her. Calchas had tried to refute this, demanding that the sacrifice be willing and aware—but faced with the close and immediate rage of Agamemnon and the distant promise of retribution from Olympus, he had relented. Like all men of religion, he was a coward at heart, hiding behind the unseen power that afforded him right and privilege.

The high king sobbed as he looked down at his child. She thought she had been summoned to Aulis to be married. He could only imagine how happy she must have been. The joy she must have felt . . .

"Father," she murmured and smiled.

"I love you," he said, hearing his own voice as a strangled sob. Calchas was still intoning the rites, but Agamemnon could stand it no more.

He rammed the dagger into his child's breast, screaming in raw anguish as the blade struck home, screaming as her blood coursed out all over his hands, bursting from her mouth as she bucked and writhed on the altar, screaming as she died under his own hand.

Screams that were drowned out as the men cheered his deed . . .

"MY king!" His guard's voice from outside.

"I'm fine," he croaked. "Fine. A dream from the . . . gods . . ." He looked at his hands in the semidarkness and imagined them still tacky with Iphigenia's blood. The only thing that could wash away the stain for a while was wine.

Agamemnon stumbled from his bed and went to the *krater*, pouring for himself the strong, unwatered Trojan stuff that allowed him a small measure of peace. And he drank deep in the night, drank and drank till all he could do was stumble back to his bed and beg the gods that he hated to send him no more dreams.

HE dressed himself and warred—as he warred every morning—with the temptation to have another cup of wine to steady himself. And it was a war that always ended in defeat. He found his shaking hands pouring a cup that he promised himself would be small. It was, but he always tipped a little more into it, wincing at the taste as he gulped it down.

Nine years, he thought. Had it really been so long? Nine summers spent besieging Troy's walls, drawing out Troy's warriors to fight on the plain. Nine winters spent in idleness, fighting suspended to the occasional raid, the Trojans using the cold months to bolster their supplies, the Achaeans hunkered down inside their fortified camp, waiting for the return of warmth. Some princes or warriors took their ships home in the cold months, but mostly they came back with the spring, lured by the scent of Trojan gold, persuading themselves that *this* would be the year the city fell. Nine years. That wasn't a war; it was a state of life, a time apart.

Time enough for a boy to become a man. Or for a man to become old. As Agamemnon had become old. He left his quarters and made his way to the ramparts of the long-established Achaean camp. *His* camp. His camp because he had to think of everything first, and first, nine years ago, had been where to position their base. War was seasonal, but Agamemnon knew, even back then, that this would be a huge investment in time and resources. As it was, the camp ran east to west with the great river—the Scamander—at the western edge. Kings and princes considered glory. Drinking water was not glorious. Washing water was not glorious. Sanitation was not glorious. But without it, they'd be finished. Even so, despite Agamemnon's best efforts, the summer always brought sickness. But at least, he thought, the death toll from it was manageable.

Agamemnon stared out over the Plain of Troy and the citadel in the distance. He'd forgotten what it had looked like when he'd first come here. There was barley now—fields of it around the city—but that would be gone soon, harvested or crushed by the feet of marching soldiers and the chariot wheels. Indeed, the plain itself was all but barren—once verdant, now flat and dead, killed by the killing that went on upon it. The only life left after the nine years of battle and foraging was a swath of green trees beside the river—both sides agreed that this would remain untouched as it was a sanctuary for the gods. The huge walls of Troy were blurred, but whether that was the haze of the morning mist or the failing of his own eyes, he did not know. He wondered if King Priam was—at this moment—mirroring him, looking out at the great adventure that had become the bane of his existence. For there was no real honor to be had in this fight anymore. No real gain. Not for men like he and the Trojan king, men who had bled out the final days of their youth on those god-cursed plains only to find that all that remained to them was obduracy and embittered pride. He was only forty-five, but at times he felt twice that. But, as Chryseis often said, it was he—Agamemnon—who bore the weight of the Achaean cause on his shoulders ("mighty shoulders," she called them), where none of the other lesser kings did. They could concern themselves with petty rivalries and their own glory-seeking; Agamemnon must carry the burdens of the entire camp. Atlas himself would weary of such a burden.

Chryseis.

Thought of her made him smile. She had come to him as a captive, a prize. Well, hardly a captive; it was she who had chosen him and not the other way around. He recalled the day she came to him, head held high amongst the downcast prisoners, her mouth slightly parted, her gaze that met his, a gaze full of promise. He did not have to force himself on Chryseis; in fact, after their first time, it was she that begged him for more.

And she was prize indeed, for she and she alone had enabled him to find at least some joy in life. She had helped him to start living again, a balm for the emptiness inside. She had helped him recover a vestige of the man that had been Agamemnon, the man that lived behind the actor's mask he wore as high king.

She drank as much as—if not more than—he did. She turned his bouts with the wine *krater* from melancholic to Dionysian.

When she was on fire with Dionysus through her veins, she did things to him—and let him do things to her—that one would only do to a slave. A *real* slave. Except that Chryseis liked it. Chryseis would suggest it. Chryseis *enjoyed* it.

It wasn't just her body and her inventiveness that fired him. It was her mind. She was intelligent, analytical, and—he knew well—shameless in her desire for self-preservation. Chryseis had chosen him because he was high king. Chosen him because here, in this closed-off part of the world that was the war, she could be his queen. Chosen him because she knew he would know this—and would accept it. Relish it, even.

He turned away from the rampart and clambered down the ladder back into the Achaean camp, aware of the eyes of the soldiery upon him; drawing himself to his full height, the king of Mycenae stood perhaps two hands taller than most men. He was, he knew, imposing—as the high king should be. And he was accorded the proper respect by his men—unlike so many of the other Achaean chiefs who chose to engender the ludicrous façade of being as one with their troops.

Hypocrites, Agamemnon thought. *Kings are only* one with their troops *until it comes time for the spoils to be divided.* Then kings would be kings and take the lion's share, while their men had to settle for basking in the reflected glory of their leaders and counting their meager cuts. At least the Mycenaean warriors knew and accepted the truth: Agamemnon, son of Atreus, was more than they. A king should act like a king—the men knew it and knew better than to be surly about it. Because he had no love for them—not the way Prince Achilles of Phthia loved his Myrmidons.

Agamemnon hated them all. Because he remembered their cheers when he'd struck the blow against his daughter—and if any man gave him cause to be punished, Agamemnon acted with impunity. They hated him, too. But even if they took a lesser share, he was making them rich, and he had learned long ago that avarice was all that drove men. Lust—for women, for gold, for power. Men were base creatures. Ironic, then, that he had to place their welfare and their objective first and foremost.

They had to win this war. Even if he didn't care if he—or they—lived or died. The gods loved a joke.

His bodyguard in tow—eight of the tallest spearmen Mycenae could muster—Agamemnon elected to tour his section of the encampment—ostensibly a random inspection, but the truth of it was that he was eager to meet with his charioteer. He was impatient but forced himself to cast an eye over the defenses and ask after the state of the men (the former he cared about, the latter he suffered). But they were in good spirits. There *was* a complaint of sickness with the animals, and Agamemnon once again had to remind them it always happened at this time of year as the temperature swung this way and that and spring spat out its rain. But, as it was, aside from a few minor ailments, the men were well—the season's fighting had yet to truly begin, and as such they were well-paid, well-fed, and uninjured.

But not if Achilles had his way.

He was pushing for a major assault as soon as the weather allowed. Which was well and good because a major assault would give the Phthian prince the chance to bathe himself in blood and glory, but of course leave Agamemnon to count the butcher's bill of an ill-conceived and hasty attack if it all went wrong.

Yet, even if he did despise the man—and Agamemnon *did* despise him—he was honest enough with himself to admit that Achilles, his companion, Patrocles, and the rest of the Phthian warriors known as the Myrmidons were superlative killers. But Achilles was all about the fight and had no comprehension of grand strategy. He was a soldier, not a general; but no one—not even Agamemnon himself—had the guts to tell him. It galled Agamemnon, but he, like everyone else, was afraid of Achilles. Because with a spear in his hand, Achilles was peerless. One day, Agamemnon thought, he'd have to have the bastard assassinated. When he was no longer useful, of course.

He pushed thoughts of the troublesome Achilles aside as he neared the horses' enclosure, his pace quickening, his lips pulled into a grin. He loved this place, the smell of the manure, the neighing and whickering of the beasts, the brusque sound of bronze saw on hard wood as the carpenters set about fixing damaged chariots. Or building new ones.

Agamemnon called to his own charioteer as he spied the lad working: a short blond youth, not over brave. Agamemnon had seen more than one prince go down to Trojan spears because of an over-eager charioteer, and he was thankful that his driver held his own personal safety—and hence his king's—in high esteem.

"My king!" The boy turned from his work and, after a moment, remembered to bow.

Given the state of the new chariot, Agamemnon was prepared to let that little lapse of protocol pass. "She's a thing of beauty," he said, running a hand over the vehicle's flank.

"And she's unique in this army," the charioteer affirmed with all the confidence of youth. "No one else rides a dual chariot, my king. I reckon they don't even have one of these in Troy."

It was true: Achaeans and Trojans both tended to use the box chariot. It was light, easy to maintain, a de facto choice. This one—the dual chariot—had curved extensions at the back, offering greater balance and making the vehicle fast, maneuverable, *and* compensating for its greater weight. The extensions were exquisitely designed, constructed (at great personal expense) from heat-bent wood, and the box was painted light gold.

"She's *faster* than a lion," the charioteer smiled. "It'll be like riding a lioness into the fight, my king."

"PULL my hair," Chryseis demanded. "Pull my hair and fuck me."

Agamemnon obliged, grasping her thick, black tresses in his fist, twisting them in his fingers, pulling hard so that she was forced to lean back toward him before he shoved her down, laying atop her. He teased her neck with his teeth and then bit her shoulder hard as he moved inside her. Gods! He couldn't get enough of her. She urged him on onward, whispering about all the things he could do to her, the things she *wanted* him to do to her, till he could no longer resist. He came into her, his cries of joy mingling with hers.

Agamemnon collapsed on top of her, still inside her, marveling at the way even their hearts pounded in unison. He kissed her shoulder, her neck. "I love you," he murmured as he rolled away.

Chryseis placed her head on his chest, her lush body pressed close to his. "And I love you, my king," she said.

"Sometimes," Agamemnon murmured, "I think you really mean that."

"I do," Chryseis protested. She was silent for a moment. Then: "It's funny how things work out. I should hate you," she said. "I'm a captive. A slave taken as a prize. Slaves should hate their masters."

Agamemnon chuckled, remembering that she had been captured *outside* the city walls—disobeying her father's command. He had been right to try to cloister her away even after the raiding season, when the Achaeans holed up in their camp and afforded the Trojans some freedom of movement. It galled him, but he simply didn't have the manpower to keep a siege up all year round. As such, the Trojans were able to resupply, allies were able to come in . . . He pushed the troublesome thoughts away. "To be fair, Chryseis," he said, "you've never much acted like a slave."

"That's true," she admitted. "But what I mean is that I have come to love my life here. In my father's house, it was nothing but rules and standing on display and never laughing. Being told I had royal blood through my mother and must be perfect as marble; being beaten when I fell short. My father telling me he'd marry me off to a prince—he thought Prince Hector would offer for me and make me future queen of Troy, and he beat me again when Princess Andromache was chosen instead."

"You could have been a queen, then?"

"I wouldn't mind being a queen, but not of Troy. In Troy, I'd still have my father standing over me with his hand out for the rest of my life, queen or no." She turned over. "Here in the encampment, I am a slave . . . but only in the eyes of the Trojans, who cannot see me. I'm free to go where I wish, wear what I wish, say what I wish, and no one beats me. I'm free to laugh out loud, drink wine, scream loud enough to wake the shades in Hades when you're inside me. In fact, I'm *almost* a queen, but . . ." she trailed off.

"But?"

"But I fear what will happen when the war is over."

Agamemnon knew where this was going. "Don't worry about the end of the war," he said after a while. "You will be cared for."

She paused, weighing his words, then changed the subject. "You know that Achilles has a new slave girl? Briseis."

"I'm surprised he bothered with a girl. Everyone knows Achilles and Patrocles are lovers."

"This one's a princess, or maybe a queen. Captured in the raid on Mythimna. They say Achilles is obsessed with her. And she's *not* in his bed. Not yet anyway. He treats her as though she were some kind of Olympian gift, something priceless." A pause. "He might even marry her, I heard."

"Once he's had her—and he will, eventually—she'll just be

his fuck piece, Olympian sent or not. And who marries their fuck piece?" Agamemnon scoffed and instantly realized that he'd fallen into her trap.

Chryseis turned her head away—a trifle dramatically. "It's amazing what love can do in such a short space of time."

Agamemnon tried—and failed—to keep the anger from his voice. "Even if Achilles did marry his new girl, I cannot be seen to be following that bastard in anything he does. I am high king," he added. "I set behavior; I do not follow the behavior of others."

Her voice dripped sarcasm. "I'm sure I understand. Even if I'm just *your* fuck piece."

Agamemnon refused to allow himself to be moved by her pique. He looked around her room—it was almost as grand as his own quarters, hung with rich cloths and decorated by expensive Trojan spoils. There was even a small statue of the sun god, Apollo. Even though he hated the gods, Agamemnon had taken it as a share of his prize and gifted it to her; Chryseis had been daughter to a powerful priest of Apollo in Troy before she had become his concubine.

He looked away from the god's impassive visage and over to Chryseis. She was sitting at her table, naked still, pouring wine from a *krater.* Agamemnon drank in the sight of her. She was beautiful—no, more than beautiful, she was magnificent. Heavy breasted, dark haired, violet-eyed, ripe, and eager. He wanted her. All the time. If there was anything good to have come out of this war, it was her. She was the only thing that brought a modicum of joy to his life. And he was being a fool—she was more, far more, than just a captive. He loved her.

"I will take you to wife when we return to Mycenae," he stated—and meant it.

Chryseis placed her wine cup down. "Don't tease me like that," she said, her eyes full of hurt. "It is not fair of you to do so."

Agamemnon looked up at the ceiling. "I'm not," he said after a moment's thought to make sure that he was going to go through with it. "You act as though you are already queen anyway," he added. "We'll make it official when the war is won." When he was no longer held beside the standard of Achilles.

He heard her approach the bed. "What about your other wife?" she asked.

"Clytemnestra despises me," Agamemnon said, squeezing his eyes shut. "How could she not?" He remembered the look on Clytemnestra's face, the horror in her eyes as he'd rammed the dagger into their daughter's chest. He heard once again Iphigenia's choking sob as her life's blood poured out in sacrifice.

Of course Clytemnestra abhorred him.

He puffed out a breath and looked over at Chryseis. Just doing so made the burden of the war, the burden of his guilt, the burden of years fall away. He reached out a hand, beckoning her over to him. "Word has it that Clytemnestra has taken a lover. I couldn't care less that she has, but it will give me reason enough to set her aside and take a new wife."

Chryseis smiled, sauntering over to the bed. Agamemnon could see that feral hunger in her eyes and knew that this round would be more exquisite than the last.

THE hall was a basic construction, to be sure, and he knew that Achilles had privately criticized him for having it built, but the timber used was taken from Trojan land—ostensibly rendering it plunder and thus giving the high king first choice on it. He knew that this right of his kingship irritated Achilles, which was why Agamemnon delighted in enacting it at every opportunity. The Phthian prince was such a preening, pouting, self-important, arrogant fool that someone level-headed needed to take him down a notch or two.

And that someone had to be the high king because the others were so in awe of his prowess with sword and spear that they couldn't see the potential destructiveness of the man's colossal ego. He was another one of those "my mother was a goddess" lunatics—the Trojans had them, too—and the ones that thought themselves semi-divine were always, *always* convinced they had some kind of grand destiny that everyone had to be party to.

Agamemnon knew differently. The gods laughed at them all. Laughed at men like Achilles with his sense of destiny, laughed at men like himself with their shattered dreams of grandeur and empire.

The flute girls brought wine and refreshments, but even before Agamemnon could begin with an appraisal of rations, troop welfare, reinforcements, and the annual animal sickness that he felt the warriors needed to know about, Achilles was raising his right hand for attention. Agamemnon was sorely tempted to ignore him but decided against it.

He knew—everyone knew—what Achilles was going to say anyway. Agamemnon saw his herald, Talthybius, roll his eyes and fought hard to resist smiling. Of them all, the herald understood this war and the machinations of the men. He was devious—rumor had it he had spies in Troy itself—he was cowardly, silver-tongued, self-serving, and utterly transparent in his desire for gold. Hence he was a man that Agamemnon could trust.

"High King," Achilles began.

Agamemnon sighed. Achilles didn't just fight like a god, he *looked* like a god. Tall, bronze skinned, dark haired, green-eyed, lithe, and muscular, his right arm a mass of crisscrossed scars, badges of honor from his many (and always victorious) combats. If there was any justice—any at all—the bastard should be hung tiny like a Hittite stripling. But there wasn't any justice: Agamemnon had seen him in the gymnasium, and Achilles' cock was as prodigious as his fucking ego.

Gods, he really hated him.

"Sure we thank you for your hospitality." Achilles gestured to the food and drink arranged on the trestle before them. "The sea gives forth its bounty . . . as do the Trojans," he added, garnering a laugh from the assembled princes, which irritated Agamemnon. "The sun warms our necks," Achilles went on, his green eyes sweeping the room. "The men are rested . . . perhaps too rested . . . after a slow winter. I think the time has come for us to push hard on the Trojans. Bring them to battle so that your brother's wife will be returned to him—and we can end this war!"

"We don't need an assault at this time, Achilles," Agamemnon made sure his voice was heavy with dismissive boredom. "My *strategy* is working. The raids are bleeding the Trojans dry—you're a spectacularly successful pirate," he added, knowing that the term would vex a *hero* like Achilles. "Besides, we have new recruits in from the mainland to swell our ranks—feckless boys with no idea of what the reality of this war is. Continuing the raiding strategy is a good way to blood them."

"There is always an excuse, Agamemnon!" Achilles snapped. "Always a reason that we should not march out and take the glory that we—kings, princes, and common spearmen—deserve. Diomedes!" he turned to the Argive king, tall and strapping in his famous lion-skin cloak. "What say you?"

Diomedes hesitated; he was younger than most, but he had a wealth of fighting experience—he'd been at Thebes before Troy, and some counted him almost equal to Achilles with the spear. "I would favor marching out," he agreed, getting a nod of approval from Achilles. "I hear truth in Agamemnon's words on feckless boys, but raiding is nothing akin to a real battle. A sword has to be tested to see if it breaks, bends, or cuts."

Achilles' eyes glittered with triumph as he turned back to Agamemnon and then to Ajax of Locris—or Ajax the Ox, as Agamemnon called him, privately, of course. Most used the epithet because of his size, but Agamemnon thought the moniker fitted Ajax's mental capacity perfectly. The huge warrior shrugged. "You know me. I'd rather be fighting," he said in that slow way of his. Agamemnon ignored him. Asking Ajax to add his wit to the argument was like asking for a contribution from a five-year-old. "We're not talking about a sword, though, are we? If the army bends or breaks, what then? Oh yes. It's very dramatic for all of you, charging off to the fight with the brazen hordes at your back. Right up until the moment things go wrong, and then what? You'd have me risk all on the throw of the dice when we're strangling the Trojans. Slowly, I'll grant you. But surely. There will be no assault," Agamemnon stated. "Not until I deem it time."

Achilles was florid. "We need to attack!"

"We need to attack, all right," Odysseus of Ithaca rose to his feet, shouting over the Phthian prince and causing all to look at him. "We need to attack the fucking wine *krater*!"

That got a laugh, and Agamemnon could see the bluster leave Achilles like air from a bladder. Odysseus was a canny bastard, Agamemnon thought. The Ithacan king was no ally of his, but he was grateful to him for cutting short the argument. Odysseus saw things with greater clarity than most of these idiots.

Achilles glared at him, and Agamemnon knew—*knew*—that he was trying to garner support for a challenge to his power. He was young. He was strong. He was a great warrior. He had divine blood. He should be the leader.

At least that's what he thought.

But Agamemnon knew the reality was somewhat different. They would not follow Achilles because, in the end, Achilles' concept of honor was too great. Achilles liked to play fair: pitched battles over sudden raids. And a high king could not play fair. The high king had to balance egos. Had to balance risk and opportunity. Had to balance the details of men lost and men replaced. Had to balance prizes.

Prizes.

That's what it all came down to in the end.

Agamemnon knew well that all these men had invested too much in the struggle to gamble on a new leader now, a leader untested and glory-drunk. He tipped back his cup of wine and beckoned for more, his eyes flicking to Menelaus, who sat staring into the distance, no doubt thinking of his lost love. Agamemnon despised his younger brother's weaknesses. Not that he'd give that voice because when angered, Menelaus was a fearsome warrior, and his wife Helen was a touchy subject. Agamemnon thought she was a troublesome bitch, but she *was* the cause of this war as far as Menelaus was concerned.

If Achilles *were* high king, he would push for single combat between Menelaus and Prince Paris and—whatever the outcome—would abide by it. If Menelaus, the rightful husband, won, Helen would be delivered and the Achaeans would return home—Troy would stand, and her gold would be intact. If Paris, the wife-usurper, won, the Achaeans would return home in defeat—Troy would stand, and her gold would be intact.

And none of them wanted that.

Too much had been lost, too many lives wasted. Even for the spearmen soldiers who fought the battles—there were unfaithful wives back home, wives with other men's children in their bellies, their own children grown, who did not know the faces of their real fathers.

Troy had to fall. And *not* because of Helen. Not because of honor, though they all pretended that was what it was about. Troy had to fall because they'd all lost too much to countenance anything else.

And the only thing that could make it right was gold. That was all that mattered now. When honor faded, when love had gone, when friends were long since ashes on the pyre, cold profit was all that remained. They would buy back their honor with Trojan spoils.

And in the years to come, bards would sing of this conflict as though it were something great and glorious. They'd sing of gods and men, of deeds great and bold. Agamemnon drank deep again as the flutes played and the drunken warriors brawled and boasted, and could not refrain from laughing aloud at the stupidity of it all.

BALANCING egos.

It irked him to do so, but Agamemnon ordered an increase in raiding activity, reasoning that it would keep Achilles' bloodlust in check, bring in some much-needed—and easy—victories and bolster morale. And let Achilles believe that his counsel had been heard. Agamemnon dearly hoped the Phthian would be killed on one of these assaults. A stray arrow, a well-cast stone, a broken chariot wheel leaving him at the mercy of rampant Trojans. But Achilles always returned in victory and was never shy about boasting about the old prophecy that Troy could not be taken without his help, his bloodline.

The priest Calchas, of course, endorsed this; Agamemnon was all but convinced that the priest had some hold over the man. He had tried many times to coerce Calchas to his side, but the man seemed so stalwart in his beliefs. It was possible that he was in Achilles' employ, or that he was simply in love with him after the leader of the Myrmidons made no secret of the fact that he liked men as much as he liked women.

That had to be it. Achilles was as handsome as a god, with a warrior's sculpted physique. It would be a festival day for Calchas if the Phthian prince ever deigned to let the priest play his flute.

That afternoon, in the quiet of Chryseis' quarters, Agamemnon put forward this theory.

"It's possible," she said, chewing on a tip of hair in that way she did when in thought. "It seems that Achilles always has the gods on *his* side. It's very convenient for him."

"And a pain for me," Agamemnon complained.

"The women are talking," Chryseis said—carefully. And that worried Agamemnon.

"About what?" he asked, pouring wine for them both. He liked to show her that despite the fact she had once been his captive that was no longer the case. They were partners in wit, in bed, and in life. She was a match for him intellectually, and that excited him—she offered a unique perspective on things.

"They say that the men are getting restless. That they're spoiling for a fight."

"They always are until it comes to it," Agamemnon muttered. "Especially the new ones who've never been in a fight."

"It's not just the new ones," Chryseis said. "Even the kings and princes now talk of our lack of action. That while we spend time raiding, the Trojans are garnering new allies. That they could be recovering their strength."

We, Agamemnon thought. Not *they*. She was saying that she considered herself Achaean now, which pleased him—even if he suspected that she had only said it to underscore her loyalty; Chryseis was nothing if not calculating and unscrupulous. Something else they shared. "My strategy is working," he said.

"If it were just the men carping, I'd understand it," she said. "But it's not. Skara told me that Ajax the Ox and Diomedes are frequent visitors to the Myrmidon section of the camp. And now that old whitebeard Nestor of Pylos and King Odysseus come, too."

"Skara?"

"Patrocles' bed-warmer, the Thracian girl with the tattoos. She leads all the women in the Myrmidon camp—well, she did till Briseis arrived."

"You're friendly with Achilles' new piece?" Agamemnon arched an eyebrow.

"Apollo, no!" Chryseis squeaked. "She keeps to herself. Quiet, strange thing. Skara, now, she and I pretend to be friends. What we're actually doing is pumping each other for information on our men—you and *him*. But she's stupid, and I'm not, though I'm allowing her to think she's manipulating me and not the other way around. So she opened up. She says Achilles' cronies are coming around to his way of thinking. That strangling Troy is not the way to finish things . . ." she hesitated, looking straight at him, "and that more direct action should be taken. With a firmer hand at the tiller."

Agamemnon rose to his feet. "So he's actually going to challenge me as high king." He laughed. "I can scarcely credit it."

"But he might just try it, Agamemnon. You should act. The stick with which Achilles hits you is inertia. Take that away from him, and what does he have? A good kill tally?" She laughed. "Men hold him in such awe, but men do not see what I see."

"And what do you see?"

"That he is merely a weapon in your armament. Like a spear or a sword, Achilles is a tool in your hand. That you hate him should not be relevant. *Use* him. We've all heard the story—Troy cannot be taken without him." She shrugged. "Give him what he wants. You are *high king*, my love. You are above the petty concerns of Achilles. He wants a legend. Let him have it. I know what you want. You want an end to this. And you want to keep your kingdom intact. You fear that a major assault—if lost—will damage us too greatly, that we will lose our grip here. But consider: we cannot do nothing. Troy suffers, yes, but I know she cannot be starved out. She will not capitulate. The deadlock must be broken."

A spike of anger flared up at her sheer gall. Love her or no, she was only a woman, and most men would give any woman who dared offer war council the back of his hand, and hard. But a high king could not afford to discard good sense, no matter how unlikely the lips that uttered it—and Chryseis, woman or no, spoke sense.

"I know nothing of strategy," Chryseis went on, eyeing him carefully, as though unsure whether to dare more words, playing the canny general in this little battle. "But it seems to me that to hand the Trojans any initiative is in error. If we attack, they must respond. Better than us responding to them?"

Agamemnon rose and held her to him. He kissed her, unsure if he was still annoyed with her for speaking out or proud of her for the same reason. Probably a bit of both. "I was lost till you came into my life," he said. "Chryseis, you give me strength that I thought I had lost forever. And perhaps you are right in this matter." She was, of course, but he didn't want her to know it. Not yet anyway. She'd work hard in bed for his approval on the matter, he reckoned, and that in and of itself was a good enough reason to hold out.

He kissed her again and then drank his wine. She watched him over the rim of her own cup, matching him sip for sip. "Perhaps my unwillingness to do battle is, in part, to spite Achilles. I know it's what he wants, and I enjoy denying him what he wants. But we're *winning,* Chryseis. Even if it is taking a Titan's age," he admitted.

Chryseis tipped back her cup. "I just want it to be over. So you can take me home." She slipped out of her robe, letting it slide to the floor with a whisper of cloth on skin. "Let us pretend it is that day," she said, her eyes burning with that fire he knew so well. She wanted to convince him.

And Agamemnon wanted her to think he would let her.

"MY king!"

Agamemnon groaned at his guard's voice from without. "I do not wish to be disturbed!"

"Forgive me . . ." He could hear the tremor in the man's voice through the door. "But a herald approaches from the city. From Troy."

"What!" Agamemnon got up too quickly and stumbled.

"The kings and princes gather, my king. I thought it wise to alert you."

"Very well!" Agamemnon shouted. "Very well." He looked at Chryseis. "Shit."

"You'll have to go," she said, pulling the covers over herself. "You cannot allow yourself to be absent."

Agamemnon cursed again. He was too drunk to deal with this kind of thing now. But Chryseis was right. He *had* to be there. And he had to look like the high king. "Bring your women to dress me," he told Chryseis.

"There is no time," she said. "I will dress you myself."

She worked fast, selecting a fine robe of purple and loading him down with jewelry while he drank as much water as he could take on, hoping it would cut through the fug of the wine. It only made him anxious to relieve himself, which was difficult enough in the heavy robe. He pissed apologetically in Chryseis' own chamber pot and then allowed her to finalize his accoutrement.

"How do I look?" he asked her as she set a diadem on his head. It tipped over his eyes, and he righted it.

"Kingly," she replied with a grin. "Best have the men take you on a litter," she added.

Agamemnon grunted. Once more, she was right.

HE hoped this would all be about a hostage exchange, something he could deal with quickly and get back inside.

The lesser kings and princes had gathered—hoping, probably, that there would be some gossip to be had or profit to be garnered. Even Achilles was there, and his presence gave Agamemnon pause for thought. Was there something afoot he was not aware of? And by his side stood Calchas.

The Trojan herald bowed as the litter approached. He was a tall man with a sonorous voice and easy manner. He was charming, and, truth be told, Agamemnon quite liked him in that he could be trusted not to put his own slant on a message given. With him was an older man who seemed familiar to Agamemnon. He was tall and imposing and one-eyed. The sort you'd not forget meeting—but yet he was sure he had never laid eyes on him before.

Probably the drink.

"What business?" Agamemnon asked the herald, trying not to slur and realizing from the sharp glances of Achilles, Odysseus, and the others that he had failed.

"Great Agamemnon," the herald began. "Ruler of Mycenae, high king who is beloved of the gods, dread leader in battle . . ." He went on in this mien for some time. Usually, Agamemnon enjoyed it, but today he just wanted to cut to the chase. Protocol, however, had its demands. "I bring with me a priest," the herald got to it at last.

"A priest?" Agamemnon arched an eyebrow: the older man didn't look like one at all. "I don't need a priest." He shot a glance at Calchas. "I have one of my own. Well—unless this one is better, in which case we might be able to make a deal."

"Dread King." The old man stepped forward and fell to his knees, arms outstretched. It was clear from the way his remaining eye glittered that the only time this one knelt was before his god. "I am Chryses," he said. "I come to ask for the release of my daughter." Agamemnon gaped at him, realizing in that sickening instant *why* the priest seemed so familiar to him. One-eyed or no, the shape of his face, his accent. Chryseis' *father.* "You have taken my child as captive," Chryses boomed. "And I am bereft without her."

Agamemnon regarded him. He didn't look bereft. He looked like a man who wanted something back simply because it had been taken from him.

"I beg of you, please return her to me."

"Beg" and "please" didn't seem to sit well with this one, Agamemnon noted. It was rather entertaining watching him act the supplicant.

"Hector himself has guaranteed a great ransom for the return of my daughter," Chryses went on, the small-time horse trader now. "It is a small thing, Dread King. You have many women, many slaves. But all I had—and all I want—is my child back." The way it was delivered, he might as well be bargaining for a horse. Fuck him. He could offer all the gold in Troy if he wanted.

Agamemnon glanced at his own priest, who gave a barely perceptible nod. "No," he said and turned away from Calchas.

Chryses' fists gripped the sand as he knelt. "You cannot know what it is like to have a child taken from you," he thundered, and the words struck Agamemnon like a spear thrust to the chest—the man's presumption angered him, the fury ignited by the wine coursing through him. He was about to send the priest away, but the bastard pressed on, his voice low now. Menacing. "I am a priest of Apollo, Agamemnon." He dared—*dared*—to address him by name. "The Far-Darter hears my words when I pray. And

I can pray for victory. Or I can pray for defeat." Agamemnon tried to respond, but his own rage strangled him.

"He speaks the truth!" Calchas shrilled. "Chryses is beloved of Apollo. Hear him, my king, hear him!"

"Hear him, Agamemnon!" This from Achilles. "Calchas knows the ways of the gods. He's never been wrong."

"Yes, he has! One prophecy after another he spouts—last time it was all about how the gates would fall if we cut down that princeling of Priam's, the young one, Troilus. Achilles ambushed him last year, and we're still waiting!"

AGAMEMNON heard himself scream in fury, silencing Calchas and the muttering around him. Gripping the side of the litter, he rose to his full height. "The gods!" he shouted. "The gods! Fuck the gods! Fuck them! I don't fear the gods. Fear them? I spit in their faces. All of them. For the gods and their mouthpieces here on earth have taken everything from me. *Everything.* I piss on them. Strike me down, Zeus!" He flung his arms out wide. "I dare you! Where is your lightning? Where is your fury? I see nothing. Only blue skies above me and a half-blind man before me with empty words and empty threats. Chryseis is *mine.* I will not give her up. Never will I give her up. And not you"—pointing at Achilles—"him"—pointing at Calchas—"nor the gods themselves will compel me!"

"My king, this is a blasphemy!" Calchas waddled out from the protection of Achilles' side.

"You're a fool, Agamemnon!" Achilles spat. "Take back your words lest you bring disaster on us all!"

"*I'm* a fool?" Agamemnon roared. "Where is your courage? Get a priest to make a threat of victory or defeat, and I—the high king—must accept it? No! It will not be so!"

"His words are heavy with truth . . ." Calchas started, but Agamemnon rounded on him.

"Speak again and you die!" Shaking with rage, Agamemnon balled his fists. "There will be no ransom!" he shouted, looking around at the pale, shocked faces of the men gathered. "No ransom. We are finished here!" His litter bearers hesitated for a moment before stooping to lift the palanquin.

"Can I see her?"

Chryses' words—so quiet in the storm—shocked Agamemnon, dousing his rage. He could not take back what he had said. But he could be magnanimous. "I don't give a damn what you do, priest. Ask her to go with you if you want. See the response you get." He gestured to the bearers, and they bore him away.

Agamemnon reached for the *krater* and drank what was left. He found himself wanting more.

WAS there any good at all left in Agamemnon, king of Mycenae? Was he a man who had used his brother's misfortune to mount a war for profit and blamed his shared capriciousness on other . . . lesser . . . men? Was he a man who had murdered his own child so that impassive gods might grant a fair wind for the endeavor?

He should have stayed his hand, kingdom and power be damned. He had killed Iphigenia because it held the alliance together. A black deed for a black soul. He had many times considered killing himself. Falling onto his own sword, washing away the guilt in his own blood. But the hard truth was he lacked the courage.

And what was he now? An aging monarch who was hated by all, and a man who openly taunted the gods in front of the men. Those who had not witnessed it would have heard the tale by now. Of how Agamemnon risked Apollo's wrath for a girl. A slave. A fuck piece. That's what they would say of Chryseis. That she was a fuck piece, one of hundreds he could choose from. Any misfortune they now suffered would be laid at his door.

How Achilles must be laughing at him. They were all laughing at him.

The door to his quarters opened, sunlight flooding in, and with it Chryseis. She was dressed in a simple shift—bereft of ornament and jewels—it only served to accentuate her exquisite beauty. And for a moment, the Furies were silent. She came to him, wordless for a time, and sat next to him on the bed, her cool fingers stroking his sweat-slick forehead, brushing away errant strands of graying hair.

"Oh, my love," she said.

Agamemnon sat up and held her close, squeezing her tight as though to gain strength from her. He wanted to weep but held back the tears—he could not stand her contempt, too. "What have I done?" he whispered.

"Nothing that cannot be undone."

He broke the embrace, suddenly fearful. "You saw your father." It was a statement, not a question.

"Yes," she replied and looked away, gazing at the stand on which he hung his armor. It was new—Agamemnon had had it made to go with the new chariot. It seemed, like the chariot itself, gaudy and overdone now. "He demanded that I leave with him. But I refused."

"Why?" Agamemnon was utterly relieved. But he had to know. "He is your father."

"He wants to love me . . ." She stopped, gathering herself. "He wants to love me in a way that no father should want to love his daughter. I saw it in his eyes all the time. I saw it again today. He asked me . . . he asked me if you raped me. I think it would have pleased him if you had. The thought of it.

"He could not keep his hands off the girls that were sent to serve in the shrine. Even Priam's daughter Princess Cassandra was fair game," she went on. "And though he wanted me, he knew that if he did, Apollo would be angered. So he didn't touch me. In that way. Instead, he took his frustration out with fists. He beat me, Agamemnon. Beat me till I was black and blue."

"Then I will kill him," Agamemnon said. "When we take the city, I will find him and take his other eye," he embellished, "so he will go to Hades blind and broken."

Chryseis shuddered as though shutting a door inside her that she wished she had not opened. "I never want to see him again," she said after a moment. "The truth is, my world is here, with you. You are my world, Agamemnon. *Our* world."

"Our world?"

"I didn't know when to tell you," she said. "But it seems that now is the time. I have missed three cycles, my love. Your child grows within me."

"A child?" Agamemnon was awestruck.

Chryseis laughed. "It happens, my king. Especially when a man ruts as often as you do."

He forced himself to smile in response; the news should have delighted him, but the Furies returned. "I don't know what kind of kingdom I will leave him, Chryseis."

"That's the wine talking," she snapped, stern now. "My father told me what you said. That you invited the curse of the gods on this army. That he would invoke Apollo's wrath on us all. Even me when I refused to go with him. He seems to have forgotten that I can pray to Apollo, too, and the god may hear me over him. I *will* pray. But you need to act on our plan.

"We know that Achilles wants to be high king," she went on. "You—in your rage for me—have handed him a sword with which to stab you. Blunt it. The stakes are raised, Agamemnon. I am to be your wife and the mother of your heir, am I not?"

She was still insecure in her position, he realized, testing him to make sure that his promise given in the afterglow of lovemaking would be honored. "You said I am your world. As you are mine. Especially now," he said. "And I promise you this: when you are too heavy with child to come to my bed, I will take no other woman to it. I swear it. You are for me, Chryseis. I love you and you alone, and I will sire no bastards to challenge our son."

Agamemnon felt a small stab of guilt at his words. Orestes was his first born. But Orestes was not *his* son. He was *Clytemnestra's* son and had suckled her poisonous hatred of him since he was a babe. Clytemnestra had taken a lover; this Agamemnon had had confirmed. Orestes would look to that man as his father. Orestes would be dreaming of kingship. The truth of it was that Agamemnon didn't know Orestes at all. His child with Chryseis would be his *real* son. He wouldn't kill Orestes, but he would banish him. He would, however, have to kill Clytemnestra and her lover. Perhaps have them drowned in that bath that she liked to make love in. A bit of panache to underscore her adultery.

Chryseis smiled. "You are a good man." The irony of her words was not lost to him. "But still, you must act. I can only imagine the hay that Achilles is making now. That you have cursed us all, that the gods are angered . . . and that bastard Calchas will be urging him on. So. Give Achilles what he wants. Give him his battle."

"After what I said in my rage, if we lose or even come close to it, it will be the end for me. And you. And our son."

"If you don't act, the result will be the same. But win and you silence him. Win and you prove that Agamemnon fears not the wrath of men or gods or priests. Win and your power is secured, and none can raise their voice against you. Not even Calchas—whose prophesies, after such a victory, would surely favor you. He's a piece of shit," she added, which made Agamemnon laugh.

"You seem awfully keen for me to push for a fight," he observed.

"I have an ulterior motive," Chryseis said. "I want an end to this war. We are winning, yes—but let us be honest: the words you spoke in your rage have changed things.

"It is a gamble, Agamemnon," she stated. "You know this. But nothing of worth was ever won without risk. You are a man. You are a king. You will be the stuff of legends. I know you scoff at tales, but think on this. Win this war and men will remember the glory of Agamemnon, the king who brought Troy to her knees. And Achilles, if history remembers him at all, will be recalled as the man whose own petty desires threatened that glory."

"I'll summon the council at once," Agamemnon affirmed.

"No." She frowned, and her brow crinkled in that delightful way. "Not yet. If you act too early, it will look like you're panicking. No," she said again. "Be kingly. Withdraw. Let them gossip—let them assume. They will be saying you've lost your nerve. Then you, my king, will strike. In the way that they least expect. By launching a major assault."

She was right. She always was. And Agamemnon realized in that moment that she had—as she always could—driven the Furies away.

"IT stinks in here," Menelaus observed as he came in, squinting in the gloom of the lamplight. "And you look like shit."

"Good to see you too, Brother," Agamemnon smiled. He was mildly drunk, sated from an afternoon romp with Chryseis, and in good spirits.

"We need to talk."

"So . . ." Agamemnon said. "Talk."

Menelaus hesitated. Agamemnon could tell that he, as the high king's brother, had been put up to this visit by the others. The truth of it was that Menelaus was weak in character. A canny fighter, to be sure, but not a leader; he might have fire in his hair, but none in his belly. Privately, Agamemnon thought it little wonder that Helen absconded. Brother or no, Menelaus was a vacillating bore. "You've angered the men, Agamemnon," he said at length.

"The men are always angry about something. Lack of booty, the slaves are too ugly, they want to go home . . . and that this war is being fought for a Spartan king's honor. Your honor, in fact."

"There's a sickness in the camp," Menelaus told him, irritatingly refusing to rise to the bait. "It's spreading."

"There's always sickness at this time of year." Agamemnon's good mood evaporated like a wine offering to Hermes on a hot day.

"I know that," Menelaus said, placating. "But the men . . . and some of the princes . . . say that the one-eyed priest's prophecy has come to pass. Men are dying, Brother."

"This is an army with a nine-year history and a two-week memory." Agamemnon reached for the *krater* and poured. He offered a cup to Menelaus, who held up his hands in refusal. "Men die of sickness all the time!" He failed to keep the anger from his voice.

Menelaus swallowed, once again the callow boy before his brother's wrath. "You have not seen how bad it is, how fast it has struck. I wouldn't come to you and bother you with it otherwise," he added with the right amount of contrition.

Of course, Agamemnon could imagine him telling the other warriors that he'd "talk some sense into my brother." Menelaus was a yes-man, always telling others what they wanted to hear. Agamemnon realized he hated him a little.

"You've been locked away in here," Menelaus pressed on. "With *her*."

"Chryseis," Agamemnon snapped. "She has a name."

“She does—and it is spoken often outside of these walls, Agamemnon. The men say that you are befuddled by her. And Achilles—Achilles claims that you have brought Apollo’s wrath upon us all for your own pleasure.”

“That’s rich coming from Achilles,” Agamemnon spat. “That bastard moons over his new slave girl, what’s her name . . . ?”

“Briseis.”

“Yes, Briseis. But I’m not allowed to find happiness in the arms of a woman. Just him? You’d think that someone who seems so keen to carve out a legend for himself wouldn’t be so petty.”

“There’s a rumor he would be a better commander than you,” Menelaus spoke carefully.

“There are always rumors,” Agamemnon said. “And there’s always a better man for the job—right up until he *has* the job. Achilles could no more run this army than . . .” he trailed off, but Menelaus had the hurt look in his eyes that said he knew the barb was meant for him. “I’m high king,” Agamemnon stated.

“They say you’re not much acting like it,” Menelaus said. “The men need to see you. The sickness is worse this spring, Brother.”

Agamemnon sighed. “I will take a tour of the camp. Check on the men.” He rose to his feet. “Inspire them with my kingly presence.”

Menelaus did not smile at the joke. “You should take your guards.”

“I don’t need protection from my own men,” Agamemnon said. But the look in Menelaus’ eyes told him otherwise. “You’re not serious.”

“The camp seethes not only with sickness but with resentment.” Menelaus’ voice was heavy with doom, and it was clear to Agamemnon that he had not come up with the phrase. It sounded like something Nestor would say—wordy and old-fashioned.

"Very well," Agamemnon said. "I'd best dress for the part." His eyes flicked over to his new armor. "Will you help me?"

Menelaus nodded. "Of course."

AT first, his tour was greeted with silence, but soon enough the muttering began. "Shall we turn back?" the charioteer whispered.

"Don't be absurd," Agamemnon snapped. He was about to speak again but was interrupted by a shout from the men.

"You brought the plague on us!"

It was greeted with a chorus of approval.

"Is she worth it?" another shouted. "We're dying because of you!"

"Give her up!"

Agamemnon did his best to keep his eyes frontward until they reached the hospital section. There were more tents than he remembered, and the whole area stank of decay and roasting flesh. The pyres *were* burning.

He removed his helmet and stepped inside the nearest tent, squinting as his eyes adjusted from bright sun to dank gloom. It reeked in here, and it took all of Agamemnon's courage not to flee. He counted himself brave—not battle-hungry like Achilles, but he'd never run from a fight. But the fear of disease, the silent killer, the invisible dart that a man could not see coming . . . that was enough to unman him.

The air in the tent was so thick that he could taste it, the rank stench of shit, sweat, and rot all-pervasive. Men coughed in throaty, phlegm-slick rattles or cried out in delirium, adding foul dissonance to this vile place. There were women present, slaves and captives mostly, caring for the men who had once been their enemies. Men who had, perhaps, taken them by force and were now at their mercy.

Agamemnon thought of Chryseis. Her love was worth more to him than anything. Even the suffering of these men. He would not give her up, he vowed, even as he toured the makeshift cots, nodding and grunting at the stricken soldiers, adopting the correct concerned expression as the surgeon told him of the virulent speed at which "Apollo's Curse" was spreading.

He said it openly to Agamemnon's face—"Apollo's Curse"—as though it was an absolute certainty that this was the Olympian's handiwork despite the truth of Agamemnon's words to Menelaus: this sickness was annual. Yes, it was worse this year, but it would pass. He listened to the surgeon and his grim prophecies and snide suggestions ("if only there was some way to appease the god") and did him the favor of not gutting him where he stood for his impudence.

"The sickness comes every year," Agamemnon told him.

"Not like this." He was old, as surgeons tended to be, white bearded, well toothed, and impertinent—also as surgeons tended to be. "The god is angry, my king. The men . . ."

". . . are not educated. Like you and I." Agamemnon decided that honey would be better than vinegar. "I'd look on it favorably if you—in your professional capacity—would remind people that the sickness comes every year and will pass as it does every year. It has nothing to do with curses and Apollo."

"Even if I believed that—which I don't—it wouldn't matter, sire." He looked as though he was going to say more, but he was wise enough to hold his tongue on that aspect. And though Agamemnon wanted to upbraid the man for his impudence, *he* was wise enough to hold his tongue, too; one day he might find himself under this man's knife, and past punishments could well be remembered. The surgeon leaned in closer. "Whatever the reason, Apollo's Curse is on us. So even if I do as you ask, my word will be worth as much as a piss in a rainstorm."

"Charming analogy. Do it anyway." Agamemnon did not wait to be contradicted; he turned his back on the man and strode from the tent, eager to be free of it. But he knew he must do his duty and visit the others. And there was part of him that wanted to, just to thumb his nose at the god and prove to everyone that Agamemnon had no fear.

Even if he did.

It took some time to visit all the tents, and as he passed from one to the next, Agamemnon noted the hostile looks he was garnering from both the sick and the hale, be they the women and surgeons who were attending the infected or those spearmen who just saw him passing by. His charioteer told him timidly that men had hurled insults at him and mocked the new chariot, which blackened his mood as they drove back to his quarters.

It was an excellent chariot.

His bodyguards were taut and alert, and Agamemnon pretended not to hear abuse and accusations hurled at him from the faceless and unseen as the chariot rolled past the men.

Worse than the sickness itself, the disease of insubordination was spreading through the camp—and Agamemnon did not doubt that this distemper was not confined to just the Mycenaeans. Soldiers were worse than crones for gossip, and he knew that everyone would now be saying that he had brought this upon them.

He dismissed his charioteer, too curtly, but his temper was short. Slamming the door of his quarters behind him, he poured some wine. He drained his cup in a single draught, squeezing his eyes shut as the calming warmth spread through him. He took a deep breath. He would have to do something, he thought as he poured again. He had his guards summon Talthybius and struggled out of his armor while he waited.

To be fair to him, the herald attended him sharply. Agamemnon liked Talthybius, even if he looked the type that enjoyed cuckolding others. He was tall, handsome, dark-eyed, and wore more jewelry than a queen and more perfume than a harlot.

"You look like a woman," Agamemnon greeted him.

"That's rich. I've seen your chariot. And your armor. You need me as herald today or friend?"

"Friend," Agamemnon said. "Wine?"

"It would be an affront to the gods to say no," Talthybius responded, making Agamemnon look at him sharply. "What?" the herald said as he took the cup. "You're not blind, deaf, or stupid, Agamemnon." He pointedly poured a libation. "To say what you said in front of the men. In front of *Achilles* . . . that was stupid."

"Don't upbraid me. I'm—"

"High king? Not for much longer if this carries on." He held up a hand to quell the outburst bubbling in Agamemnon's craw. "I'm not your enemy," he said and seated himself in Chryseis' favorite chair. "But you do have them. And the sickness is spreading. I know it comes every year," he added. "But it's worse this time. Men are dying of it. Cretans. Mycenaeans. The Spartans. Ajax's lot. It's spreading like a pox from a dodgy whorehouse. Naturally, the Myrmidons are untouched." He drank his wine and poured more for himself. "You have to give the girl up."

Agamemnon bit down an angry response. The untrustworthy herald was one of the few men he trusted. Because Talthybius had only Talthybius' interests at heart, of that Agamemnon could be certain. "I will not give her up," he stated. "I intend to marry her the moment I'm back through the Lion Gate."

"She's a *woman*," Talthybius waved that away. "You'll tire of her eventually. I hear she's got your bastard in her. Once that pops out, things'll be different. She'll turn into a mother, and the child's interests will be at the forefront of her mind."

"You don't know Chryseis." The look on Talthybius' face told Agamemnon that the rakish bastard would love to know her in all sorts of ways. And he knew that Agamemnon knew it. Chryseis probably knew it, too. And knowing Chryseis, if she thought the idea would entertain him, she'd do it. He pushed the image of a diverting little threesome aside. "Even if I did give her up, what good would it do?" he asked. "It won't stop the sickness, and it'll make me look weak in front of the others."

"I'd give more of a shit about holding on to power. There's talk that Achilles is going to make a play for leadership. And after your little rant, the more religious amongst us might well be swayed."

"You?"

"Don't be an idiot. Achilles is too honorable—the man has a bronze pole of righteousness crammed so far up his arse I'm surprised Patrocles can fit his cock in there. You're the right man for the job. Or," he looked Agamemnon in the eyes, "at least you were. But you're losing your grip. This girl is making you crazy. Give her up so we can get back on with the war and go home. Think of the gold," he added. "Think of the history, too. You'll be remembered as the man who razed the city that couldn't be razed. You'll be a legend. And I'll have gold beyond the dreams of avarice. Everyone'll be a winner."

"Forget Chryseis. For now," Agamemnon said, forgiving the herald for the exasperated roll of his eyes. "I'm planning on announcing a major assault."

"What! With a third of the men down sick?"

"What else would you have me do? The Trojans won't be expecting it, and it'll prove Achilles wrong. But I need a favor."

Talthybius' eyes lit up. He would press for more of a cut of Agamemnon's booty, the high king knew. "Go on."

"I know you treat with the Trojans," Agamemnon spoke the truth that everyone knew. It was convenient to pretend that it didn't go on, but this was how ransoms were negotiated. That quiet, dark-skinned son of Priam's—Hellenus—was occupying the Talthybius role for the enemy, he knew. He recalled the

Trojan prince when they had first met in Sparta. An honorable man, he'd thought. But war had a way of changing men for the worse.

"How could you say such a thing?" Talthybius laughed. "Perish the thought. But let's pretend that I do. What do you need?"

"I'm going to go with this assault. And you know before a major battle there's the possibility of single combat for Helen," Agamemnon said. "If Paris ever found the balls—which I doubt—Menelaus would probably win. Then . . ."

Talthybius paled. "The war would be over. Honorably."

"Exactly. Imagine all this blood spilled for not a single piece of gold from that cursed city. We can't allow that to happen. If Menelaus wins . . ."

"I think I can help," Talthybius said. "In fact, I know I can. But it'll cost you a share."

"Why am I not surprised?"

Talthybius laughed. "Because I'll have to pay someone to get the job done. I take it if by some chance *Paris* wins, you'll have someone to take care of matters on this side?"

"Of course," Agamemnon smiled. "You. With Achilles spreading righteousness and honor faster than this plague, I'd rather have a man like you take care of both aspects."

The herald grinned. "Because I'm not righteous and have no honor?"

"It's why we get on so well."

Talthybius got up and placed the wine cup on the table. "About the girl," he began.

"Chryseis."

"Give her up, Agamemnon. You'll win back the men if you do. I'll put it about that she's to be your wife, that your love for her is greater than that of Menelaus' for Helen. Or Achilles for that

Briseis. She's a strange one," he added. "Skinny as a boy, and they say she drives a chariot like one too. Bet that's why he can't take his eyes off her." He regarded Agamemnon, and the high king saw genuine compassion in his eyes. "Look, I know what you've given up for this war. I've never forgotten it—that day at Aulis. The others have, I think. And now they ask more of you. I think you deserve some of your own tragedy to be remembered. I'll do my best for you. But . . . you know I'm right in this."

He left Agamemnon alone with the wine *krater.*

Agamemnon took the jug with him and sat on the bed, staring at the floor, his hair hanging about his face. He could see the gray in it, so he sat up and drank. "The Curse of Apollo," he heard himself say aloud.

Talthybius was right about the personal cost to him. He *had* given up so much and earned no thanks for it. Rather, he'd earned contempt of those far beneath him.

What about the price demanded by the gods? The blood of Iphigenia. The murder of his own child? She was worth more to him than the paltry lives of faceless soldiers, of men who were born to serve their betters. Men who were afforded the opportunity to have a little glory, lightening what would otherwise be a life of inconsequence. They should be thanking him. *Thanking him?* They should be venerating him.

Which of them had given up what he, Agamemnon, had? Petty men with petty complaints, petty lives, and pettier deaths. And now they wanted him to sacrifice again? He would not do it. He had given up too much already. He was high king, and he would prove it to them all. To all the men and the Achaean kings and princes. Especially to Achilles, so smug in his virtue.

The Phthian prince's face swam before his eyes as he fell back on the bed. But so it faded and was replaced by Iphigenia's. Then came the Furies, fluttering around the periphery of his consciousness, waiting for him to slip into the grip of Hypnos, where they could bind him and rend him at their leisure.

HE looked up to see Chryseis sitting in her chair. "Get me some wine," he said, forcing a smile, but the look on her face froze him to the bone. Her eyes were bloodshot, her face red and puffy. "What is it? Who has upset you? I'll have them punished."

"The men are dying," Chryseis whispered. "They are blaming you, and Apollo doesn't hear my prayers. I cannot stop this."

"It will pass, my love. This will be forgotten in a few weeks. I plan on the assault, as I have said—"

"You're not listening to me!" she said and burst into tears. "You're not hearing me!"

He rushed to her and took her in his arms. "I will make it right," he soothed, kissing her raven-colored hair. "I will make it right."

"You can't!" she sobbed. "My fucking father—gods curse him. He brought this upon us!"

"No he didn't . . ."

"Don't tell me this is the usual sickness. No one thinks that. The *men* don't think that. They think it's me. They think it's me . . ."

"What are you saying?"

"It might be true," she sobbed. "What if it *is* true? That I have brought the curse." She looked at him, her face red and mottled, her eyes shot with tears. "I have to go back."

The words struck him in the heart with a blade of ice. "No," he said. "No, Chryseis, you cannot. I will not allow it. We are to be together. The child . . ."

"Stop it!" she screamed. "Stop it! My heart is broken! But we must do this, Agamemnon. If not, they will kill us anyway. Sooner or later. I have to go back," she said again, and this time

Agamemnon's tears fell with hers. He held her close, as though somehow this closeness would make it all stop, make the curse end, and make it all well again.

But he knew it would not.

Agamemnon held his love and wept, his heart breaking as he kissed her, hating that everyone was right and he was wrong, hating that he had given everything for a war he no longer believed in, and hating—above all—the gods themselves.

They spoke for hours, both making promises that they knew would be hard to keep: how Agamemnon would find her at the end of the war and bring her home, how he would give it all up and they would live together with their child.

But they both knew that her one-eyed father, Chryses, would make that impossible—that Agamemnon would probably never find her. But he promised and vowed that he would upend the earth itself searching for her until, after a while, the wine allowed the grief to pass and the anger to vent.

"That fucking Achilles," Agamemnon spat. "He will take this as a victory. Then he'll ride to glory on the back of my leadership. I hate him, Chryseis."

"Then hurt him," she hissed. "Hurt him as we are hurt."

"How?" Agamemnon was so drunk he was struggling to think straight. "How? I cannot beat him in a fight; the men love him, and Calchas ensures the gods love him, too. All I can hope is that a spear finds him in the battle and I will be rid of him."

"Then don't let him fight in the battle."

"I cannot order that. The men wouldn't stand for it. Don't you know the prophecy that he and Calchas keep spouting? Troy cannot be taken without his blood and his 'divine' aid."

"I know a way," Chryseis' voice was ragged from tears and rage. "You make his notion of honor work against him and *for* you. Do as I say, and at the end of it, the men will hate him and look again to you."

"What must I do?"

"Make love to me for the last time." She smiled through her tears. "And my last gift to you will be your redemption."

HE did not drink that day nor the next. Nor the day after; though he shook and craved for it, he did not allow a drop to pass his lips. And of course, word reached him that, as promised, the sickness had begun to dwindle and the deaths were fewer. The news seethed through the camp like the plague itself had once done. Apollo's eye was turned from them, the curse lifted.

It made Agamemnon all the more bitter because he knew if they could have delayed a few more days, he'd have been proven right, Chryseis would still be at his side, and Achilles would have looked a fool.

Achilles.

Agamemnon's smile was cold when he thought of the Phthian prince. He would have his vengeance upon him. Thanks to Chryseis, unscrupulous to the last, he would tear Achilles' heart out as his own had been torn. And then Achilles would know loss. Achilles would know the emptiness of honorable words. Agamemnon would make a pyre and let the bastard burn on his words of honor.

The days without booze allowed Agamemnon to think more clearly. The pain of his loss was more, but he knew that no amount of wine could blunt it. No amount of wine could drink away the old wound of Iphigenia nor the fresh one of Chryseis.

All he had was vengeance and hate. There was nothing left. Vengeance against Achilles and vengeance against the Trojans. If not for them . . . if not for Paris . . . none of this would have come to pass. He would raze that city, and he would bathe himself in

Priam's blood. He would butcher the old man's children before the Trojan king's eyes so that he, too, would know pain and loss. And then he would spill the old man's gizzards and drag him to Apollo's temple as offering. Before he stood in the face of the god and laughed.

Agamemnon called a council on the fourth day, and none refused it. They came to the council hall in good spirits, and he saw forgiveness in the eyes of some, pity in those of Achilles' lieutenant, Patrocles. A good man, save for his loyalty to the Phthian. Agamemnon wished it was Patrocles who commanded the Myrmidons; *that* would have made life much simpler. But of course, Patrocles wasn't Phthian and hence could not lead them. Still, he certainly looked like them; at his age, he still had the muscle of a man in his twenties. The only incongruous things were that Patrocles often had a smile on his face and knew the meaning of manners. He gave Agamemnon one of those smiles now, and a part of him was grateful. More than a part: thanks to Patrocles' bed-warmer, Skara, Chryseis had been able to find the knife with which he could stab Achilles.

Achilles.

Agamemnon's eyes met those of the Phthian and saw smug triumph in them.

He allowed the men a chance for small talk and gossip before he called them to order. "The sickness has passed," he said to grumbles of approval. "The men are recovering, and it is my intention to seize the initiative of this war and launch—as some of you have been pushing for—a major assault. It is time to end this."

"It is high time," Achilles said. "But I give thanks to the gods that you have reached this decision." The Phthian prince glanced at Talthybius, and Agamemnon guessed that the herald had been true to his words and put about the truth about his love for Chryseis. “I know what you have given up,” Achilles said. “It could not have been an easy thing.”

Agamemnon’s grip tightened on the arm of his seat. How dare he? How dare he act conciliatory? Easy, he thought, to be the bigger man when you have given up nothing. He breathed in through his nose and let the air slip from his mouth, calming him. And he forced a smile. “Yes,” he said. “About that. As high king, the right of spoils are mine. As many have pointed out, Chryseis was merely a prize of war. A trophy, if you like. And now I find my share lacking. I demand recompense. You all swore an oath—and now I will claim my prize.”

“If it is in our power, we must grant it,” Achilles said, looking around for support. The men agreed. It was right and proper.

“I’m glad you see it that way,” Agamemnon said. “I am now without a woman. Hardly fair.” He made a show of thinking as he looked into the green eyes of Achilles—eyes, it was claimed, that came from his mother, a sea nymph. Eyes that grew wide as realization began to dawn. Agamemnon savored the look of growing horror—the powerlessness, the color draining from his cheeks as the sick dread was welling up inside him. He didn’t need to ask Achilles how it felt. He already knew. “Briseis was also a prize of war,” he said with a faint smile. “I’ll take her. As is my right. On the oaths you swore.”

Achilles rose to his feet, taut with rage, and his hand twitched as though going for his sword. Agamemnon felt a stab of fear in his breast; the man was lethal, a warrior who killed with impunity—to be the object of his wrath was dangerous. Patrocles reached out and touched his commander’s arm, stilling him. An act for which Agamemnon was profoundly grateful.

“High king,” Achilles spat contempt. “High king? You are not worthy of the title. Does your greed know no bounds? Briseis is mine.”

Agamemnon had expected wild rage. Fury. But this was not that. This was stone-cold wrath, and it was unnerving to see the iron control the man had over himself. But he could see the pain in the Myrmidon's eyes. The slight to his precious honor must be killing him.

"You will not have her," Achilles said. "I will kill any man that tries to take her from me."

"You swore an oath of fealty. To me," Agamemnon said. "You will abide by it, or all will know that the honorable standards you set—standards that inspire us all, I'm sure—are in fact merely empty words. How, then, will you be remembered, Achilles? As the man who refused his king—a king he mocked for loving a woman—the gift of a woman that he himself holds dear. A *slave.* No. I will have Briseis. I'll treat her well," he added. "I'm sure that in time she will come to . . . enjoy my company."

That one hit home, and Agamemnon saw the fury in his enemy's eyes. "I curse you," Achilles said. "By my mother's blood, I curse you."

"A bit late for that." Agamemnon looked upward. "As you and others have had it, Apollo got there first. I've made my sacrifices. Time for you to make yours. Or are we no longer honorable men?"

Achilles was white in the face. "You dare speak of honor? You, who are a drunkard, a coward, an indolent bastard who hides behind the deeds of others. Honor—"

Agamemnon shrugged. "Honor demands you obey."

He could see it. Crippling Achilles. Consuming him. Honor was a spider's web, and the leader of the Myrmidons—named after obedient soldier ants—was now trapped inside it. There was nothing he could do but capitulate. He knew it; Agamemnon knew it; everyone knew it.

Capitulate. How does it feel, you bastard? How does it feel to lose?

Peerless Achilles defeated by his own notions. The cost of losing

Chryseis was too high for Agamemnon to enjoy it, but he savored the other man's impotent rage as he would the finest wine.

"I will do as honor demands, Agamemnon." Achilles was trembling with suppressed rage.

He opened his mouth to speak again, but Patrocles—ever calm—rose and gripped the Phthian's arm. "As Achilles says, so it will be. Honor will be satisfied."

Achilles shook him off, unready to be silenced. "Know this," he spat. "All of you. Mark my words and mark them well. I have no issue with the Trojans—they never came to my lands, never burned my fields, and never hurt my people. I have no more quarrel with them. I am done with this war. I will watch from my black ships as they burn yours, Agamemnon. And I will laugh in your face when you come to me on bended knee and beg me to save your army." He stormed out of the hall, leaving a shocked silence in his wake.

Agamemnon allowed him his moment. Allowed Achilles' words to resonate with the men. Allowed them time to realize who was in control—and who was not.

Patrocles, red in the face, cleared his throat. "I will speak to him," he said. "You've wounded him, Agamemnon, and you know how he can be."

"I've put up with *how he can be* long enough, Patrocles. How you bear him, only the gods know." He paused. "Go on. See to him." Patrocles nodded and rushed from the council.

"The rest of you," Agamemnon raked them with his gaze. "This is the man who had designs on my place. Say what you will of me, but ask yourself this: Is that the kind of man you want as your leader? Is that the kind of man who you'd trust with your lives? The lives of your men? You heard it from his own lips. He wants us to lose. Because of a woman?

"I'm aware of the irony, kings and princes. The spear cast at me is now cast at him, and he acts like a petulant child. Yes. I reacted with fury when I faced the decision he now faces. That I will admit. But I did not abandon you as he has. I did not threaten you with defeat—yet Achilles would see all our endeavors here fail. Or at least that's how he would have it.

"We can't win without him? What does that say of mighty Ajax? Of Diomedes? Of Odysseus? Of all of you? What? That you are *lesser* than Achilles? That you are unmanned without him? If you think that, then let us depart. Let us return home like whipped dogs and try to ignore the Furies that will haunt our dreams for what we have given up here.

"I say that we take the fight to Troy. I say that we defeat them on the field of battle. I say that we take what is theirs and sear our names into great tales with blood, fire, and glory. And I say that all will remember us. And none shall speak of Achilles but to say that he was the only one of us who ran."

They cheered him.

They, who not days before were cursing his name, cheered him. Agamemnon had always known that men were base. That he was so utterly correct both pleased and saddened him at the same time.

CHRYSEIS had been sure: deny Achilles his prize, and Achilles would withdraw from battle—handing Agamemnon his victory and redemption. In that, she had been correct.

However, neither she nor Agamemnon had counted on the intensity of Achilles' wrath. Agamemnon counted himself brave; but he was honest enough to know that even on his best days—which were fewer and farther between—he had no chance against Achilles.

Hard as that was to admit, he consoled himself with the fact that on *most* men's best day, they'd have no chance against Achilles.

But now Agamemnon had to drive it home to all that it was the high king who controlled things. And do to that, he would have ensure that Achilles' humiliation was utter.

He would have to violate this Briseis—even if he knew it was beneath him and she didn't deserve it. But her degradation would be Achilles', her shame would be his, her submission his own.

Agamemnon drank—too much, he knew, but he drank anyway, and by the time they brought her to him, he was drunk.

He regarded her as she stood before him, head held high, her eyes meeting his own. As Chryseis had done when she'd chosen him. But there was no hunger in this one's eyes. Only contempt. Briseis was tall and handsome enough in the face, chestnut haired, long-legged. But her build was lithe and muscular, altogether too boyish. Nothing like Chryseis, who was soft and curvaceous, as a woman should be. "So," he said. "You're the one."

She didn't respond. She just held him with her murderous gaze, and Agamemnon could see in her eyes the thousand ways in which she wanted to kill him. Where, he wondered, was the fire that he needed? He *had* to do it.

"Take your clothes off," he said.

She snorted in derision and undid her *chiton.* It fell to the floor with a sibilant whisper of cloth. It was like looking at a dickless boy, Agamemnon thought. He drank some more wine, willing his cock to even twitch at the sight of her. But it did not.

It wasn't just that she was unattractive and sexless. It wasn't even that she hated him. Agamemnon had fucked plenty of slaves that hated it—and him—and he cared not a jot. It was that he knew in that moment that fucking her wouldn't be a victory for him. That fucking her wouldn't break her. It would lessen *him.* Lessen him because that's what everyone would expect him to do. *And* they'd expect him to brag about it.

It was all of that.

But most of all it was that she wasn't Chryseis. She was in fact the object of Chryseis' revenge, and every time he tupped her, he'd be forced to think of what he had lost.

But for all that, he still had to humiliate her—and in doing so, humiliate Achilles. What was it he had said once to Chryseis? *"You've never much acted like a slave."* No. She had not. And nor did this one. Chryseis had told him she was a princess. Unused to work. Unused to hardship. Achilles treated her as though she were "an Olympian gift," Chryseis had said. Well, Agamemnon hated the gods. Hated Achilles. And hated this Briseis because it was plain that she did not fear him.

He wouldn't touch her. But he *would* break her. He'd break the arrogance. Break the pride. Break the woman. And in doing so, break Achilles. "You're nothing," he said. "From now on, you will clean chamber pots. You will carry my shit. It's out back. Put your clothes on, see to it, and get out of my sight."

"What?" she said, her eyes widening in shock. In realization. In horror.

"I said you will clean my shit. And then men will know that what Achilles values and holds dear . . . his pride . . . his honor . . . *his* Briseis . . . is all shit to me. You will be the lowest slave in this camp. You will be . . . nothing. Go on," he waved a hand, "get on with it." Her shoulders sagged, and Agamemnon was pleased. She dressed and moved to the back of the hut, going to the anteroom where he made his toilet.

Briseis was prepared for rape. He knew it now. She had armored herself against it, and he had out-maneuvered both her and Achilles. His "Olympian gift" would carry Agamemnon's shit for the remainder of the war.

As she emerged with the chamber pot in her hands, he burst out laughing. It crept up on him, and he found he couldn't stop, even as she left to dump his waste. Agamemnon clutched his sides in hysterics, knowing that the sound of his laughter would echo in her ears as she carried his shit away.

THE pennants hung limp, bereft of wind to stir them; the smoke from the hecatombs a funeral pall hung thick over this obscenity, filling the throats and watering the eyes of the eager scum who watched.

They brought Iphigenia to him, and she lay on the altar. He could feel the hilt of the dagger in his sweat-slick palm, the dampness of the tears on his face, the pounding of his heart in his chest.

He raised the knife and brought it down . . .

Iphigenia was gone; in her place a deer. The beast did not make a sound as the blade ended its life, its blood spraying him, neither warm nor cold. Agamemnon staggered away from the altar, looking around in confusion. About him, the air swam, the gathered throngs becoming as smoke, fading away. He dropped the knife, and it clattered on the stones, a tinny sound, too loud in the silence. He looked at his hands, bloodless now and clean.

He was alone. Everything had vanished save for the mist. He could feel the ground beneath his feet, solid and firm, but the mist swam about him.

He felt no fear and was acutely aware that he should be terrified. Perhaps, he thought, he had been struck down as he had committed his foul deed, and this was Hades' realm. If that was so, then he counted himself blessed and started walking.

As he did so, the mist swirled about him, and he saw shapes in it, the figures of men and women, sometimes making out their faces. Here was his own father, there that idiot Heracles with his club, solid for a moment, but as he focused on them, they became insubstantial and faded into nothingness.

After a while—he could not say how long—the ground beneath his feet shifted and became less solid, each footstep crunching on sand

and shale. The mist began to recede, and he saw that he was on the bank of a river, its water black and as unmoving as glass.

The Styx, he reasoned. So he, Agamemnon, high king, was dead.

"No," he heard Iphigenia's voice. "You are dreaming, Father."

Agamemnon turned and saw her standing before him, perfect and unsullied, her chiton *white as purest snow. He heard himself cry out, a strangled gasp of disbelief, and he ran to her, pulling her to him, holding her tight, tears running unchecked down his face. "My child," he sobbed. "Oh, my Iphigenia!"*

It was a dream; her words cut through him, but this was a dream unlike any other. Always there were Furies, the guilt, the self-loathing, the darkness. But this was different; he could feel her in his arms, and Agamemnon thought his heart would break for joy. He knew it could not last, but he was determined to hold on to it for as long as he could.

He looked at her and kissed her face, her hair, her cheeks, and pulled her close once again. "Let me die," he said. "Let me die so that I can be with you. I miss you so much," he sobbed. "I am sorry. So, so sorry."

"I know," she said and pulled away from him. "I forgive you."

"I cannot forgive myself."

"I know that, too." She smiled at him as would a parent to a child who had learned a harsh lesson. "Walk with me. Time is short."

Agamemnon did as she asked, his hand reaching out to hers as it had done so many times when she was small. It was such a natural thing—their hands fitted together perfectly then. As they did now. "I've made mistakes," he said after a while.

"You have," she agreed.

"My ambition blinded me."

"Perhaps. But then, you are not the only man of ambition, Father. Men are weak, petty, and vain. They lust. They plot. They scheme. And they do vile, vile deeds and cloak them with the veneer of honor or acquiescence to the gods." She looked at him. "As you know."

"I would undo it. A thousand times, I would undo it. I would burn in Tartarus to bring you back."

Iphigenia smiled. "It's over there." She pointed to the west. "So I'm told. I don't think that you will end there, Father. But you will pay for what you have done, of that I have no doubt."

"I will pay my debts." Agamemnon shrugged. "Nothing is worth anything, Iphigenia. You are lost to me. The woman I love is taken from me. The man who should be my staunchest ally in winning this war hates me—as I hate him. My fellow kings and princes maneuver for profit and gain. Across the field of Troy, Priam squats over a treasure beyond imagining. And that is what all this is about." He laughed, a harsh sound in the stillness. "Treasure. Legend. It's all dust in the wind, isn't it?"

"I don't know about that." She smiled. "Time will tell."

"Why am I here?"

"Because you need to forgive yourself. You are guilty of many things, Father. Accept your guilt. There is nothing . . . nothing . . . you can do to change what you have done. But you can change what you will do. You are high king. You know the realities of that role. You know that honor is hollow. But you know also that you of all men must maintain a veneer of it. That you must wear ten thousand different masks for the ten thousand different faces that bend their knee to you.

"Be cruel if you will. Be strong. But above all, be king."

Agamemnon pulled her close and held her . . .

And hit the floor with a thump.

He had fallen asleep and fallen off his chair. His brazen wine cup lay next to him. He pushed it away as he sat up, and it rolled across the planks, its sound as tinny as a dropped dagger on stone.

His robe was wet, and he stank. He realized in horror that in his drunkenness he had pissed himself. Pissed himself and puked all over himself—wine-dark, stinking vomit coated him, spattered all over the floor, wet, rancid, and bubbled with urine.

Agamemnon sat in his own filth and cried. Cried because he had fallen so low, cried because his actions sickened him, cried because his beloved child was nothing more than a dream.

A vision.

It was more than a dream, he realized. She had come as a vision, and her words were true. Her compassion for him—she, whom he had killed—was boundless. She had forgiven him and asked him to forgive himself. That he could not do. Could never do.

But he still had vengeance. He still had hate. And he had a war to win.

Agamemnon staggered to his feet and tore off his robe, wiping the puke off himself with it before hurling it to the floor. He tipped water over himself, cleansing his body if not his soul.

Men often spoke of their legend; they had grand dreams of how they would be remembered, how they would be venerated, how their stories would be told through the ages.

They would tell Agamemnon's story, all right. He would be remembered for his cruelty because, as clarity burned through him like Apollo's sun, he knew without doubt that Troy would fall at his hand. And he would take out all his anger, his grief, and his suffering on that cursed city.

IN the first ranks were his spearmen. The best of the best, elite because they had survived. They had stripped bodies of armor and equipment, and some had kit that would be the envy of a minor prince. Behind them, the less experienced and new. They had little armor and paltry, round buckler shields. In time, if they survived, they would be warriors, too. Next the archers and slingers—looked upon with contempt by spearmen, they always seemed to enjoy their lowly status and bragged that their kill tally would always be more than that of a base infantryman.

The truth of it was that they were all part of the whole: spearmen would struggle without the support of the skirmishers, and all the skirmishers could do when facing the phalanx was run away when their ammunition was spent.

It had been a week since he had had the vision of Iphigenia. A week to cleanse himself. A week to fight the Furies and not seek solace in the wine *krater*.

And now . . . now . . . Agamemnon had not felt this way in *years*. He felt strong. He felt free. He lusted for battle, for vengeance. And he felt young. His armor, new and burnished, fit him well. His shield was light and strong, two circles atop each other, bull's hide and bronze on a wicker frame, shaped so a spear could be thrust easily from behind it.

From the chariot, he surveyed the host.

His host, he reminded himself. Girded for war, they marched across the plain toward the Trojans, advancing through trampled mud and stands of barley. Agamemnon fancied that Priam's men were afraid. Afraid at his sudden change of tactics, afraid that Agamemnon was now so confident in the support of the gods that he would fight without the vaunted Achilles. Afraid, above all, that they were going to lose. Because they knew that annihilation would follow their defeat. Their lines were as long as his, he noted. But they were thinner. Honor compelled them to meet the Achaeans on the plain.

Honor seemed to have a way of undoing men.

The charioteer steered the horses with his usual skill and efficiency, and despite himself, Agamemnon laughed aloud. "It is a good day to fight!" he shouted. Some of the men heard him and cheered.

To his left was Talthybius—a bow and arrows secreted in the chariot—and to his right, Menelaus.

"It is good to have you back, Brother!" he called across.

Agamemnon took it in the spirit it was meant, though Menelaus' assessment was not entirely accurate. He was not "back." He was different now, a man not only clad in bronze but bronze from within. He imagined his heart hardening, turning to metal so that it would not feel the loss of Chryseis. That it would not hold him in check with pity or mercy for his foes. That it would not be pierced by arrow, spearhead, or sword.

Agamemnon turned to look back over his shoulder at the Myrmidon section of the encampment. He could feel Achilles' eyes on him, hoping and praying that he would fail.

He would not fail.

How it must be destroying Achilles, Agamemnon thought. The man who defined himself by his skill at arms, sitting out the greatest clash in a generation. His men, undeniably the best fighters amongst the Achaeans, forced to watch as their so-called inferiors fought their way to victory. What was it Diomedes had said—a sword had to be tested?

Not Myrmidon swords. Not today. Not in this war. And Achilles would—in time—go to his grave with the question whispering in his mind: *What if?* The ultimate test had come . . . and Achilles would not be tested.

"My king!" A bark from Talthybius.

Agamemnon turned his eyes to the front and saw a lone chariot driving toward them. The Trojan herald, he guessed. Agamemnon raised his arm for the army to halt, which took some time. Men couldn't just stop on command; only the Myrmidons seemed to have mastered that. But it was tidy enough for Agamemnon's liking. He nodded at Talthybius, who drove forward to converse with the Trojan.

"Maybe they're going to offer us a treaty," Menelaus called.

"There will be no treaty, Brother," Agamemnon shouted back. "Only the return of Helen or the utter destruction of Troy will suffice. My fury at these people is great. My *men* have suffered too much to allow them to blind us with trinkets and tokens. What is theirs will be ours!" Those that heard him cheered and were soon spreading the word to those that didn't, and soon a chorus of approval rippled down the lines as men from Ithaca to Sparta to Aulis acclaimed him.

Agamemnon cared nothing for their paltry approval. All that mattered was winning. All that mattered was blood. All that mattered was Troy.

The conversation between the heralds was brief, and soon Talthybius was heading back; he drove with skill, wheeling his chariot so he stopped close by Agamemnon. The expression on his face did not bode well.

"What did he say?" Agamemnon asked.

"That Prince Paris challenges King Menelaus to fight." Talthybius was grim. "That if he wins, we must depart and pay tribute. And if he loses, that Helen will be returned. And they will pay tribute."

Agamemnon ground his teeth. He had made provisions for a duel, how to manage the outcome, but now his impatience for a battle was surging too high. He wanted a clash of spears and shields that crossed the entire field, not one spear on one shield. Besides, why had Priam capitulated now of all times? It didn't feel right.

It occurred to him that Priam may not have acceded to this. That it could be some scheme of Hector's. That one was as honorable as Achilles; perhaps he had pushed this on his brother because he saw—as Agamemnon had seen—that a duel was the cleanest way to end things and leave Troy intact. Except of course, Agamemnon couldn't allow that to happen.

Talthybius met his eyes. "All is in order," he murmured, his gaze flicking to the Trojan ranks. So. Talthybius' assassin was in place should Paris somehow carry the day.

"Tell them I agree," Agamemnon said.

BUT one could never tell. The rumors were that Paris was a coward, a fop, a lover of the finer things, and certainly he'd looked that way at nineteen when Agamemnon first clapped eyes on the Trojan prince. But they had been here for so long, and Paris was still alive and had fought in at least some of the engagements. Perhaps he'd been honing his skills for this moment? It was at least a possibility.

He saw the ranks of the Trojans begin to part: Paris making his way forward. His eyes flicked to his brother. Menelaus was pacing back and forth like a lion in a cage, flexing and relaxing his shoulders, his fist gripping and then releasing on the haft of his spear, his breathing deep and calm. He carried the old-fashioned tower shield, a huge board of ox-hide over a wooden cross. It afforded greater protection than the newer double-hooped ones, and Menelaus was hefty enough to wield one for a long time.

The Trojans began to cheer, making Agamemnon look back to them. Paris emerged from the ranks. He was clad in expensive armor—bronze scales over leather, on his shoulders a spotted leopard skin. His helmet was bronze, decorated with jewels and sporting exotic feathers; the sort of thing that Talthybius would covet. His shield was impressive, though—a tower that looked to be strong and well made, its bull's hide recently redone so that it shone.

But for all that, he didn't look dangerous; especially not when compared to Menelaus, who was now being acclaimed loudly by the Achaean host. At once, a contest between them and their Trojan counterparts began, each side seeking to outdo the other both in cacophony and quality of insult. Not that they could understand each other, Agamemnon thought, but with all the gesticulating, arse-flashing, and genital grabbing that was going on, the meanings were certainly clear.

Menelaus strode toward Paris, eager to begin the thing, but Paris backed off, slowly at first and then with greater haste, retreating to the safety of his own lines.

The cheering died down. Men looked to each other, confused. Menelaus thrust his spear into the ground and opened his arms wide, as confounded as the rest.

Agamemnon stood taller than most, and the chariot gave him a vantage point. He kept his eyes on Paris as he wove his way back through his ranks; he stopped by a huge warrior—Hector, Agamemnon identified at once. Hector, the prince of Troy . . . Agamemnon wondered idly if Hector might be assassinated somehow behind those high walls. That'd break the spine of the Trojans in a night. It was worth a try. Such deeds won wars.

Hector was gesticulating, clearly in anger. At one point, he reached out and shook the younger man, then slapped the palm of his hand on Paris' gaudy war-helm. He pointed toward the Achaean lines, and Agamemnon noted Paris' shoulders slump as the Trojan prince trudged back through his lines. His men cheered him as he came, but it was muted and soon drowned out by the chorus of abuse from the Achaeans.

Paris, it seemed, was a coward, after all. Menelaus, on the other hand, while he may have been weak and indecisive when it came to being a king, at least could be counted on to fight. He was a boor, but he was strong and too unimaginative not to be brave.

A hush fell as the two warriors circled each other, Menelaus shouting insults, threats, and imploring Zeus to grant him revenge on "the man that had stolen his wife." Which, Agamemnon ruminated, sounded better than "the man who fucked my wife so well she left me."

Paris, for all his timidity, had not folded in the face of this verbal assault. In fact, Agamemnon saw that it had perhaps stung him. Hurt his ego—which, if his armor was anything to go by, was prodigious. With a snarl, he drew back his arm and hurled his spear.

Menelaus' shield swung out and swatted the spear aside with contempt. He took a few quick steps forward and cast his own weapon, which flew as though Ares himself had given him aid.

The men of both sides were cheering now, on their feet, jumping up and down, screaming advice, making bets, and generally enjoying themselves. Agamemnon could hardly begrudge them because they were usually the ones at most risk. A battle of champions (if Paris could be called such) was spectator sport.

Paris' shield came up, but at no angle—an amateur's mistake. Menelaus' broad-headed eight-footer passed through it as easily as Paris had between Helen's legs. Agamemnon heard Paris squeal—actually *squeal*—in pain as the spearhead ripped into his shoulder. The sound of it fired Menelaus; he dragged his sword from its scabbard and began raining blows on Paris' shield. Paris turned and ran away, pursued by the man he'd cuckolded.

"By the gods, Brother!" Agamemnon roared. "Finish it. It is an embarrassment." This said, he glanced at Talthybius, who sensed it and met his eye. The herald looked to the Trojan ranks for a few moments. He nodded, satisfied, and jerked his chin, clearly indicating that his assassin was in place. Agamemnon tried to follow the vague direction, but there were too many men moving and jumping about, and his eyesight wasn't what it once had been.

He turned his attention back to the fight—Menelaus was bearing down on Paris, who, it seemed, was at last struggling to free his own blade.

He loosed it just as Menelaus reached him and swung it with a strength clearly borne of desperation. And it could have been a killing blow because Menelaus, in his eagerness to spill the Trojan's blood, had lowered his shield.

But he was fast. His own sword came up and parried the blow, the impact so great that it sent Paris' weapon spinning from his grasp. Agamemnon glanced once again at Talthybius.

"It's not over yet, my king," he said.

Paris was backing away, wracked with pain from his wound, visibly sobbing. The Trojans roared him on. Even if he was a weakling, he was a prince of Troy, and he bore their honor. Honor that was cowering behind its tower shield, desperate to survive a fight it couldn't run from.

Agamemnon was growing to love honor. It made fools of men more than a woman could.

Menelaus stalked his hated enemy, sword poised, waiting for a clean opening to present itself. But the tower shield was huge, designed to protect a man from nose to shin, and if he wasn't engaging, all that remained was for the attacker to wear him down. And that could take a while, Agamemnon thought.

Menelaus clearly realized this, too. Roaring with fury, he closed in and grasped the top of Paris' shield with his left hand, pulled it aside, and brought the blade of his sword down on the younger man's helmeted head with tremendous force.

The clash was brazen, piercing the shouts of the men with a keen note. Paris fell to his knees, leaving a dumbstruck Menelaus standing over him—and staring at the broken nub of his sword. A fitting metaphor, Agamemnon reckoned.

It was hardly a contest. It was a farce, and Agamemnon was desperate for his brother to kill Paris so the real battle could begin. The subsequent loss of Menelaus would be unfortunate, but then, without Menelaus, the Trojans would have no one to give

Helen back to, and Agamemnon could wage the war in honor of his dead brother.

Menelaus was now dragging Paris back toward the Achaean lines, too furious to bask in the adulation of the soldiery. He had grasped the Trojan prince's war-helm and was pulling him along on his arse as Paris gagged on his chin strap.

Which, of course, broke.

Some of the men were openly laughing now; Agamemnon would have joined them if the implications of Paris actually surviving this weren't so serious. The Trojan prince was up and running toward his own lines. Menelaus cast his shield aside and lumbered after him, inducing more hilarity from the Achaeans and heaping intolerable shame on the Trojans. All of a sudden, Menelaus slowed his run and began to stagger like a drunkard. A black arrow protruded from his side, and blood coursed down his leg.

Agamemnon sighed in relief and lifted his voice. "The Trojans have betrayed us!" he screamed. "They broke their oath! Kill them before the gods! Kill them all!" He raised his spear.

"What about Menelaus?" Talthybius shouted.

"Get him a fucking surgeon!" Agamemnon snarled. "Forward!"

The charioteer flicked the reins, and the horses responded. Agamemnon heard his men roaring in fury now. The Trojans were dressing their lines, but the ease of Paris' defeat had surely sucked the morale from them.

Agamemnon's face split in a fierce grin, the daemon of combat rising within him. Now he would give vent to his hate. His frustration. His loss.

The Trojans would pay.

The sound of the lines colliding was like slamming the doors to Tartarus, a mighty crash intermingled with the pitched screams of men. After the initial clash, there was no end to the cacophony, no raising or lowering in its intensity—just a constant deluge of noise that drove a man mad with battle lust or fear.

Agamemnon's spear was red to the haft in sixty heartbeats, men falling around the dual chariot as though he were reaping grain. He screamed in fury, each blow a punishment for what had been taken from him. Hatred seared through him, giving his arm a strength he had not known since his youth.

"Iphigenia!" he cried. "Iphigenia!" From now on, her name would be his battle cry. For if he fell, the last name on his lips would be that of his beloved child. Who had, perhaps, forgiven him. "Iphigenia!" As far as he was concerned, this entire war could be sung to future warriors as the *Song of Iphigenia.* A song of dishonor rather than heroism, of dishonor and murdered innocence. A song of wasted years.

A chariot sped toward them, its driver wild-eyed, screaming as his champion readied himself.

"Hold fast, my king!" Agamemnon's charioteer shouted. He pulled hard on the reins and the dual chariot—much heavier than the box—slid along and smashed into the Trojan vehicle.

The impact overbalanced the Trojan champion, and Agamemnon reached out and tore him from the chariot car, sending him facedown into the dust. The high king rammed his broad-bladed spear into the man's back, through his armor, feeling the blade grate on his spine. The warrior may have screamed, but it was drowned out in the tumult of battle. But he was dead; the ripe smell of his bowels opening as he went to Hades told Agamemnon that. He twisted the spear and pulled it free, turning to see the two charioteers wrestling like flute girls playing at Amazons. He stuck the Trojan fellow in the side and laughed as he fell.

He took a moment to survey the field. He spied Diomedes and his lion-skin cloak in the thick of it, a whirlwind of death, men, and champions falling to his spear as though he were Ares himself. It seemed to Agamemnon that Achilles wasn't needed, after all. Diomedes plowed on, killing and killing and killing.

"Go!" Agamemnon yelled to his charioteer, blood pounding within him, his desire hot for more death.

And more death he sowed. There was no weariness in him, no sapping weakness, no thirst to slake. Only the desire to kill. His chariot was slick with the blood of the enemy, his spear coated in it, his armor burnished in it.

It was slaughter without end, and Agamemnon drank it as he had once drank wine. And he was drunk.

When the horses were blown, he leaped from the chariot car and fought on foot, screaming Iphigenia's name as he made murder amongst the enemy. He rammed his spear into the belly of a man who wailed like a boy as Agamemnon dragged his guts out with the bronze barb of the warhead, turned, took a blow on his shield, and then smashed it into his assailant's face. Agamemnon kicked him in the balls and thrust the spear into his back when he went down, sending a geyser of black blood skyward.

"Agamemnon!"

A challenge.

With a roar, he turned to see Odysseus and Ajax the Ox before him. "What the fuck are you doing!" he screamed, his throat ragged from his war cry. "Get back in the fight, you gutless cowards! We're going to break them! The day is ours!"

"It's not, you fool!" Odysseus grasped him by the shoulders. "The Cretans are breaking, the Athenians, too. It's you and Diomedes who've done the damage for us, *but our men are weak from the plague*!" The way the ugly little Ithacan said it—so pronounced—cut through Agamemnon's battle rage, dousing the fire with ice.

"What?" He blinked. "No . . . we're winning. Diomedes . . ."

"Diomedes almost killed Aeneas of Dardania," Ajax the Ox noted. "Knocked those sea-colored feathers right off his helmet." Which was off the subject and garnered him an annoyed look from Odysseus.

"Look around you," the Ithacan said as Agamemnon's charioteer drove back toward him—clearly on Odysseus' orders. "Look!"

It was true. Around him, he could see that the Trojans—far from being broken—were making a fight of it. And in that moment, Agamemnon realized that his fears could come to pass. That he could lose it all here and now because if his men broke, it would be all over. He would not be avenged, and Achilles could laugh and spit on his corpse and go on to say that he was the greater man. That his precious honor had proven him right.

That, Agamemnon could not countenance.

And then, as it had before, honor came to his rescue.

"Hear me!" a voice boomed out in accented Achaean. "Hear me!"

A huge figure strode from the lines—almost as huge as Ajax. Prince Hector. The fighting began to slow, and the men pulled away from each other, their battle lust spent.

Agamemnon looked around. It was utter carnage. Bodies, many stripped of armor, littered the field. The ground was black with blood, and the flies were thickening already. The stench . . . shit, puke and copper . . . hung in the air like an obscene hecatomb.

"Many are dead," Hector intoned. "Yet no victory is won . . . for either side. The day started with a duel . . ."

Hector looked around, realization dawning in his eyes. Agamemnon saw that the Trojan prince had lost his nerve and thrown his dice too soon. If he had waited, the Achaeans could well be in flight. But he hadn't. And victory, that fleet-footed whore, had vanished.

"The day started with a duel . . . and should finish with one!" Agamemnon shouted in order to make sure he left Hector with no way out. "After your brother's shameful display, it surprises me you make this offer, Prince Hector. But *we* will accept it because I am a man of . . . honor."

"*You* will face me, Agamemnon?"

"I am a man of honor," Agamemnon said again. He felt a stab of fear pierce his heart of bronze. He was no match for Hector, but he could not admit it, nor could he run. "As the kings and princes of my council are men of honor. I propose we draw lots, and whosoever draws Hector's name will have the honor of killing him before his city."

That at least lowered the odds.

Hector accepted, as Agamemnon knew he must. The high king was glad of the respite. The more he looked around, the more he saw how exhausted the Achaeans were. The Trojans, too, were in a state: a hard day.

Later, the result of the lots was called by Talthybius, and Agamemnon allowed himself a laugh at Odysseus' snide "nicely done" as Ajax's name was called out as "victor." The Ithacan was too wily not to have guessed that the lots were rigged, given that Talthybius was the man assigned the job of drawing them.

Agamemnon's legs were sore from the day's fight, and he no longer felt young. "You're an intelligent man, Odysseus," he said quietly. "You should understand how the game is played."

"Oh, I do," the little Ithacan said. "I do. It's one of the reasons you're still high king. I know you, Agamemnon."

He didn't extrapolate. He didn't have to. Agamemnon knew that Odysseus despised him, but the man knew—as Agamemnon himself knew—that the high king could not play fair. The high king had to balance egos. Had to balance risk and opportunity. Had to balance the details of men lost and men replaced. Had to balance prizes.

Because that was what it all came down to in the end.

Even now Hector and Ajax were chatting like old friends, each promising to honor the other's corpse and stating what prizes they would take from each other.

"King Menelaus survived," Odysseus said conversationally. The look in his eyes told him that he at least suspected Agamemnon had orchestrated the "treachery."

"I'll sacrifice to the gods in thanks," he muttered, the flick of his glance telling Odysseus that he didn't care what the little man thought. Or the gods, for that matter.

"Who do you think'll win?" Odysseus asked as he lowered himself to the ground.

"I don't know," he said. "Look at the size of them. It'll probably go on all night."

"Fancy a cup of wine?"

For a moment only, Agamemnon was tempted. But only for a moment. He shook his head. Besides, the offer had been made from sufferance on politeness. Even if Odysseus was one of the few who realized what kind of man it took to be high king, it didn't mean that he looked on such a man with any kind of empathy. Odysseus still despised him as much as the others, perhaps even more so—precisely *because* of his insight. But he would be an ally from now on. He had intelligence. Agamemnon would use that.

He gave the Ithacan a nod and walked away as the combat began. He thought of Chryseis and what might have been. He thought of their unborn child and what might have been. He thought of Iphigenia and what might have been.

What *should* have been.

And then he thought of Achilles, who he hated and who hated him. Achilles, who would die. Because men like Achilles . . . Hector . . . Ajax . . . they always died. Because they had honor.

Men like Agamemnon survived.

He had come full circle. Once, it had been ambition that drove him, the desire to be remembered as the high king who brought Troy low. Ambition, hope, love, and yes, honor, had been drained out of him, soaked into the Trojan ground. It was a bleed that had begun when he agreed to the sacrifice at Aulis and had finally run dry the moment that Chryseis was taken from him.

He had become a shell of a man. A man without honor. A man without care. And he was prepared to do what it took . . . *anything* it took . . . to achieve his aims. He recalled the promises that he made to Chryseis. That he would find her, would upend the world looking for her when this war was done.

Promises he would not keep.

Because his love for Chryseis had made him weak. And a high king could not afford to be weak. A high king could not afford to love. Ultimately, to be high king was to be alone.

It was a liberating realization.

THE FOURTH SONG

THE GAMBIT

by David Blixt

Everything terrible that happens to us,
To the World,
All our Tragic,
Happens,
Because we Loved something
We had No Business Loving.
—Sean Graney, *All Our Tragic*

HECTOR

"APOLLO be my speed!"

Leaping from my racing chariot, I cast my spear at the height of my arc. Suspended between sky and earth, I felt all potential futures in the instant. Victory, triumph, exultation. Failure, defeat, destruction. Unity, separation. Joy, sorrow. Life, death. Everything was possible.

Hurtling through the late morning air, the ash-hardened pole topped the Achaean camp wall, its bronze head piercing a Spartan throat.

The dead man clutched feebly at it, then clawed the air as he toppled back behind the pirate's ramparts. Only as he fell did I recognize him. His name was lost to me, but years ago, at Odysseus' wedding, we had sung wine-soaked ballads together. Now I had stopped his voice forever, and with it, his song.

Hellenus would have lamented. Paris would have crowed. Aeneas would have prayed. But it was not for Priam's heir to indulge in sentiment. To me, the man's passing meant one less Achaean to fight.

Yet, for the briefest of moments, I felt—actually felt—the spear's tip at my neck. I gasped, as if the wickedly sharp bronze point had thrust through my tender flesh. Imagination, surely. The result of a restless night poised on a sword's edge. A dark chord in a bright song, a shadow on a sunlit day.

Landing on the earth, knees bent and shoulders squared, I fixed my shield. No time now for shadows of the mind. Under the unrelenting sun, my armor stinging where it touched my skin, I drew my sword and held it high. "Form up!"

Eager Trojans flocked to my back. Out of my vision's sharp edge, I noted approvingly that my half-brother Cebriones was steering my chariot behind our line to await my call. The horses needed a rest. We had already met Agamemnon's pirates in the open, pressing them until their backs were to their walls. What came next was not for chariots. As Agamemnon had discovered to his frustration, the best chariots in the world meant nothing against walls.

The pirate king had blundered. Yesterday he'd risked a direct assault on Troy, then compounded his blunder by remaining too long in the shadow of our walls. Pride had compelled him to throw living men after the dead. But the walls of Troy had laughed Achaean chariots to scorn. Trojan spears and stones from on high had claimed hundreds of enemy lives. When our forces streamed forth from the Scaean Gate, Agamemnon was forced to abandon his wounded and dead. The plunderers found themselves plundered, and dozens of my Trojans were now adorned with Achaean armor and weapons.

By nightfall we had driven them west across the Scamander, chasing their dust all the way over the Plain of Troy and around north to the safety of their camp.

That camp lay upon the western cape of the bay. Not fearing approach by the sea, they had only walled up the southern edge of the cape. Those walls were temporary things, constructed by Nestor to protect their tents and ships along the sea-facing shore.

The old soldier had done well enough, erecting an eighteen-foot wall with a chasmous ditch before it. But the ditch wasn't as wide as it should have been, and the walls were not stone, but rather a patchwork of thatch, plaster, and rocks. Sturdy, but far from impenetrable.

But the fortitude of those walls had not mattered, as the strength of Agamemnon's army had prevented us from making a full assault.

Recent events altered that equation. Eris had sown her discord among the Achaeans. Young Achilles had taken himself from the field, and with him his Myrmidons. Rumor said Agamemnon had nursed his outrage with drink, and Odysseus was considering going home.

With these reports in mind and night falling on us, I decided to risk a gambit of my own. Ordering our soldiers, tens of thousands strong, to pass the night on the throsmos, the high ridge at the very edge of the Plain of Troy, I returned to inform the king of my intentions.

The gambit was simple. I meant to take advantage of the Achaean disorder and turn this day—Apollo's Day, the longest day of the year—into the fulcrum of the war, the lever that would shift the world.

After an hour of argument, Father had approved my plan. I had returned to the throsmos to pass a restless night in jangling anticipation. Win or lose, this day would change everything.

Sensing the danger, the Achaeans had come at us with the dawn, bellowing their war cries as they spilled out their main gate. Their plan had been sound—drive us back across the Plain to the Scamander, there to slaughter us as we bunched up at the ford.

Anticipating their intent, I placed dozens of men in the scrub and thickets of the swampland along the edges of the throsmos. With the blinding rays of ascendant Apollo in their eyes, the Achaeans did not see the threat. The moment they reached us, Agamemnon's forces were beset on three sides, arrows and spears coming down like thunderbolts. Our soldiers were fresh and jubilant, the rising sun warming their backs all through the struggle.

After a morning of hard and costly labor, we forced their retreat.

Now, with Apollo's chariot directly overhead, the Trojan army was ready to end this war, once and for ever. Today, Apollo's Day, was the be all, and the end all.

Dust had hardly settled from my leap when my fellow Trojans

rushed to join me. Familiar faces, they showed their teeth inside the cleft of their helms. Most were spattered in crimson, but the blood was not their own.

Paris was beside himself with joy. "We have the cowards on the run!"

Aeneas vibrated with passion as he prayed, "Mother, give us strength!"

To my right, Hellenus was silent, yet I knew my most dependable brother was ready to fight for a city that did not value him half as much as it should.

Like him, I allowed action to be my voice. Wading into the Achaean rearguard, I let my blade carve out my song. For that is what combat truly is—a song. A tale told to the music of blood, with the victor as bard, shaping the narrative.

The first stanza of this day's song had finished in a triumphant crescendo as we drove our foes back. Now the second stanza began as we approached their walls, facing a combination of their bravest and their slowest. Their leaders injured, these last sea-dogs formed a rearguard while their gasping army sought shelter in their walls.

Directly before me were Gerenians, wearing Nestor's colors and crests. A tall people, lean and hard. Further back were the forces of the Thessalonian king Eurypylus, casting spears over their comrades' heads.

I felt the music as I plunged into the fray. Here, like individual notes in a score, each action told a story, the call and response of desire and denial. The extended arm, reaching out in a stab, sang out, *I want your life*. The bent arm, pushing away in a block, responded, *You cannot have it*.

Ducking a spear thrust, I surged forward, closing distance to render the Gerenian's longer reach useless. In his desperate attempt to claim the honor of killing Hector of Troy, he had over-extended himself. I did not bother with my shield. Rising, I took his useless spear haft on the shoulder of my armor and drove my sword's point through the soft underside of his chin, pinning his mouth shut. Another singer silenced. His eyes widened in terror before he fell slack. I was already moving on, not bothering to claim his armor. My song would not be bettered through besting some young Gerenian who had desired my death too much, and been denied.

Desire and denial. The whole of war—indeed, of life—comes down to those two words. For me, Hector of the Shimmering Helm, the key was not allowing my desires to rule my actions. Too well I know the damning spot next to my name. Hector is too dour, too brooding, too contained. Perhaps it is so. But in the labyrinth of my thoughts, it always seemed better to control my desires than to let them control me. Only sometimes, with Andromache, when I feel secure that my desires will not overwhelm us, have I ever allowed them to billow my sails.

My wife watched me now, I knew. Cursed with excellent eyesight, my beloved stood behind Troy's walls under Apollo's sun which freckled her nose, tracking the progress of my silvered helm amid the churning dust and riot of spears. But at such a distance, she could not hear the music I made. The glorious music, the tremendous, swelling, contradictory chorus of war. *War is glory, war is life. War is terror, war is strife.*

Desire, and denial. That was the story of this gods-damned war.

All around us, the music continued. Some men raised their voices in triumph, others in agony. Swords made a symphony of sounds as they struck metal, or wood, or flesh, or bone. I heard the twang of Paris' bow, and near the gate I saw the Thessalonian king reel back, struck in the shoulder. "Got him!" said my brother, smugly.

As we carved our song on the hearts of the Gerenians and Thessalonians, I heard Ajax's voice booming inside the ramshackle

Achaean walls, urging the straggling pirates to safety from our swords. The remaining Gerenians hopped back out of our reach, then turned to flood through the gate to their camp.

"They're retreating!" I heard Paris gleefully shout, "Give chase!" As ever, his desires overwhelmed his sense. The result of never being denied. Given his head, Paris would run us into disaster. It was his nature.

"Belay that order!" I bellowed, checking my own advance. Hellenus and Aeneas did the same.

My prettiest brother almost carried on past me, forcing me to block his path. Incredulous with fury, Paris protested, "Hector, we have them on the run!"

"Into a trap. Look." The noontime sun showed bristling spears atop their wall, poised to give their brethren cover. "Our father has lost enough sons today."

That brought Paris up short. "Who?"

"Antiphus and Isus." Our full brother, our half-brother. I'd seen them fall at the throsmos.

"Who slew them?" demanded Paris.

"Agamemnon."

"Damn the spears, we must avenge them!" Again Paris surged forward.

I spun him around and barred his path. Desire and denial, personified. "Beyond that wall, brother, Ajax has already lined up ten dozen men to cut us down as we funnel through the gate. We'll stumble over our own dead as we are cut down."

Paris understood danger when it came to his own skin. Yet he struggled purely for show, knowing I would not let him pass. "So we give up?"

Piqued, I released him, then caught his elbow as he staggered. "Not at all. We drop back out of spear range to ready our assault. Go."

He obeyed with the sullenness that, sadly, was the core of his nature. I remained, watching the last of the rearguard hustle through the gate.

Ajax appeared in its mouth to offer me a wry salute. "Next time, Hector!" Then he swung the palisade doors shut, single-handedly lowering a bar across them. The man's strength was obscene.

Turning, I issued quick orders. "Tend to the wounded, send all prisoners to Troy for ransom."

Paris still fumed. "I can't believe we're not pressing our advantage! We had them on the run!"

"We're not finished," I said grimly. "Today, if Apollo wills it, we decide this war. For now, put that bow of yours to good use—if any damned sea-dog raises his head over that wall, put an arrow in his eye."

My brother and two dozen others took up their bows and watched the walls, which kept their own archers crouched below the ramparts. Bows were not much favored in war. Skillful archers were respected, of course, but much the same as a talented dancing girl or gifted musician. They were for show, or for hunting, not for war. Distance fighting was cowardly. There was no glory in that music. War was not for stringed instruments. War was a song composed of bronze trumpets, iron blades, and the drums of horses' hooves.

Still, strings could make you just as dead. Another of my half-brothers had taken a bolt meant for me, clear through his throat. That long-armed bastard Teucer—my own cousin!—had cowered behind Ajax's shield as he fired off shaft after shaft, murdering a dozen great men. I'd achieved a little justice with a well-placed rock that both snapped Teucer's bow and rattled his skull. Served him right for fighting against his mother's people!

Shamefully, Paris was just the same, shooting from a racing chariot. My brother justified the weapon's use by invoking

Apollo's killing of the Python, but I couldn't help being reminded of Eros' annoying little bolts. Never putting himself in harm's way, Paris fought the same way he had absconded with Helen—hit and run. He could never stand up for his actions.

I knew I shouldn't be disappointed. Born with a preternatural skill for the bow, the skill had shaped his character.

And he *was* skilled. Just this morning Paris shot from the back of a racing chariot and struck no less a warrior than Diomedes, pinning the great soldier's foot to the ground. After some choice insults for Paris, Diomedes had torn his foot free and been carried off on Menelaus' chariot.

Cebriones come trotting up on foot. "The horses are being watered for when we need them."

"You read my thoughts, brother. Gather the family, and all the kings. With haste!"

Word spread, and they flocked to me. Hellenus and Aeneas first, then more of my kin joining the client kings and princes. While we waited, I said, "Antiphus, Isus. Who else have we lost?"

"Doryclus was cut down by Ajax," said Hellenus.

We brothers shared glances. Our father was losing both legitimate and natural sons this day.

"No time for lamentation. We'll honor him by winning. Take charge of his men." Hellenus nodded. "Who else?"

"Charops and Socus of Lycia," replied Hellenus. "Cut down by Odysseus."

I scowled. "Sarpedon will be furious."

"At what?" demanded King Sarpedon of Lycia, arriving. Troy's client king was older than most of us, and haughtier. His gleaming lacquered armor was famous, but had been made when he was younger. Though not fat by any means, the king had thickened in middle age, and his multi-hued breastplate no longer fit as it should. Yet he wore it, a badge of pride, clinging to glories gone. Like Nestor, he thought surviving past wars gave him status. Every army had one.

Hellenus repeated the news, adding, "Socus got a blow in as he fell."

Helm off, Sarpedon nodded his salted locks approvingly at the last act of his fallen subject. "Odysseus was badly injured, I hope?"

Hellenus shrugged. "Menelaus carried him off on a chariot, bleeding."

"Please, Mother, let it be a cut that festers," prayed Aeneas.

"Who else?" I asked.

"Agamemnon killed one of the Thracian twins," said Hellenus. "In answer, the other drove a spear clear through Agamemnon's right arm. The pirate king retained strength enough to cut off the other twin's head, but then his arm went limp. That's when he leapt on his fancy chariot and sounded the retreat."

"That's how it started? Good." Agamemnon's injury brought me pure satisfaction. His sea-dogs had seen their leader hound flee with his tail between his legs.

By now all the leaders were gathered. Sheltered behind raised shields, I gave urgent orders. "Agamemnon, Diomedes, and Odysseus are all injured. Achilles is off the field. Of their best leaders, that leaves only Ajax and ancient Nestor. This is our moment. We must strike now. If we give them time to breathe, we lose."

"Strike how?" demanded Sarpedon. One of the greatest fighters on our side, the Lycian king was an uneasy ally. Like Aeneas, he claimed to be descended from the gods, though his bloodline was more grandiose than mere Aphrodite. He said he was descended from Zeus himself. It made him prideful. In battle, he preferred setting his feet and holding ground against all odds. Yet the older man persisted in blaming me for any losses incurred by his refusal to give ground. Just this week the Lycian king had denounced me for acting like Agamemnon, using Troy's allies to fight our battles. That accusation stung like a serpent's tooth.

I answered Sarpedon plainly. "We assault the wall, both east and west. Two parties will make feints to draw Ajax away. Once he's gone, we break the gate."

I expected an argument. Instead, Sarpedon said, "Once inside, what is your plan?"

I told him. His resistance fell away and he offered a mad grin. My brothers, too. Even Hellenus liked my plan.

Sarpedon volunteered to lead one of the feints. "It will be an enormous risk," I warned him.

"If your gambit succeeds, it will be worth it." The Lycian king set out, leading his two thousand spearmen west along the wall. Briefly I wondered how he would span the ditch in front of the wall. But a good leader issues orders and allows his men to figure out how to enact them. I sent the Paeonians to go with him, then ordered the Mysian commander east with an equally large contingent of Arcadians.

My family and our soldiers remained before the Achaean gate. The real danger—and therefore the real glory—would belong to the Trojans.

This was not pride, but simple good sense. Agamemnon was suffering from disaffected allies. I would not emulate his mistake.

It also worked to our tactical advantage. Conditioned to think like their leader, the Achaeans would see the allied assaults as the real threat, while we Trojans appeared a mere holding force, preventing any wily Achaeans from spilling out to harass the attackers' flanks.

I turned to my brothers. "Now, while they're looking the wrong way, get started."

Grinning to a man, they set to work. I had to remain visible, so I strode forward to study the gate. I had an idea how to breach it. It was difficult to focus on the task, however, as my mind was already inside those makeshift walls, ending the war.

I thought again of the rumors that had reached us. It was hardly credible that the Achaean leaders had fallen out over a single enslaved girl. Yet it appeared to be true. The Myrmidons had not been part of either yesterday's attack, or this morning's fighting.

The irony was stark. A war begun over a stolen woman faltering because of a stolen woman. While other Trojans chuckled down their tunics, I alone understood this was our best chance to break the Achaeans' spirits. For young Achilles was a warlike wonder of the world. On the battlefield he was unique. He did not concern himself with desire or denial. To him they were the same. A desperate defense became a killing stroke in the space of a heartbeat. In battle, Achilles was above petty wants and fears. He simply existed. With him at their head, the Myrmidons were virtually unbeatable.

However, if the sword of Achilles stayed in its sheath, the balance of power shifted. Our men gained heart, while the Achaeans lost theirs. Who would have thought that the magnificent warrior Achilles would be the Greeks' greatest vulnerability?

For Ilium's sake, I was perfectly willing to take advantage of their tragic foolishness, and thanked the gods for Agamemnon's pride. With glory aplenty to be had, he squabbled over the lion's share—and, like lions, he ended in carving his own pride to shreds. Agamemnon desired victory over Achilles more than he desired victory over us. That would cost him.

Desire and denial. I wished I could say the philosophy was my own invention, but it had come from a bard my father once employed. A line he sang stayed with me:

All that is tragic
comes from desiring
what we should not.

How painfully correct. This whole conflict was born of unchecked desires. Paris desired general adulation, specifically our father's approval. Father desired war. That pig Agamemnon desired power. Achilles desired glory. Menelaus desired revenge and the return of his property.

And Helen? What did Helen desire? Not Paris, not really. According to Andromache, Helen claimed she longed for freedom. Perhaps that was what she told herself. But I had beheld the savage joy in her eyes when men were bloodied in her name. It was my opinion that Helen desired revenge—revenge on a world that made her a prize. Eris personified, a sower of discord, we were all reaping her planting.

One night not long past, I had explained all this to Andromache. Caressing my aching temples, she had said, "And what do you desire, my love?"

"You," had been my immediate reply. "You, and our boy." Our siege-born son Astyanax, whose entire life had been bounded by war. I had feared greatly, risking my wife's tiny frame in the birthing bed, but she'd borne the pain like an Amazon and laid Troy's heir in my arms. He had my hair, but his mother's freckles. So small then, he was walking now. And if this war did not end, he would soon be fighting in it. A terrible inheritance.

When I was with them both, it felt true that they were all I wanted. But in the shadowed recesses of my heart, I wondered. What did I truly desire? If I prided myself in one thing, it was my ability to balance my passions. I had never suffered an excess of lust, or thirst, or rage. Anger, to be sure—I was far from bloodless. But it had never caused me to lose my head.

It's what made me a good soldier. My desire for glory never outweighed my sense, nor did my desire to live overwhelm my courage. My song was a harmony of high and low notes, without discords.

A good example was my duel with Ajax. He'd sought to overpower me from the first, and I desired nothing so much as to match him, strength for strength, blow for blow. But that was prideful. Worse, it leaned into his assets, not mine. What was I good at? Patience. Endurance. So I decided to outlast him. Without retreating—Paris had done enough running—I avoided Ajax's sweeping hacks. Desire, and denial.

What did Ajax desire? To be strong. He was that, to be sure. And nothing more. Ajax thought power came from the sinews of his arm. In a tavern brawl, perhaps. But in war, muscle, however impressive, was just meat. For all his fearsome power, Ajax had no patience. Probably felt he didn't need any.

A man's fighting style reveals his character. Ajax mistook strength for skill. Had he married true training with his size, he would have been unbeatable. But he relied on his gods-given nature, thinking nothing needed improvement. Chasing me, he had worn himself down. By the time night fell, I was aching from a few fierce blows, but he was panting, desperate for breath. With neither of us in condition to continue, we agreed to clasp arms and share honors.

This caused Odysseus to quip, "The whole war in miniature—power versus fortitude, ending in a stalemate. How the gods must be laughing."

I had never much liked the clever Ithacan king. Perhaps the events of his wedding made me spiteful. Still, Odysseus understood patience. He also understood how a body works. Power comes from hip and shoulder, not bicep. Used together, the whole body was stronger than its individual muscles. Odysseus' trouble was that he thought too much. Waiting to be attacked, he was all about denial, not desire. He was so focused on countering the other man, he had no desire of his own.

Or so I had thought. As Ajax and I traded honors that night, I replied to the Ithacan, "Let us hope the war also ends with enough honor for all."

Odysseus had shaken his head of oiled, dark curls. "Honor be damned. I just want to go home. We all do."

We all do. Like Athena from the hard cranium of the Thunderer, the idea for this day's attack leapt fully armed into my mind.

The question had always been, how do we defeat these sea-dogs? Their objective was simple enough: to take the city and plunder it, killing us all. What was our objective? Survival? Was it enough to outlast them? We had done so for nearly a decade, and still they showed no sign of leaving.

Wars are won in two ways: by achieving your objectives, and by preventing your enemy from achieving theirs. Desire, and denial.

Odysseus' casual remark had revealed what the Achaeans truly desired. I was a fool for not seeing it earlier. Dispirited, still recovering from their recent illness, the pirates were sick at heart of this endless, unwinnable war.

They desired to go home.

To break them, we had to remove their ability to do that. Hence this day's gambit.

How does one hurt a pirate?

By destroying his ship.

MENELAUS

MY charioteer reined in my pair of sweating steeds near the medical tents. Behind me, Odysseus clambered down to the earth, his wounded side obviously causing distress.

It did not prevent him talking. Nothing could keep Odysseus from talking. "Day three-thousand, six-hundred and forty-three, and I'm finally wounded. Bastards couldn't wait one day more."

Stepping down after him, I ignored the Ithacan's verbal rubbish as I sought my brother. Following his bellowing baritone, I made my way through dozens of lightly injured soldiers, as well as those past care, until I spied him. Agamemnon was seated on a barrel far from the tent flap, away from groans and odors. My brother had no love for the injured. I told myself that was the reason he had not visited me after that treachery during the duel with Paris. In truth, I had been grateful for his neglect. The placement of my wound had been more embarrassing than painful, making it appear I had pissed myself with blood. I had not deserved such insult.

Sewn and bound, that wound barely troubled me this day. Whereas Agamemnon's was fresh, and clearly distressed him. Like all men with no patience for others' woes, he was deeply affected by his own. As a surgeon poked at his arm, Agamemnon cursed at him, at the Trojans, and at the gods. "What a time to give up drinking!"

Spying me, he cursed me as well. "There's the bloody cuckold! Where in Hades have you been!"

"Lending me one of his broad shoulders," said Odysseus, arriving in my wake to offer my excuse. Which I resented, as it assumed I required one.

Agamemnon turned his ire towards Odysseus. "What's the matter with you?"

Kneeling, Odysseus allowed his armor to be removed, hissing as his bloody tunic was peeled away from his injury. "Sss-side."

"Mortal, I hope."

The Ithacan grinned. "No such luck. Glanced off my ribs."

"Always were a lucky bastard." Agamemnon lifted his arm to

show his own wound. It evidently hurt, for my brother shouted, "Trojan whores!"

Odysseus cocked his head curiously, then loosed a single laugh, which caused him to wince again.

Agamemnon snarled. "You laugh at my pain?"

"Misheard you," said the Ithacan, speaking in staccato bursts. "Thought you said horse. Funny." He clutched his ribs. "Ow! Athena, relent! How can I survive without laughing?"

Odysseus really did have the most inappropriate sense of humor. I wondered if he had ever suffered at night, as I did, thinking of my failings, my humiliations, the injustices I continued to endure.

As the King of Kings barked at the apprentice surgeon working on his arm, Odysseus looked around for assistance. "Where's the healer?"

Agamemnon hooked his left thumb over his shoulder to the medical tents. "Nestor took him inside, arrow through his clavicle. The wife-thief does love his bow!"

My face turned red. Ten years, and my brother still did this. He couldn't just name Paris. No, he had to remind everyone that the pretty Trojan prince had stolen my wife. That I was the Cuckold King. My successes were greeted with nothing more than a curt grunt, while my failures were made into a mosaic of words, tile by tile creating a picture of the world's greatest buffoon. He would always close by saying, "No wonder Helen abandoned you!"

Part of me understood his intent. He was stirring our soldiers' spirits, reminding them of the cause of this war. The Trojans accused us of being thieves and pirates, yet they had brazenly stolen my most precious possession, a wife of such beauty that she could only be descended from a god.

I remembered the first time ever I saw her, pouring wine for her mortal father. Her white-gold hair spilling past her shoulders as she bent, her creamy bosom tantalizingly revealed by the falling folds of her shift. I had desired her in the instant. I did not even mind she was taller than I. It was a glorious fantasy to imagine scaling that magnificent height—or better, taking her legs from her and bringing her low, beneath me, where she belonged.

Then, thanks to my brother's machinations, fantasy had been made real. How I had loved fucking the daughter of Zeus! It was as though I was sticking it to the entire universe, forcing respect where none had been given me as I claimed my divine gift, proving my right to rule again and again upon her alabaster flesh.

How humiliating, then, to have her stolen. How that humiliation was amplified by her willingness to be taken. To know Paris was now the one sticking it to her. Did she do more than just lie there for him, her expression enigmatic, half bland smile, half grimace? Did she enjoy him, encourage him, cry out for him? Did she ache for his touch as much as she had recoiled from mine?

My humiliation was not simply that engendered by the rejection of a woman. I had been gifted something divine, only to have it snatched away. It was as if Zeus himself was laughing at me. Overnight I had gone from important to impotent.

Worse, all the kings fighting beside us had been suitors to Helen. That they were here now was only because they had sworn to uphold my marriage. In the eyes of each and every one I beheld the disdain, the certainty that if any of *them* had been Helen's husband, she would never have left.

They were wrong, all of them. None here could have pleased her better than I had. She'd have lain under any of them, smiling that same enigmatic lip twist as they rutted in her. I never knew what was going on in that bitch's head when she smiled—no one could. Haughty Helen, who thought her own thoughts, walked her own path, lived her own life.

I desperately wanted her back.

My brother knew it, and it served his purposes to wage this war in the name of my marriage. But he also disdained me for it.

Hence his constant reminders of my cuckoldry. Deep down, I knew he enjoyed twisting the knife. He did not respect me. No one did. Not Helen. Not Paris. Not Achilles. Not Agamemnon. All I desired was respect, and they refused to give it to me.

Lost in my own stewing, I barely noticed Agamemnon's head snapping up, and it took me a moment to focus on what had alerted him. Not the sound of war, but a voice my brother loathed. "What is that damned whoreson Calchas doing now?"

"Putting heart in the men," said Odysseus laconically.

Agamemnon grunted. "Perhaps he's not entirely worthless, then. So long as he doesn't demand I cut off my arm to save the army. You hear me, fellow!" he raged, slapping his surgeon across the head. "Save the arm or be buried with it!"

Drawn by my brother's ranting, Diomedes limped up to us, leaning heavily on a spear. The foot that Paris had pierced clearly pained him. Observing the wounds of Agamemnon and Odysseus, he said, "Damn. That leaves only Ajax."

His meaning was plain. Of the great Achaean kings and heroes, only Ajax remained.

And me, I thought fiercely. *And me!* I was also a son of Atreus, a king in my own right. But did the Argive leader take notice of me? Of course not. No one valued me. To them, I was a pathetic figure to be paraded out to move soldiers to pity and outrage. I had not deserved such insult.

My kindling ire was forestalled by Odysseus, who said, "No. There is one more."

Fool that I was, for a moment I thought he meant me. Then Diomedes said, "Achilles."

"Achilles," agreed Odysseus.

"We don't need him!" declared Agamemnon, a little too hastily.

Diomedes said nothing.

"We don't!" my brother insisted, looking to me to back him up. I shook my head, which could have meant anything.

Studying the inside of his eyelids, Odysseus said, "You're absolutely correct, Agamemnon. We do not need Achilles. But we could certainly use his men."

Diomedes remained expressionless. "They won't follow anyone but him."

Odysseus shrugged, which made him wince. "Then we'd best hope Ajax can hold the gate. Ah, I hear a familiar gait and grumble."

The old blowhard Nestor arrived, blinking at us under the midday sun. My brother greeted him with short-tempered impatience. "If you're whole, old man, return to the battle!"

Outraged yet inured, Nestor flapped a hand. "As soon as my chariot is mended. Wheel's threatening to come off."

"Take one of ours," offered Agamemnon with surprising practicality. "We're not using them, and we cannot rely on that meatheaded mountain to hold the Trojans off forever. We must give the impression we are not failing, as much for our men as theirs."

Diomedes drew himself up a little straighter. "I might be able to ride a chariot. I won't be worth much, but the men would see me."

Agamemnon shook his grizzled head. "If you don't fight, the men will wonder why, and panic. We all know how excitable these sheep can be."

"Hm." Odysseus was staring at his armor in the dust. "I may have an idea."

"Of course you do." My brother grimaced. "What is it?"

"I was picturing Nestor riding in one of our chariots. That was the flint that sparked the idea."

"No one cares where the notion came from! Out with it!"

"We collect the best soldiers from our ranks and put them in the best armor."

"What good will that do?"

"It will have a threefold effect," said the Ithacan king patiently. "First, some of our best men are poorly armed, so they fall sooner than they should. Imagine how brave they would be with proper protection. Second, it will be seen as rewarding their valor, giving them heart."

I found those arguments weak. Evidently Agamemnon agreed, for he was sneering as he said, "And third?"

"Well," said Odysseus, gesturing to his own armor lying in the dirt, "my armor is fairly distinctive. So is yours, Diomedes, and of course Agamemnon's . . ."

We all saw it then. Dress men in our armor and send them into the field, giving heart to our soldiers and breaking the spirits of the Trojans, who thought our leaders bested.

"Deception," said Diomedes with real revulsion.

"And a clever one at that!" hooted Nestor. "Amuse the enemy."

Before my brother could decide, I said, "I have another suggestion."

They all looked at me. They had forgotten I was even present.

"I could go. I could lead the men."

"You?" Looking me over from heel to head, Agamemnon clicked his tongue once. "What can you do? Besides, you're still sporting that injury. You'd just be another target for the bride-thief's arrows. He's already stolen your wife. He'd be all too happy to steal your life." Dismissing me, my brother looked to the commanders he actually valued. "Well? What about Odysseus' idea?"

"I like it," said Nestor. "It reminds me of the time Theseus came to Athens in disguise—"

Diomedes cut across him. "It dishonors us."

"Will losing honor us more?" asked Odysseus.

Agamemnon scowled suddenly. "Damn it all! Here comes Achilles' better half, doubtless sent to find out what's happening! Damn him!"

I turned to see Patrocles approaching with an urgent gait. Encased in unsoiled Myrmidon armor, the handsome man looked fresh and strong.

Odysseus traded a glance with Nestor, who said, "I'll divert him, great king, before returning to the fray."

Agamemnon grunted in something near gratitude. Nestor went off to intercept Patrocles, and I saw them conversing as Nestor led the handsome fellow out of Agamemnon's sight.

My brother was about to offer his verdict on Odysseus' idea, without even asking me my opinion, when the arrival of the Athenian commander forestalled him. "Kings! The wall is breached! Sarpedon has broken through! And—"

"Out with it! And what?"

"The Trojans have firebrands!"

Odysseus hissed, and Agamemnon said softly, "The bastards."

In confusion, I said, "Torches, in daylight? What, do they mean to burn the walls?"

"Idiot! Dolt! Clod-pole!" Agamemnon unloaded his fury on me. "They mean to burn our ships!"

Despite the heat, my blood froze in my veins. Without ships, there were no supplies, no reinforcements. No return home.

"And on Apollo's Day," murmured Odysseus, "giving them extra hours to achieve it. Hector, I didn't know you had it in you."

Agamemnon rounded on him. "Damn your admiration! As soon as that wound is tended, put your idea into action. Shut your mouth, Diomedes, I don't want to hear it! This is no time for scruples! If you will not help us, at least find Teucer and send him and his bow to aid Ajax. We must protect those ships at all costs!"

I waited for Agamemnon to give me an order. When he turned to me, I straightened, ready to prove my worth. Perhaps he would want me to don his own armor.

"Brother, go to my tent, make sure Briseis is still there. I don't want her using the battle to sneak off to the enemy. Or, worse, Achilles."

"Why me?" I demanded.

He laughed nastily. "Think of it as a test! There's no one else who has more experience of women escaping him. I want to be sure that, when we do regain your wife, you'll be able to keep her!"

The other kings all laughed as I accepted my latest humiliation. Sent to make sure his stolen prize did not escape. My brother had not even sent me to protect our own ships. I was that inconsequential.

I did not deserve such insult.

PATROCLES

"APOLLO'S blessings upon you, Eurypylus! Here, allow me!"

Returning from my troubling conversation with Nestor, I spied the Thessalonian king among the wounded. He was struggling one-handed to remove the shield which dangled from a shoulder pierced by an arrow. As I assisted him, he favored me with a gruff nod. "My thanks, Patrocles." An old injury in his face twisted his mouth into a distended grin, which belied the groan he loosed as the shield came free. "That coward Paris!"

Deaf to his weakness, I said, "Tell me, friend, the state of the battle?"

"Doubtful," he admitted. "All the kings have been wounded in some way. That mountain Ajax held the Trojans at bay practically single-handed. But Sarpedon and his men used their spears to vault over the moat on the western end of the wall, near our ships. Sarpedon himself burst through the wall like Heracles, tearing the wattle apart with his sword and pushing until the section collapsed."

"He wasn't repulsed?"

"Oh, he was. But the distraction allowed Hector to break the camp gate."

My eyes grew wide. "How?"

"Heaved a stone the size of my head and broke the bar. It was valiantly done. Perfect throw."

"So Hector is in the camp?"

Eurypylus flashed his remaining teeth. "His men may be, but he is not. Ajax picked up the offending stone and hurled it back. Struck Hector smack in the center of that fancy lapis armor and laid him out." The Thessalonian king's carved grin turned down as his jaw tightened. "But more of Priam's sons flooded into the camp with torches. They're heading west for the shore, and our ships."

Blood drained from my heart. "They're what!?"

Eurypylus snorted. "Not good, is it? You'd think they'd want us to be able to piss off, eh? I stayed as long as I could stand, but my men were falling just to protect me, so I fell back." The Thessalonian king gave me a look so pointed it cut me to the quick. "Tell me, will this stir Achilles to action? Or is your friend determined to spite us all for his pride?"

"That is unfair."

"Unfair! I brought forty ships to this war! Is Achilles going to let them burn over a woman?"

Head low, I shook it doggedly. "The fault lies with Agamemnon."

"Agamemnon is wounded, after fighting like a hero! Little though I love the man, if we are defeated, the blame won't lie with him!" Eurypylus used his good arm to point. "See there!"

Following his extended finger, I beheld plumes of smoke down by the shore. He was correct. Someone had to do something.

Absently, as if it were a chance remark, I said, "Nestor told me the other kings are considering dressing others in their armor, to make it appear they're still in the fight."

"That's a bloody terrific idea!"

"You think so? Is it not dishonorable? To let another wear your armor is a sign of defeat."

"Not at all! Armor given is perfectly honorable. Only having your armor *taken* signals defeat."

He was on the edge of making a suggestion, the same one Nestor had made. But Eurypylus balked at pleading. He chose to shame me instead. Hefting his shield from the dirt, he said, "I'll give this to the fittest one of my men. My breastplate and helm as well. What matter how glorious the armor, if it goes unused!" With that, he staggered off.

I returned to our section of the camp, along the northernmost edge of the cape, far from the contested gates and fighting. My cheeks burned as hot as the Trojans' torches. My shame was not for myself, nor even for the Myrmidons, all of whom were bristling to unsling their spears and race into this fight. My shame was for the man I loved best in all the world. My friend. My companion. My lover.

From the beginning, Achilles and I had shared everything. Training under Chiron's watchful eye, we had vied and competed, laughed and bellowed, as we became versed in the hunt. I was older, but Achilles never got on with boys his own age. He already surpassed them physically. With every year that passed, Achilles grew in strength and skill, and soon he was beating me in nearly every contest. I quickly realized there is no shame in losing to the best. I remember envying his skill, yet I was never jealous. What is the point of being jealous of a bird because it can fly? It is only doing what it was born to do.

More, he lifted me up so that I could fly alongside him.

I liked to think that I had a similar effect on him. Tethered by a bond beyond mere words, we made each other better. We shared so many memories, from our training days to our adventures on the battlefield. He made me a better soldier, and I made him a better man.

As we both matured, we initiated each other into the joys of the flesh. I loved everything about him, from those pale green eyes right down to that hard, lip-less sword-stroke of a mouth. Not as handsome as Paris or even Diomedes. Yet he was attractive. Talent, skill, confidence—these are far more appealing than physical beauty.

Harder to love were his bouts of anger, his impulsiveness, his recklessness. From me, he learned compassion towards the vulnerable, and how to be vulnerable himself. With me, and me alone, Achilles shared his innermost thoughts, his dreams, his frustrations. His admiration for his father, and his filial fear that he would surpass his father in greatness.

He even told me of his mother, who had tried to drown him at birth. "Out of love," he'd insisted. "Or at least, her perverse notion of it. She wanted to make me immortal by making me leave life as perfect as I'd entered it." I had wept for him then, and watched the wariness which infused every dealing he had with women with greater understanding.

In a way, his mother had succeeded. Whether by birth or by the hands that shaped him, Achilles had a streak of immortality in his mind. On the field, he could snatch victory from the jaws of defeat through absolute belief in himself. It offered him a kind of invulnerability.

Yet I, who knew him best, understood that it was off the field of battle where he was vulnerable. His body was armored, but his image of himself was prone to pricking. In this matter with Briseis, his pride was his weakness. It was not as though he was unaware.

He had even admitted that he knew he was being stubborn. He simply found it impossible to swallow Agamemnon's insult.

Where in the body does pride lie? In the heart? In the liver? It was as if Achilles was already a statue, a colossal figure made of stone, not flesh, and all these petty creatures were chiseling and chipping away at the highest part they could reach, no higher than his ankles, to topple him. Without realizing that, if Achilles came crashing down, they themselves would be crushed.

One cannot truly love someone without understanding them. So I felt his pain.

But, for the first time in our history, I also felt ashamed of him.

Approaching his tent bearing the news of the Trojan attack, I encountered six men I knew well. Five Myrmidon captains alternately paced or stood before their commander's tent, fully armed. Each commanded the crews of ten Myrmidon ships, about five hundred men when the war had started. Now they were like hounds straining at their leashes. Phoenix, the eldest, who had helped raise Achilles, twitched his wrists with imagined strokes from an undrawn sword.

Achilles' charioteer, Automedon, squatted on his haunches, drawing racing horses in the earth with a piece of driftwood. Spying me, the red-headed youngster bolted upright and scuffed the drawing with his toe. The others straightened, but allowed Phoenix to greet me first.

"Greetings, Patrocles, son of Minoetius. How gravc gocs thc world?"

"Some men who belong in graves are having trouble finding them," I answered.

"Because the best guides are not leading them there." The rebuke was plain.

"Truth is truth," was all I could say.

"Tell me it is not ships that burn to the south."

"I would," I answered, "but untruths wear on my soul."

Phoenix clamped his jaw so tight that he resembled Achilles. "It's a long swim home."

All the commanders burned with the same shame scorching me. A week earlier, Agamemnon had been the one suffering those internal flames. Now, through some terrible alchemy, it had been transferred to us.

Passing the captains, I lifted the flap and entered our commander's tent, feeling the weight of their expectations heavy upon me.

In the stifling air within, Achilles sat upon his ornately carved, backless ivory chair. The open flap cast my shadow across the furs at his feet, but he did not acknowledge me. Instead, he held his lyre in one hand, absently running his nails across its nine strings.

Before him stood his armor. Inherited from his father, the glorious shell rested upon a stand shaped like a trident, reflecting the roseate warmth of a half dozen lamps. Atop the frame rested the well-forged helm, its dyed horsehair plume bristling to bring terror to all foes.

Achilles stared at the armor intently. There was longing in his gaze, and curiosity, and regret, and despair.

In that olive voice, smooth and rich and delicious, he said, "Tell me."

I did so, without plea or rebuke. I knew he'd been listening to the horns and the shouts, the clatter of countless swords and shields, the thudding thunder of hooves. I wondered if he could tell the battle's progress just by those sounds. The song of war was a special Siren's song to Achilles. It harmonized with his hot blood. Its descants delighted him. Its melodic refrain summoned him. Resisting it cost him pieces of his soul.

I finished my report. Plucking one lyre string at a time, Achilles summarized. "The Trojans are in the camp, though not yet in great numbers. All the leaders are wounded, save Ajax, who does his best to preserve a thousand ships."

"Yes."

Achilles shrugged. "We are far up the line. Even if Trojans are on the beach, it will be nightfall before they can reach us. Our ships won't suffer."

"They say Hector is wounded," I added.

A fleeting smile. "The best is bested? Then what's the point?"

"Our men are anxious to fight."

"My men are anxious to fight for me," he countered, now pinching two strings at a time. "Not for Agamemnon."

My men. Not ours, *mine*. It hurt, but I understood. It was his pride that suffered, his name. That was my lot—I could not share his glory, but neither could I shoulder his shame.

I braced myself. "Achilles . . ."

"You are clearly dying to say something. Speak freely."

Taking inspiration from the lyre in his hands, I invoked future bards. "Songs will say you dishonor our age."

"Songs will say the age dishonors me."

I opened my mouth, but he forestalled me. Pressing his palm against the strings, he ended their vibrations. "I didn't intend this to go so far. I did not intend never to fight."

"I know. But if not now, when?"

"When our ships are threatened."

"That will be too late."

"I thought Agamemnon would return her."

"I know."

"But, having already backed down once, he cannot, can he?"

"He can."

Achilles looked at me curiously, then nodded. "But he won't."

"No, he won't."

His gaze returned to his armor. "Troy never wronged me as much as Agamemnon has."

It was true, of course. What had Troy done to us? Why were we even here? We had not sworn to uphold the marriage of Menelaus and Helen. We had come to Ilium seeking adventure and glory, like in the days of heroes. I wondered if the true story of Jason and Theseus was as sordid as present events, or if the world was indeed in decline, as Nestor claimed.

Achilles continued to stare at his golden shell of war, as if seeking something in the embossed field of stars there. A flaw, or an answer.

"It misses you," I said.

Achilles shook his head. "It has no feeling. It is just a thing. There is no heart within it."

"No," I agreed. "But there should be."

Achilles closed his eyes. Each breath was deliberate.

I knew the signs. Any moment now he would rage, tear his hair, howl at the gods.

Yet I mustered the courage to push harder. "You heard what they're doing. Trading armor."

"I heard you. I just don't see the point."

"The best fighters take the best armor. It gives the men heart."

"An Ithacan idea if I ever heard one."

I said, "Let me."

His jaw muscles flexed, but Achilles said nothing.

Squatting on my haunches beside him, I dared what no man else might. "Let me don your armor and lead the Myrmidons to save the day, drive the Trojans out of the camp. The sight of your golden helm alone will drive them out. We can save the ships, and be in a position to demand anything from Agamemnon. Even Briseis. You can have her back without being forsworn."

Lipless mouth sealed, he shook his head.

"Why not?" I pleaded.

Opening those pale green eyes, Achilles looked into my heart and said the only words that could ever wound me.

"Because I do not trust you."

It was worse than rage, worse than the tempest of his fury. It was like having my heart crushed by the hand of Atlas. My breath became trapped in my lungs. My blood ceased to flow. My muscles turned to stone. I could not even muster the strength to alter my expression, much less speak.

Something of my pain must have reached him, for he amended his statement.

"I do not trust your motives."

That turned the knife. The soul who knew me best in all the world did not trust my motives. Somehow I scraped speech from my constricted throat. "What do you think my motives are?"

He rose and stepped away, as if his words would be less damaging if directed to the tent post. "That you love me, I do not doubt. But I wonder if you do not see this as the moment to eclipse me. I refuse to lead the Myrmidons, so you step in, and are hailed as the hero. Leaving me even more impotent than I am at this moment," he added angrily.

He glanced at me, expecting denials and finding none. Taking my silence for guilt, he continued on, the fire of his temper feeding itself. "You have long enjoyed the secrets of my heart. Then came Briseis. With her, I was able to speak as I could speak to no one else. How could that fail to make you jealous? Replaced in my affections, you must want to punish me." Fists clenched, he turned on me. "After all, you helped take her away from me! You brought her to Agamemnon! Now you use her name to bargain for your own glory, at my expense!"

Here was the familiar fury. In a moment, he would be howling at me, banishing me from his sight, calling down curses. It had happened before. Always before, I had given way. One does not fight thunder by shouting, but by letting the storm pass. Always before, he had summoned me back. I never sought an apology, and he never offered one. The very act of summoning was the apology.

To spare us both, I had taken to leaving when I saw the signs. When his beautiful green eyes turned red, I made it my practice to depart and await his call.

It was on his tongue to banish me.

I should have gone.

Instead I hit him.

It was a glorious blow. Rising from where I crouched, I struck his chiseled chin with all my might in an uppercut that slammed his teeth together and lifted him off his feet. He landed sprawling, but unlike every other time I had seen him knocked down, he did not rise. Shock kept him pinned to the furs as I stood over him, trembling with rage.

"You bloody fool!" I shouted. "Is the well of your love so shallow, that only one may drink from it before it goes dry? Do you think so little of me, that I could be swayed from loving you if you showed affection elsewhere? This is not a marketplace, where loyalty and love are bartered and, once sold, are gone forever. The harvest of my affection is infinite, even if yours is not!

"You arrogant, conceited ass! I am glad for you! It has been an honor to be your sole soul-friend. But you do not realize the cost. I know you, Achilles, son of Peleus! I know how lonely you are. How much it takes for you to trust another person—especially a woman! You think I am jealous of Briseis? Are you jealous of my Skara? Of course not! I love Briseis, Achilles, because you love her! Because she lifts a burden you have carried for too long! Because with her in your life, the weight of your pride is halved between us!

"How could you believe I could want to eclipse you? That's like a feather wishing to be the bird! I am not myself. I am yours. I am yours, Achilles, whether you want me or no. My love is unalterable—even if yours changes with the tide."

Achilles recoiled as though struck a second time. I confess to a certain level of satisfaction at that moment. I had wounded him.

Lowering my voice, I pressed on briskly. "Today you find yourself on a summit with no descent. Whatever you do, shame awaits you. If you fight, Agamemnon wins, and you are shamed. If you refuse to fight, your honor is diminished, and you are shamed. But my solution is your bridge to liberty. I don that armor there and lead the Myrmidons to drive the Trojans out. You are not forsworn, and Agamemnon is eclipsed by your shadow. Think of it—Achilles is so fierce, just his armor is enough to make an army run."

He didn't laugh, though he did release a wry snort. By now he had hitched himself onto his elbows. Leaning hard on one, he raised a hand to his jaw, testing. "You hit me."

Gloating would turn him sour. Apologies would lessen the moment. I said only, "Yes."

Rising to his full height, he looked me up and down. "What are you waiting for?"

I braced myself. "What?"

Achilles pointed to the armor. "You struck me down. It is the custom for the victor to take the vanquished man's armor."

I paused only a moment, not comprehending. Then suddenly it came to me. I grinned. So did he.

As I began stripping off my own armor, he resumed the commander's role, issuing orders. "Here's what we'll do. While you arm, I'll go out and make a speech. I'll instruct the men that, when the order is given, they are to go forth and drive the Trojans from our camp. But—" he paused to be certain he had my full attention

"—none must pursue the enemy past the Plain of Troy! We will save Agamemnon, but I refuse to win his war for him."

I finished removing my leg greaves. "Agreed."

"Assuming I can make my mouth work." He touched his tender jaw, working its hinge back and forth. "The swelling is going to be fierce."

"Good," I said, which made him laugh. The years fell away, and we were young again. Soul-bonded with the purity of youth and love and fellowship.

He walked up and kissed me. Not passionately, but with fond familiarity. He winced. "Ow. That hurts."

"Sorry," I said automatically.

"Worth it." With a wink, he exited the tent and told his captains to gather the men.

Swelling with pride and love, I lifted the armor of Achilles from its frame and began working the silver clasps.

HECTOR

HOVERING on the edge of consciousness, the night's wicked dreams abused my heart once more. In the dream, my body was limp, lifeless, unable to draw breath. Looking down, I saw my blood spill over my armor, which for some reason was covered with stars.

Filled with bitter resignation, I stared along the haft of an ash spear, into eyes so green they seemed to glow . . .

A blow to my face brought me around. At once I grasped my neck, but there was no wound, no spear. My armor was mine own. Only now the blue lapis was spider-webbed with cracks from the rock Ajax had hurled at me.

"Hector, you're alive!" Paris leaned back after slapping me, just a hint of disappointment tempering his relief. "Your poor armor!"

"It did its job." Events came rushing back. Knocked flat by a one-handed throw, I'd had enough wit to curl beneath my shield against the ensuing shower of spears. Carried to the back of our lines, I'd vomited blood. I must've passed out, for I had dreamed a dream of death so real . . .

But there was no time for dreams. I had a war to win. "Help me up. Where's my chariot?"

Relieved, Cebriones helped me into the chariot, Paris behind me, and we joined the rush back toward the shattered Achaean gate.

"What's happening?"

Gripping the guard rail, Paris spoke with eagerness. "We followed your orders! After you were carried off, Aeneas tried to burn the gate to widen the gap, and Hellenus led a wedge of men with torches down to the seashore to burn their ships!" The smoke ahead of us verified this statement. "But Sarpedon was repulsed from his breach, which let Ajax focus on pushing our men back. His spear missed Polydamas, but he practically beheaded one of Antenor's sons, and he's killed another half dozen men. He pushed Aeneas back and has planted himself in the gap where the gate stood!"

"You mean Hellenus is cut off?!"

"It's not my fault! I'm telling you, Ajax is unstoppable! The giant was joined by Nestor, and they're defending the gap with everything they possess!"

I wanted to say, *While you remain safely away from the bloodshed you caused.* But there was no point, and no time. Hellenus needed our aid. I shuddered to think what Cassandra would do if I allowed her twin to fall. And it would grieve my wife mightily.

Far greater than personal considerations, the outcome of the entire war was in the balance. I had gambled our victory on this day. Clearly, if it was meant to be, it was up to me.

A generous gust of wind cleared the smoke, and I took in the battle's current state at a glance. Paris was correct, our forces were on the verge of retreat. To my left, Sarpedon's Lycians were making a good stand, fending off Nestor's Pyloans with ease, despite being outnumbered. But to my right, the Arcadians and Mysians were struggling. Ajax himself was planted like a massive oak in the center of the gate, creating a barrier as much mental as physical. And beside him . . .

I squinted, disbelieving my own eyes. Somehow the injured Agamemnon, Odysseus, and Diomedes were healed, and back in the fight!

Or were they? I knew those Achaean leaders by their fighting styles, and a single jab of these men's spears told me they were not the pirate kings. Skilled soldiers, to be sure. But these were other men dressed in the kings' armor.

My first impulse was to reveal the trick to my men, to whom it must seem our foes were magically healed. It was vital to dispel such awe, and the news would rekindle their fury. But I also saw the opportunity. Their ploy—doubtless dreamed up by the too-clever Odysseus—was a double-edged blade. "Cebriones! Get me close to the man in Agamemnon's armor!"

As Cebriones used his scourge to change our steeds' direction, I stood tall and, removing my helm, bellowed, "Trojans!"

All eyes turned. There was no mistaking, it was me, returned from seeming death. I was greeted with cheers from our allies and silence from our adversaries.

Helm back in place, I gripped my spear and crouched. Paris loosed arrow after arrow, carving a path toward the man disguised as the self-proclaimed "king of kings." At the last second Cebriones hauled the reins to the left, kicking up a spew of dirt as he lurched us into a turn that nearly capsized our two-wheeled vehicle.

I leapt, using my shield to scythe the air, beating away the defending spear-points and sword-tips, and buried my spear right in the heart of Agamemnon's armor.

The man wearing it staggered back, gouts of blood gushing from his lips. To both my men and the enemy soldiers, it appeared that we had just won the war. Then the fellow, grasping to life, pushed the helm from his head. I knew him at once. Periphetes, son of the herald famed for announcing Heracles' twelve labors. A better soldier than his father, he died wearing a king's armor.

The trick was revealed. Shamed by their commander's cowardice, the Achaeans fell back to where Ajax stood, giving his impression of an immovable object.

I followed at a jog. Falling in, my brothers and comrades took up my pace, invigorated by outrage. The Achaeans cast spears, but our relentless advance threw off their aim. Or perhaps it was Paris and his fellow archers who broke their concentration with a shower of arrows. Whatever the cause, we batted aside the seadogs' miscast missiles and pressed our advance on the gate.

Ajax howled orders out of a throat grown ragged, and I broke into a run. "Apollo be my speed!"

We met the Boeotians first. My thrown spear killed their leader. My sword cut down the man to his left, while on his right, Aeneas skewered two men on the length of his spear, leaving them to stagger confusedly in confusion before they bled out. Woe betide the Achaeans this day. Aeneas was furious at his brother's death, and Aphrodite's son was as unforgiving as she.

We carved our way to the broken and burning gate. Even the wind was on our side, bringing billows of smoke to choke our foes while clearing it from our path.

As the Achaeans broke, Ajax himself retreated, not foolish enough to try to hold the expanse alone. Even a great boar will die in a thicket of thorns.

Trojans flooded into the pirate camp like the sea through a shattered hull. "Left! Left!" I bellowed. "Don't stop! Punch through to the shore! Reinforce Hellenus!"

My men obeyed, heading for the seashore. High to our left, the wall's defenders hurled spears down on us, but Aeneas led a contingent to sweep them from their own ramparts. To our right, tents were ablaze, evidence of Hellenus' passing. Racing along in his smoking wake, I plucked up a burning piece of timber and held it high. "Speed to the ships!"

The Achaeans raced westward, to the safety of their fellows among the boats, swelling their numbers. This was not the place where the battle would be won or lost, and both sides knew it.

At the western edge of their camp, we slowed as we encountered the sandy slope down to the beach. The midday sun reflecting off the water made me squint. Stretched out along the shore, a thousand beached black ships stood tall.

The penteconter was a vessel of fifty oars, a full hundred feet in length. Out of the water, they stood as tall as three men. Most of the beached vessels stood upright, but every fifth or sixth ship was overturned, creating a makeshift dome. Used as housing for the warriors they had ferried to our shores, they were connected by a series of bridges, creating a ziggurat of crisscrossing planks overhead. While their commanders had grand tents or even full houses on our shores, the Achaean soldiers existed in an upended world. On land as well as at sea, their ships were their shelter.

The nearest penteconters smoked, and my heart lifted as I spied Hellenus still living, still fighting, still showing himself to be my most dependable brother. But his men had suffered badly, and now had their backs to the ships they had set ablaze, using the flames to act as a buffer against the encroaching Achaeans.

Feet churning black sand in sprays behind us, we bore down on the Achaeans facing Hellenus, their backs turned invitingly towards us. In seconds they were either cut down or melting away under the hot sun. Our aim was clear, and the Achaeans showed a desperate desire to protect their precious vessels, swarming up over the hulls and brandishing long spears and oars to keep us at bay.

Reaching Hellenus, I bashed my forearm against his shoulder. "What, did Cassandra predict you'd win the war single-handed?"

Sagging, Hellenus shook his helmeted head, too breathless to speak. I felt a stab of concern. "Tell me you're not hurt!"

Again he shook his head, then gathered enough air to say, "Thanks to Euphorbus."

I glanced to his elbow, where stood a too-handsome Trojan spearman. He was a favorite among the ladies of Troy—and several of the men—for his wondrous curls of long, dark, luscious hair. That feature was hidden now under his helmet, which bore a dent spattered with blood.

"Good man!" Clapping Euphorbus on the shoulder, I told them both, "Rest now, while we spread our flames of victory." I turned to see my chariot bearing down on me. Our charge through the gate having opened a path, my loyal half-brother had followed, Paris riding behind him.

Chariots would be slower on the beach, but given enough room to maneuver, they were a welcome means of pressing the enemy.

As they slewed alongside, I leapt into the basket called the cockpit. Tossing a wave to Hellenus, I focused on a nearby Thessalian penteconter whose prow I recognized from years before. It had been the leading ship to land upon our shores. Its king, Protesilaus, had been the first of Agamemnon's pirates to fall in the war, at my hand. Only fitting that his ship follow his example.

As Cebriones brought us alongside the dark vessel with its glorious golden prow, I pressed my brand against a patch of tar. Wonderfully waterproof, the substance was also known to be highly flammable, and I expected it to catch alight at once. So I was frustrated when it only bubbled and hissed. Clearly I had to find another method of playing Prometheus.

"Bring me around the stern!"

MENELAUS

"TRADING armor didn't work? You astonish me! Fucking Odysseus!" Agamemnon used his good arm to swat his leg in frustration. "It's no surprise, is it? It's because Zeus hates me. I know he does. Look at them. Just look!"

Peering between patches of smoke, we watched the Trojan chariots descend to the beach, cutting a swath through the forces of Nestor and Ajax, scrambling to defend our ships from above.

I spied Hector, who had been rumored injured, riding around the lead Thessalian ship. "At least he doesn't seem able to spread the fire," I observed with satisfaction.

"Now you've done it!" snapped Agamemnon. "I swear, you're a living jinx!"

Hector's chariot was just turning under the elevated ship's stern, where the tiller hung low, closer to the sand than any other part of the vessel. With a mixture of horror and awe, I watched as Hector grabbed it one-handed and, lifting his legs, let his chariot continue circling while he hung beneath the dead king's ship, holding his firebrand to its nether parts. Protected as he was from above by the shape of the ship, his men rushed to hold off our earthbound forces from spearing him with their darts. It took several seconds, but smoke began to rise from the

Thessalian vessel's stern, first in wispy octopus legs, then full inky clouds.

By this time Hector's chariot was completing its second circumference of the ship. The Trojan prince could have dropped to the earth and then clambered aboard, but he opted for a more flamboyant return. Dropping from the tiller as it passed, Hector landed upright in the cockpit, his brand still aloft. Carried away from the latest burning ship, Hector pumped his free fist in the air, and his men cheered him.

"Now there's a prince!" growled Agamemnon with grudging admiration. "A man who can get things done."

My brother's jibes frayed my heartstrings. "I'll stop him."

Agamemnon simply laughed. "Good luck with that, my warhungry brother! Shout yourself hoarse—mayhap you'll scare him to death!"

Stalking towards my waiting chariot, I seethed. I did not deserve such insults.

PATROCLES

WITH the silver ankle-clasps of the greaves secured behind my heels, I strapped on the golden breastplate I knew so well. Leaner than Achilles, and two inches taller, the armor was a little loose around my chest and gapped at my midriff. This upset the weight distribution system, forcing my shoulders to bear what should have been on my hips. With time, I might have corrected it. But I was in a hurry.

Outside, Achilles was addressing the Myrmidons. Not a born orator, his plain, blunt style befitted his nature. It was why his men loved him, and Agamemnon hated him. Achilles never tried to be something he was not.

"I know you want to fight!" Achilles told two thousand soldiers. "Of course you do—you, the bravest men in all the world, desire nothing more than to show these Trojan louts how real men do battle! For once they've ventured out of their walls, and you're all like my horses, straining to run full out, while I, your charioteer, haul on your reins to prevent you! Well, no more! We fight!"

As the Myrmidons cheered their throats raw, I belted on the fine bronze blade with its silver-studded hilt. Making sure the shield was ready, I raised the helmet with its bristling horsehair crest and settled it on my head. It fitted perfectly. The narrow vertical gaps focused my world, and made my beating heart reverberate in my ears.

Inside the helmet, Achilles sounded very far away as he continued to rally the troops. "They dare threaten our ships? The thread that connects us with our homes, our fathers and our sons? They want to sever that tie, prevent us from departing their blighted land! That cannot be endured! So, my Myrmidons, I release the reins! Not to fight Agamemnon's war, but rather to preserve our hope of returning to our homes victorious and triumphant!"

As the men beat their spears on their shields, Achilles stepped into the tent and started at the sight of me. "Ah! You look well. I had no idea I was so impressive."

"You're not," I told him. "It's the man who makes the armor."

"Ha!" Achilles flashed his teeth in a rare smile. "Remember—save the ships, don't win the war." He frowned at my armaments. "You don't want my spear?"

I shook my head. "That's too far. I feel like I'd be tempting fate. Besides, I'm used to mine. Don't worry, I'll make you proud!"

"I don't doubt it. Just drive them off, don't try to win the war yourself."

"Yes, dad!"

His laugh rang, and I remember thinking that, should I fall, I was glad his laugh was the last of his voice I would hear.

Only that is not how the story unfolded.

Encased in Achilles' glittering golden armor, I emerged into the daylight. I felt the sun's rays reflecting off the polished metal, blinding those near me. Let Hector dress himself as the sky, or the sea. I was fire. I was light. I was life.

The watching Myrmidons gasped. Having just seen Achilles disappear seconds earlier, it was as though their leader had been transformed by the gods. I raised a lone finger to my lips.

Understanding the trick, they began to laugh. They could now fight without staining their commander's honor.

Grabbing a pair of spears from a rack, I climbed into the cockpit of Achilles' chariot. "Automedon, take us to where the fighting is fiercest!"

The charioteer obeyed, and the Myrmidons surged behind us, aimed at the heart of the battle.

This was the moment for which I had been born. My hour to shine brightest in all the world. To be more than a shadow of Achilles. To bring him honor.

It was my only desire.

HECTOR

CHOKING on an errant gust of smoke, I felt my breath leave—and not return. For a terrifying moment, the bellows of my lungs did not rise or fall. They simply ceased to work. Surrounded by a cloud of darkness, my breathless self was again returned to the terrors of my restless night, dreaming of death. Not the deaths I brought the enemy, but a death all my own. Again the stab to my throat, my choking gasp. But now, behind the veil of smoke, other senses struggled to fill the void. I felt the ghost of a scratch at my ankles. It felt like rope tied around them. As if I were about to be dragged away behind a chariot.

Then all at once we were clear of the cloud, and I could breathe once more. Involuntarily my hand sought my throat, but it was whole and unmarked. Nothing encircled my ankles save the buckles of my greaves and my sandal tops.

I had dismissed it earlier, ascribing these visions to an uneasy night and an exhausting day. But it had felt more real this time. As though I was drawing nearer the event . . .

A spear tip caught my eye an instant before it arrived to spit me. I batted it aside with my shield. And just like that, I shook off these fancied disasters of my mind and focused on bringing disaster to the Achaeans.

The strife on the beach had transformed into a perverse parody of a battle at sea. Achaeans ran between their ships across a maze of airborne bridges, while our chariots swarmed below, like sharks circling doomed vessels. We wove and dodged as they swung out with spears and pikes and oars, attempting to prevent us from drawing near enough to set them alight.

How strange it must have been for those pirates! Used to vessels built for speed, they were suddenly stationary, helpless to give chase. The attackers had become defenders.

It rapidly became clear that our desire was greater than their ability to deny. Some of their ships were side-by-side, with no space for a chariot to pass through.

Stung, perhaps, by my display of valor, Aeneas was the next to brave all for glory. Abandoning his chariot to race afoot between two pirate hulls, Aeneas set both alight, the nearness of the hulls sheltering him against attacks from above. Flames devoured both wooden hulls, sending plumes of black smoke billowing skyward, a sacrifice to almighty Zeus. Aeneas emerged blackened but unhurt.

His deed was emulated by others, forcing the beached sea-dogs to drop down to the sand and defend their vessels.

Upturned ships proved more difficult to burn, as their defenders could muster beneath the sheltering beams, creating a forest of spears with a hard shell atop. But just one well-thrown brand would begin a fire on the hull, trapping the defenders beneath a burning shell.

Soon three dozen ships were blazing. Trapped Achaeans were forced to either burn alive or abandon their ships, leaping to the dark sand as if it were the sea, to be speared like fish by our men.

We cheered each burning vessel, while our foes redoubled their efforts, fighting back with increasing desperation. Ajax was in the thick of it, leaping from ship to ship, swinging a timber big enough to be a foremast, knocking men from their chariots, battering back our soldiers.

Even as we advanced our victory, I kept an eye on our right flank, where stood the enemy camp. There was a world where the Achaeans mustered enough men to pen us down on the shore and cut us off from Troy. It was vital that our path back to the gate remain clear.

A bellow turned my head. As if bringing my fear to life, Menelaus was leading a charge of chariots to cut us off. Preparing to leave the beach to intercept him, I saw there was no need. I was beaten to it by Hellenus, who cast a spear that neatly pinned the Spartan king's wheel through the spoke. The chariot flipped, casting the broad-shouldered Menelaus hurtling through the air.

I had a cruel moment of hope. Menelaus dead, nothing remained to bind the pirate kings to this war. But the man was beloved of some evil god, for he emerged from the wreckage unscathed and cursing as his soldiers bore him back to be checked for injuries.

The arc of my chariot brought me near the ship Ajax was defending. I threw him a taunt. "That's the man whose marriage you're sworn to protect?"

"You don't understand honor, Hector!" Out of reach of the massive timber he swung as a weapon, Ajax could only hurl words back at me. "But I'll teach you! This time you won't have night's cloak to hide behind!"

"No need!" I shouted over my shoulder as I was carried away. "Your burning ships will light the night for our victory!"

Fire knows only desire. Once kindled, there is no denying it. If these arrogant pirates ever breached the walls of Troy, their desires would run unchecked. So did ours that afternoon on their usurped beach. Already fifty ships were ablaze. With each burning vessel, Agamemnon's army felt the fist of Troy tightening on its throat.

I was exultant, earlier injuries forgotten, evil portents ignored. I was outside myself, seeing the moment as if from on high, as the Olympians would see it. No longer the moody prince, whose song was forever played in a minor key. For a shining moment, I was the greatest warrior on earth. I was Ares come to life. Heracles, Theseus, Jason, even Achilles—none of them could touch me. I was all I ever wanted to be. My whole world was in harmony. The thunder of my blood, the roar of the sea, the crackle of the flames, the thud of hooves on sand, the screams of the vanquished, the shouts of the victorious—all blended into a grand symphony of warfare.

How fitting. On Apollo's Day, the god of music was using us as his instruments to compose the greatest song of all.

The song of war.

Then, like castles in the black sand, it all came toppling down.

Out of the cacophony of battle, Apollo added a new instrument to his composition. From the north, amid a rising swell of cheers, horns blared a peculiar tune, a triple note that lingered, then repeated.

We all recognized it. The notes that called the Myrmidons.

MENELAUS

COVERED with dirt and ridicule, I staggered along the camp's edge to rearm and gain fresh horses. My charioteer had been trampled, yet, miraculously, I had emerged unscathed, as if Poseidon himself had protected my body. The shame was that the fickle god had not preserved my honor, which was as mangled as my broken chariot.

My latest charioteer was yoking steeds to a working set of wheels when Agamemnon arrived, arm now in a sling. Instead of rejoicing in my salvation, my brother chided me. "So much for dealing with Hector."

I bristled, but said nothing.

"Tell me, whose ships are burning? Which king must I reimburse?"

In the middle of the most dangerous day of this entire war, that was Agamemnon's chief worry? Still, I answered him. "Nestor's."

"Oh terrific!" groused my brother, the king of kings. "The old fart will never shut up about this!"

"Brother," I said, putting real urgency in my tone, "we are in true danger. Even if the Trojans don't reach our own ships, it will only take a few hundred torched vessels to strand the bulk of our army here. The men will lose heart."

Agamemnon waved me off as he would a horsefly. "Or they'll fight all the harder! Hector is doing us a favor. I should have burned all our ships when we arrived. Leave the men no hope of going home—unless we win!" Suddenly his chin lifted. "What noise is that?"

"Cheering," I said.

Agamemnon cuffed the back of my head. "I can hear that, fool! But it's not coming from the beach. It's coming from . . . Quick, boost me!" With my help, he clambered onto the wheel of my new chariot and stared north. On my toes, I peered in the same direction.

The acrid smoke from our burning ships did not disguise the sight awaiting us. The cheers grew in volume, drawing nearer as more and more of our battered army saw salvation.

The Myrmidons had emerged. Fresh, armed, and ready, they jogged in good order towards the heart of the fighting.

At their head, unmistakable in his golden armor, rode Achilles.

I would be a liar if I said I did not experience a wave of relief. With Achilles on the field, Hector and his Trojans would swiftly be forced off the beaches. Our fleet was saved.

My brother sputtered. His skin turned crimson, then purple. For a second I believed he was suffering a stroke. Then, in his most quiet, most dangerous tone, he said, "Damn him. Damn Achilles for all time."

PATROCLES

I stood in the chariot and felt the adulation, the joy, the euphoria that greeted Achilles whenever he entered the fray. Back in Opois, I had been celebrated, but never, never like this. Even knowing it was not for me, it was intoxicating. I raised my spear, and thousands of voices roared in joyful reply. My simple ruse was giving heart to an entire army.

Automedon was struggling with the reins, our horses surging across the packed sand, as eager as the Myrmidons to enter the fray.

It was my honor to lead them into battle, to defend our ships and our honor. I prayed to Apollo to grant me strength to carry this formidable burden for just this one day.

So far the day had gone all Hector's way. With Agamemnon's soldiers and allies treed like cats up in the ships, Troy's forces had been free to have their pleasure. That now changed. Sight of us caused them to abandon their assault upon our ships. Otherwise, with two thousand Myrmidons falling on their flank, they would be forced to bunch together beneath the very ships they were assaulting, with Ajax and Nestor hammering them from above while we picked them off below.

How it must have galled Hector to pull them back! Already he had decimated our fleet. Nearly a hundred of our thousand ships were burning. An hour more and we might have lost all.

Yet, wisely, he did not risk his men. Had he stayed, we could have smashed their army there and then.

But Hector did exactly what he should. Not a panicked retreat, but an orderly withdrawal to regroup, reassess, and attack again.

It was up to me to deny them a second bite at the olive.

Spearing straggling Trojans, we traversed billows of smoke as we chased them off the beach. I meant to drive them up the slope towards the gutted camp, into the funnel of the broken gate. Simple logistics would slow them down at that spot. I meant to clog that portal with bodies, preventing their return with a barrier of their own dead.

Without warning a wall of bristling spears sprang up between us and the fleeing Trojans. Ahead of me, I saw the Lycian prince, Sarpedon, gather his warriors to block our charge. He knew as well as I that chariots were of no use against armed men who stood firm. Achilles' horses were bred for speed, not size. With both hooves and wheels struggling on the sand, we would never gain the speed needed to break Sarpedon's spear wall.

Automedon altered course, carrying us along their line as I cast one throwing spear after another into their ranks. Each spear claimed a life. When I ran out of spears to throw, I hefted my war spear and caught one of Sarpedon's men in the mouth like a fish, hauling him through the air, only to cast him aside.

To their credit, the Lycians did not break. Every second they held gave Hector time to regroup. If I wanted to expel these Trojans from our camp, I had to break these men here.

What would Achilles do? That was simple. He would beat them himself by taking on their strongest man in single combat.

As if in answer to my thought, Sarpedon stepped out of his protective wall of spears and, bellowing a challenge, cast a throwing spear. It missed me, but sailed over my shoulder to wound one of the horses. The beast bucked and fought, veering us back north, away from the enemy.

No! Refusing to lose the initiative, I dropped off the open back of the chariot, my legs already pumping—a dangerous maneuver, like stepping from a speeding ship onto a quay. One trip would have brought the deception crashing down with me—Achilles never fell on his face!

Ahead of me, Sarpedon waited, strides ahead of his line of spears, completely exposed. An invitation to single combat.

I waved the Myrmidons to halt their attacks. In return, Sarpedon began jogging across the sandy earth to meet me. The firelight reflecting off his lacquered armor made it appear he was charging straight out of the sun.

But his fire was only reflected. In facing me, he was racing into an inferno.

A dozen paces away, Sarpedon cast his war spear. Ducking low, I closed the gap between us swifter than he expected, and he barely got his shield up to block the thrust of my spear.

Sidestepping, he drew the sword strapped beside his muscular thigh. "Well met, 'Achilles!'"

So Sarpedon, at least, suspected the trick. I laughed. "I'll take that name out of your mouth!"

We came together like glorious waves, the sound of metal on metal ringing in my borrowed helmet. My spearhead met his shield. I batted away his sword with the spear's end, and we began our deadly dance, the music of swords and screams ringing in our ears.

The song of war.

HECTOR

IT was not Achilles.

At first, I'd been fooled. The man was a gifted soldier, his movements uncannily like those of Achilles. Enclosed in that golden armor, he looked for all the world like the young man everyone called the greatest warrior in the world.

However, as I watched from further up the slope, I began to suspect the trick when he left his chariot. Whoever it was, he was taller than Achilles, his thinner frame adding to the illusion of height. Moreover, that glorious golden armor did not flow with him, but fought his movements, gapping at the belly and armpits.

The instant he met Sarpedon in combat, I was certain. While we are all taught the mechanics of fighting from boyhood, no two warriors fight the same way. And that man, brilliant fighter that he was, lacked the divine streak of genius that Achilles owned.

Which made him no less Sarpedon's equal. The pair danced to the music they made with equal skill, sword and shield against spear. All around the fighting slowed, men stepping away from their sparring partners, pausing in mutual consent to watch the contest between these two brilliant warriors.

What struck me was that both combatants wore ill-fitting armor, though for different reasons. Achilles' borrowed armor was loose on the man who wore it, whereas Sarpedon's armor was too tight. Made for the Lycian king in his youth, the gleaming armor was ill-fitting for his age, and gapped at the belly as he lifted his arms. The real Achilles, I felt sure, would have already taken advantage of that fact and killed Sarpedon dead. But these two were fairly matched, dancing around each other in disguise. One man pretended to be an absent warrior, the other pretended to be his younger self.

At one moment, the man in Achilles' armor turned so that his breastplate caught the firelight, and I felt an ethereal finger pinched the string of my life. His breastplate was covered in a field of stars. Just like the one I wore in my dream of death. What did that mean?

Then the man leapt into the air in a perfect imitation of Achilles, and suddenly I knew who it had to be. Patrocles! No one else fought so like Achilles. Patrocles, wearing Achilles' armor—astonishing! I would never have imagined Achilles consenting to such a blatant deception. Nor that Patrocles would participate.

Again I was faced with the dilemma of revealing the trick. If Sarpedon cut down Patrocles, the deception would work in our favor. For, as obvious as it was to me that a substitution had taken place, there were countless soldiers out there who would be so blinded by that glittering armor that they took in nothing of the man within.

I decided to say nothing. Real soldiers would know the truth. Only fools would think Achilles had emerged from his tent to win Agamemnon's war.

MENELAUS

"THAT bastard Achilles! May his eyes be thrown to the crows!" shouted Agamemnon.

He and I pressed our backs against the wall of his makeshift palace, watching the duel unfold.

"Sarpedon is fierce, but aged," I assured him. "He's no match for Achilles."

My brother rounded on me. "You burden to the earth! Do you honestly believe I am afraid of Achilles *losing*?"

"Then what are you—"

"Victory!" he bellowed. Realizing his words might carry, he brought his voice under bronze control. "It's victory I fear, you fool! Don't you see? We were close to beaten! All that stood between us and surrender was Ajax and his men. At which moment that son of a deluded whore chooses to bestir his puckered ass, sallying forth to rescue us all! To rescue *my* army!"

My brow furrowed. "Brother, if they had continued burning ships—"

"—we could have blamed it on Achilles' refusal to help!"

I was utterly confused by his thinking. "But he *is* helping."

Agamemnon threw up his good arm in frustration. "Yes! *After* we had all been beaten. You cannot be so dense that you don't see what's happening! This is exactly what he planned. At the moment when we all stand on the precipice of defeat, he nobly sets aside his pride to rescue us. He will win this duel, and then single-handedly reverse the winds and blow Hector and all the Trojans from our camp. Demonstrating to all the world that, when all was lost, Achilles was the only one who could save us from our own folly! Our own incompetence! That young bastard! So perfectly timed! And do you imagine he will stop there? No! He'll push the Trojans until their backs are against their impenetrable walls and slaughter them all! In the rush, he might even do the unthinkable—take the city!"

"But, brother," I said, "if that happens, we will have won!"

"No—HE will have won! Without us! Without ME!"

In a stupefied horror, I finally grasped what my brother was saying. Winning the war was not enough. Agamemnon himself had to be holding the reins when we did. In a war nominally waged for my honor, my brother cared more for his pride than our victory.

I have not deserved such insult.

Furious, Agamemnon tried to move his injured arm, in some vain hope that the gods had healed him to allow him to lead a charge. He winced, barely clamping his mouth shut on an agonized howl. He shook his head, cursing.

Then he looked to me, and, for what felt like the first time, it seemed he actually saw me.

"Menelaus. Brother. You're our only hope." Clamping his good arm behind my neck, Agamemnon yanked me close, forehead to forehead. His breath made me start to recoil, but he held me fast. "Let him save the camp, the ships. But, whatever happens, Menelaus, don't let him give them chase. Whatever you must do, prevent Achilles from winning this war!"

I broke into a sweat that defied the heat of the day. Was he truly giving me this order?

He saw my hesitation and clutched me tighter. "Do you want Achilles to be the one who saved your pride? Do you want to be beholden to that man, who disdains your marriage, your brother, your king? Who is so petty as to start a needless quarrel over a woman?"

That smote me. Did Agamemnon not understand what he was saying? If my brother disdained Achilles for being affected by the loss of Briseis, at heart he must also disdain me for being affected by the loss of Helen.

This war had suited his ambitions, that was all. I was nothing to him.

"I have not deserved such insult," I muttered.

Thinking I responded to his words, Agamemnon's wide face broke into a fierce grin. "No, we have not! Go! Go, and prevent us from being made ridiculous!"

PATROCLES

THERE are perfect moments, moments hewn from the air to become ephemeral waves of joy. They are too few in life, and therefore precious. Until now, mine all involved Achilles. First sight of him. First night of him. First fight alongside him.

My fight with Sarpedon was one such moment. Made all the more glorious as Achilles was not involved. This moment belonged solely to me. My heart struck a steady rhythm as I stabbed and evaded, feinted and blocked. I was outside myself, part of a larger something that was almost divine. Apollo himself was giving me strength.

A Myrmidon war spear was not meant to be thrown, but wielded two-handed. Its wicked tip flared out like a laurel leaf before coming to a sharp point. The butt end was capped with a metal knob that acted as counterweight, perfectly balancing the weapon. Sharp at one end, blunt at the other.

Sarpedon stabbed at my chest. Using the spear's shaft to beat the blow aside, I immediately brought the tip down upon his head. Meeting it with his shield, he rolled his wrist to slash at me, but I snaked the spear's tip inside his guard, aiming for his exposed thigh.

He should have blocked with his sword and used his shield to batter me. Instead, he gave ground while continuing his stab, though now I was out of reach. It told me something, and I decided to test my theory.

Advancing, I swiped, forcing him to repeat his retreat. He lunged again, and I danced sideways, circling him and barely missing his kneecap. Backfooted, he tried to regain the lead in our dance, and I wasted several seconds blocking, dodging, and weaving his expert cuts and thrusts.

He was no fool, Sarpedon. As brilliant a soldier as stood upon Troy's shores.

But I had spied his weakness.

Sarpedon planned his moves.

Old Chiron, the horse master who had trained Heracles and Jason, had reluctantly agreed to teach Achilles, and by extension, me. Gruff and honest, he'd peppered us with sayings. "Breathe, or die." "Extension, not tension." "Distance is danger." Or his favorite, "This is so simple, even Heracles could do it!"

One such saying confounded me until I survived my first battle. "Set goals, not plans." It was the best advice I had ever received. Because, while it was important to know your desired outcome, the path there was best discovered in the moment. A man who plans a battle becomes committed to that plan, tries to make it happen even when it should be abandoned.

Sarpedon was such a warrior. Even forced to retreat, he'd executed that useless attack. Which informed me he did not react to opportunities. He lived a second ahead of the fight, not in the moment. He reacted to patterns. He made plans.

Knowing what was about to happen, I almost pitied the man.

I launched into the attack Chiron had dubbed The Star of Pain, a six-part attack that traveled down and up the body on opposite sides, high-middle-low, low-middle-high. Like a lever with a center pivot, each block Sarpedon performed brought my next attack singing in.

Skilled, Sarpedon parried the first five blows—shield, sword, shield, sword, shield. By then the pattern was obvious. My next move should have been to swing the butt end to rattle his skull. Already his sword rose to knock it away. Thinking ahead, he was probably planning a counterattack.

If so, he never got to perform it.

Changing course, I pushed hard off my left foot, ramming my shoulder and hip into an enormous thrust just below Sarpedon's abdomen, where his lacquered armor gapped.

As his sword sliced empty air, the tip of my spear punched through leather and cloth, into his belly.

Sword high, shield wide, Sarpedon looked at me, stunned, wondering how I had beaten him.

I continued my drive forward, pushing him stumbling backwards until he gave way and collapsed. His mouth opened, but his vocal cords were battling an eruption of blood. Blood won.

His silence was measured against the gasps and shouts of his men. The Lycians cried out in horror as their commander's lifeblood spilled to blacken the sands even further. I placed a foot on the dying man's chest and yanked my spear free. A welter of blood followed it, droplets flung skyward like a sacrifice given to the gods.

I let out a victorious roar, turning to face the whole Trojan army, brandishing my spear and shouting a challenge to any who would face me. Let Aeneas come. Let Hector himself.

The dying king stretched an arm for his comrades. "Glaucus! Don't—let—dishonor!" Then, with a final violent vomit of blood, Sarpedon fell dead in the sand.

Vibrating with exultation, I reached down to claim his gleaming armor, as was my right after single combat. The death of Sarpedon was the victory of Patrocles of Locrus, son of Menoetius the Argonaut. This glory was solely mine own.

The Lycians' outraged screams seemed distant, immaterial. There was thunder in my ears, a rhythmic hammering of blood and power and life, a Siren's song calling me to further glory. Measured against that Zeus-like rumble, the frenzied shouts of the Lycians were nothing to me but the buzzing of gnats.

I watched them surge forward to protect their dead leader's

honor. Behind me, Myrmidons raced to meet them. Under the punishing heat of the afternoon sun, we smashed together over the armor of a dead hero, honoring him by soaking the sand around his corpse in other men's blood.

"Do not stop until every Trojan lies beside him at our feet!"

HECTOR

I watched Sarpedon fall. Days earlier, he had complained to me that we Trojans allowed our allies to do the fiercest fighting, keeping ourselves safe. His death seemed a final, vindictive indictment of my leadership.

The Lycians waged a pointless war to recover his lacquered helmet and breastplate. I had never truly understood the posthumous battle over a fallen warrior's armor. Among impoverished soldiers, looting corpses made sense. But a prince taking a foe's armor was uncomfortably vainglorious. I felt the same about men who collected trophies, or pissed on their slain foe. So unnecessary! What did it matter? The man was already defeated!

Yet often the fiercest fighting took place over the arms of men who no longer required them. As though the corpse's comrades could make symbolic restitution to him by keeping his shell safe after the threads of his life had been cut. I wondered how many men had fallen vying over a dead man's armor, raising its perceived value by the ever-increasing price paid. So foolish! Wasteful! I prayed that, should I fall, there would be no quarrel over my corpse . . .

Again that shimmer of unreality, a flash of sensation more true than real. The instrument of my death being torn free, leaving me to fall. My dying self, split at the throat, hitched by the heels behind a chariot. This time sight and touch were joined by hearing. My ears rang with my wife's howled protest, my father and my son both calling out my name, my country gasping in terror at a future where my gambit had failed, and my lifeless self was dragged away from them.

Dragged behind the same golden chariot Patrocles had ridden onto the beach.

The chariot of Achilles.

Terror took hold of my ribs and squeezed, constricting my very vitality. *Imagination, Hector? Now? You've never been fanciful in your life!* Were these dark visions the product of exhaustion? Or was I in tune with the god whose day this was? It is claimed that Apollo has the power to peer into the future, seeing which grain will grow and which will not. At times, it is said, he grants this power to mortals. Some claimed this was the affliction that beset my sister Cassandra . . .

"Hector!" Paris was shaking my shoulder. "We should go!"

Roused from my crushing fantasy, I nodded. But instead of falling back as he intended, I ran forward to join the Lycian ranks. However stupid I found it, the enemy desired Sarpedon's many-hued armor. It was Troy's duty to deny it them.

Besides, if we could make the Myrmidons break now, we could reopen our path to the beach. My original plans cast to the wind, it was time to make the best of what Apollo offered us.

My men followed my lead, and more, and more. For nearly an hour, ten thousand men stabbed, threw, battered, kicked, kneed, bit, and howled over a dead king's armor. The heat choked us. The sun burned us. Countless cuts bled us. Yet we fought on.

Patrocles fought fiercely, with Ajax, Nestor, and Menelaus joining him. Our side fought just as bravely, with Hellenus, Aeneas, and even Paris joining me in the scrum. The Myrmidons were fresh, but were fighting uphill. Bodies mounting, we climbed over our own dead to hack away at the emboldened Achaeans. There was no room for finesse, no great deeds. Just the brutal business of war.

The song of war is, at its heart, the drum of men's hearts, counting each precious beat as its last.

Then, above the thunder we made, I heard two simultaneous cries, one of triumph, one of anguish. Sarpedon's body had long vanished beneath a mound of corpses, but his breastplate suddenly emerged in the grip of some bloodied Achaean. The man was cut down, but he managed to toss the breastplate to one of his comrades, who passed it off down the sea of Achaean soldiers, out of our grasp.

In that instant, everything hung in the balance. Sarpdeon's men could have surged forward and, in their rage, set fire to every rotting, broken, scavenged plank of every ship in Agamemnon's fleet. Their desire for vengeance could have been everything.

But men are fickle creatures. Sarpedon's soldiers had pinned their hopes on saving their dead commander's armor, and with it, his honor. Seeing that honor vanish on a sea of bloodied Achaean hands, their hopes were snuffed out like a pinched candle. There is nothing so crushing as a heartfelt desire, denied.

A cut lyre string makes no noise. A horn without breath is silent. Suddenly the song of war was sung all from the other side.

Our men did not yield to outright panic. They fell back in good order. My aching legs carried me back to where Cebriones waited, reins ready to take us back to the safety of Troy's walls. He said, "It was a glorious day."

I shook my head. A piece of battered metal. Of minor intrinsic value, turned priceless through the cost paid to attain it.

Such a stupid thing to lose a war over.

MENELAUS

I confess, my voice was raised with all the others as the Trojans withdrew from our camp. The waves of battle had taken me far from the Myrmidons, but I saw Sarpedon's armor carried away, and felt the heart go out of Hector's men. I was even caught up in the surge to chase them, driving the Trojans from our camp and away from our precious ships. This day was as close as we had ever come to losing this war in battle, and the relief I felt was intoxicating.

Until I saw Achilles' chariot giving chase.

Recalling my brother's instructions, I called for my own chariot. To onlookers, it appeared as though I was joining the routing of the Trojan army.

But my eyes were fixed on the back of Achilles.

PATROCLES

"APOLLO, averter of evil, thanks unto you!" Blood singing, I shouted my praise to the god whose day it was. Such a glorious day! I had done what I'd promised. I'd driven the Trojans from our camp. I'd saved our ships, and with them our hope of home. By my own hand, I had slain forty-nine men. To me, and me alone, belonged the glory of this day.

And Apollo's Day was far from over! Pulse fast, heart rejoicing, I did not hesitate to give chase. The shouts of warriors filled the pitchers of my ears like wine, bringing me intoxicating courage. I could taste victory on my tongue. It had the tang of copper.

Exiting our burning gates, I felt no guilt. If, in the back of my mind I heard Achilles' injunction, it was drowned out by the joyous blare of our trumpets.

Ahead, the Trojans turned east, descending the throsmos to

the Plain of Troy. As we followed, the land opened before us like a flower, giving the horses room to run. I decided I would give chase up to the Scamander. The natural barrier served as an excellent marker, beyond which I would not go. Achilles would not blame me. I did not intend to steal his glory, but rather prove myself worthy of him.

In a series of arcs and swoops, we harassed the Trojans across the no man's land. Here, just the day before, Agamemnon had launched his assault, only to be driven back. Now it was our turn to kick up the earth in pursuit of a retreating foe. Chasing them across the Plain, I wished for more throwing spears. Many clustered together defensively, but Automedon managed to trample a few stray soldiers beneath our horses' hooves.

Arriving at the river, Trojans made a stand as their lead elements began wading across the ford. Slowed by the water, they made perfect targets. Having killed four more men in the chase, I lamented that the rest of their army was about to be out of my reach, and looked around for some way to get past them, cut off their retreat.

I spied an unused ford further south. "There! Take us across there!"

Automedon urged the four great steeds across the Scamander, kicking up massive waves on either side of us. The spray of water was welcome as it struck my legs and arms, a moment's relief from the heat of the sun and the sweat of war.

Free of the river, Automedon wheeled us north, directly for a cluster of Trojans struggling through the mud to reach dry land. They were headed northwest, where loomed the magnificent walls of Troy. The dead from the previous day's fighting had already been dealt with by the Trojans. If theirs, carried back for rites. If ours, plundered and left to rot. Tonight, Troy could watch us do the same to the men we now cut down.

Suddenly I spied Hector's chariot. Having crossed already, he was looping back to protect his men. As we raced north along the Scamander's banks, he was driving west, back towards the river, aiming to cut across our path.

An ambitious voice sang a seductive note in my heart, wordless but clear. Defeat Hector, and I could crush the Trojan spirit. Capture him, and what could not we ask for his safe return? Capture him, and we could end this war. Glory, victory, honor, success.

In that moment, it was all I desired.

Seized with sudden inspiration, I leapt from Achilles' golden chariot and bent low. Scooping up a shining black stone, I spun and hurled it.

Not at Hector, but at his charioteer.

HECTOR

"CEBRIONES!" The stone struck my half-brother just between the eyes, denting the helmet and sending forth a spurt of blood.

I lunged to catch him, but he toppled over the chariot's side like a diver into the sea. But it was not water that greeted his limp form. He landed on earth churned from yesterday's fighting.

The flapping reins unmanned, my horses continued their course. Twisting, I saw Cebriones in a heap, with Patrocles closing in on foot. Having failed to overturn my chariot, the impostor Achilles was already racing to capture my half-brother.

Priam had lost enough sons this day. Jumping from the back of my chariot, I forced my weary, trembling legs into a run. With every stride, I closed the distance between myself and the figure in the golden armor.

But not fast enough. Patrocles was closer to Cebriones, and my watery stalks could carry me no faster. In desperation, I shouted:

"Patrocles! Turn and face me!"

Startled, the man within Achilles' armor glanced over his shoulder. Inside the arcs of the helmet, his wide eyes showed surprise that the trick had not worked on me. Slowing his pace, he called to me, "I'm glad you know! Fitting!"

Easing to a trot, I changed my angle of approach, trying to edge around him to protect my brother. To distract him, I said, "Where is Achilles?"

Patrocles circled along with me, allowing me to place myself between Cebriones and his spear. "Honing his sword for a better fight!"

I spat at his feet. "A true leader leads!"

The truth of my words hurt him, yet he rallied. "You are not worth his effort, Hector!"

"I am, in fact. As you shall learn." With that, I stepped in and, weary as I was, engaged the golden-clad impostor. I hoped that in beating him, I would also beat back these disquieting images of death.

MENELAUS

MY chariot was just cresting the Scamander's eastern bank when I saw Achilles face Hector in single combat. I swear I actually felt my brother's fist at my throat, heard his insults in my ear. *You swine! You let Achilles kill Hector! This will now be his war! He will forever eclipse me, the greatest of all kings! All thanks to your pathetic incompetence! No wonder Helen left you!*

I was so distracted that I was nearly knocked from my chariot by a spear. It struck my armor a blow across the chest that rocked me back, forcing my free hand to grasp for the rail.

Eyes darting to the spear's origin, I recognized the muddy

spearman. It was the Trojan with the dancing girl's hair, Euphorbus. I threw him a rude gesture, then ordered my charioteer, "Steer us towards that duel!"

Slicing my sword from side to side, my attention was pinioned to the unfolding duel. It was not as imagination would have me believe. I had thought Hector the taller of the pair, but Achilles seemed to have that advantage, as well as a longer reach. With those factors in his favor, he should be winning against the exhausted Hector. Yet somehow the pair seemed evenly matched.

Sidestepping a stab, Achilles turned his back to me, and I spied a curious space between his helmet and his back-plate. Perhaps a strap had come loose. Whatever the reason, Achilles' armor did not fit him as it usually did. Normally molded to his frame, the golden armor was now gapping along his shoulder blades.

Like Athena from the brow of Zeus, an idea came into my brain. A notion Odysseus would have been proud to have conceived. It would take skill both physical and mental to pull off. Success would silence my brother's insults forever. Failure would open me to worse ridicule than I had yet endured.

But at least then I would deserve it.

PATROCLES

SWEAT poured down my brow, my breath was ragged, my muscles screamed in protest. My heart pounded in my chest, a primal drumbeat urging me forward. The tension was palpable, an unspoken battle of wills as we danced to the music made by our weapons.

It was thrilling. Never before had life been so sweet, so vital.

I thrust for Hector's throat. Leaning back, he made to block with his shield, as I knew he would. Spinning left, I swung the spear's butt end in a vicious blow to his left knee. It was there, exposed, ready for shattering. I was certain I had him.

That was when Hector did something I could not credit. Off-balance, his weight going the wrong way, he threw himself into the air as an acrobat might, spinning like a hurled spear. For three beats of my hammering heart he twisted in the air, feet towards me, head towards Troy, my blow hissing the air where his leg had been.

Any other man would have fallen in a heap. But somehow Hector's foot found the earth with surety, and suddenly he was upright again.

I stood immobile for a moment, as did he, both awestruck. I could see the delight in his features at having achieved something impossible. The thought flickered into my head, *I wonder if Achilles could do that.*

The moment ended. Hector attacked, plunging me back in the thick of the fight.

At least, my body was fighting. My mind, however, was no longer in the instant. Recalling Achilles' warning against chasing glory, a vicious seed of doubt planted itself in the fertile land of my imagination.

You have gone too far. You have reached beyond your grasp. You have wanted more than you deserve.

No. I denied any fear that clouded my purpose. I tried to tear it out, keep it from taking root. I was Patrocles. I was relentless, unyielding, a fire that refused to be extinguished.

Yet the saucy doubt persisted. *You have gone too far. You have wanted what you should not.*

At the end of a particularly vicious flurry of blows, Hector and I staggered apart. Out of distance, panting for breath, we hurled insults in place of blows.

Hector began. "What's the matter—Patrocles? Weary already?"

"With laughter!" I retorted. "You make a—fine acrobat, Hector. But I've seen—roosters with better fighting skills."

"Whereas I applaud yours! Still, little wonder the—shadow of Achilles can mirror his movements. I just didn't know shadows—could wear armor!"

"This shadow is cast by great Apollo to make you a shade!"

"Has Apollo made Achilles ill, then, that he lets another wear his armor? Sick at heart, perhaps, that he hitched his star to be dragged in the dirt behind Agamemnon's chariot!"

That hit too close to home. "Now, by Apollo, I swear it will be you, Hector, dragged behind Achilles' chariot, with my name on your dying lips!"

HECTOR

THE words struck me like a thunderbolt. An invisible hand clasped my heart. Time stood still as every hair on my body stood upon end.

My senses filled with the flashes that had plagued me all through this long day. Only now they came together, like the pieces of a mosaic. In themselves, they had small meaning. But taken together, they crafted a story of death.

I gasped as a wickedly sharp bronze point thrust through the tender flesh of my neck. My body went limp. The bellows of my lungs ceased to work. Unable to draw breath, I looked down and watched my blood spurt over my stolen, star-filled armor. Filled with bitter resignation, I stared along the haft of an ash spear, past gleaming lacquered armor, into eyes so green they seemed to glow.

Colder than death, the eyes held no forgiveness.

The spear was torn free, and I fell. Ears ringing with Andromache's howls and my name being called, I felt the scratch of rope binding my ankles. Just as darkness closed in, I felt the jolt of the rope going taut, but I was spared the sensation of being dragged behind the golden chariot. Spared, by Charon's icy embrace.

I couldn't comprehend what was happening to me. I felt at once both separate and united with all of creation. A moment of beauty and terror in equal measure. Was this death? No, the hammer of my heart struck its anvil in rapid beats. Breath heaved, muscles ached. I blinked, and sight was restored. All my senses were alive—as was I.

Before I could even attempt to make sense of it, Patrocles was upon me with his long war spear. I defended myself instinctively, shaking off the shadow that had crossed my soul.

MENELAUS

WE made a full circle around Achilles and Hector. I could not hear their voices over the din, but it hardly mattered. Insults were traditional, and rarely taken to heart. Soon enough they were at it again, Achilles attacking with ferocious skill, catching Hector back-footed.

Agamemnon was correct. Achilles was about to win this war. It was up to me to prevent that.

All around, men on both sides watched the duel unfold. This clash of heroes had been avoided for nine years, because, I suspected, no one wanted to know which would prevail. Now that it was here, all eyes were drawn to it.

Yet I did not sense the awe such a moment should inspire. As the two figures engaged there on the field before Troy, as Apollo drove his chariot slowly westwards toward the horizon, as the most dangerous day of the war took its toll on all involved, the duel felt—hollow. A cheap imitation. Like a cheap sword that does not chime as it strikes a shield. It was not what we thought it would be.

Which made my plan all the more appealing. Circling the combatants in my chariot, I craned around for the right man. A Trojan warrior, with a spear, and a decent reputation.

As if summoned, the dancing girl in warrior clothes came into view. Determined to fight me, Euphorbus was chasing my chariot afoot. He had clearly set his heart on ending the war by ending me. After all, with me dead, Helen had no husband to whom she must be returned.

I hesitated. To reach my aim, I had to risk my life. But so be it. I felt no uncertainty. Live or die, Agamemnon could never again disrespect me to my face.

Timing was vital. First, the bait. I made another hand gesture at Euphorbus, jerking my fist sideways and using my mouth and tongue in conjunction so that I appeared to be sucking a cock. Childish, it was enough to make him redouble his pace.

"Slow down," I said over my shoulder. My charioteer obeyed, allowing Euphorbus to gain ground. Hacking at other Trojans, I pretended not to notice his approach, and feigned surprise as he leapt aboard my chariot. He tried to run his short throwing-spear through my shoulder, and was surprised when I parried the thrust with my sword. My free hand gripped his spear haft hard, and we struggled.

My charioteer was ready to come to my aid, but I shouted, "Keep going!"

Locked in struggle with Euphorbus, my eyes flew to the great combatants, gold versus azure, their glittering helms reflecting Apollo's descending beams as they stabbed and dodged, cut and blocked, elbowed and twisted away.

So focused was I on picking my moment that I nearly lost all. Euphorbus dropped one hand from his spear to draw a dagger, and I barely dodged his upswing aimed at my throat.

Blocking his downward thrust with my sword, I recognized my moment. Achilles ducked, and for a split second, the flutter of a fly's wings, his back was turned.

My chariot was still moving. So was he. Another second and the chance would be gone.

Now, or never.

Calling upon all my strength, I wrenched Euphorbus' throwing spear clear of his grip, then plunged forward, dragging him with me even as I released it. For all the world, it appeared as if he had hurled the weapon.

The next instant I stabbed upwards with my sword, directly through Euphorbus' neck, showering me in his blood.

I didn't bother to even look at his death. My eyes were on the dead man's spear, thrown by my own hand. It traveled straight and true a few short feet—

—planting itself in the gap in Achilles' armor.

PATROCLES

A vengeful god had smited me. That was how it felt. Pain erupted through my body, shattering my nerves, overwhelming me. My back arched, my arms flew wide. Gasping for air, I turned my head to see a Trojan spear sticking out of my back. I reached for it, which only sent a firestorm of pain through the nerves in my arms and back.

To the watching Achaeans, Achilles had been struck down. Around me, I heard gasps of shock, groans, even wails. The glorious sounds of war faded, replaced by a terrible calm. Men stopped fighting. Some even dropped their arms.

The Myrmidons knew who it was under the armor, but that did nothing to lessen their grief. For they had loved me. Loved me enough to follow me into glory.

Achilles had been right. As I knew his soul, he knew mine. Deep down, in a place I refused to admit existed, I had craved glory. He had warned me not to chase it. I had failed to listen.

Desires that deep, when unburied, consume.

Still, for one brilliant moment, glory had been mine. And glory, once gained, is eternal.

I staggered forward, vision blurring. Fumbling at the spear lodged between my shoulders, I somehow released a clasp and felt the golden breastplate come free. The embossed stars fell to the trampled earth. A perfect symbol of my hopes.

I fell into Hector's sweating arms, face pressed against a breast made of stone, now cracked and flawed. I dragged my eyes up to look into the Trojan prince's horrified eyes.

Then I watched his horror fade, replaced by a cold determination.

Achilles, forgive me. I never meant to trap you so. All I ever wanted was your love and respect.

Now I see I wanted it too much.

HECTOR

FOOLS say life is long. Yet momentous events often hinge upon a decision lasting no longer than the flap of a woodpecker's wings.

The moment the spear landed, my enraged soul traced its source to dead Euphorbus, falling from the back of Menelaus' chariot. An accident, then. A spear in the back of a duelist was beneath any Trojan.

Suddenly Patrocles was in my arms, looking up at me with a question.

A question whose answer would determine the war.

I could have taken the wounded Patrocles prisoner. He might

conceivably survive a spear in the back. If so, he could be ransomed back to Achilles, perhaps in return for the Myrmidons abandoning Agamemnon's cause.

But his wound was gushing blood, and already his face was pale. Most likely he would die, and the eventual demise of Patrocles within Troy's walls would do us no credit, nor no material good.

Whereas the death of Achilles on the battlefield, here and now, could reverse the winds of war, blowing us all back into the Achaean camp to finish what we had begun.

If it were to be done, it could not be accidental, nor lingering. To work, his death had to be deliberate, and immediate.

Seeing the answer in my eyes, Patrocles rebelled, trying to pull away. Yanking his helmeted head close, I whispered, "What I do, I do for Troy."

Then I stepped back, letting Patrocles fall to his knees before me. Dropping my sword and shield, I hefted his spear. I felt the weight of thousands of eyes upon my shoulders, carrying a decade of expectation, of hope, of rage, of dread.

Patrocles locked eyes with me. In desperate pain, he gasped, "You did not—defeat me. This is—Apollo's victory. And Achilles—will make you pay."

I said nothing as I rammed the spear clean through the unprotected chest of Patrocles.

MENELAUS

I watched the stabbing of Achilles with a delight I dared not show. How my brother would sing my praises! After this, he would be unable to deny me my due! I had removed forever the one man who dared challenge his authority.

It could never be known, of course. The rest of the world had to think me the righteous slayer of the villain who stabbed Achilles in the back. I, his murderer, would be hailed as his avenger.

But Agamemnon would know. As would I.

PATROCLES

ACHILLES. I regret only the price my death will force you to pay. Forgive me.

HECTOR

LEAVING the body speared, I reached for the golden breastplate.

And paused.

The stars. This was the armor I would die in.

I wavered. As surely as I knew my name, I knew that touching it would seal my fate. If I reached for the stars, I would fall.

Yet the chance was too good to miss. My gambit might yet succeed. Clutching the armor, I hefted it high over my head.

In answer, my soldiers shouted my name. "Hec-tor! Hec-tor!" All around me it grew, echoing back from Troy's walls, where jubilant Trojans choked back their sobs of joy to shout my name as well.

To them, I was the greatest man alive. I had defeated Achilles.

But true soldiers knew it was not won from the man himself, but from an impostor. Worse, an impostor not bested by me, but by a blow to the back.

Stolen armor. Stolen honor. It was the choice I had made. In order to end the war.

Sick at heart, feeling death and dishonor swirling around me, I raised my voice. "To me, Trojans! To me! For Apollo!"

They swelled in response, forming up to return once again to the Achaean camp, this time to finish them.

That was when we heard the scream.

MENELAUS

STILL filled to overflowing with my triumph, my head was wrenched toward our camp by a cry like no other I had ever heard. The call of a soul that has lost itself. I thought I had understood loss when Helen was taken from me, when I wrenched open the door of her chamber and our daughter let out a wail to see her mother gone. But I had not understood grief until I heard that terrible cry.

There, on the throsmos, stood—

Achilles.

Blinking, I squinted again at the impossible sight. Yet there was no mistaking him. Achilles stood there, across the Plain of Troy. In a plain tunic, carelessly belted with a cord, he cut a more menacing figure than any blood-soaked soldier bedecked with spears and spikes.

What is this magic? Trying to make sense of what was happening, I looked back to the dead figure at Hector's feet. The helmet was still in place, but the shape of the chest, the length of the arm, showed me what I should have seen before.

Patrocles.

Their duel now made sense. I even recalled Nestor being deputed to tell the young man of the plan to swap armor. I had simply never imagined Achilles would do such a thing.

Achilles, who now began to run across the Plain at full speed, unarmed and unarmored. How could he be armored, when his famous golden breastplate and helm were held by Hector?

He plucked a spear from the ground without looking at it. The weapon seemed summoned to his hand.

Achilles was coming to have his revenge. Woe betide any who stood in his path.

Worse, damned be he who had shed the blood of Patrocles.

In that moment I realized no one could ever know my part in this day's fighting. Not even Agamemnon. No one, ever.

For Achilles was about to bring death to Troy.

HECTOR

I watched Achilles come with true despair. Victory had been within my grasp. Thinking him dead, all the sea-dogs would have broken. We could have brought fire to their remaining ships, then offered them terms for surrender. It could have all ended.

Now the spell was broken, replaced by something far more terrible. How many men, on both sides, thought this was Achilles reborn, resurrected by his mad mother who had tried to make him immortal by drowning him?

Wonder and amazement held every man on the battlefield as Achilles crossed the plain. I was among them, watching this thing, this perfect instrument of war, come to carve his song on our bones.

On my bones.

My death had stalked my mind all morning. Now it came for me as Achilles reached the river. He did not slow. I saw my half-brother Lycaon wade bravely back in to face him, only to be speared in the belly. Lycaon fell to his knees and, though I could not hear his words, I saw him throw his hands wide in a plea for mercy.

Achilles pulled a sword from the water and cut off Lycaon's head.

More men rushed in, and from the bank one warrior threw spears from each hand. Achilles beat them aside with the same blows that ended the lives of his nearest enemies. Then he came for the warrior, who managed to block Achilles' attack three times before spilling his guts to the fourth sword stroke.

Bodies were piling up in the river. Stunned, only now did the Achaeans begin to fight alongside their hero. Newly heartened, they meant to slaughter us.

I started forward, only to feel several hands restraining me. I fought them, shouting, "Let me go!"

"You can't go back there!" cried Paris.

I struggled to free myself from their preserving grasp. "I have to face him!"

"Then do so when you are as fresh as he!" shouted Hellenus in my ear. "He hasn't been fighting since dawn!"

"It's me he wants!"

"Yes! So it's you we must protect!"

My own strategy. To win, deny your enemy his objectives.

Every fiber of my being desired to wade into that river and face Achilles, come what come may. But I was Hector, and Hector never gave in to his desires.

Desire, and denial.

I gave up struggling and ordered a retreat to Troy's walls.

Behind us, Achilles incarnadined the Scamander with blood.

MENELAUS

TERRIFIED, I watched as Achilles threatened to do that which my brother most feared—win the war single-handed. I had sworn to my brother that I would not allow such a thing to happen. But he seemed unstoppable, soaked to his shoulders in Trojan blood.

By now the exhausted Ajax had come, and Nestor with him. Under their eyes, how could I possibly stop Achilles?

It turns out that I did not need to stop him. He might have indeed won the war that day, had victory been his goal. Instead he carved out a passage to where lay the meat that had once been Patrocles, and there simply stopped. Had Paris still been on the field, he could have ended the life of the unprotected Achilles with an arrow there and then.

As Achilles stopped, so too did the rest of our soldiers. Nestor urged them on, but without Achilles at their head, they fell to looting, leaving the Trojans to flee unpursued to the safety of their precious walls.

Achilles did not care about his foes' flight. His whole world had shrunk to the lifeless lover before him. He sank to his knees, shoulders slumped, just staring. When Ajax came close, reaching out a comforting hand, Achilles snarled and almost removed that appendage with his sword.

I remained well out of his reach, but I heard Ajax say, "Let's take him back. Let's take Patrocles back to your ships. I'll carry him."

"No." Achilles' voice was hollow, his vocal cords ragged. "I will."

Tenderly, Achilles gathered Patrocles in his arms and carried him all the long way back to our camp. We followed him like lambs, leaving the Trojans to watch as we ceased to fight in order to mourn one man.

A man dead by my hand.

That thought troubled me over the ensuing hour. My bowels turned to water at the very notion of Achilles discovering my deed. Almost as bad was the thought of Agamemnon learning what I had done, and its effect. I had managed to do the one thing he wanted to avoid—I had brought Achilles back into the war.

Avoiding my brother, I distracted myself by overseeing repairs to our burnt ships, seeing which could be salvaged.

Odysseus was there ahead of me, his tunic tied at his waist, his bandaged ribs visible for all. Letting men know he'd been wounded and still found work to do. In his hands, everything had a purpose.

I felt little love for him at the moment. It had been his genius notion for us to trade armor. If not for that, I would not now be dreading some witness coming forward to declare what I had done.

The Ithacan asked me what had happened, so I told my version of the event, noting that I had taken the life of the man whose spear had landed in Patrocles' back.

"Which brought Achilles roaring out of his tents. It's funny—I mean, not funny ha-ha, but ironic."

"What's that?"

"The fallacy of sunk costs. A thing only has value because we say it does. Be it gold, or jewels, or spices, or art. We create the value by showing how much we're willing to give for it. This whole war in a nutshell—each death justifying the next, until there is no one left alive."

"What are you talking about?" I demanded.

"Nothing of use to you," said Odysseus, not unkindly. "Listen, we must talk. Your brother is with the surgeon. Placing maggots in the wound to keep him from losing the arm."

I shivered with disgust, despite understanding that maggots only ate rotting flesh. Odysseus looked tempted to make a jest, doubtless about the vile creatures not knowing where to stop eating, but he restrained himself. I said, "Achilles is with Patrocles' body?"

"He is. There will be a funeral later tonight. We must all attend. First, there is a matter I must discuss with you. Come, walk with me to the shore, where the wind will blow our words away."

My innards squirmed. Did he know? Had someone told him what I had done?

Stopping where the sand was still damp from the outgoing tide, he nodded at the red horizon. "The sun is almost down on this, the costliest day of the war, for both sides. Fitting, in its way. Apollo has always been on Troy's side, so it was on his day that we came closest to defeat. Now, I don't know if Zeus intervened, or Ares, or whoever. We'll pray to all of them. But gods are fickle. Tomorrow they may turn against us. As it is, we survived today only through chance. Before today we won every engagement, yet we sit on the cusp of defeat. It isn't enough for a man to win. His foe has to lose. For victory, a foe has to be one of two things—dead, or broken. By broken, I mean admit they've lost. They need to submit.

"It's something your brother understands. From the moment Agamemnon drove his blade into his daughter's bosom, I've known that he understands what it takes to win. He showed the world he was willing to do anything—anything at all—to achieve victory. That he was willing to give up what he loved most. That he was willing to lose personally, so that the cause could win."

I tried not to think of my niece. A sweet soul, she had died for a war waged in my name. Sad, but if she was the price of my honor, I wasn't going to protest her death.

"Unfortunately, we have two leaders treating each other like foes. Agamemnon has achieved a victory over his rival by removing the thing Achilles wants. Achilles did the same by refusing to fight, therefore denying Agamemnon victory."

Odysseus checked over his shoulder before continuing. "The death of Patrocles, while a tragedy—who didn't like him?—is the best thing that could have happened for our cause. And if you tell Achilles I said that, I'll tell him the words belong to Agamemnon."

"What are you driving at, Odysseus?"

"I'm saying, my friend, that if we are to end this bloody mindless rutted-wheel of a war, everyone needs to lose something. With Achilles, that has already happened. He has two choices now. Either sail home, or seek revenge. We must ensure that he stays to call for Hector's blood tomorrow. Hector is the hope of his people. Remove him, remove their hope. I think even Priam would break if he lost his heir. Now, Achilles' rage is greater than his pride. But, just to be on the safe side, we must give his pride a sop, a fig leaf, the smallest concession."

"You mean Briseis."

"I mean Briseis," agreed Odysseus. "It would look like an act of kindness, of camaraderie."

"Agamemnon won't do it."

"Oh, I think there is a compelling argument that will move Agamemnon."

"Then why don't you use it?"

"Because it must come from you, King Menelaus. It can only come from you."

I listened, and flushed with shame and humility as he explained. Because of course Odysseus was correct. It was the obvious argument.

Back in the commander's tent, his wound bandaged, my brother was in a thoughtful mood. To my surprise, he still eschewed wine, even to dull his pain. I recounted the battle, omitting the part to do with me, and then laid out exactly what Odysseus proposed.

Unaccountably, Agamemnon was agreeable. Only later did I realize it was because something had been stolen from Achilles, something that hurt him deeply. Agamemnon, who had begun this war with a similar wound, however self-inflicted, took pleasure at the thought of Achilles' pain. They were now even.

The same proposal had been put to Achilles by Nestor. Bereft,

Achilles had agreed. So it was that I escorted Briseis to the Myrmidon encampment.

As we walked I studied her, this scrag of a slave girl who had almost cost us the war. She was nothing special to look at. I could see no value in her. But Achilles and Agamemnon had made this pathetic, prideful little bint the most valuable woman in our camp. By Odysseus' thinking, because Achilles valued her, she was priceless.

What did that make Helen? For her a thousand ships set sail, bristling with spears. For her, my brother had sacrificed his own daughter. For her, two armies had fought for a decade. By this measure, Helen was the most valuable woman in all of history. And she was *mine.*

Patrocles was laid out on a bier made of spears and planks from his ship. All the kings save Agamemnon were present, with gifts to honor the man who had saved the Achaean fleet.

Achilles knelt, holding Patrocles' lifeless hand. When he saw Briseis, he did not react. She crossed to his side, and knelt beside him. Together they looked upon the body of Patrocles. That was when I heard her speak for the first—and last—time. "My love, your friend is dead."

Like a lost child, Achilles said, "He was just here."

"Now, he is only thought." She took both Achilles and Patrocles' hands in her own. "Of all men on this earth, he was dearest to me. For, more than any other man, he showed me kindness. When my husband and brothers were killed, he took me in hand and told me not to weep, for I was to marry you. You, who slew my husband. He was so happy for me that my tears refused to come. He said he envied me, for you were the greatest man on this earth, and I would bask all my days in the light of your sun. Even when he was forced to escort me to the envious Agamemnon, he was kind to me. I love you, my lord. But I should not love you had he not shown me you were worthy of such love. I will mourn him forever. More than any man, he was kind to me."

Achilles wept. When at last he could find breath, he faced her, still upon his knees, and traced the line of her face with a tender finger. "You must go."

"So I am told. But I wish I could stay. You should meet your child."

I jolted with surprise. No wonder Achilles had wanted her back!

But he did not seem to want her now. "It has been agreed. Neither of us shall have you. It is the price. The price of pride."

"You have paid too much already."

He wept then, his forehead against hers. "Make sure no one else dies for my pride." Then, kissing her with those thin lips of his, he gestured for her to be taken away. Out of the camp, and out of all our lives.

It had been the argument Odysseus had given me, the one Agamemnon could not deny. Here we were, waging a war over a woman taken from her rightful master. He could not, in good conscience, do the same. Even so, we all knew Agamemnon would never return the girl to Achilles. So clever Odysseus proposed she be sent away. Achilles wanted the girl. Agamemnon wanted the girl. Would it be enough if no one possessed her?

Achilles had almost cost us the war, had lost his best friend, his lover, and dozens of other brave heroes, all for her. And now he was letting her go.

So in the end, Briseis received what no one else had: freedom. Which was what Helen claimed to want above all else.

I was struggling with these thoughts when I heard Achilles speak my name. "Menelaus."

I stepped nervously forward. "I'm here."

Rising, Achilles plucked a spear from the earth. "I heard what you did."

My legs turned to water. How had he heard?

Slowly he approached me, spear held across his body. "You took something from me."

Suddenly dry, my mouth produced no sound as he came to a halt before me.

"You killed the man who felled him. You took the first part of my revenge. I am furious that he did not die at my hand. Yet I appreciate your act. For that, I thank you, and present you with this. I know he would want you to have it." And he passed me Patrocles' spear.

"Thank you," I managed to gasp as I took the spear from his grip. I nearly dropped it.

"I need new armor." Glancing down, Achilles saw Sarpedon's armor, laid out at Patrocles' feet to honor the man who took it. The defeated Lycian king's lacquered armor gleamed with a prism of colors under the lamplight. He plucked it up. "This will do."

Achilles looked around the tent, fixing each of us with his steady glare. "One of his murderers is dead. Tomorrow, I shall be avenged upon Hector."

I stood there, filled with relief that I had not been found out. Yet there was a gnawing pit inside my soul that writhed with shame.

Holding the spear of the good man I had wrongly killed, I understood that I would have to carry it with me forever. A reminder of what I had done.

I deserved such insult.

HECTOR

FROM high upon Troy's ramparts, Andromache found me watching the sun set on the longest day I had ever endured.

Rather than speak, she wrapped her arms about me, nestling her head against my chest.

"Where is Astyanax?" I asked.

"With your mother."

"Good." Hugging her close, I rested my chin on her head. "How are things in the palace?"

"Emotions are high. The temptation to celebrate is tempered by the losses, and—"

"And the threat of Achilles' wrath," I finished for her.

She stepped back, and I released her so that she might look at me. "You need not face him."

I said nothing.

"You were injured today. There is no shame in refusing a duel when injured."

I shifted my gaze to the last crimson sliver of the sun, setting in the western sea.

"You nearly won the war today! That is more than enough to ask of you!"

"Nearly is not enough," I said.

Andromache bit her lip, fighting back the tears pooling in her eyes.

"Astyanax," I said, thinking of my son's name. It meant "high king." "I hope it comes true for him."

"Someday, I'm sure," Andromache said, pretending not to understand what I was saying. "But you will be the next high king."

I said nothing.

"Hector, you can defeat Achilles!"

I wanted to laugh. Not because I was joyful, but because it's what one does to break a tense moment. That, or else change the subject. "Do you know where Cassandra is?"

"Lurking, somewhere. Why?"

"I owe her an apology."

"For what?"

"For not understanding."

My whip-smart wife, who loved me so much it pained her, took my meaning at once. "You've had a vision."

I nodded. "Apollo's gift. On this, his day, I begged him to make me his vessel. He must have listened. As long as I did him honor, he was with me. But he showed me glimpses of how my fate would change if I wronged him . . . then I killed Patrocles."

"Was that not honorable?"

"It was wrong. I knew it was wrong, and I did it anyway. At the time, I thought it would inspire the men, reverse our fortunes. In that moment, Apollo left me. But not before revealing the consequences of my deed."

"Tell me." Such bravery. Even sensing the worst, she did not shy away from it.

I closed my eyes. Behind the veil of my eyelids, I saw it all again. The vision that had struck me when Patrocles had called down his curse upon me. I forced myself to watch it all. The fierce duel. My death at Achilles' hands. Him making good Patrocles' threat and dragging my body behind his chariot.

There was more. As Achilles turned the Scamander red with blood, I had seen it all again, and more. As my body was dragged around the city, Cassandra tore at her hair, Hellenus wept, Paris vomited, and Helen gazed on like a medusa, her stony glare offering no remorse.

I had seen my father, great Priam, haughty and arrogant, break. Then, darkness.

Would the Achaeans make him beg for my body? Would stony-faced Achilles spit on my father as he went on bended knee? Or would he mingle tears with Priam, as my father embraced my killer in arms that had never so embraced me? Would he do me the honor with my funeral rites that he had denied me in life?

Apollo had not shown me that. On his day, the bright god had only shown me my death.

Andromache did not need to hear the details. Answering her, I said only, "I will face Achilles. I will lose."

She clutched my hands in hers. "It is just one of your dark moods. Just your imagination!"

"Isn't that what we said to Cassandra?"

She flinched, then yanked my arms with surprising strength, bending me until our faces were scant inches apart. "Don't make it true by thinking it!"

I took her freckled face in both my hands. "Darling, I will fight with all that is in me. Do you think I want to leave you, leave our son, our family? Well, maybe Paris." We smiled at the weak humor. "Darling, in another time, we might have lived to be a hundred years old, with children and grandchildren and great-grandchildren. The glory of Troy could have lasted a thousand years." I laid my forehead against hers. "But when you see fate, fate sees you."

Andromache wept, clinging to me, while I watched night fall.

Tragedy comes from wanting something too much. The greater the desire, the more brutal the denial.

As it turned out, I was not the balanced, measured soul I always claimed to be. For I did want something too much. I had wanted to break the stalemate. I wanted to be the one who altered the course of the war, hasten it to its end. I had been willing to risk everything just to bring change. I had wanted Apollo's Day to be the lever with which I would move the world.

Be careful what you wish for, they say.

My gambit had reversed the winds in our sails. Thinking to take advantage of the division in the Achaean ranks to defeat them, what I had actually succeeded in doing was unite them. Achilles would not leave, not now, not where Patrocles' grave stood within sight of his killer. Injured, Agamemnon could now allow Achilles to lead the army without dishonor.

Apollo had composed his greatest ballad this day. It was a glorious song, and terrible. It sang of war and death. Of love and grief. Of desire, and denial.

Tomorrow, Apollo's chariot would drag the sun from its bed in the east to start a new day.

The song of war is not a song we are meant to survive. Yet it plays on. Its music never ends.

Only men end. And with them, their desires.

THE FIFTH SONG

THE BOW

by Libbie Hawker

He that fights fares no better than he that does not; coward and hero are held in equal honor, and death deals like measure to him who works and him who is idle.
Homer, the *Iliad*

PENTHESILEA

EVEN before she reached Troy, her song was one of mourning. She had followed the sun for days, for weeks, riding slowly on her gray mare through a world grayed by her sorrow. She had ridden that route before—ten years gone, a lifetime past—when, in a joyous train of women-warriors, she had followed her sister Hippolyte west, past the sunrise reach of the dark sea, down through the steep green mountains edged in mist to hot plains tufted in sere yellow grass. And on and on to the city of Troy, to its golden shore, where a ship had waited to carry them farther still, to Sparta.

Then, riding behind Hippolyte, Penthesilea had been happy. They all had been as happy as girls dancing at a wedding—they *were* going to a wedding, the wedding of the king of Ithaca to a cousin of Zeus-born Helen of Sparta. By day, the young women that had comprised Hippolyte's honor escort had ranged out over that vast plain, racing their horses under the high blue dome of the sky. By night, they had sparred with their spears in the starlight and told bawdy jokes around the cook-fire. Penthesilea had never felt so free before.

She had begged her parents, the leaders of their tribe, to allow her to accompany Hippolyte on her mission of goodwill to Sparta. In truth, she had been too young to make the trip. She had not yet killed her first enemy in battle, and so she was not a warrior, not yet fit to represent the dignity of their Cimmerian tribe. But Hippolyte had argued for her—splendid, straight-backed, sharp-eyed Hippolyte, who by Penthesilea's age had already killed three warriors, and who could coax any favor from their parents' hearts.

"Penthesilea can oil my spear for me," Hippolyte had said, throwing an arm around her younger sister in a way that suggested she would take the girl with her whether their parents agreed or not. "Besides," she added, off-handed and cool, "it's only some damned Achaean wedding. What trouble can my little sister make at a wedding?"

All those days, as Hippolyte's party had ranged out over the baked, golden plain, laughing and carrying on like colts in a springtime meadow, Hippolyte herself, the gift-bearer, the ambassador, had maintained a straight-backed dignity, a watchful aloofness that suited their lineage. But whenever Penthesilea had caught her sister's gaze, Hippolyte gave her a secret smile, and her dark eyes shone.

Now, aching with weariness, though she had never pushed her horse faster than a trot, Penthesilea remembered the brightness of the world ten years past and shuddered. Then, these plains had been golden and blue, and tiny birds had skimmed in front of their horses as if wishing to race them at a gallop. Every time those birds would pivot on their small, sharp wings, their feathers would catch the sun and their bodies would glint with a sudden flash of green, malachite beads scattered over the dazzling plain. There were no birds now, no precious beads, no rush of wind in her hair. There was only the heavy drone of unseen insects in the grass, the steady plodding of hooves, a weight like a broken brick in her heart. And all the color was gone from the gray, gray world.

Penthesilea didn't notice that her horse had begun to climb a hill, but soon enough the mare's leisurely pace became a labor, tearing Penthesilea's thoughts away from the dark and bitter past.

She reined in on the crest and regarded the city of Troy in dull resignation. The slope fell away again below the gray mare's hooves, a gentle but inevitable stoop into yet more of that dry, hot expanse of knee-high grass. And another rise, edging more steeply to the west, to the foot of the long, pale wall that ringed the great city of Troy like a lazy snake. Even at a distance, Penthesilea could see the flat roofs of a thousand houses, dots of glaring sunlight floating above the black score-marks of streets and alleys. Troy itself climbed the eastern face of the hill, until, at the highest point of the stony bluff, an inner wall encircled the palaces of the rich and mighty, the temples of the gods, protective as a mother's arms. She could see the cool shade where the land dropped below the city's western wall, a scarp that faced the sea winds. Beyond Troy, the sea was a colorless shimmer in the unrelenting sun.

Penthesilea closed her eyes and breathed deep. Below the dry scent of baked earth and dying grass—the pervasive odor of the plain—she could smell the salt of the water and the faintest hint of spice from the city itself. Then the wind rushed at her more strongly, insistent, and Penthesilea noted the heavy, cloying stench of death in the air.

She had long since earned her place as a Cimmerian warrior; the smell of death was nothing new to her, nothing shocking. But it never failed to sicken her a little, to make her mouth flow with saliva and her stomach tense with wariness. She turned her head and spat into the grass. The taste of death was always foul; even now, when death and war were all she sought.

She squinted under her hand. The siege tents were obvious, the Achaean camp like a small city of its own across the plain from Troy, squatting beside the mouth of the river. There was no use trying to count the Achaean forces. On the edges of their sprawling camp, she could see tiny men like ants laboring around a nest, hauling wood from the stand of trees that still clung to the river's bank, building pyres to burn their dead.

So there had been a recent battle. Which side was growing more desperate, Penthesilea wondered. Was Troy fighting harder to break the grip of the siege, or was the pot of High King Agamemnon's fatal patience finally, after so many long years of leading this war, boiling over?

It makes no difference to me. If Troy falls or if it stands, my purpose will be satisfied. She tapped her mare's ribs with her heels, and the gray horse started down the long slope.

Before long, Penthesilea reached the pale track that curved under the city's walls, following the narrow bend around toward the great gates. She could see Achaean warriors on the plain, picking at the remains of a battle like vultures, scavenging what they could of weapons, provisions, armor spotted with old, dry blood. The men looked up from their grisly chores as she passed, shading their eyes to squint after her—these westerners were always transfixed by the sight of anyone on horseback, particularly a woman—but it was clear from her felt tunic, her pale trousers, and her long black braid that she was a Cimmerian, and therefore not party to this conflict.

Yet.

She spared hardly a glance for the Achaeans who straightened from the bodies of the dead. She paid no mind to their whispers of *Amazon.* She had far greater concerns than these men, than their scorn for her misunderstood people.

She proceeded along the narrow road toward the city's main gate, followed by whispers and stares. A few men trailed her on foot, curious and cautious. But no one accosted her until she reached the Scaean Gate.

The great square frame of the gate itself towered over the city's wall, its soaring lintel carved with a likeness of Poseidon. The dual doors were at least six times the height of a man, stout black wood strapped and studded with bronze, which had long since traded its glow for the patina of age. Two pillars of brilliant red flanked the gate, and high on the wall another rank of crimson pillars, the façade of some temple, peered over crenelated notches. The red of those pillars, stark and bloody, was the first color Penthesilea had seen since leaving her tribe.

A man shouted down from the wall. "Who are you, stranger?"

Penthesilea called back, spacing her words carefully so the man could understand. The Trojans, she knew, considered the Cimmerian accent thick and barbaric. "I have come from Scythia to speak to my cousin."

"And who is your cousin?"

She drew a deep breath, conscious of the few Achaean warriors milling far behind her, men clustering, increasingly curious. Her spear was strapped across her back, easy to draw if she was attacked, and her mounted vantage gave her superior reach on any Achaean sword. But they outnumbered her, and they had arrows.

She sent up a hasty prayer to the gods—if any gods still deigned to listen to one as cursed as she. *I must reach my cousin. If I am to restore my honor, I must reach her and swear to her service, or all is for naught.*

The shout came again from the top of the wall. "Who is your cousin?"

She could delay no longer. She swallowed hard and shouted back, "Helen."

There was silence on the wall for a long time. The gray mare swished its tail in the sun. Finally, with a clatter and a groan, the Scaean Gate edged open, and men with shields appeared. They formed a protected path for her, facing outward, short swords raised—though none of the Achaeans who lingered beyond the road's edge raised anything sharper than a curse.

Her chest expanding with relief, Penthesilea squeezed the mare with her legs and trotted through the Scaean Gate.

Penthesilea was made to wait for more than an hour in the courtyard of Troy's great palace. Long after her horse was led away to the stables—the famous Trojan stables, where, it was said, the best war horses in the world were trained—she sat, still and quiet, on a small limestone bench in the shade of a pillar. She watched the pillar's long shadow creep across the courtyard pavers, silently marking the passage of time.

Without her horse beneath her, Penthesilea felt small, diminished. The city of Troy was very large indeed—far grander than any town or encampment she had ever seen in Cimmerian lands. Yet despite its great size, despite the palpable weight of the palace and the huge stone wall, Troy held an atmosphere of quiet despair. There was no soft laughter of servants among the shadows. No men's voices drifted from high palace windows. In the far distance, from the direction of the red-pillared temple she had seen from the gate, Penthesilea could hear a faint din of rattles. Even that act of worship had an air of fatigue, the listless drag of exhaustion.

Penthesilea hadn't known what to expect of Troy. She had never been to the city before. Ten years prior, on that joyful ride with Hippolyte and her escort of warriors, they had passed the shining city on its grand hill and ridden straight for the shore. There they had boarded the ships that would carry them all to Sparta, to the wedding feast where Hippolyte was to present gifts to the king of Ithaca and his bride. Penthesilea had hated travel by boat, no matter how beautiful the sea and its islands were. Men were never made to rock upon the waves, and waves lacked the predictable rhythms of a horse's gait.

But horses cannot run on water. Huddled in her narrow band of shade, listening to the wan, distant chime of rattles in the temple, Penthesilea felt as much out of her element as a horse trying to canter over the wide, ever-moving sea.

Something prickled along her scalp, then crept down her spine. It was a sensation she knew well from battles and raids: the feeling of being watched. She looked up sharply, squinting at the bright glare of sunlight on stone. Across the courtyard, between two pillars, a woman stood alone, watching Penthesilea with an unreadable expression. She was darker than most Trojans—reason enough to stare, for few people as dark as she ever visited Cimmerian lands—and had the black, tightly curled hair of a Nubian. But she was dressed in the manner of a well-born Trojan woman, a tight bodice over a long, flowing skirt with intricate embroidery at its hem. The skirt had once been black but had faded to some sickly shade of darkness that was not quite gray. In places, where the woman's knees would have pressed it often against a stone floor, it was so worn that it seemed almost pale.

What kind of woman would go about the Trojan palace dressed in sorry rags? Penthesilea stared openly at her, counting her heartbeats until the woman turned abruptly and drifted away into the palace's shadowed depths.

"My lady."

Penthesilea jumped at the voice. The woman in the ragged skirt had so unnerved her that she hadn't heard the slave approaching. Inexcusable carelessness for a warrior of the steppes; Penthesilea's face heated as she rose.

"Princess Helen will see you now," the servant said and turned on her heel. Penthesilea followed her long, fluttering skirt into the cool halls of the palace. The woman moved with quiet efficiency, yet there was a tightness to her shoulders that Penthesilea couldn't help but notice. Nor did she miss the way the servant wrung her hands as she walked.

Something had gone desperately wrong in Troy. Have I come at the wrong time? Would the gods be that cruel to me—have I earned their ultimate scorn? Or have I come at the perfect time?

They reached a bronze-strapped door, and the servant pushed it open, stood aside to let Penthesilea in.

She blinked and swallowed hard at the sight of Helen's chambers. Save for minor differences in style—the lusher, bolder colors the Trojans favored, the more ornate decorative flourishes—she could have been staring back through time, ten years into the past, to see Helen in the women's quarters of the Spartan palace. A western woman's necessaries were strewn all around the room: the high square frame of a loom, a patterned cloth abandoned halfway up its taut warp threads. A couch for lazing. A small table with a polished mirror made from Aegyptian electrum. A handful of women scattered around the room, occupied by the tasks that western women found so compelling: dropping their spindles to whirl at the ends of their fine woolen threads, whispering, staring morosely at nothing.

Helen stood in the middle of her chamber, slender and elegant and golden, unmarked by ten years' passage. She dressed like a Trojan woman; that was the only difference in her, the only change Penthesilea could discern. Helen's lovely face even held an expression of faint dissatisfaction, a dull surprise as if she, too, was startled to find this chamber so familiar.

The door shut behind Penthesilea. She bent before the daughter of Zeus, lowering her gaze to the floor.

"I remember you," Helen said. Her low, perfectly controlled voice filled the chamber, though it was not loud.

Penthesilea straightened, met Helen's clear, gray gaze. "Ten years ago, I came bearing gifts for your cousin Penelope when she married the king of Ithaca."

"Yes." Helen's mouth curved slightly, a tiny smile. "You played with my daughter, Hermione. You showed her how to hold a spear."

Penthesilea opened her mouth, ready to make some polite but meaningless reply. Then she saw the shadow of pain pass over Helen's face. It was fleeting and small and quickly banished. But it had been real. She nodded instead of speaking.

Helen turned, gestured toward her two couches with an unconscious grace. She sat, watched Penthesilea stumble awkwardly toward the other couch. "Remind me: your name."

"Penthesilea, Lady."

"Of course. But it has been so long since I've seen you. A cousin, am I correct?" She tipped her golden head to the side. "At least, according to Cimmerian beliefs."

Penthesilea's heart leaped in her chest. Had she ridden all this way for nothing? If Helen didn't accept her, didn't believe that they were kin, then her last hope for redemption was lost.

"A cousin," Penthesilea said, a touch more insistently than she'd intended. "All the world knows that you are Zeus' daughter, and many generations ago he sired my line, too."

Helen's smile was cool, amused. "What, then, can I do for you, Cousin? Why come to Troy, now of all days?"

Penthesilea breathed deeply, steadying herself, as she breathed in battle to steady her spear arm. "I have come to serve you. To pledge myself to you as your guardian and warrior."

The soft whispers from Helen's companions vanished into silence. Even the faint hiss of thread through the spinning women's fingers stopped. Penthesilea could feel many eyes upon her now, but she did not break Helen's steady gray stare.

"Why would I need another warrior?" Helen finally asked. "I have warriors inside Troy's walls and outside, too—all of them fighting for me."

The words should have been a boast. Penthesilea had no doubt that her golden cousin had intended bravado. But Helen spoiled the effect by swallowing—that long, smooth swan's neck tensed, and for just a moment, and between two beats of her heart, Penthesilea could read something blunt and bitter in Helen's face. It was not regret—not quite. It was the dullness of exhaustion, the helpless despair of a woman who had long since grown tired of her circumstances.

Penthesilea gave an uncomfortable shrug. "This is war, Lady. Who cannot use another good fighter when the world is all blood and fire?"

One of the other women, leaning against the window frame with her arms folded tightly around her body, muttered so softly she nearly went unheard. "Nearly ten years of war." Penthesilea glanced at her, trying to place that small freckled face—she, too, had been at the wedding in Sparta; what was her name? The woman continued to stare out the window; the beam of sunlight in which she stood picked out the freckles on her pale cheeks and sharp nose and set a warm glow flaring through her nut-brown hair. But her eyes were swollen and red from many hours of weeping.

Penthesilea knew what it was to cry that way, to pour out a river of tears so deep and fast it choked off breath but was still not deep enough to drown sorrow. She stared at the freckled woman, her stomach tightening with a new anxiety. Something had indeed gone amiss in Troy—something still more terrible than a near decade of war.

Finally, she turned back to Helen. "Let me fight for you, Lady, daughter of Zeus." If she served her family loyally, then the worst of her wrongs would be undone—or so Penthesilea prayed.

Everyone in her tribe had told Penthesilea it wasn't her fault. Even while her mother and father and her other sisters mourned, smearing ashes on their faces and eating black dirt from their trembling hands, still they insisted it was an accident, the kind of misfortune that could have befallen any warrior.

But their insistence had been no comfort to Penthesilea. She couldn't stop herself from reliving that terrible moment when, in the midst of their raid, she had flung her spear toward an enemy—and some unseen force, the wind or the whim of a cruel god—had taken the weapon on another course. Even when she rode out of her tribe's encampment forever, her muscles and bones remembered again and again the feel of the throw, the shaft of her spear gliding confidently from her hand. And the cold that seized her heart when the throw went awry and her own spear buried itself in Hippolyte's straight, proud back.

The sound of Hippolyte's dying scream had followed Penthesilea down the mountains and over the dry, hot plain. It seemed to hang even now in the rafters of Helen's chamber. She could feel the scream vibrating with her pulse, hear it rushing in her ears.

I killed my sister. It won't matter to the gods that it was an accident. It doesn't matter to me. I killed her, and if I do not restore my honor, then I will never see Hippolyte in the afterlife. I will never have the chance to beg her forgiveness.

"Please, Lady." Penthesilea hated to beg, but she would do what she must for the sake of honor. And service to her family was the last honor she could hope to claim. "Let me be your warrior."

Helen's expectant silence stretched on. Penthesilea pressed her lips together to stop them from trembling and cast about for something more to say. But the small, freckled woman who stood beside the window, wrapped in her own misery, gave a sudden gasp, and Helen turned to regard her.

"Andromache?"

The other made no reply. Helen stood smoothly and glided to her side. She, too, looked out the window, then clicked her tongue in disgust. "So the black beetle is creeping through the garden today."

Penthesilea went to the window, too, though she had not been asked to join her cousin. Outside, the sun was hot on the well-groomed squares of faded flowers and bristling herbs, the paths of crushed white limestone that led from one half-dried patch to another. A figure moved out from behind a scraggly laurel tree, drifting with no obvious aim. Penthesilea sucked in a startled breath: it was the dark woman in the ragged black dress.

The dark one stooped, examined some half-dead stick of a plant, and drifted to another garden bed. A young man entered the garden, too, his clothing impeccably clean and perfectly arranged. He called out a greeting to the woman in the garden—the salutation was ignored. Then he approached, holding out a dipper dripping with water, a friendly offering in the afternoon heat. Still, the woman paid him no mind.

"Coroebus of Phrygia," Helen said wryly. "He thinks he's going to make Cassandra his wife. It doesn't matter how many times that wretched creature looks right through him; Coroebus keeps trying."

The finely dressed young man stood poised and hopeful for a moment longer. Then, as Princess Cassandra turned away to pluck at the leaves of a laurel tree, he flung the water into the garden bed and marched away in defeat.

Helen's small laugh barely stirred the air. "I wonder. Is it love that's blind, or madness?"

"Madness?" Red-eyed Andromache's voice was dull. "Cassandra saw this all and tried to warn us, and yet no one listened. Are you certain she's the one who's mad?"

"No one *should* listen to that creature," Helen muttered. "She scratched my face and tore out my hair, the wild bitch."

"And she told us all to send you away." Andromache rounded on Helen, dullness burning up in a flare of anger. "She said you would bring us nothing but war—*death.* She was right."

"Go," Helen said shortly.

Andromache stepped closer to the golden beauty. The rage in her eyes was so terrible that Penthesilea stepped back. Andromache motioned abruptly to one of the slaves lingering along the opposite wall; the woman rushed forward, and Penthesilea could see that she carried a child in her arms. Andromache took the child and held it close—like a shield, Penthesilea thought, or like a token of hard-won victory.

"You do not order me about," Andromache said quietly to Helen. "If not for the death and destruction you brought, I would be queen of Troy. You do not order me."

"All the same," Helen said levelly, "go. You've stirred my anger enough that I might strike you. I shouldn't like to do that."

Andromache's eyes narrowed. Her child made a grizzling sound, a growl to reflect his mother's rage. "It's you who should be struck. And struck down. If the gods had any mercy at all, they never would have sent you to doom us."

Helen held herself in icy stillness, and Andromache stormed past her, out the chamber door, which she slammed hard in her wake. Penthesilea expected Helen to say something unkind now that Andromache was not there to defend herself. Instead, Helen sighed.

"Poor thing. It's only grief that makes her forget her courtesy."

"Grief? Who has she lost?"

"Her husband, Prince Hector—King Priam's heir, the future king of Troy. Just a month ago, he was struck down by Achilles, that cruel madman the Achaeans so love, the beast on whom they hang their hopes."

Penthesilea raised her brows. It was strange to hear Helen, an Achaean herself, speak of her own people as if they were as foreign as Aegyptians. Perhaps she believed she truly was a Trojan now.

"I confess I didn't think Hector could be killed," Helen said quietly. "For so many years, he was our champion, our shining hero. With him to inspire our men, we knew Troy would stand forever. And like that"—she snapped her delicate white fingers—"he was done. How can a hero be killed so easily?"

Penthesilea, of all people, knew how little death cared for the glory of those it claimed. If death stayed its cold hand and spared heroes, Hippolyte would still be alive. She would still raid across the wide steppes, would even now be teaching her young daughters how to hold a spear.

Helen folded her arms around her slender body, just as Andromache had done, and gazed out into the garden. Cassandra, her faded dress like the feathers of some haggard crow, stooped and plucked up a green sprig from one of the herbal beds. She held it to her pretty nose, inhaled, then let the sprig fall to the garden path.

"So many years," Helen said softly. "And in all that time, I never doubted, never feared. But now Hector is gone—Hector, of all men. And for the first time, I . . ."

She didn't complete the dark thought, but Penthesilea heard her words all the same: *Now I fear Troy will fall.*

Penthesilea tore her eyes from Cassandra, eerily compelling in her faded garb. Instead, she studied Helen's face in profile, the pale, delicate skin flawless in the sunlight, the gray stare steady and calculating—and also tired.

I was wrong, Penthesilea realized. Helen had changed, after all. Her calm surface was only a mask. Beneath, a steady current of weariness ran like the rush of a river. That hadn't been a part of Helen before, at the long-ago wedding feast. The war had worn her down, as it had worn all of Troy down—and all the Achaean forces, too, Penthesilea suspected.

"Your hero Hector is gone," she said. "But new heroes can rise. Hope is not lost."

Those words were a kindly lie. No Cimmerian tribe had ever allowed such folly as a near decade of war; surely, both the Achaeans and the Trojans were fools or madder than Cassandra in the garden. If two factions could claw at one another for so long, then surely there had been no hope to begin with for either side. But it suited no one's purpose, least of all her own, for Penthesilea to say so.

Helen turned to her with a tiny smile. It might have been mocking. "And you believe you are that hero, Amazon?"

Penthesilea bowed her head. "I make no claims on that front, Lady. But you are my cousin, and if you'll have me, I will be yours, loyal and sworn. I'll fight wherever you tell me to, and I'll fight in your name alone."

Helen's gaze flicked momentarily across her chamber to the women spinning on the far side of the room. She drew closer to Penthesilea and whispered, "And if I go back to my rightful husband, King Menelaus—back to the Achaeans, will you fight for me then?"

Penthesilea blinked in surprise. "Are you considering—?"

"Flight? Of course not. How could I? My father-in-law watches us all like a hawk."

Helen laughed lightly, as if she'd caught out Penthesilea in a jest. And maybe it had been a jest, after all. Smooth and cool as cream, Helen was nearly impossible to read.

"It makes no difference, Lady," Penthesilea said firmly. "My spear is yours, wherever you bid me throw it. The Cimmerians take no part in this war; you know that well. I've come to you for reasons of my own."

Helen sobered. "Troy may be doomed. You realize that, don't you?"

"I do, Lady. All I want is a chance to serve you with honor."

The woman's smile was brittle and small. "And you believe I will confer honor on you?" Helen was not the same woman Penthesilea had thought to find at Troy. But her true nature made no difference. All she needed was a kinswoman to honor now that she had ripped her own family apart.

"I believe you are the very image of honor," she finally answered. And that, too, was a lie, but the gods would hardly think a lie as great a sin as Hippolyte's death.

Helen turned back to the garden, to Cassandra swaying in the laurel's dappled shade. "Very well, Cousin. Then you are mine. I accept your pledge."

PHILOCTETES

HE bit back a curse as he stepped down onto the beach. Pain leaped from his right foot and lanced up his leg with a long, searing throb, but Philoctetes refused to let that agony show on his face. The two honor guards sent to escort him to the tent of King Odysseus of Ithaca were young and looked hotheaded. They were exactly the sorts to gossip about other men's weaknesses. Beyond the beach, where the Achaean tents were arrayed, he could hear men's voices raised in a ragged rhythm, chanting their warriors' songs.

He snorted in disgust. There were many reasons to sing, many great and terrible things to sing of. But war was not one of them.

Hades damn every last one of the gods. Philoctetes clenched his jaw, waiting for the pain to subside, to retreat once more to the pooled ache in his foot, the ever-present but manageable irritation that had dogged him for nearly ten years. *Hades damn himself, too.*

A voice hailed him, and Philoctetes looked up. The young page who had accompanied him all the way from the island of Lemnos was leaning over the rail of Odysseus' warship. The boy's golden-brown curls were a sunlit dazzle against the ship's black hull.

"What is it? Odysseus has summoned me to the high king's quarters; I mustn't keep them waiting." *Much as I'd like to.*

"Your bow, Prince Philoctetes." His first instinct was to refuse the bow. Leave it aboard the ship, his home for nearly a month, ever since word had come to Lemnos—since Philoctetes was dragged out of obscurity, back into this gods-be-damned, interminable jape of a war.

But this *was* war, and even when war was at a slow simmer, one could never quite predict when the pot might boil over. Philoctetes was old enough to know that much.

He nodded impatiently. The boy swung his legs over the side of the black ship and jumped down, agile and confident as a dancer. And why not? He was an island lad. Lemnians were never intimidated by the sea or seafaring, while Philoctetes, a rather useless and forgotten prince of Meliboea, had always harbored a creeping suspicion of Poseidon and his watery realm. A near decade on the island of Lemnos, nursing the snake bite on his foot that never quite healed, hadn't been enough to change Philoctetes' nature.

The boy handed over Philoctetes' bow and quiver. "When will you be back, my prince?"

"I don't rightly know. Whenever Odysseus is done with me. Don't hold supper, but stay here on the ship. A camp full of lonely soldiers is no safe place for you. I'll send word if I'll be holed up past midnight."

WHEN Odysseus' men had come for him last month, cajoling him out of his small but pleasant home on the southern coast of Lemnos, they'd told Philoctetes he was wanted as an advisor. "There's no man in all the world who knows archery as you do, my lord," the messenger had said. "And our high king and his allies need your expertise now."

No doubt a novel tactic was being planned even now in one of those tents—a more creative means of breaking Troy and bringing this long, grinding war to a close. How would bows and arrows play the crucial part? How could archers assault that high, walled city? Philoctetes couldn't see a clear advantage for archers—not from this perspective, trudging over sand as it gave way to rough grass. With every step, the pain in Philoctetes' foot stabbed upward again. He resisted the urge to curse his foot, to curse the snake who had bitten him nearly ten years past. He shouldn't curse the wound, he knew. It had kept him out of the conflict for these many years; it had brought him more peace and quiet than any other man had known since that treacherous bitch Helen fucked off to Troy a decade ago.

Yet here he was, being rowed for the shore where the siege still endured, where Troy still stood in defiance. No man can escape the bonds of an oath—not forever, not even with a crippled foot.

That damnable oath—now *there* was a proper target for Philoctetes' curses. It was nearly twenty years since he had been made to swear it—he and how many other good men? A dozen? More? He could no longer remember all the princes of all the lands who had traveled to Sparta to compete for Helen's hand, hoping to claim the throne along with the beautiful, golden-haired princess. Philoctetes had had no interest in the bride, but Sparta, with its strategic location and powerful army, would have been a welcome addition to Meliboea's holdings—or so his father had reasoned. And so the duty of courting Helen had fallen upon his only unmarried son, Philoctetes.

He'd been twenty-five then: too old to stand out beside the pretty and lively younger suitors and not nearly old enough to garner the respect the older men enjoyed. His indifference to Helen's charms surely set him at some disadvantage, too. The games and the boasts and the attempts to win Helen's attention quickly grew tiresome for Philoctetes. It had come as a relief when Odysseus had proposed his clever solution to their conflict: the drawing of lots and a binding oath that each suitor would come to the winner's aid should any ill ever befall Helen's future husband.

Philoctetes had nearly trembled with relief when he'd pulled one of the short straws. Odysseus, too, had held up a short straw, laughing and shaking his head good-naturedly. Philoctetes couldn't say how Odysseus had managed to rig the lots, but even after so many years, he had no doubt that the outcome had been determined not by the gods, but by dark, smirking Odysseus. Menelaus had chosen the long straw, and Helen's father had beamed, and Odysseus had clapped the victor on his shoulder and said with a laugh, "The Fates have made their will known."

But Odysseus hadn't wanted Helen, either, had he? Not truly. Perhaps he had seen something in Helen that the other suitors had missed. Perhaps he had noted, those many years ago, the calm and icy directness of Helen's gaze, as young as she was. Perhaps he had read the danger in her—a book that was open to keen Odysseus but closed tight to lesser men.

Whatever sly trick Odysseus had wrought, all the suitors had ended up swearing on a sacrificial horse to answer Menelaus' call should any harm befall Helen of Sparta. Philoctetes could still feel the flesh of the dead horse beneath his foot, could still hear the buzzing of the flies. The bloody haunch yielding a little as Helen stood upon it, the flies droning along as he recited the words.

An oath as great as that one couldn't be broken lightly. An oath of that magnitude couldn't be broken at all.

"I actually saw Hector's body," one guard said to the other, tramping, oblivious, ahead of Philoctetes. "A great, gaping wound right here." He tapped his throat. "Prince Achilles' spear must have torn through the back of his neck."

The breath froze in Philoctetes' chest. An ache uncurled inside him, stronger by far than the lingering snake bite and more persistent in its poison.

Achilles.

After so many years, his very name still had the power to stir Philoctetes, to send that golden glow racing through this body, to cut him wide open with longing. Strange—almost ten years, and Prince Achilles of Phthia was still everything to him. The whole world. Reason enough to turn his back on Meliboea and remain on the island, where memory of the young warrior's beauty still lingered in every grove and meadow.

It was stranger still when Philoctetes considered that Achilles was only a fleeting memory now, a patchwork of images barely connected by time and place. That summer, after the emissaries sent to Troy to retrieve Helen had failed, Odysseus had sent Philoctetes to Lemnos to conscript men for the upcoming war. And Prince Achilles of Phthia had arrived with a captive youth, whom he never quite managed to sell into slavery. Somehow Achilles and his band of boys had brought Philoctetes into their midst. He was incongruous among them, a thickening goat twice their age with gray streaking his hair and beard, but all through the long, hot days of summer he had run with them, laughed with them, hunted and sang war songs with lads who were barely old enough to grow a few wisps of hair on their own chins. And he had felt like a boy again himself for those precious months—too soon gone. He had fallen in love like a boy, too. Fallen and landed hard and never picked himself up again.

Achilles—the wind tossing his soft waves of hair as he sang beneath an olive tree, as the leaves tumbled down around him. His hand on the shaft of a spear, skin smooth as only a boy's can be, save for the red of an insect bite on one of his knuckles. The broadness of his shoulders disappearing into shadow as he led his captive youth away from the fire—his willing captive, the luckiest man the gods ever made. Achilles, the smell of dust and sweat. A high, soft laugh like a woman's, rising like sacrificial smoke to the gods. Piercing pale green eyes turning to Philoctetes in the firelight, holding his gaze for a moment, the weight of words unspoken between them. And then an owl called in the dark forest, and Achilles looked away, laughing, always laughing.

Then a hunt for rabbits in a farmer's field. And a snake coiled tight among the wheat. A fire in Philoctetes' heel. He woke two days later in bed in his borrowed home, head swimming, choking on the taste of vomit, and the summer was over, and Achilles was gone.

But Philoctetes had never stopped loving him. It was as hopeless then as it was now, for during that blissful summer, Achilles was already too old for Philoctetes to take him as a lover. Not that a man like Achilles would deign to love someone as unremarkable as Philoctetes. Achilles was half-god, and anyone who set eyes on him knew it without being told. Splendid in his strength, beautiful in his arrogance, Achilles could reduce the greatest of men to nothing with a look. And Philoctetes—well, the best that could be said of him was that he was handy with a bow and made a tempting target for vipers.

Of course Achilles was here now. How not? He was the greatest warrior in the known world—Philoctetes had heard the tales of Achilles' career unfolding, even on Lemnos. War was his natural element, and now, after a near decade of conflict, Troy was war itself.

Philoctetes had heard how Achilles had defeated Mythimna and Mytilene, cutting down their king, who was armored and mounted on a chariot while Achilles was afoot and naked. Philoctetes' imagination had fed on that feast for several sleepless nights, but he had seen nothing of the beautiful hero, naked or clothed, since that long-ago summer.

But Achilles is here. Now. In this camp.

Or so Philoctetes hoped. According to the messengers who'd fetched him from his island, it had been a full six weeks now since Hector had been slain, perhaps more. Had Achilles departed? What more could a man accomplish after slaying a foe as powerful as Hector?

Philoctetes' escorts chattered on, sharing the excitement of war as only fresh young men can. The nearer they drew to the Achaean camp, the thicker Philoctetes' anxiety became. He was once a decent warrior—serviceable enough, but no hero. Those days were far behind him now. He couldn't even walk without limping, and he had lain low, allowing this conflict to pass him by like a gentle breeze. Not that Meliboea would have had any use for him, one prince out of many and crippled by a damned snake.

He only wanted the sanctuary of his island now. All the way from Lemnos to Troy, he'd felt like a dead man being ferried across the Styx. The world into which he was going, dragged on by the power of Odysseus' thrice-damned oath, was not a world he could recognize. If Achilles was no longer at Troy, then what was there for Philoctetes?

He was sweating with the effort, and his whole leg burned by the time they found High King Agamemnon's quarters. A grinning Mycenaean spearman, no doubt one of Agamemnon's favorites, raised his spear in invitation, and Philoctetes stepped inside. A scattering of brightly colored but well-worn rugs made a passable floor, and strewn over that floor were chests and casks, lamps on iron tripods, a few articles of clothing piled near a stool, waiting for slaves to come for the washing. One chest, unlocked, its lid thrown back, revealed a bronze breastplate embossed with the image of the lion of Mycenae. The interior reeked of burnt oil, metal, and the breath of many men.

Those very men clustered around a table, heads together, talking over a map or a scroll. At the sound of footfalls, one looked up, met Philoctetes' eye, and gestured the others to silence with a simple lift of his hand.

Agamemnon of Mycenae rose slowly from his seat. It had been years since Philoctetes had seen him, but he recognized the man on the instant: tall, whip thin, long of face and longer of nose, his mouth pinched and tight. Gray feathered his temples, but far more gray had invaded Philoctetes' hair since he and Agamemnon had last met. The eyes were still the same, though—chestnut-brown and commanding in their intensity.

Philoctetes bobbed his head in greeting.

"The old prince of Meliboea," Agamemnon said. "We feared you'd forgotten about your oath to Menelaus."

"Forgotten? No, my king." *Would that I could.* Philoctetes took a few steps toward the table, doing nothing now to disguise his limp. "But as you can see, I'm not much use on the battlefield anymore."

Another man stood, and Philoctetes recognized him, too. Not nearly as tall as Agamemnon, whatever Odysseus lacked in height he made up for with a bull's chest and shoulders. Age had touched him less than any of the others; he still wore a proud crown of thick black hair, and his smile was as bold and mocking as it ever was.

"Not much use?" Odysseus said. "I think you're wrong about that, Brother."

Philoctetes cringed inwardly at the familiarity, but he was a prince of Meliboea, even if he had spent a decade languishing unwanted on an island. He had more sense than to show his discomfiture to Odysseus and his friends. "Your messenger said my skill as an archer is needed. But I confess I can see no way to—"

Agamemnon silenced him with a wave of his hand. "It's not your *skill* we need now, though the gods know it's laudable enough. This"—he tapped one of the documents spread on the table before him, a scrap of textured Aegyptian papyrus—"is a note sent by one of my best servants. It's a notation of a prophecy recently given by Chryses."

Philoctetes noted the dark spark in Agamemnon's eye, the tightening of his lips; he had no liking for this Chryses, whoever he was. But he thought it prudent to keep his observations to himself. "I'm afraid I don't know that name."

"Of course not." Odysseus laughed quietly. "You've been holed up on your rock almost since this war began."

"Chryses is a priest of Apollo," Agamemnon said. "Trojan and lacking an eye to make him even more useless. But still, his people give great consideration to his prophecies. I have no admiration for the man." His eyes narrowed as he spoke those words, their corners tensing with a sudden energy that Philoctetes couldn't help but notice. Agamemnon was tempering his words. It was clear that he hated the priest of Apollo.

"But," Agamemnon said, "a prophecy can be a useful tool if it's widely believed. His words seem to suggest that under the right circumstances—well, he is most insistent, Philoctetes, that this war can be ended—that Troy could possibly fall—if we only hold the right weapon."

"I'm glad to hear it, my king. But what do I have to do with it?"

Odysseus leaned one elbow on the table, fixing Philoctetes with a dark-eyed stare. "The war won't end, so the old Cyclops says, until we have the bow of the greatest hero of them all. The bow of Heracles."

Philoctetes felt his heart still for one moment—a moment that stretched to an uncomfortable, impossible length. His grip tightened on the bow; he resisted the urge to hug it to his chest like a possessive child.

"How did you know," he asked softly, "that I have Heracles' bow?"

Odysseus must have noticed the whitening of Philoctetes' knuckles, the way his fist clutched hard at the polished horn. "What," he said in disbelief, "*that's* not the very bow, is it?"

"It belonged to Heracles once," Philoctetes said. "It's mine now."

"It's rather plain, that's all." Odysseus cast a smirk at the bow. "I'd expect a hero's weapon to be grander—a little silver on the grip, maybe, or at least a pair of tits etched on the limbs somewhere."

The men laughed. Philoctetes did not.

Of course men like these expected grandness from a hero's

weapon. But a bow was a bow; its purpose was utility. All it had to do was fire an arrow.

Men like these expected grandness from their heroes, too. But a man was only a man. Heracles, beneath his lion-skin cape and his roaring laugh, had been just a man, too. Big as he was, his legend was bigger still, even while he lived. But Philoctetes had known him well—had run with him and fought with him in the days before Helen and the drawn straws, before the oath that had doomed the world to war. Heracles was called a hero. All the world had thought him invincible—Heracles himself had often behaved as if death could never touch him. But in the end, poison had taken him in agony, and when his servants and his followers saw the great man weakened and in pain, crying out for mercy, they had fled in fear and disbelief.

Only Philoctetes had stayed by his side until the hard and horrible end. Philoctetes had built a pyre to send that invincible hero's smoke up to the gods. He'd helped Heracles climb atop it and lay down at his side to hold his friend and comfort him until death finally released him. And when finally the hero's suffering ended, Philoctetes had lit the pyre and walked away.

But before he'd expired, Heracles had taken a key from a string around his neck and pressed it into Philoctetes' hand. Back at Heracles' hunting tent, abandoned by the servants, silent as a tomb, Philoctetes had found a locked chest. Inside the chest was his friend's favorite bow: plain, polished horn, simple and serviceable. Exactly what a bow ought to be.

It was a good bow, and Philoctetes, with his lifelong love of archery, knew how to appreciate its craftsmanship, how to use it well. It had been his pride during his free days, during those months of summer when he had ached with the blissful pain of love and dared not confess his longing to anyone. He had only told a few people how he'd acquired the bow. Only his dearest friends.

He swallowed hard, holding Agamemnon's stare, and when he spoke, his voice was hoarse and gravelly. "How did you know that I have the bow of Heracles?"

"I told them." A voice from behind him at the tent's entrance. A voice he hadn't heard in ten years, but still he recognized it on the instant. It sent fire through his veins and squeezed his heart with a merciless fist.

Philoctetes turned. Achilles stood in the lamplight, gazing at him steadily, his face devoid of all expression but somehow still tinged by weariness and grief. His hair tumbled in waves toward his shoulders; what had once been the wisps of a boy's beard had thickened to the full, rough shadow of manhood on his exquisitely sharp and strong jaw. The smell of dust and sweat and summer heat struck Philoctetes like a blow, though it was only a memory—only a memory. His disbelieving gaze fell to Achilles' hand, hanging loosely at his side. All the softness of youth was gone; the skin was callused and cracked and hardened by war. And there was no red welt on his knuckle. Of course there was not.

But it was Achilles—it was Achilles.

Philoctetes heard Agamemnon's voice, muffled by the pounding of his own heart in his ears. "So will you fight for us, then?"

He didn't tear his eyes from Achilles' face—couldn't have done it, even if he'd wanted to. But he answered Agamemnon without hesitation.

"Yes, I'll fight for you. However I can."

PENTHESILEA

PENTHESILEA woke late in the afternoon—or perhaps she didn't wake at all. Ever since Hippolyte's death, sleep had mostly evaded her, and when it came, it was shallow and fleeting, laced with dark dreams and haunted by the sound of her sister's final breaths.

She rolled over on her cot, its frame creaking, and stood on legs that trembled from grief and exhaustion. Her stomach felt hollow and sick at the same time. In all the days since she'd arrived in Troy—half a moon's turn, now—she had eaten very little and drank only when Helen demanded that she take water or diluted wine sweetened with plenty of fortifying honey. Her appetite was small; there was no room inside her for anything but sorrow, no matter how Helen chided her to eat, arguing that a trembling, stick-thin warrior would do her no good when the time came to fight. Who knew when that would be; there had been no fighting at all since Penthesilea had arrived two weeks ago. All Troy seemed too sunk in stillness to venture outside the great gates, even for a raid.

The cot was set into a small servant's alcove in a corner of Helen's great chamber. Penthesilea lingered behind the alcove's curtain, listening. There was no murmur of women's voices in Helen's quarters, no cries or accusations from Andromache, whose eyes were still red whenever Penthesilea saw her. There was only the slow, resigned clacking of the loom.

She pulled the curtain aside. Helen stood at her loom on the far side of the chamber, her straight and slender back to Penthesilea, passing the shuttle slowly through a forest of white threads.

"Awake?" Helen asked in that remarkable voice—carrying, strong and smooth, but never loud. She did not look around.

"Yes," Penthesilea said.

"Good. The gods know I could stand some company."

Penthesilea went to her, padding across the chamber in her bare feet. She wasn't used to moving in such absolute silence, but she had taken all the ornaments out of her hair, all the discs of silver and shell. She was in mourning, and the bright music of their movement was unsuited to her grief. She would be in mourning forever.

Penthesilea looked over Helen's shoulder at the cloth growing slowly on the loom. Surely, even a slave girl could have done better. There were slubs in the fabric, and the pattern of keys and suns had broken here and there. It was careless work—distracted work. Helen was capable of doing much better, but the woman's sigh as she passed the shuttle again, her distant stare out her chamber window into the sun-beaten garden, told Penthesilea that all effort and care were beyond Helen now.

"Your maids, my lady?" Penthesilea asked.

Usually the talk and laughter of Helen's servants made weaving more bearable for her, carrying her sharp mind away from the drudgery of the task. But Helen sighed in the silence.

"I sent them away. They're fools; I can't abide their mindless chatter today. There's fresh water in the ewer, though. Drink. You won't be any use as my personal warrior if you die of thirst. Or starvation. You'll be sure to eat well tonight, won't you?"

Her tone was cool and detached, but Penthesilea had known her cousin long enough now to hear the subtle note of concern. She gave a tiny smile of gratitude for Helen's care.

"I will, if it will please you."

"Excellent. Though I still don't know what I'm to do with my own sworn Amazon. At least you are a novelty. There's precious little novelty in Troy anymore."

The shuttle passed through the threads again.

Penthesilea poured a cup of water and drank. The water was cool and sweet; it felt good in her throat. She'd been thirstier than she knew. She drank another cup while Helen watched with approval.

"Look at me," Helen burst out suddenly. An unexpected bitterness tinted her voice. Helen rarely showed any emotion, even when Penthesilea was sure it was rippling under her cool surface like wind across the grass. "Look at me. Weaving. I hate weaving. It was all I did back in Sparta. I swore when I left that place that I'd never touch a shuttle again, that I'd burn any loom they put in front of me. Yet here I am, doing it anyway, after all these years. What else am I to do?"

Penthesilea leaned against the windowsill, her back to the garden, watching her cousin and waiting. More was coming; she was sure of that.

Helen stared past Penthesilea, out into the garden with its laurel tree and its dappled shade. But she seemed to see nothing except the private images that tumbled through her memory.

"I wonder," she said, and now her voice was not smooth and grand. It was small and cracked, very nearly broken. "Does my daughter weave?"

"I remember your daughter well," Penthesilea said. She remembered, too, the blankness in King Menelaus of Sparta's eyes when she had congratulated him on the good fortune of having a daughter. Achaeans did not value daughters as Cimmerians did. "She was lively and red-haired. A pretty little girl."

"Little, yes. She's not a little girl any longer. All this time, I've tried to send for her. So has Priam. We've offered riches Menelaus could hardly refuse. But he did refuse—turned us down every time. All to spite me—only to spite me."

Helen drew a long, shaking breath. When she spoke again, she was calm, composed. "Hermione is fifteen now. Ready to marry, and she *would* be married, no doubt, if her father weren't off at war."

"Perhaps she enjoys the maiden's life," Penthesilea offered.

"Yes." A quiet laugh, wry and self-deprecating. "Would that we were all so lucky to avoid marriage and remain free." The shuttle moved again in her delicate white hands. "Still, I wonder if she weaves."

Penthesilea helped herself to another cup of water. "Would you want her to weave, my lady? If you despise it so?"

She didn't look up from her loom, but one corner of Helen's mouth curled, and those sea-gray eyes sharpened. "Since when does it matter what a woman wants? We all end up in drudgery, one way or another. I suppose it's all the gods made us for, after all. Even me, Zeus's own daughter." She set the shuttle in its holder and picked at the skewed threads of her tapestry. "One would think the daughter of a god could manage to weave like Arachne. Apparently not."

"You're only distracted, my lady. This war—"

Helen cut her off abruptly, shaking her pale gold curls. "This war. This war like every other war."

Not exactly like every other war, Penthesilea thought soberly. *It has dragged on for nearly ten bloody years.* But she knew better than to say such a thing to Helen.

"What is the point of war?" Helen asked.

Penthesilea knew she was not meant to answer. There was no good answer she could give anyway. She knew the point of battle in her homeland. Among Cimmerians, raids brought honor and opportunity—the chance to raid in return, to raise the honor of one's family ever higher, like a banner against the sky. But what indeed was the purpose of this endless conflict? The king of Sparta would have said the purpose was to win Helen back. But any king with a speck of sense would have declared Helen unfaithful and unworthy—would have taken another wife, less beautiful but also less troublesome.

What was the purpose of war in Troy, in the Achaean lands? Where was the honor in years of deaths, in an endless siege? Penthesilea gazed out over the garden toward the wall of Troy beyond. There were children in that city who had never known a world without fighting, who could never recall a time when their home was not besieged.

"This curse has followed me all my life," Helen said, joining Penthesilea at the garden window. A warm breeze lifted the scent of herbs from the beds, a soothing fragrance. Helen seemed not to notice.

"What curse, my lady?"

"Womanhood." She pressed her lips tightly together. For a moment, Penthesilea wondered if Helen would spit out the window. "What I wouldn't have given to be born a Cimmerian like you. Women are *more* in your land, aren't they?"

"More?"

"Yes. More than spoils—treasure. More than prizes to be won. All my life, I've been a pretty little bauble, something to be haggled over, something to be stolen. First, when I was merely a child, then again when the suitors came for me. And here I am, languishing at Troy, where I thought I could be free—where I thought women could be more than just spoils. But I am still the prize. Nothing has changed."

Penthesilea bit her lip. She cast an uneasy glance at Helen from the corner of her eye. There was truth in her words—there was nothing but truth. Penthesilea could offer no comforting denial.

A tap sounded at the door, startling both women out of their bleak reverie. "Come," Helen called.

Penthesilea expected a slave or two, bearing wine or a meal. Instead, it was Helen's husband, Paris, who entered. Penthesilea had seen little of him since she'd arrived in Troy, for Helen kept to herself whenever she could, and Penthesilea remained close by her side. For all that he was Helen's husband, Paris seldom passed his time in these rooms.

The prince of Troy was as finely formed as a statue, perfect in his proportions and gleaming with ornaments and fine white linen. His gleaming hair, wavy as the sea, was combed into place with lotus oil. He was a pretty man—there was no denying that. But no Cimmerian woman would bother to bed him. Beneath his ostentatious, swaggering confidence, the faltering heartbeat of a coward was plain to hear. Such a man's seed could never sprout strong daughters. What good was a man like Paris?

He came toward Helen grinning, his arms outstretched as if to embrace her, but Helen stiffened as he approached, drawing her typical icy aloofness tight like a fur cloak in winter.

Paris' hands fell back to his side, but his grin remained firm.

"My lovely," he said.

Helen allowed him to kiss her cheek—that, and nothing more. "What brings you here?"

"A man may visit his wife in her chamber. If the gods have made new proclamations forbidding it, I haven't heard." Paris laughed with a note of pure confidence. His charm was palpable, even cloying. "You haven't been seen out in the garden or walking the palace for several days."

"Should I go wandering about like Cassandra?"

"Fresh air is good for the body and the mind," Paris protested. "A stroll in the garden would brighten your moods."

"My moods do not need brightening, thank you." Helen returned to the window, gazing down on the garden she spurned.

Paris stepped closer and took her by the elbow, a commanding grip. Helen pulled her arm away with a smooth, unthinking motion, not deigning to meet his eye.

"Then brighten your people's moods," he said. "You know Troy has been under a dark cloud since Hector's death. They need to see their great beauty out there"—he nodded toward the garden, to the city beyond the citadel—"you, confident and smiling, among them."

Helen's laugh was short and sharp. "I am not their beauty, and well you know it. There is not a tongue in Troy that hasn't cursed my name. The city despises me, Paris—everyone in it. And so what has this all been for?"

She gestured out over the city, toward the wall and what lay beyond—what none of them could see but which they could all feel like weights around their necks, dragging them down into dark water. The ranks of tents waiting like wolves on the plain. The black ships anchored in the bay.

"Troy may yet win," Paris said jauntily. Penthesilea could hear the waver in his words.

She expected Helen to give another of her cold, bitter laughs. But she only shook her head slowly. "No, Paris. Not now. Not with Hector dead. He was our hope, our pride. Our gift from the gods. He was our future king."

"I'm tired of hearing about Hector," Paris hissed. "He wasn't the only son of Priam, you know. He wasn't our city's only hero!"

"Oh, do we have another?" Helen arched one thin golden brow in dark amusement. "Tell me—who is he? That sour-faced prig Aeneas, perhaps? Your little brother Polites, now that he's all of fourteen?" She held Paris' eye with a merciless stare. "I haven't seen a hero in Troy since Hector fell."

Paris' face darkened; his lips thinned as if he'd bitten into a sour fruit. "My own wife believes me a coward—is that the way of it?"

Helen's only answer was a tiny, needling smile.

The prince dropped his forced cheer like a hot brand. He drew close to Helen—so close he seemed suddenly menacing, and Penthesilea moved toward him, ready to defend her cousin.

"Go outside," Paris said flatly. "Take the air. Show your face. I'll hear no more of this moping in your chamber. It's not a request, Helen. It's a command from your husband. Since you've failed in every other way as my wife—failed to give me children, failed to keep warming my bed as is your duty—you will give me obedience."

With that, he turned and stalked out the chamber door.

"Fool," Helen muttered before the door had closed.

When they were alone again, she sighed and turned to Penthesilea with a weary shake of her head. "Hector. He could never pretend liking for me, considering the trouble I brought in my wake, but I always held him in high honor. What are we without him? I can't tell you how *precarious* Troy seems now, as if there's a great blade hanging over all our heads, and any moment it might drop. I almost wish it would just so the waiting would end. Just so it would be over."

Penthesilea hadn't been in Troy long, but she knew at once what Helen meant. The days of mourning Hector, of cowering under the blow of his loss, seemed to be coming to an end. Conflict was gathering its strength once more, preparing to strike again. The whole city felt like a crouching animal—waiting, tensing itself for some terrible blow. Hector had been their shield and their mighty arm. There was no shield now, no defense, even with Troy's vast and soaring walls. The gods had turned their backs on the city. Achilles, god-born, had taken Hector away.

"You mustn't speak that way," Penthesilea said. "The blade won't fall. I won't let it."

Helen turned to her, pale as bone. "You won't? What can you do, Penthesilea—anything more than Paris can? What can a *woman* do?"

Helen's slaves entered the chamber then, bearing an early evening meal. Despite her promise to eat, Penthesilea slipped back to her sleeping alcove while Helen was distracted, pulling her saddlebags from beneath the wicker bed. She found her bag of bones in their soft-worn leather pouch and hid the pouch in her fist. Then she hurried outside and crouched on the other side of the laurel tree's trunk before Helen could note her absence.

Penthesilea spilled the bones into her palm and stared at them for a long time. They were marked all over with the symbols of divination, the symbols rubbed with charcoal so they stood out starkly against the smooth whiteness. She hadn't cast bones since long before her sister died, and she didn't know whether the gods would still work their powers for her—for Hippolyte's killer.

"Do it."

Penthesilea, squatting on her heels, looked up in alarm. The laurel's shadows played over the face and bare breasts of the woman in the faded black skirt. At close range, she could see that the woman's feet were bare, hard and dry at the soles.

Cassandra.

Penthesilea hadn't seen her since her first day in Troy, but she had heard plenty of talk about the seer. Some still called her mad, though from what Penthesilea had gleaned from the gossip, Cassandra was the sanest person in the city. She had heard, too, that Cassandra used to be barred in a cell—for her own good, she wondered, or to save her family's reputation? But since the pall of Hector's death had fallen over the city, no one had thought to lock the dark woman in her prison.

"Cast the bones," Cassandra said.

Penthesilea hesitated.

"It makes no difference to you whether Troy stands or falls, isn't that so?"

Penthesilea nodded. She struggled to find her voice, but Cassandra seemed to have stolen every word from her throat.

"So long as you are loyal to the daughter of Zeus," the woman said, "your purpose will be served. So cast the bones."

It seemed as if some other hand tossed the bones into the dust, and Cassandra leaned in to read the divination even before Penthesilea did.

"What do they tell you?" Cassandra asked.

Penthesilea stared. She was barely passable with divination. She examined the pattern, counted the pieces lying flat and the ones propped up on their ends, squinted at the incised charcoal symbols, searching for their meaning. Spear, man, horse, black, hollow, carrion crows. It made no sense to her.

She looked up at Cassandra in desperation, hoping the seer had some advice to offer.

"You already know what you *want* to do," Cassandra said. "Tell me."

"Restore the balance," Penthesilea answered. Her voice was as dry as the bones themselves. "If I can kill the one who killed Hector, then the balance will tip back in Troy's favor."

"That is the way you Cimmerians do it, isn't it? An enemy tribe kills your best warrior, so you raid them and kill their best fighter in return."

"That's how honor is maintained."

"I see." The wind blew; light and shadow slithered across the seer's dark features, her wide, staring eyes.

"If I kill the man who killed Hector, then Helen's fears will be soothed."

"And then you will have served your cousin well."

"Yes. That's all I care about now. I don't care about Troy—not truly. Troy matters nothing to me."

Cassandra nodded, a simple acceptance of Penthesilea's honesty.

"They say you are a seer. Tell me: If I fight the Achaeans' best warrior—this man called Achilles—will I win?"

Cassandra's fierce, staring eyes softened with a sudden smile. "I don't know, Amazon. That, of all things, wasn't given to me to see. But does it matter? Are you so keen to go on living?"

Penthesilea knew the answer to that question. She gave it at once, and the word raised no fear in her belly. "No."

"It's death you seek," Cassandra said. "It's not Helen you serve, but your slain sister. Her death, not Hector's, is the balance you seek to right."

Her throat too dry to speak, Penthesilea nodded.

The seer offered her hand. Penthesilea took it—it was softer and warmer than she expected—and allowed herself to be pulled to her feet. She tugged at the skirt of her tunic, straightening it over her breeches, suddenly conscious of the way she must look to the seer of Troy. She left the bones where they had fallen.

"The morning," Cassandra said. "That's when you must face Achilles."

Penthesilea felt the truth of her words. She didn't bother to ask Cassandra how she knew, which god whispered into her ear. The morning—it felt right. It was right. And whether she died or Achilles did, a balance would be restored.

"I'll send a messenger to the Achaean camp for you," Cassandra offered. "I shall tell them that Troy's best warrior is coming to avenge Hector's death, outside the Scaean Gate when the sun rises."

"Am I?" Penthesilea blinked at her, startled. "Troy's best warrior?"

Cassandra's full lips bent in a smile. "We'll find out, won't we?"

Then the seer turned and walked away, the hem of her old, ragged skirt rippling in the garden's dust.

Penthesilea stood and watched Cassandra as she crossed the garden. Then the seer vanished amid the bright white of sun on limestone and the all-consuming blackness of shadow. With every step the dark woman took, the weight of grief lifted from Penthesilea's heart.

She could smell supper drifting from Helen's chamber, roasted meat and onions and sweet honeyed wine. Her stomach rumbled;

she turned away from the laurel tree and left the divination bones untouched.

That night, with her stomach full and her heart soothed, Penthesilea slept well for the first time since her sister's death.

PHILOCTETES

DUSK approached, dragging its heavy blue cloak over the Plain of Troy. Released at last from Agamemnon's quarters, Philoctetes limped outside into the first breath of evening's oncoming coolness. The sky was the deep blue of indigo dye with a last flush of gold on the western horizon. Philoctetes breathed deeply. Beneath the stench of many men, their beasts, their latrine pits, he could detect the coolness of the River Scamander. And even the smell of a war camp was a relief after the close air inside Agamemnon's tent.

Achilles had long since departed. Once satisfied that Philoctetes and his bow had in fact come, the great hero had simply turned and stalked out of the high king's quarters, swallowed up in a blaze of late-afternoon light. But the pounding of Philoctetes' heart hadn't slowed, had only increased as he'd sat listening to the other men talk of their strategies and their plans for the bow of Heracles.

Philoctetes gazed out over the water. Odysseus' ship waited patiently among the others, somehow far blacker than the rest. He must send a messenger to his page—tell the boy not to expect him back any time soon. He didn't know how long he would be in the camp; the other men had reached no consensus on how they might employ the bow. But Philoctetes was certain he wouldn't be set free until Odysseus and Agamemnon had tried every trick they could scheme up between them, and then a few more. For all Philoctetes knew, he might never see the deck of that ship again nor his page boy nor his small, peaceful home on Lemnos' southern shore.

He headed toward the river, drawn on by the coolness of the water and the paltry screen of the few trees that still stood in that plundered woodland. As he made his slow way through the camp, he could feel men turning from their nighttime tasks and their cook-fires to look at him—to look at the simple horn bow that swung from his hand. Warriors ceased their joking as he passed; an expectant silence trailed him through the ranks of tents and shacks and the rows of bedrolls.

The river called him on, but before he reached the bank, the faint singing of a lyre captured his attention. He paused, looking around. This was surely the camp of Achilles' Myrmidons; it stood in better order than the squalor of the other Achaean warriors, the tents well pitched, the men moving about disciplined and quiet—quiet enough to hear the lyre. The notes were soft, not as if the music were muffled or at any great distance from where he stood, but as if the player plucked softly at the strings. His eye fell on a grand tent—a palace, as war tents went. Philoctetes forgot the river and limped toward the great tent.

A servant stopped him at the door, a young man, reddish-haired, slight of frame, moving with the stiffness of recent injuries. Despite his youthful appearance, he had been active in battle.

"Is this Achilles' tent?" Philoctetes asked.

At the sound of his voice, the lyre ceased to sing. Achilles—unmistakable to Philoctetes' yearning ears—called from inside the tent. "Automedon."

The youth nudged open the tent's flap and gave a nod to the lamp-lit interior. "It's the prince of Meliboea," he said. Then he turned back to Philoctetes with his brows raised. "I think."

Philoctetes restrained a chuckle. "You're correct, lad. May I see him?"

Achilles said, “Let him in.”

Automedon drew the flap aside, and Philoctetes stepped through, hesitant and wondering, like a man stepping fully awake and lucid into the realm of dreams. The ground was covered with far finer rugs than had floored Agamemnon’s tent, the space opening into other rooms, more tents and shacks all built together. Light from half a dozen lamps filled the room with a rosy glow. Spoils of war furnished the place as richly as any prince’s villa: trunks strapped with silver and bronze, a bedstead carved with lion’s feet, strewn with cushions and plush animal skins.

Achilles himself lounged on an ornate ivory chair, his legs crossed casually at the ankles, a nine-stringed lyre resting in his lap. His broad chest stirred with his breath. Those unforgettable eyes, piercing and green as the sea, fixed Philoctetes in silent contemplation, and again the memory of Lemnos came back to him, Achilles in the firelight, Achilles ten years younger. Achilles, about to speak, then turning away with a careless laugh. Philoctetes couldn’t tell whether the inaudible humming in the air was the dying echo of the lyre’s strings or the rising ache of his own foolish old heart.

“It’s good to see you again,” Achilles said quietly.

The tent flap thumped softly shut.

“You still remember me?” They were pathetic words and weakly said. Philoctetes could have kicked himself, but he could think of nothing else to offer.

Achilles’ broad shoulders jumped once, a silent laugh. “Of course I do. Sit.”

Philoctetes tried not to limp as he made his way across the patterned rugs to the chair Achilles indicated. There was a jug of wine on the table and cups stacked one inside the other.

“May I?” Philoctetes jerked his head toward the wine. “My throat is very dry.”

"Help yourself, but none for me. Wine has lost all its savor."

Philoctetes poured and drank. The wine was exceptional—as one would expect in surroundings such as these. Achilles watched him steadily, saying nothing as Philoctetes tasted the wine, betraying none of his thoughts or feelings with the slightest flicker.

But then those eyes lowered to the bow resting across Philoctetes' knees.

"So you do still have it. The bow of Heracles."

"Of course." Philoctetes set the empty cup aside. The wine burned in his throat, a pleasant warmth already fortifying his wobbly courage. "You don't think I would have gotten rid of such a treasure, do you?"

Achilles smiled. A rare thing, his smile—if memory could be trusted. "I remember you shooting rabbits with it. And the rest of us teased you that a hero's bow should be used for a nobler purpose. And you said, 'There's nothing nobler than supper, lads. If you don't believe me, I'll keep all the meat for myself, and you can dine on roots and berries tonight.'"

"I remember," Philoctetes said. *I remember you singing beneath an olive tree. I remember the leaves falling at your feet; even they couldn't resist you.* He forced a smile. "Do you recall . . ."

They went on that way for some time, recounting the summer of Lemnos when they had left all thoughts of war behind, for a few months at least. The longer they reminisced, the younger Philoctetes felt. Year after year fell from him, peeling back and tearing itself away. He was like a snake, shedding its dull old skin to reveal brighter scales beneath. Another cup of wine vanished, and then Achilles rose and poured for himself, carrying his smell of dust and sweat and warm metal into Philoctetes' vicinity. They laughed—cautiously at first, then with growing humor. And before the night had gathered, they were like young men again—both of them, even Philoctetes.

They were like younger men, but they were not men untouched by war. Even as the wine flowed and Achilles' laughter grew louder and more frequent, a shroud of sorrow clung to him, shadowing his face and edging all his words. And after a time, all the stories of Lemnos had been recounted, and silence fell over them both.

Achilles rose slowly from his ivory chair. He opened an ornate black trunk and stood over it, staring down at its contents, hair obscuring his face. Philoctetes couldn't see what was in the trunk, so he left the bow lying on the table beside the wine jug and joined Achilles, his skin tingling from the other man's nearness.

The trunk housed a set of armor, more beautifully made, more intricately decorated than any Philoctetes had seen before.

"By Zeus," he muttered, gazing down at the layers of bright enamel over embossed figures so delicately made it seemed only a god could have crafted them.

Achilles lifted the shield from its trunk. He turned it in his hands like a wheel, and the many delicate figures spun and tumbled before Philoctetes' eyes. Achilles stopped turning the shield; the scene that was upright depicted a wedding. Guests dancing merrily and a bride and groom standing side by side, bright and resplendent in their glittering colors.

Achilles touched the bride with one finger, and Philoctetes' heart made a bitter stutter-step.

"Briseis," the warrior said.

"Your . . . your wife?"

He smiled ruefully, shook his head. "No. Mother of my child."

"Your son?" Philoctetes remembered—he had learned in the summer of Lemnos that Achilles had a son, even then, young as he was. He'd fathered the boy when he wasn't more than a boy himself—fourteen, fifteen at best—and had never seen his get. Philoctetes had assumed the woman who'd birthed Achilles' son had meant nothing to him. But watching him now, the way he touched the woman on the shield with such tenderness, Philoctetes wasn't so sure.

"No—not that son, at least. My first son, Neoptolemus, is old enough now to be a warrior himself. I hear he's sent word to Agamemnon that he'll be joining us soon."

"This child, then," Philoctetes said. "A boy or a girl?"

"Good question," Achilles answered. "I don't know yet, and I'll never find out."

"What do you mean, you'll never find out?"

"You know the story. The prophecy."

Yes, Philoctetes knew the prophecy: that Achilles would die young and in the glory of war, but his name would live forever. He'd heard Achilles speak of it on Lemnos. Achilles hadn't seemed troubled by the prospect then. But when a man is young, he thinks he will go on being young forever. He thinks glory and greatness are his due and all he will ever require.

"I won Briseis in battle," Achilles said, grazing the image of the woman again with his rough fingers. "She was a queen, but she came to me a slave. Still, she never held herself like a slave, never had the look of a conquered woman."

He paused.

"Honorable," Philoctetes said. It seemed he was expected to say something.

"And strong," Achilles agreed. "Brave. The things a woman ought to be, but so often is never allowed to be."

Philoctetes nodded. Achilles of all people would know; he had been raised among women, his mad mother's attempt to thwart the fate of his early death.

"But do you know why I liked Briseis? Because she could dance."

Philoctetes chuckled, startled out of the sober mood by the unexpected image of Achilles, the irrepressible god-born hero, leering at a dancing woman like a common spearman in a tavern.

Achilles shot him a piercing stare, and the laugh died in Philoctetes' throat. He swallowed hard.

"When I played my lyre and Briseis danced, she was so beautiful, so alive. I almost felt alive then, myself. Almost."

"You are alive," Philoctetes said quietly.

Achilles shook his head. "No." He lowered the shield back into the trunk and shut its heavy black lid. "No. If I ever was alive, I'm not any longer. This war is almost all I've ever known, and even before it started, it dictated my fate. And what is it all for? For the pride of Menelaus, for the gain of Agamemnon. For nothing."

He turned and stalked back to his ivory chair, sank onto its seat. For a moment, he sat staring blankly into the flame of the nearest lamp. The lyre lay forgotten between his feet.

"But war is all I'm good at, Philoctetes. All I'm good for."

"Surely, that is not true."

"All my reputation—my livelihood itself—depends on playing this game. On allowing myself to be woven into this pattern, set in the warp and weft of the world from the time I was a child. Maybe before that. All this, just for the glory of two men."

Philoctetes sank slowly on his own chair. He rolled his cup between his hands, but he had no more thirst for the wine. "I've often wondered if Agamemnon and Menelaus think themselves god-born, like you. What else could make them go on fighting for so long? Helen herself certainly isn't worth it."

One side of Achilles' mouth curved up in a wry smile. "God-born? Like me? That's what they all say, isn't it? It's what my mother always claimed: that she was a goddess. And I have seen enough strange things in my life, experienced enough, to believe her. Yet more and more often, I can't help but feel that I'm just a man. Like Menelaus and Agamemnon. Like you. Like Hector."

His voice sank to a gravelly depth on that final name. Philoctetes traced the rim of the cup with an anxious finger.

"Odysseus told me how you made an end of Hector," he said, not cheerfully as a young warrior might, but gently, sorrowfully, for he sensed that Achilles took no joy in that victory.

"I did make an end of him. And by all the gods, I wish I hadn't." Achilles raised a hand as if to forestall Philoctetes, though he'd had no intention of protesting the younger man's words. "I don't regret avenging Patrocles—not for a moment. He was my dearest friend, one of the only men I still respected in all the world."

More than a friend, Philoctetes knew—a lover. Prince Patrocles of Aegina had not come to Lemnos that summer; he had been recruiting spearmen elsewhere, but Achilles spoke of him often, and the affection in his voice had been plain. How Philoctetes had envied the absent Patrocles, who had been fortunate enough to know Achilles when he was still beardless, young enough to lie in a man's bed without dishonor.

"Patrocles died because of me," Achilles went on, "because I was too proud and ill-tempered to do my duty. I wished to defy my fate, and Patrocles paid the price at the point of Hector's spear. No, I don't regret avenging him.

"But do you know what Hector told me when we stood face-to-face? He said, 'We two know this war to be foolish. We two can end it.' And he was right. We could have put a stop to it all by simply throwing down our weapons and refusing to fight. I knew his words were true in the moment. But Patrocles was dead. So instead of ending this gods-damned war, I killed Hector."

The pain in Achilles' voice was so raw that Philoctetes felt it stabbing in his own chest. He struggled to find words, but the gods gave him nothing to say.

"What does it matter?" Achilles went on. He nudged the lyre with his toe. "I'm already as dead as Hector."

"No."

"I have been for years, my friend. This war, and my prophesied fate, have ground all the life out of me, if there was ever any life to begin with. Perhaps if I'd let Hector live—perhaps if we had forced some peace between us, without regard for what Priam wanted, or Helen or Menelaus and Agamemnon . . . perhaps then I might have evaded my fate. But I played into the gods' hands, and now I will die here on the Plain of Troy."

Philoctetes' hands ached with the desire to reach out to Achilles, to touch him, to feel the life that was in him and to make him feel the leap and power of his own pulse, too—to show him that he still lived and would go on living. But he was an old half-crippled man, not beautiful and dancing like Briseis, not a stalwart spear-brother like Patrocles. He was nothing beside the hero—who, even in his despair, slouching on his ivory throne, was more beautiful to Philoctetes than any sunrise and every song.

Useless, he told himself bitterly. *You snake-struck, useless old fool.*

But how, after all, could one comfort the god-born?

"This war will never end," Achilles said dully.

"All wars end sooner or later."

"Not this one. Not in my lifetime."

"Stop that, Achilles; you'll live to see an older age than I will."

He shook his head slowly, staring into the lamp again, distant and dark. "I think of this child of mine, the one Briseis will bear. Will I send my son—or my daughter—out into battle to be killed, just as Priam did to Hector?"

"Priam may have lost many sons, but he still has a few more."

"And I alone killed four in a single day. One of them his heir, who would have struck a peace with me if only I'd listened. What will become of my child? Whose spear will strike him down?"

"No one's," Philoctetes said firmly. "We'll end the war long before that. Before your Briseis even feels her first labor pain, if the gods are good."

"If the gods are good," Achilles said with a bitter laugh. "When have they ever been good?"

He stood abruptly and moved toward his bed, half-hidden now by night's shadows. "I'm tired, Philoctetes."

"Then sleep, my friend." He rose and gathered his bow.

Achilles turned back to him, a startling, piercing pain in his eyes. "Stay."

Slowly, Philoctetes lowered the bow back to the table. Achilles had no desire to bring him to his bed—he was sure of that. He only wanted the company, the comfort of a friend's presence. Of life in his tent. But it was enough for Philoctetes. He nodded and shrugged to hide the grateful flush that was rising to his face. He turned away and said casually, "Well and good, if you wish it. I'd rather sleep in your tent than on Odysseus' ship. I'll just duck outside for a moment."

Achilles grinned, jerked his head. "The latrine pits are that way."

But it wasn't the latrine pits Philoctetes wanted. The isolation and clear, cool flow of the river still called to him; he dragged his foot through the final fringe of the camp until a darkness deeper than the night closed over his head—the stretch of trees, well thinned by many years of siege, that clung to the Scamander's banks.

The night sounds of the camp dwindled behind him, replaced by the whisper of the river. Philoctetes sank onto a flat, cool stone and watched the river's surface, the reflection of a thousand stars rippling with the water's flow. The smell of mud, of damp leaves, was sweet and soothing after the stench of a war camp. He closed his eyes and drank of it deeply, clinging with desperate hands to his memories of Lemnos. Again he saw the olive leaves falling, and again he heard the strum of Achilles' fingers on the lyre.

"You will not die here," Philoctetes whispered. "I won't let you." But he didn't know how one old man could stop the motion of fate, its inevitable turn like the shield rotating in Achilles' hands.

He heard a soft rustle on the river's bank and opened his eyes. A small black thing hopped and bobbed at the water's edge. Starlight glinting off the river limned it in silver, so its shape was clear, but it took Philoctetes a heartbeat or two to truly recognize what he was seeing.

A crow. A carrion eater. And at night, when such an evil bird should have been in its roost.

Uneasily, Philoctetes lowered his hands to the stone, ready to push himself up and hobble away from this place. But the bird saw his movement and turned its head, pinning him in place with its stare. He could see the moon glowing in the small black bead of its eye. The crow flipped over a dead leaf with its beak, hopped again along the gravelly strand, then pointed its dagger bill directly at Philoctetes. It called once, harshly, into the night.

Philoctetes lurched to his feet. The crow startled and flapped away, but the damage was already done. The omen was given, the bones of fate cast.

"I won't let him die here," Philoctetes shouted after the bird as it winged off across the river.

But he was one man alone, who had nothing to fight with, nothing to shield Achilles, save for love—the most earnest yet the weakest shield a man could hold.

He went back to Achilles' tent as quickly as his burning foot would allow.

OVER all else was the sound of Achilles in sleep, his breaths even and steady. He slept heavily and undisturbed, as if he were already dead.

When the horses began to stir and nicker, Philoctetes knew dawn was approaching. He rolled from his pallet as quietly as he could and stood slowly, his old bones protesting at least as much as his foot did. Someone was padding quietly from the far side of the huge tent. Through darkness that had just begun to give way to the pale dawn seeping in from outside, Philoctetes made out the now-familiar silhouette of Automedon, stretching his thin arms over his head as he crossed the gloom.

Together they stepped outside.

"Did he sleep well?" Automedon asked quietly, toeing the remains of a long-dead fire in a charred, shallow pit.

"Far better than I did," Philoctetes answered.

"I'm glad to hear it. He hasn't rested well since Hector, you know. The army is still giddy over Hector's death, but I think Achilles—"

Rough shouts cut Automedon short. They turned and gazed in the direction of the camp's gates and soon saw a commotion of Achaean spearmen approaching the Myrmidon camp, materializing out of the shadows. At the center of the shouting crowd strode a Trojan herald with his formal staff, escorting a tall, harsh-faced warrior whose helmet bore a crest of sea-colored feathers.

As they drew nearer, Philoctetes could make out the warrior's shouts over the tangle of gruff Achaean voices. "Peace! I have only a message! A message for Achilles."

Automedon started toward the knot of men, no doubt to quiet them. But the damage had already been done. The tent flap opened; Achilles stepped into the gray morning chill. He didn't look like he'd been recently asleep. His dark hair was unmussed, and there was not so much as a wrinkle evident on his deep red tunic. He had even found time to don his sandals.

The band of Achaeans gave a collective shout when they spotted Achilles. He held up a hand to quiet them.

"Aeneas of Dardania," he greeted the harsh-faced man in the tall blue plumes. "I see you didn't die of that wound I gave you six weeks ago. Did your mother, Aphrodite, heal you with magic balm?"

"You will not profane the name of my mother, Ishara, with your crude Achaean terms—"

Achilles cut him off. "What do you want?"

The Trojan removed his helmet stiffly. "I come bearing a message from the Lady Cassandra, daughter of Priam." His voice was harsh as the crow that had cawed at Philoctetes last night.

Achilles gestured impatiently. "I am sent to tell you that Troy's best warrior comes to challenge you at sunrise. To avenge Hector's death."

"You?"

"I would count it hubris to call myself Troy's greatest warrior. Helen of Sparta"—the distaste in his voice was clear as he emphasized her proper title—"has seen fit to bestow the compliment on a recent new ally."

The watching Achaeans cursed in mocking tones. Achilles said nothing but folded his arms across his chest, waiting for silence to return.

"On your side of the Scaean Gate," Aeneas added.

"Troy's best warrior," one of the Achaeans said, laughing. "You mean the best among the scraps they have left. Achilles killed *Hector*, man! Are you Trojans so eager to cross the Styx?"

Achilles gave a rough, jerking nod. "Tell Priam, or his daughter, that I accept."

Philoctetes clutched the tie of his own leather belt to keep his hands still, to keep himself from bursting out with disbelief before all these men. The sight of the crow came back to him, its keen, glittering eye, the sharpness of its beak.

"Now let these men go back to Troy," Achilles said to the scouts. "Accompany them to the gate, but do not abuse them."

Achilles turned away and vanished back inside his tent before Aeneas could even don his helmet. Philoctetes shared a wary glance with Automedon, then he, too, ducked into the tent.

"Don't do it," Philoctetes said quietly.

Achilles turned, went to one of his lamps on its iron tripod, touched the sulfur-dipped stick he'd lit on the fire's embers to the lamp oil. Light bloomed, and the tent's interior was suddenly there, blinked into existence as if willed by a god.

"I will do it." Achilles lit another lamp.

Philoctetes followed him across the tent, pleading as softly as he could. No one outside the tent should hear—not even Automedon. But Philoctetes was desperate for Achilles to listen.

"It's just a feint by the Trojans. Just a play to keep the war going on forever. You remember what Hector said. You told me yourself that you should have listened to him."

The twig burned down to Achilles' long, graceful fingers. He shook his hand vigorously, and its flame snuffed out.

"And I told you, too, that this is all I'm good for. War is all I know."

"You could know more, if only you wished it. You could know a better life."

Achilles smiled, but not mockingly. "Like your life? Living alone on some rock in the sea?"

"I have known peace," Philoctetes said sharply. "Peace in a world full of war. Who else can say as much? Not you. And that child your Briseis carries—would you rather your son know peace or war?"

"If I have a son, he'll be expected to fight like me. He'll be expected to follow in my footsteps. There is nothing *but* war for a man like me, and the same will be true of my son."

Heart pounding, Philoctetes edged closer, staring up desperately into Achilles' distant, angry eyes. "And if your child is a girl?

What future for your daughter, Achilles? Will she be spear-won, too, like her mother? Will she become a slave, to be traded like a horse or a pound of tin?"

Achilles huffed a short laugh. He turned away, pulled open the black trunk where his magnificent armor lay. He lifted out the shield and examined it in the lamplight, then set it gently aside. He bent to retrieve another piece of armor, but Philoctetes' hand snaked out of its own accord and caught Achilles by the arm. His muscle was hard beneath Philoctetes' fingers, and his flesh was warm—alive, no matter what Achilles felt inside. He was still alive, for as long as Philoctetes could keep him safe. But how much longer could he manage it?

Achilles turned, brows raised in surprise, and gazed down at Philoctetes. Then his eyes fell to the hand that still clutched his arm. Philoctetes did not remove it—could not have, even if he'd wanted to.

"I'm afraid," Philoctetes admitted in a whisper.

Achilles turned toward him. "Of what?"

"I fear you'll be killed." *The crow as good as told me so.*

Achilles bent his neck. For a heartbeat, Philoctetes thought the great hero was hanging his head in shame or yielding to his warning and giving up on Troy's new champion.

But then he drew nearer and nearer still. Achilles' lips brushed Philoctetes' cheek, just above the graying bristle of his beard.

"I know, my friend," Achilles said. "But I'm not afraid."

He straightened, turned back to his trunk. Philoctetes was left in mute shock, the warmth of Achilles' kiss still burning on his cheek, his hand still tingling with the feel of the man's skin. He swallowed hard, fighting down the loss that surged in his chest.

"I'll count it a great favor," Achilles added, "if you'll help me with my armor.

PENTHESILEA

THE sun was just beginning to rise behind the walls of Troy when the Achaean hero Achilles, flanked by chanting, cheering troops, presented himself at the Scaean Gate. Penthesilea watched the crowd from the wall beside the gate's great crest. The Achaeans gathered, jeering and howling, around the two red pillars that flanked the gate. The pillars were mostly lost in shadow, but even through that dimness, even from her high vantage, Penthesilea could not escape their frank color, the evocation of blood about to be spilled.

Gleaming in his many-hued armor, Achilles halted twenty paces from the pillars while the remainder of the Achaeans held back, contenting themselves with the insults they hurled at the city. A stocky, graying man limped up beside Achilles and squinted up at Troy's walls, where the sun blazed.

"That one, the gray one, expects a crowd," Cassandra said from her place beside Penthesilea. "Priam and his queen, at least; perhaps Paris and Helen. But he sees only the two of us. What do you think he makes of us, Amazon?"

Without a crowd to watch the fight, Achilles no doubt suspected a trap. Penthesilea watched the warrior go still, almost as if he hesitated. Even most of the Achaean troops quieted. She could hear the rattle of armor and weapons as they shifted, gazing about the plain warily, fearful now of an ambush.

A slender, auburn-haired man sidled close to Achilles. He leaned close to speak into the hero's helmet, into his ear. Achilles listened but then shook his head in denial or refusal. He steadied himself, his legs wide in a powerful stance, his hand firm on his spear. There was a readiness in his stance that chilled Penthesilea's blood even as it stirred her admiration. The man was ready to die—eager for it. He stepped forward and raised his voice to address Cassandra and Penthesilea, two women alone on the wall.

"I am Achilles. I've come to meet Troy's best warrior. Let him come out and fight me, as agreed."

Cassandra turned and gazed at Penthesilea. She did not ask her to reconsider nor question whether she was ready. The seer only looked at her, silent and serene, and Penthesilea knew it was time.

She descended the long stairs to the court below while Cassandra gave the signal to the gatekeepers. The black Scaean Gate screamed like a chorus of the damned as it swung open just wide enough to reveal the lone figure of Achilles, backed by the crowd of Achaeans at a safe distance. Penthesilea stood in the gateway, braced and ready, never taking her eyes from the warrior in the gleaming, lacquered armor. She heard the gate close behind her.

Achilles held out his hand; the auburn-haired youth delivered his spear, then took the graying man by the shoulder and pulled him back, well away from the ring of Achaeans that now rushed forward to form before the closed gates. It was an arena walled by shouting, cursing, taunting men and floored by cold earth, still in shadow beneath the towers of Troy. Cold fear warred with readiness in Penthesilea's gut. A fist seemed to reach up from her middle, seizing her heart, but she willed it to go on beating. All the chants of the men sounded like the screams of carrion crows.

The Achaean men and even Achilles himself seemed to stare right past her, waiting for the gates to reopen and disgorge a hero. Anger flared in Penthesilea's heart; she would not go to her death invisible. She would let the gods see her, make them know her, so there could be no doubt who had set the balance to rights.

She slung her spear casually over her shoulder and strode out into the ring of Achaeans. Silence washed like a wave around the ring as the men finally *saw* her—as they realized that she was the hero come to fight the great Achilles, and no other.

She might stand as tall and proud as any warrior, but even through her strange, flowing trousers and oversized tunic, through the simple scale vest, they could all read the curves of a woman's body. Penthesilea had braided her long black hair and bound it up around her head where it would not impede her, tucked beneath the small cap of hardened leather that served as her helmet. Her olive skin, broad nose, and catlike eyes would mark her as a Cimmerian to Achaean eyes. She could guess their thoughts—*Troy's best warrior isn't a Trojan at all. Troy's best warrior isn't even a man!*—and she laughed at them, laughed at Troy and Sparta, letting her teeth flash in the rising sun.

She had small bronze-studded bucklers strapped to each forearm, but that was the extent of her armor. She halted several paces from Achilles, aware that she looked hopelessly slight and poorly protected against his obvious bulk and power. She tossed her spear in her hand, testing its balance, then gave it an experimental swing. She laughed again, louder this time—loud enough for the gods to hear.

"An Amazon?" one of Achilles' men muttered. "What's Priam playing at?"

Achilles looked up at the wall again. Penthesilea knew he would see nothing there—no one but Cassandra, staring back at him.

"I don't want to fight a woman," Achilles shouted up at the seer.

"You speak to *me*, Achaean rat," Penthesilea shouted. It felt good to call out her defiance to the hero. It made her feel strong, alive. Her accent might be thick, but she knew Achilles would understand her well enough. She advanced on him, spear poised and ready. "It is *I* who will send you to the afterlife, to plead on your knees before your gods for their mercy!"

The ring of Achaeans erupted in laughter. Penthesilea ignored them all. She circled Achilles, but as she passed nearer to where his two attendants stood—the auburn-haired and the gray—she caught the older man's eye. Only for a moment; she didn't allow her gaze to stray from Achilles for longer than a heartbeat. But what she saw in the grizzled man's eyes made her heart lurch, almost made her flinch. His pain was palpable, and such a perfect reflection of her own loss that it shuddered the breath in her throat. The joy of the fight and the certainty of deliverance slipped away from her. She felt the weight of grief dragging at her spirit again, trailing behind her as she moved, making her clumsy and slow.

She pushed the feeling away with brutal determination. There would be time enough to acknowledge her sorrows when death came to claim her. For now, she must fight—must give the gods a good show and prove her bravery, prove she was a worthy warrior after all. She must not lose sight of honor. She must not let the balance tip so far from level again.

Penthesilea glowered into the shadow of Achilles' helmet.

"Do you see me, Achaean dog?" she taunted. "Your death is coming at the hands of a woman! You'll bleed out under the point of a woman's spear!"

Achilles said nothing. He circled to keep her within his sights, but his spear remained low, his shield tentatively high. He made no move to fight her. As Penthesilea turned him to face the rising sun, the light revealed his eyes. They were as pale green as new grass, and he watched her with an intensity that took her aback. It was not the bitter glare of enemies about to meet in war. It was wide-eyed, awed, like a man struck by love's arrow.

"Gods," he murmured, so softly she could barely hear him over the noise of the crowd. "Gods, but you're alive."

Alive. Only if the gods were cruel. Only if she couldn't right the balance.

"Come," she shouted. "Are you brave? Or are you weak? Show me, Achilles! Show me your true nature!"

But his spear remained stubbornly low. He made no move to advance. "I won't fight a woman," he said again. "Go back to Priam and tell him—"

"Fuck Priam!" Penthesilea yelled. "And fuck Troy, too!"

The circle of Achaeans cheered heartily at that. She advanced on Achilles, a few dancing steps, then a few more. She was within the reach of his spear now. "I don't fight for Priam," she said. "I fight for Hector only. His blood cries out for justice, and I will give him that!" *Hippolyte's blood cries out for justice, and hers is the only voice I hear.*

"Hector is dead," Achilles said calmly. "What's done is done. And if you have no love for Troy, then you had no love for Hector. Tell me why you really fight, woman."

For one brief moment, no longer than the beat of a blackbird's wings, Penthesilea hesitated. Her eyes widened, holding Achilles' steady green gaze. But in the next moment, her grief and rage came pouring back into her. The pain gave her life, and she could feel that life emanating like lightning from her eyes. Achilles sucked in a breath, as if struck again by awe—by longing. His own gaze softened and his mouth fell. The tip of his spear drooped ever farther toward the earth.

"You are too beautiful to kill," he said.

"Damn it, Achilles!" The graying man threw himself forward, as if he sought to plant himself between Penthesilea and the warrior. His hands reached out as though he wanted to drag Achilles from the ring, even if it shamed him in front of all the these Achaean sea-wolves and Troy, too. But the younger one—the auburn-haired man—grabbed him roughly, held him back.

Penthesilea laughed hoarsely. She spat at Achilles; the spittle struck him on his enameled breastplate. "Do you fear a woman? Are you such a coward? Does Agamemnon keep your balls pickled in a jug of wine?"

"Go back to Priam," Achilles tried again. "There's no honor for me in this—in killing a woman in single combat."

"Honor?" Her teeth clenched; she could barely force the words out. "What about my honor? What about my sister's honor?"

Achilles, still circling slowly to face her, cast her a look of pure confusion.

"You will fight me," she insisted. "I will not go back to Troy in disgrace. You will die to avenge Hector, or I will die to avenge Hippolyte. One way or another, I will have my honor, Achilles. For life without honor is not worth living."

Penthesilea struck first.

Her spear flashed in the sun as it darted toward Achilles' legs, seeking to sprawl him in his heavy armor. Achilles danced back, parrying the blow. Her spear whirled over her head so fast it whistled, and in a blink she attacked from another angle. Achilles' shield deflected her blow with a loud clang.

The men in the ring hooted and cheered; the fight was on, whether Achilles willed it or no. Blow by blow, strike by parried strike, their clash shifted subtly. Achilles' reluctance to fight a woman wore away as Penthesilea proved her skill. Her attacks came ever more quickly; with minimal armor, she was agile and light, and she knew that all the watchers could see her dexterity, could appreciate her lethal swiftness. She was as good as any of the men who stood watching—that, she knew. She thought she might be as good as Achilles himself. But she didn't need to best him. She only needed to provoke him.

The clang of spear tip against armor echoed from the Scaean Gate. Then a high, panicked shout came from the same direction. Penthesilea spared the briefest glance at the wall, seeing in a moment that more people had joined Cassandra. White-haired Priam was easy to recognize, as were Paris and Helen, who hurried to stand beside him, both of them gleaming like treasure in the rising sun. Helen leaned over the wall, her mouth opening in another cry, though over the noise of crowd and combat, Penthesilea could not make out her words.

Penthesilea drove at Achilles with naked fury, and finally the last of his reluctance vanished. The rhythm of battle seemed to fall over him as a drummer's beat captures the minds and bodies of dancers. He no longer retreated before her attacks, but drove at her with brutal speed, his spear slicing the air, singing against her bucklers, sending jarring blows up her arms to rattle her bones. His warrior self was at the fore now, eclipsing all thought, all hesitation.

Penthesilea feinted right, then dodged left, hurtling herself toward Achilles' spear. It should have been a good move—to push herself in past the man's reach, blocking use of his spear arm with her own body, forcing him to turn and expose his back to her weapon.

But Achilles, enthralled by the battle's rhythmic dance, seemed to know what Penthesilea intended almost before she did. He was ready for the move. His spear swept low, knocking her feet from beneath her; she fell upon her back, her leather cap rolling away as her head struck the hard ground.

Ignoring the shock of the impact, she began to roll at once, gathering herself to spring up and fight on. But Achilles was ready for that, too. As her left arm reached across her body, the unprotected spot just below her armpit was exposed. Only for an instant, but an instant was all a fighter like Achilles needed. He drove his spearhead in deep.

Penthesilea froze, never knowing whether it was pain or relief that stilled her—agony or the bliss of forgiveness.

Silence fell over the ring. She opened her mouth to speak, to call out Hippolyte's name. But only a weak sound emerged, a whimper of surrender to her fate.

She sagged back against the earth, Achilles' spear still quivering in her body. The shudder of the blow that ended her pain sang a sweet song along her limbs, sweeter than the rhythm of hooves across the steppe.

PHILOCTETES

WHEN the Amazon's blood darkened the ground, the life seemed to drain out of Achilles, too. He stood over her, panting, his fists slowly unclenching, his head, in its plumed helmet, drooping. The shield slid from his arm and rolled along the ground on its rim, then wobbled, teetered, and fell flat.

"No," Achilles said. His voice was quiet, but so was the Plain of Troy. The word carried far.

He dropped to his knees beside the dying woman. "No!"

"Gods' sakes," Automedon hissed at Philoctetes' side. "Come on."

They went to stand at Achilles' side. He didn't look up. His mouth hung open; his eyes were stark with grief, with a terrible self-loathing.

The woman rasped on the ground, blood thick on her lips. Her braid had uncoiled itself from her head and lay like the shadow of a snake in the dust.

Automedon planted his foot on the woman's chest and seized the spear. "Brave," he said to her kindly. "And worthy."

But the Amazon didn't hear. Her black eyes already stared into a misty distance, and just before Automedon pulled the spear out, sending the last gush of blood from her side and from her mouth, Philoctetes saw her smile. Whatever glory or absolution the woman had sought in battle, she had found it in the end. It was a small mercy that would, Philoctetes suspected, comfort Achilles not one bit.

The light faded from the Amazon's eyes. As it went, it wrenched a wordless howl of anguish from Achilles' throat. It was high and harsh, just like his laugh—almost womanish in its pitch and its passion. Before either Automedon or Philoctetes could stop him, he stooped and gathered the dead Amazon to his chest. He rocked her, smearing his breastplate with red, then bent and kissed her, painting his lips with her blood. He left his tears to run down her cheeks.

"Gods!" Achilles screamed. "Why, gods! It was supposed to be me—me!"

Automedon threw down the spear. "For fuck's sake, Philoctetes! Get him out of here!"

Philoctetes grabbed Achilles by the arm, trying to pull him up, to tear him away from the Amazon. But Achilles batted him as if he were a fly, and Philoctetes stumbled backward, crying out at the pain in his foot.

He glanced up at the wall. Helen and the woman in black had both vanished, but Priam was there, still as a statue, watching.

And Paris was beside him. Paris, too, looked down in perfect stillness for a moment. Then, as Achilles' cries of sorrow rose again, Philoctetes could see the Trojan prince's shoulders tremble, then bounce with the rhythm of his laughter.

It was Automedon who convinced Achilles to relinquish the woman's body, though how he managed it, Philoctetes never knew. When Achilles was on his feet again, Philoctetes wedged himself under one of his arms, supporting the warrior as if he were injured—though he had sustained no physical wounds that Philoctetes could see. With Automedon on the other side, they shouted and cursed until a way parted through the crowd of staring warriors, and they guided the grief-blinded hero back to the Myrmidon camp and his tent.

Once there, Achilles broke away from his friends and staggered to his ivory chair. He sat, no longer wailing, the tears drying on his face.

There was a cacophony of voices outside as the throng grew. Word would soon spread through the whole Achaean army, Philoctetes knew: vile talk that Achilles had shamed himself with this display of grief, and before the walls of Troy, too.

What will Odysseus think when he hears? What will Agamemnon think?

"I'm going out there," Automedon said. "I'm going to shut those bloody shits up. Otherwise, the gods only know what kind of stories will fly around camp." He cast a long, sympathetic gaze at Achilles, hunched silently on his throne. "Take care of him, Philoctetes."

How? he wanted to ask. But Automedon was already ducking through the tent's door, already yelling for the nearest spearmen to bugger off, to remember their loyalty and their pride.

Philoctetes limped across the bright rugs, passed the nine-stringed lyre on its stand. He stood before Achilles, and Achilles stared through him, seeing nothing but the horrors in his own mind.

"Up, my friend," Philoctetes said briskly. "Let me get you out of your armor."

There was a lengthy pause, filled with Automedon's shouts as he drove men well away from Achilles' tent. Philoctetes thought Achilles would refuse or simply go on staring until the war ended and Troy and Sparta and the whole damned world crumbled to dust. But then he pushed himself up from the ivory chair, slowly, silently. He held out his arms, and Philoctetes began to unbuckle the plates from his body. One by one, he laid the pieces aside. They would have to be cleaned of the woman's blood before they could be stored again.

"Did you see her?" Achilles asked quietly.

Philoctetes did not hesitate in his work. "Of course I saw her."

"Did you truly *see* her? There was such a light in her eyes. Such sorrow. She was alive, Philoctetes. The battle was her dance—like Briseis, dancing."

Achilles fell silent. His arms were bare now, but he seemed not to notice; he held himself in the same position, arms stretched to the sides, eyes staring blindly.

"I killed her," he said softly. "I killed life. I killed beauty. She is dead—beauty is dead. Because of me."

Philoctetes pulled the last buckle apart and eased the breastplate from Achilles' body. He turned it as he laid it on the carpets so Achilles would not be forced to look upon the Amazon's blood.

He could think of nothing to say to Achilles. He watched him in pained silence for a moment, then held out his arms to embrace him.

With a high, broken sob, Achilles fell into Philoctetes' arms. His great, strong body was heavy in his grief; Philoctetes' leg throbbed as he strained against the weight, holding Achilles upright. He stroked his back, the skin still flushed with the heat of battle, slick with sweat.

"It will be all right," Philoctetes said.

Achilles shook his head; his sharp chin dug into Philoctetes' shoulder. "It won't. It was supposed to be me; don't you see that? It was my death the Fates foretold. But instead, I go on living. And I am tired, Philoctetes. Tired of war. Tired of life."

"You mustn't speak that way. Please." *I couldn't bear it if you died.*

"When will the gods end my misery?"

"When they end this war," Philoctetes said. "When it's all over, you'll come to Lemnos with me. And it will be like it was that summer. Hunting, laughing, singing by the fire. You remember. Don't you?"

Achilles pressed his eyes against Philoctetes' neck. The tears were hot as they tracked down into the collar of his tunic.

"But this war will never end," Achilles whispered. "And neither will my pain."

AGAIN the Scaean Gate opened with its hellish scream. Philoctetes approached warily, limping over the hard-packed ground, skirting the stain of livid red that marked where the Amazon had fallen. At once, nearly a score of Trojan troops surrounded Philoctetes, hands on the hilts of their swords, eyeing him darkly as they escorted him to the citadel. Their pace was brisk, and it was all he could do to stay on his feet, to walk—in his poor, crippled way—without crying out from the pain.

The soldiers conducted him through the limestone arches of the citadel gates, across a courtyard paved in smooth white marble that glared in the brightness of the sun. Philoctetes' leg was screaming by the time he was ushered into the high palace of Priam. When two carved, gilded doors were opened to reveal the dark length of Priam's megaron, Philoctetes sighed in relief. The soldiers parted, and he was allowed to continue at his own pace, albeit with a pair of armed Trojan scowlers for companions.

Philoctetes moved slowly, heavily, holding the messenger's staff before him. Priam sat in dignified silence on his throne, his white hair and beard almost luminous against the shadowed stillness of the room. Golden Paris stood to one side of the throne, fidgeting, smirking, nearly bouncing on the toes of his sandals like an untrained boy.

"I remember you," Paris said almost eagerly. His grin was wide with amusement. "The old mattress. The shaft-planter."

Philoctetes did not dignify Paris with a reply. He couldn't help but recall the last time he'd seen the Trojan prince, at the wedding of Odysseus and Penelope. He remembered how Paris had taunted him at the archery contest—had tried to humiliate him, in fact, before the eyes of the whole celebration. The same mocking light glittered now in the prince's eye.

Priam's mouth thinned, and his white brows rose when Philoctetes dipped his head in courtesy. "My king. I've come with a message."

"A message?" Age had graveled the king's voice, but it was still thick with power. "From whom, I wonder? Agamemnon sends that smarmy herald Talthybius when he wishes to treat with me." The old man's eyes narrowed, glinting with amusement. "You stood with Achilles this morning, at his . . . *display* before the Scaean Gate."

"Yes, I—"

Priam raised a hand, callused and broad despite the age spots that peppered his skin. "Perhaps your message is from Achilles, then."

"My king, I'm afraid the message is mine alone. I hope you will listen, although I am not a great man."

Paris snorted, ruffling his gleaming curls. "A great man like Achilles?"

Philoctetes ignored him. "I am a prince of Meliboea, and over many years I've seen enough battles to sate any man's thirst for blood. I know Troy must have long since grown weary of this war, as we all have."

Again Paris interjected. "When we heard there was a messenger outside our gates, we assumed you came from one of the commanders. But now you tell us you act on your own whims." He turned to Priam. "This man is wasting our time, Father. Send him away. Better yet, send him back to Agamemnon with his head in a sack."

"The high king won't much care if you kill me," Philoctetes said. Which was not true; Agamemnon apparently believed in the power of Heracles' bow. He wouldn't like to see its owner—and the best archer in the army—divested of his head. But neither Paris nor his father needed to know the special store Agamemnon placed in Philoctetes and his bow.

"I am a friend to Achilles," Philoctetes went on. "He confided something important to me—something I believe you should hear, too."

Paris' smirk slid from his face, and he stilled himself, his pale eyes watching Philoctetes with a sudden greedy intensity. No doubt the prince of Troy thought Philoctetes was about to turn traitor and spill out the great hero's deepest secrets now that Achilles had made a spectacle of himself before the city's walls.

Priam gestured: *Out with it.*

"Hector spoke to Achilles before their final battle," Philoctetes said. "And he offered Achilles peace."

Priam leaned forward on his throne. "Peace?"

"An end to the war, my lord."

"I am aware of what the word means, Prince of Meliboea. How exactly did Hector think to make this peace?"

"By refusing to fight. He urged Achilles to walk away from the battle, and together, with their mutual refusal, they would bring an end to the conflict."

Paris and Priam both stared at Philoctetes in frank disbelief.

"It is true," he said. "And what's more, I believe it was a good plan. I believe it would have worked if Achilles hadn't been so distraught over the death of one who was close to him—a man whom Hector killed."

"Do you think," Paris scoffed, "that wars end as simply as that? Do you think warriors merely agree to stop fighting, and that's that—all slights forgotten, all bitterness turned sweet?"

"No," Philoctetes said. "But a refusal to fight any longer, a decision to spill no more blood on either side: that would be a start to the process. From there, we could—"

"Tell it to Agamemnon," Priam said. "Don't tell it to me. Look around you: this is a city under siege. We have held for long years, but we are still besieged. Whenever we spill blood, it is in defense of our city, of ourselves. It's you who are the aggressors. It's you who make the cuts that spill the blood."

"Perhaps the high king will agree to—"

The king laughed bitterly. "Agamemnon will agree to nothing. He will not give up until my city falls. His greed is too strong. You don't think it's his brother's wife he fights for, do you? Helen was never anything to him but a convenient excuse. No, it's the tin trade he wants to control and access to our strait and all the rest of the goods that flow though Troy. One haughty cunt like Helen isn't worth all this fuss. No woman is, no matter how beautiful. But wealth, trade—that's worth waging an endless war for. And Agamemnon will not stop until he controls it all."

Paris stepped forward, drawing closer to Philoctetes than the latter liked. The younger man's smirk stirred a thrill of loathing in Philoctetes' veins. The memory of the archery contest, and Paris' disrespect, was closer to the surface than Philoctetes had thought.

"But Agamemnon may have no choice but to turn tail and run now," Paris said. "His greatest warrior is reduced to nothing, weeping like a woman over some Amazon bitch. Soon every Achaean out there on the plain will be weeping, too."

"Quiet," Priam said. He raised his chin in Philoctetes' direction—as much of a gesture of apology as a king ever gave. "My son is hot-tempered and has lived a soft life." Paris' cheeks flared red, but his father went on relentlessly. "For too long, he has gotten by on charm and left real men's work to his brothers. But now the best of his brothers are dead. And it's time for him to prove himself a worthy son of Priam."

Philoctetes could feel Paris' rage, a simmering heat that made sweat bead on Philoctetes' back. He would not look at the prince, hoping his refusal to see the younger man's mortification was enough to stay Paris' wrath.

"Father," Paris said in a strangled voice.

Priam stayed his protest with another curt gesture of that powerful hand. "If you think Achilles is so reduced, so womanish, then go and kill him yourself, Paris."

Philoctetes swallowed hard and did not look at Paris, but the younger man's stillness told him everything he needed to know. The charming prince whose charm had finally worn thin, the eternal favorite of his father finally swatted down in displeasure.

"Hector didn't fear to challenge Achilles," Priam went on relentlessly. "Even that Amazon didn't fear. Surely, you are brave enough to take on a broken hero. Surely, you are a son of Priam."

"My lord," Philoctetes said quietly, "perhaps I should be dismissed before you discuss strategy—and the assignment you give your own son . . ."

"Do you think I'm a fool, Prince of Meliboea?" Priam's mouth curved in an unexpected smile. "Do you think my mind has rotted with age? Paris has strutted about this palace from the day he returned from exile. If he thinks himself a hero worthy of immortal songs, then let him prove it. If he fails, then he'll find himself on a funeral pyre. Just as Hector did. It is all one to me now. Troy has a surplus of princes, and even now, after ten long years of war, I do not lack for sons."

Paris stared goggle-eyed at his father. Then he turned to Philoctetes, and his look melted into hatred and rage. Without another word, the prince spun on his heel and stalked out of the room.

Philoctetes relaxed a bit with the prince gone from the megaron.

Paris was a braggart, and all braggarts were cowards. He would take himself off to sulk somewhere, for an hour or a day or a week. But he would never have the courage to challenge Achilles to a fight.

"My son is a fool," Priam said tiredly. "He still thinks this war is about him. But it never was."

"No, my king. Not truly."

"You've brought your message, Prince of Meliboea. I'll consider what you said." But the weariness in the king's voice, and the way he drooped back in his carved chair, told Philoctetes he wouldn't consider the proposal very far. Priam was too convinced that there could be no compromise with Agamemnon and Menelaus. He believed too strongly in the war's perpetuity, in the hopelessness of his position. "Now go back to your camp."

"WHERE were you?" Automedon stood and offered Philoctetes a wineskin.

He drank deeply, then passed it back to the young man. "You wouldn't believe me if I told you."

Automedon jerked his head toward the tent. "He has stayed inside all day, but he's been asking for you."

Philoctetes reached up and scratched the place on his neck where Achilles' tears had run, leaving traces of salt on his skin. He could almost feel the wing-beats of the crows high above, but he refused to look at them again. "I'll go see to him, then."

Philoctetes had hoped he might find Achilles' spirit restored, some of his agony soothed away by the healing power of sleep. But Achilles sat on the edge of his bed, hands hanging limply between his knees, and staring blankly, as before, at nothing. Philoctetes glanced around the tent and saw that the armor was cleaned and stored. Automedon's doing, no doubt.

"Where were you?" Achilles asked dully.

Philoctetes drew a deep breath and considered giving the same answer he'd given to the young man outside. But he remembered the weight of Achilles, sagging in his arms. There was something more than friendship between them now. Perhaps it was not enough for Philoctetes—not what he truly wished for. It was real, though, and he cherished it.

"I went to the city," he said. "I carried a message to King Priam."

Achilles looked up at him. The dullness fled from his eyes, and he held Philoctetes in place with the force of his stare. "What message?"

"I brought him Hector's offer—of peace, of a cessation of all fighting. I told him what Hector told you: that we could decide to end this fight if we simply chose not to fight any longer."

Achilles nodded, thoughtful and silent. Finally, he asked, "And what did Priam say?"

"He found little hope in the plan. And Paris—"

"You spoke to Paris, too?"

"It was not my preference," Philoctetes said wryly. "Paris is more boy than man, and more shit than boy."

"He'll be one of the only heroes Troy has left now that Hector is dead."

"I don't think Troy accounts Paris a hero, however highly he thinks of himself."

Achilles hesitated, then asked, almost timidly, "Did Paris say anything about me?"

Philoctetes didn't want to answer that question.

"I heard he was on the wall this morning," Achilles said. "I heard he saw . . . saw everything."

"He was on the wall," Philoctetes admitted.

"And what did he say about me?"

Philoctetes sank wearily into his chair. "Achilles—"

"Tell me," Achilles insisted. His sharp eyes narrowed, and

with a note of triumph in his voice, he said, "If you love me, Philoctetes, then tell me what he said."

His heart pounded; his throat tightened so abruptly that he was sure he could never force the words out. But Achilles was watching, so at last he nodded. "He said you are broken. He said you . . . you wept like a woman."

Achilles rose slowly from the bed. He stalked to one of the lamps and stood before it, arms folded, staring into its flame. "Perhaps I did," he said softly. "That Amazon would have wept for me, I think, had she killed me. She was a woman, but her tears would have been worth something. But you're right, Philoctetes. Paris is more shit than man." He drew a measured breath. "And he's the last hope Troy has, isn't he?"

"I don't know. That's the honest truth."

Achilles stared at him; Philoctetes couldn't look away and couldn't hide the flicker in his eyes that said there was more—information he was holding back.

"Tell me," Achilles said.

Philoctetes sighed.

"Priam told Paris to fight you. One on one, as you did—"

"With the Amazon."

"With Hector."

Achilles straightened, turned away from the lamp's flame. "Well, then. Perhaps Priam is right. I should call Paris out in combat—I should face him. And let the gods do whatever they will."

"Paris is far too cowardly to face you."

"He will if I call for him. Priam will force him out of the gate. I'll make the challenge at dawn."

Philoctetes shook his head, his body trembling with exhaustion. "No, Achilles. That's not the way to win this. You need time to recover from what happened this morning—time to regroup. There's no sense in risking yourself again; not until you're in a better frame of mind. In the meantime, we can take Paris out from afar."

Achilles turned to him, one brow raised in cool amusement. "A bow shot? No, old friend. After all the grief he's wrought, I want the satisfaction of looking into Paris' eyes when he dies. I want to see the life leak out of him."

"You only feel that way because he insulted you. But what are words from a man like Paris? Nothing. Less than nothing. They're mindless, harmless—like a breeze."

Achilles shook his head and returned to his brooding study of the lamp's flame. "A bow shot doesn't make the right death. Not the death Paris deserves."

Philoctetes held his tongue, but he was an old enough man to know what the young did not: that death is death. And a bow could do the job as well as a spear.

Achilles reached for his sword belt with sudden energy. He buckled it around his waist.

Philoctetes lurched to his feet. "What are you doing?"

"Going out," Achilles said. "I've been in this damned tent all day."

He made his way to the tent's door, and Philoctetes hurried after him.

Outside, Automedon rose from the fire pit. "Supper's not ready yet, but—"

Achilles waved him to silence. "Save it. I'm only going out for a stroll along the river. To clear my head. I'll be back by the time it's ready." He narrowed his eyes at Automedon. "Don't let anyone follow me. I don't want to deal with any of those limp-cocks who saw me fight this morning."

"Understood," Automedon said. He passed a wary glance to Philoctetes.

High overhead, where the smoke from the fire dissipated on the gathering breeze, a crow called—and Philoctetes shivered.

"I'm coming with you," he said to Achilles.

"No. I'm going alone. You'll stay here, Philoctetes—that's an order."

"But I—"

"No."

Achilles strode away, heading toward the thin strip of trees that edged the Scamander. Night's shadows were already beginning to pool between the trunks of trees, but the late sun was bright on Achilles' back, and his back was straight and proud. He looked more confident, more whole than he had that morning. Philoctetes wanted to believe that the worst was beyond them now. But a cold stone sat in his gut, and the crows overhead were still calling.

He turned back for the tent, found his bow where he'd left it beside the half-empty jug of wine. He strung it with a sure, practiced motion and secured his quiver across his back.

"Philoctetes!" A shout from within the camp. Philoctetes turned to see Odysseus striding toward him. "Let us talk, friend," Odysseus called. "I have a few ideas about that bow of yours."

"Blast!" Automedon looked ready to spit.

"Odysseus can wait," Philoctetes said. "I've something more important to attend to now. Make and excuse for me, Automedon."

Automedon nodded. "Stay as close to Achilles as you can."

"I'll do my best. But this foot of mine—"

"It doesn't matter. You have your bow. Use it well if need be."

"Let us pray there's no need."

The memory of Paris' hate-filled stare burned in Philoctetes' mind as he limped after Achilles. And even though Philoctetes was certain that Paris would make no move against Achilles, the gods alone knew who else might be out there, laughing into their hands over Achilles' tears, his unmasked pain. Only the gods could say who might stumble across the Achaean hero and think him broken, an easy target.

Beautiful, strong, and whole, Achilles left the Myrmidon camp behind and moved with ease through the thin lines of trees, gliding smoothly along the river while Philoctetes fell farther and farther behind.

I should have sent Automedon to protect him, he thought, cursing himself bitterly, *and stayed to handle Odysseus on my own.* But even as he lashed himself, Philoctetes savored the sight of Achilles moving free and alone through the sparse woodland. The years fell away; it was Lemnos again, and summer, and the murmur of the river over rocks was the laughter of happy young men for whom the world could never be cruel or bruising. From somewhere—carrying faintly from the distant camp or from the walls of Troy, or perhaps singing in his own heart, he could hear the long, lingering notes of a lyre and a high, sweet male voice raised in song.

The faster Achilles walked—the farther he went from Philoctetes—the lighter his step became. He was outrunning his sorrows, the feel of the Amazon woman dead in his arms, the grinding weight of the war. He was little more than a boy again, hunting rabbits in a field. Philoctetes' breath burned in his chest as he struggled to maintain a safe distance between them—a bowshot's length. That distance would have to close as night came on and visibility was reduced. Never once as the shadows deepened did the broad, brilliant hero turn to look over his shoulder. He only pressed on, going aimlessly toward whatever relief he found in the twilight shadows, in the soft singing of the river.

Achilles approached a great tree, fallen across the bank—the victim of some long-ago windstorm or perhaps a lightning strike. Philoctetes leaned against a nearby jut of stone and panted, trying to ignore the ache in his foot. He watched distant Achilles consider the tree, searching for the best way over or under.

A steady movement on a narrow trail, well beyond the fallen

tree, caught Philoctetes' eye. He froze, every hair on his body standing on end, and stared. While Achilles still inspected the tree, the thing in the brush beyond wavered through shadow, bobbed, seemed to dissipate for a moment, then coalesced into the unmistakable shape of a man—one man, walking alone through the trees.

Philoctetes held his breath. The man passed through a slanting beam of gold, the last vestiges of the sun's fading light. The fallen tree's root ball must have blocked the man from Achilles' view, but to Philoctetes, the gleaming curls were unmistakable.

Paris.

Philoctetes squinted at Paris, trying to gauge the distance, trying to feel the wind's direction. But his heart was pounding with such a desperate fear that he knew he couldn't trust his own senses. He opened his mouth to call a warning to Achilles—and then snapped his teeth shut again. There might be more men following Paris—scouts, soldiers. And Achilles was unarmored, with only his short sword and Philoctetes to protect him.

Philoctetes could see that both men stood with swords drawn, crouched forward, ready to fight. Paris was far better protected, with a reinforced vest and a short skirt of bronze scales protecting his thighs. He bore a bow and quiver as well as his sword.

Achilles glanced down as Philoctetes burst out of the trees like a haggard old deer. "Get back, Philoctetes."

Paris spared no glance for Philoctetes, but his mouth tightened in a spiteful grimace. "The old messenger, the old post-hole. Stay and watch, graybeard. I'll give you a message to carry back to camp." He made an experimental lunge at Achilles, who knocked his blade back with offhanded ease.

Paris edged back, shrugged his bow and quiver from his shoulder, let them fall to the ground. He crept toward Achilles again, sword raised.

"Alone, Paris?" Philoctetes called. "Out to prove your heroism by yourself? Or did your father send real warriors with you to be your nursemaids?"

Paris grinned humorlessly. "You'd like it if I told you, wouldn't you?"

Paris and Achilles circled, backs stiff, eyes blazing, like two dogs hackling before a thrashing, snarling fight. The moment Paris' back was turned to Philoctetes, he slid his bow down from his shoulder and pulled an arrow from the quiver on his back. He nocked quickly and melted back against the tree, ready to draw in an instant, watching for his moment. He knew that when it came it would be fleeting and precious. He mustn't waste the shot.

"When I kill Achilles," Paris taunted, "will you wail over him, old man? Just like a mourning girl—like Achilles himself cried over that Amazon?"

"You know nothing," Achilles grated. "Nothing of beauty, nothing of life."

"I know plenty of death."

Paris drove for Achilles then, and despite his evident softness, his habitual avoidance of battle, he was well trained, as any prince should be. His attacks were fast and relentless, his determination to strike Achilles down palpable and terrifying.

But Achilles had earned his reputation and his songs. Even without armor, he threw himself fearlessly at his enemy. Their swords rang and rattled through the trees as loud as thunder.

Philoctetes kept the bowstring taut, just on the point of a draw—but the combatants whirled and tangled too quickly, too close. He couldn't be sure of a shot, couldn't fire without the risk of striking Achilles.

Paris surged in a flurry of fast blows; Achilles parried in a blur of bronze. Then Achilles struck fast and hard from above. Paris raised his sword just in time to keep his head in one piece.

Achilles' blade slid down Paris' with a cold, slithering note; in the next moment, Paris screamed, reeling back as his sword fell to the earth. A red line tracked across the back of his sword hand, weeping blood. Achilles kicked the downed sword; it skittered across the bank and splashed into the river.

Paris, clutching his wounded hand, grimaced at Achilles. He wavered on his legs, as weak and wobbly as Troy was now that Hector had fallen.

"Yield," Paris gasped.

Achilles' ripple of laughter filled the night. "No."

"My father will ransom me."

"What do I want with Trojan gold?"

Achilles charged, his sword rising to deliver the killing blow. Paris staggered back with a wordless cry of fear. He tripped and sprawled backward, rolling as Achilles thundered past.

With another easy laugh, Achilles turned and stalked back to his prey. Paris hunched on the ground, shivering, cowering . . .

And as Achilles reached him, his hand flashed out like a viper's strike. He pulled an arrow from his dropped quiver and drove it with desperate, savage force into the only part of Achilles' body he could reach: the tendon just above his heel.

Philoctetes grunted in disbelief at the sight. Even in the twilight, he could see how the arrow's head slid through the tendon like a knife through soft cheese, severing it completely. Blood gouted, and Achilles' foot dangled, utterly useless, as he jerked up his leg in shock.

Then Achilles loosed a bellow of pain. His sword dropped beside Paris; he staggered across ground trampled by their fight, his movements grotesque and desperate, his foot dragging behind him. Then his leg gave out. He fell heavily to the ground.

The breath left Philoctetes' lungs in a painful rush. But he saw Paris rise and lunge for the dropped sword. He raised his bow and fired—and the arrow snicked past Paris' shoulder as he dodged away.

"Bastard!" Philoctetes roared, snatching another arrow from his quiver.

He drew again, but Paris was already flinging himself at Achilles—wounded, unarmed, unprotected.

Philoctetes leaped forward, his bow arm trained on Paris with a shot that would have been true and fatal. But his wounded foot gave way, and Philoctetes staggered, yelling in pain as another shot sailed past the Trojan prince's body.

The blade flashed in the fading light. Achilles' body jerked as his own sword came down to slice cleanly across his throat. The hot-copper smell of blood assailed Philoctetes; this time when he cried out, it was with a different kind of pain, an agony a thousand times more searing than the snake's bite.

Paris stood slowly. Violent shivers racked his limbs, and the sword dropped from his hand. His armored vest was darkened, shining with Achilles' blood. Droplets clung to his face and hair.

"Leave," Paris said hoarsely. "Go back to Agamemnon. Tell him Achilles is dead."

A hard force of grief surged in Philoctetes' gut, nearly choking off his breath, but he did not leave. He stepped forward. He couldn't look down, couldn't bear to see the terrible stillness of Achilles' strong, beautiful body. But he could look at Paris. He could see him clearly now. He did not give him the courtesy of looking away, as he'd done in Priam's megaron.

"Go," Paris said, his voice rising. He fell back a step before the rage in Philoctetes' eyes. "I have my honor now. It's all I need. Don't make me kill you, too." He seemed to realize then that he'd dropped his sword; his eyes hunted for it.

"Honor." The word was barely more than a whisper, rasping

from Philoctetes' throat like a blade. Why did the Amazon's dying whimper leap up so clear in his memory?

Philoctetes slung his bow over his shoulder as he advanced on Paris. The Trojan shuffled backward, eyes flicking to his fallen sword several paces away. In that moment, as his eyes lowered, Philoctetes sprinted toward him.

There was no pain in his foot now. He ran like a youth, fierce and strong. But he was not a young man. He had lived long enough, seen enough, to know that Paris was a man like any other. He was a man like Achilles, like Hector—mortal and soft inside his armor, and Paris' face could be broken like any other man's.

Philoctetes fell upon him, roaring with fury. He smashed the golden prince's face with his fists again and again. The strong, arched nose broke with a sickening crack, and blood gouted hot and fast; the lips that had so often smirked and grinned split until Paris' teeth cut into Philoctetes' knuckles. He beat his ears, his high cheekbones, the eyes that had watched Achilles in his grief and had seen only weakness instead of strength.

Paris clawed and shouted and spat, and finally he wrenched out of Philoctetes' reach. Philoctetes hunched, wrestling with the grief that stole his breath, tears stinging his eyes.

Paris stared at him for a long, long moment. And then his bloody mouth curled in a mocking smile.

"I see," Paris said thickly. "I do."

Philoctetes shook his head.

Cold eyes flicked to where Achilles lay. "Did he give it to you every night, or did you give it to him? A man like him, raised to be a woman, I would guess he'd be the one taking it, not giving it."

An icy calm took hold of Philoctetes. He pulled another arrow, nocked and raised his bow. "When we traded bow shots in a training yard in Sparta ten years ago, you told me you could plant a shaft anywhere. Would you like to find out where I can plant mine?"

Paris' broken lips twitched. He spat blood on the ground, then said slowly, "You came to my father with a message of peace. You said we could end this war if we only decided not to fight."

Philoctetes gave a startled laugh, pure disbelief. "You think to strike a peace *now*? After what you've just done?"

"Let me go." The boy was trembling now, his words all but pleading. "And I swear to you, I'll convince my father to end this war."

"Hector was wrong, you know," Philoctetes said. "And you were right. This war won't end just because two men lay down arms."

"The war will end when I want it to," Paris said. But his voice was half a sob. His breath rattled as he drew it in sharply. "I'll give Helen back, I'll—"

"You are the maker of this war, Paris, the author of our suffering. But it won't end when you decide. It won't end with you giving up your stolen wife. It will only end when you are dead."

"When I die—and that day won't be today, old man—at least I'll die with honor. I claimed my honor today." Paris drew himself up, mustering the courage to glare his defiance at Philoctetes, at the arrow aimed at his throat. But Philoctetes noted the rapid blink of his eyes, the trembling in his limbs. Behind the mask of blood and bravado, Paris wore his fear plain on his face.

Fear—as all men feel. Even heroes.

Philoctetes heard the Amazon's cry again, faint in his mind. He heard her words, too. *A life without honor isn't worth living.* If anyone had lived without honor, it was the Trojan who stood before him now.

"Go back to Troy," Philoctetes said. "Tell your father what has happened here."

Paris hesitated, licking his ruined lips with a nervous tongue.

Philoctetes lowered his bow. He jerked his head toward the city, its pale walls barely visible through the trees. "Run."

Paris took one step back, then another, not daring to turn away from the old archer. But as Philoctetes remained still, bow lowered toward the ground, Paris turned and stumbled back the way he had come.

Philoctetes raised the bow of Heracles. He drew the string smoothly to his cheek.

Paris heard the creak of the bowstring; on the instant, he gave an undignified shriek and moved faster, as fast as his battered body would allow.

But it wasn't fast enough. Philoctetes loosed; at such close range, the arrow punched through the heavy leather vest into Paris' back. A good bow—made of horn and sinew, not of ibex or exotic wood, not decorated with silver or gold. It did all that was required of a bow—the only thing that was required.

Paris fell facedown on the ground. Philoctetes went to him slowly and fired one more shaft into his back, but the prince of Troy didn't flinch as the arrow drove into his body and pinned him to the earth. He was dead already. He was dead from the moment he had raised Achilles' own blade against him.

Philoctetes dropped the bow in the dirt. It was, after all, just a bow. And Heracles had been an ordinary man, for all his songs and fanfare. Paris was an ordinary man. And Achilles, too.

The bow was useless to him now, for a man couldn't fire an arrow into his own heart. Philoctetes still had his dagger, a small but wickedly sharp blade. He drew it from his belt and stared down at its point, gleaming in the fallen sun.

Life without honor is not worth living.

He'd heard that refrain all his life, it seemed—from everyone who fancied himself a hero. From Achilles. From Heracles, long ago. From the Amazon woman who had fought and died with such beauty, such grace.

Paris had been a man devoid of honor. But to shoot him from behind, as he ran in fear—that was dishonorable, too.

A hero would do it now, Philoctetes told himself dully. *Open his veins. Die a grand and moving death, with his beloved's body in his arms.*

Slowly, reluctantly, he sheathed the knife. He wasn't a hero. He was a man—an ordinary man, as they all were, whether they knew it or not. And ordinary lives were worth living.

He still couldn't bring himself to look at the ruin of Achilles' body. It was not the way he wanted to remember his beloved. It wasn't the way he wanted the world to remember Achilles, either—as a hero, a legend spun out of his own control.

When the war is over, he promised Achilles, looking away, *I'll see that the world remembers you. As you truly were, my love. Not as the hero they made you.*

He found the trail in the shadowed dusk, following it numbly through the shadows of gathering night.

The camp was somewhere ahead, and Odysseus was there, too, waiting, wondering where his hero had gone. Philoctetes could hear a lyre in the distance, faint and melancholy. A wind moved off the river, tugging leaves from the trees, scattering them in his path. As they fell down around him, brushing his cheek, he smelled dust and sweat and summertime, and though the twilight stole the color from the world, still the leaves that fell were as green as olives.

THE SIXTH SONG

THE HORSE

by Victoria Shecter

"Alas," Odysseus said to himself in dismay. "What will become of me? It is bad if I turn and run, but it will be worse if I am left alone and taken prisoner . . . But why talk to myself this way? Cowards quit the field. A hero must stand firm and hold his own."
Homer, the *Iliad*

ODYSSEUS

"THERE is no honor in deceit," Diomedes huffs as we scale a drainage path on the south side of Mount Ida.

This again.

I say nothing, for what is there to add? Diomedes of Argos is the greatest of warriors under High King Agamemnon's command now that mighty Achilles is dead. And the great warrior has made it clear that he does not like my tactics. But I no longer care about his preoccupation with honor—I care only about results. Honor took us into this war, and honor has kept us here for far longer than anyone ever dreamed possible. And whether it requires lying, cheating, or trickery, the only honor that matters to me now is the kind that ends with me going home.

To Penelope. To Ithaca. To my son. To my father.

When our climb grows steep and our worn sandals slide on rocky soil, Diomedes curses under his breath. By the gods, unless there is combat involved, he's as fussy as a virgin on her wedding night.

His complaints make me miss Achilles. Despite his monstrous pride, at least our fallen hero never whined as much as does Diomedes. And yet I can't seem to shake the young king of Argos. Like an annoying rash, he keeps coming back. He insists on joining my expeditions lest I find some adventure without him and earn the fame that eludes me but collects around him like thunderbolts at the Cloud-Gatherer's feet. And all the while, we both pretend that as long as he *complains* about using trickery, it does no harm to his honor.

"And if anything stains this fur," Diomedes continues, "I will kick my foot up your arse so high you'll be sneezing leather for a week."

Very heroic of you. Again I keep my tongue, even though I want nothing more than to rip off my friend's prized lion-skin cloak and shove it down his noble throat.

Who, I ask you, dons such a conspicuous thing to go on a *secret* mission? I wear my lowest man's dirtiest rags. Why? So I do not *stand out.* Because the point is to move *undetected*, not draw the eye like golden Zeus on his fucking throne.

One of my scouts earlier reported that a man in finely woven clothes and gold jewelry had left Troy and was headed toward the mountain. When I set off to investigate, Diomedes insisted on accompanying me. I paid little attention because I was too preoccupied with questions. Who from the palace would leave *now*, and for what purpose? Have the Hittites finally decided to send reinforcements to the Trojans? By the gods, we are too damned close to lose now just because a bunch of spoiled, perfumed foreigners from the east finally found their balls.

A small temple to the local gods sits on the eastern summit of Mount Ida, so there is a chance this official is only a priest trying to carry out the business of worship despite the dangers of ambushes by our men. Either way, we must know.

We spot human waste and the occasional carcass on this little-used path, more evidence that either some of the abandoned villages are repopulating or there is a meeting of some kind convening. My heart pounds with the chase, and I speed up, crouching carefully.

Diomedes grunts in protest. What, is it unseemly to crouch and run like a beast? Even when you are dressed as one? Gods, but I am so, *so* very tired of heroes and their preoccupation with their image.

Diomedes' lion cloak is the perfect example. He claims he slaughtered the great beast with his bare hands. But I was there. And it was no such thing.

It was in the early days of the struggle against Troy, when it was all a great adventure and we all "knew" we'd be home with ships full of gold within the year, two at the most. Diomedes and I had gone on a raid for supplies. We'd come across a small village recently abandoned—the young men to fight for King Priam and the women and children for the safety of life inside the gates of Troy—leaving only a pair of long-haired elderly caretakers of the sickly temple lion to fend for themselves.

The men I quickly dispatched, without Diomedes' help, by the way. I began loading up an abandoned cart with goods, food, and weapons. Diomedes, of course, refused to help with such "base" work.

Instead, he circled the lion. Did I mention the creature was blind and dying? Diomedes claims the "great beast" attacked him. What actually happened was this: my hero friend approached the tethered sleeping cat and gave it a cautious kick on its bony rump to see if it still lived. The old lion raised its massive shaggy head—blinked once, looked at him as if to ask, "What took you so long?"—and dropped it back down with a heavy, hopeless thud. Diomedes leaped on it and cut its throat.

The beast's roaring was insufferable—Diomedes', I mean. The lion barely had enough strength to flick the tip of its forlorn tail in relief at being put out of its misery.

Of course, there was no one left alive who could identify this "mighty beast" as the gelded, pitiful, starving thing it was. But the skin looked majestic and fearsome when he brought it back to camp, holding it aloft like a triumphant god while I stumbled like a peasant leading the half-starved, overburdened line of donkeys and rickety carts loaded with the goods that kept us alive. But then again, I was only a farmer-king of rocky Ithaca, not the golden ruler of Argos. How much someone who *looked* like a god could get away with! The back-slapping by his sycophants only encouraged him to exaggerate his kill until, by the end of the night of wine-soaked celebration, he was virtually Heracles strangling the Nemean lion.

At the feasting, others asked me if I'd seen his extraordinary battle with the beast. "He's lying," I'd said plainly, staring into the fire. The men roared with laughter. "He said 'he's lion,'" they claimed. "Oh, that Odysseus and his word play! He is so right. Diomedes is indeed the LION of us all."

What could I have done except laugh and hold out my cup to honor the hero as he weaved, grinning drunkenly with pride? Even in those early days, the boys needed a hero to believe in. Plus, no matter what I said after he'd made his claims, I would have sounded unmanly. Jealous. Spiteful. Womanish. Better to play along. I've learned well enough that honor is more self-claimed than won. And he who claims it first wins.

That very night, jealous Prince Ajax of Locris began plotting a lion hunt so that he, too, could earn the praise of his fellows. Never mind that we'd hunted the region dry of all game within months of arrival on the Plain of Troy. He would not be outdone by Diomedes.

Eventually, I had to tell Ajax that all of the lions were now *inside* the Scaean Gate at the palace bestiary, so his only chance to outdo Diomedes would be to keep fighting until we took the city. I would personally release the palace lions, and he could hunt them then.

This appeased him. *Stupid ox.*

The Trojans had, by this point, likely already killed and eaten most of their nonworking animals inside the gates. Besides, lions will be the last thing the big man will chase once he has his pick of gold and women inside the city.

If we can ever manage to find some way to break through those cursed gates, of course.

As always, I find myself wishing our heroes spent half as much time killing the sons of Troy as they spend trying to surpass each other in these ridiculous games of one-upmanship. We would have been home long ago if they had.

We climb onto a rocky outcrop on the edge of the trail path. After detecting movement below us, I signal Diomedes, and we crouch behind a strand of stunted cypresses, waiting for our quarry.

I freeze like a rabbit under the shadow of a hawk, but Diomedes twitches and fusses like a flea-covered rodent. He'd stepped on the tail end of his cloak when he crouched, and he's trying to adjust himself so as not to scuff it. The resultant rustling explodes like a lashing of storm waves on a rocky shore. I grip his shoulder hard to quiet him, but he backhands my arm off, making even more noise. Meanwhile, our quarry nears. He will be an easy catch—if Diomedes doesn't scare him off first. By the gods, if I have to sprint down this mountain because my partner has scared off our prey, I will kill—but then something strikes me.

I have an idea.

As our victim grows ever nearer, I remove my dagger. Thankfully, Diomedes also stops moving at the sound of the climber's heavy breathing.

Hold, hold.

Just as the stranger comes upon us, I prick the tip of my dagger sharply into the meaty part of Diomedes' ass.

He jumps and roars in surprise and outrage, tripping over his tawny pelt so that he tumbles and rolls directly onto the man's path, looking like a giant sow trying to escape a furry yellow sack.

The man freezes as if confronted by a real beast. Every boy in every land knows the rule—never run in the presence of a giant cat; it only spurs them to the chase. The man is clearly still trying to understand what the tumbling, cursing creature is before him, giving me the distraction I need to circle behind him and put a dagger to his neck.

"Do not move," I drawl.

"What in the name of all the gods is that thing?" the man breathes, staring wide-eyed as golden Diomedes straightens, red-faced and furious, slapping at the dirt besmirching his beloved cloak.

I quickly divest our prisoner of his spear, dagger, and axe. The man has an odd spicy scent that pricks at my memory. "What in Hades is that smell?"

"Cinnamon," the man explains in a low, cultured voice.

Ah, the wiry black hair, the Aegyptian oil, the dark-skinned face. I know this man! I turn him around and begin to laugh. "Prince Hellenus! Son of Priam, it is good to see you again. But why are you out here alone on this abandoned mountain path?"

"I'm headed to the temple to pay my respects."

"Ach, no need to pay your respects to me, my old friend," I say with a wide grin. "But thank you. I am honored."

He blinks, not getting the jest, nor recognizing me, it seems.

His handsome face—more angular and severe than I remember it—darkens. "Who are *you* to speak to me this way?"

"You wound me, friend," I say with a mocking smile.

After I bind his arms with the pretty but strong leather belt I rip from his waist, I stand up straighter and cross my arms in the noble gesture of kings and warriors. "For I am Odysseus, king of Ithaca, and this is Diomedes, king of Argos. You, sir, were present at my wedding."

The man's eyebrows rise. "King Odysseus? In slave's rags?"

From him, too? I ignore the obvious point that if he had clothed himself in rags, we would not have gone after him. At the same time, I signal Diomedes to secure the area in case his guards are hiding. "How come you to travel by yourself? Where are your men?"

"I am alone," Hellenus says, then adds, after watching Diomedes, "Is he the son of Heracles?"

This makes my partner smile. I close my eyes and sigh, but fuck him, he really does look impressive with his spear planted and lionskin cloak billowing behind him. Though it doesn't stop me from enjoying a small sense of superiority that Hellenus has no memory of meeting godlike Diomedes so many years ago at my wedding.

Still, despite my affection for the Trojan prince—for I remember him as a smart yet haunted young man—I press my weapon harder against the knob of his throat. "Where are your men?" I repeat. A prince of Troy does not travel alone, even a minor prince like this one.

"I told you," he says. "I left alone. I was angry."

I look up into his sunken eyes, registering with vague irritation that, once again, yet another princeling towers over me. "What are you angry about?"

"Helen," he says.

I snort. "Welcome, then. *Everyone* here wants to wring her pretty little neck."

"Why are you angry at her?" Diomedes asks, scowling mightily. "We are preparing an offer for a trade now that Prince Paris is dead."

Paris' death—now that was a gift from the gods. Or more accurately, from gray-bearded Philoctetes, safe-keeper of Heracles' bow—and more importantly, another man of practicality like me. He could've acted the hero and avoided shooting that soft Trojan prince in the back after the man felled Achilles. A hero always fights face-to-face. Yet Philoctetes acted for the greater good, and not just to improve his own personal reputation. He dispatched that pretty princeling like the rat he was.

Still, the old, limping fool came back from the site of Achilles' and Paris' deaths seemingly more broken than before.

When I put a hand on his shoulder in commiseration at Achilles' pyre, he backhanded me away with surprising force. "Do not," he'd growled without even looking at me, "ever touch me or come near me again, you backstabbing, piece-of-sheep's-shit herder-king. Are we clear?"

I put both hands up and took a step back, leaving him be. Of course, he's never forgiven me for leaving him at Lemnos after that terrible snake bite that kept him from joining the high king's fleet years ago, but in my defense, I thought I was doing him a favor. I assumed he'd make it back home and escape this folly of a war without any loss of honor or dignity. But he never left. You'd think I'd torn him from the arms of his most beloved the way he continues to fume at me.

Still, in the month that has passed since Paris' fall, there has been a good deal of arguing in King Agamemnon's hut about what we might trade for Helen—or even whether she is worth anything at all at this point. Though I learned quickly enough not to give voice to *that* thought in front of her long-jilted husband, Menelaus of Sparta.

"There will be no trade," Hellenus nearly spits. "Because Helen has remarried."

"What?" I croak. "That can't be . . . I don't understand—explain."

"My brother Deiphobus. We both sought to marry her. He won. I lost. And so I removed myself from the palace for a time to serve the priests of Cybele at the mountain's summit."

"She married Deiphobus?" I say after picking up my jaw. "What in Priam's prick was she thinking?"

Hellenus winces at my words but ultimately ignores the insult to his father. Before I can say anything else, Diomedes punches Hellenus in the back of the head, which sends him hurtling into me, his chin smacking my forehead. I curse, though part of me acknowledges that this is one of the few times being short is an advantage. If I'd been of height, the snap of his head would have surely broken my nose. Instead, it only grazes my forehead.

I struggle to hold our captive up. "Diomedes, control yourself," I bark. "Reserve the violence until we *need* it." Hellenus rubs the back of his head, cursing in his mother tongue.

"We do need it!" Diomedes roars. "The negotiations for that witch were tied to our demands on the tin trade! We were finally going to break all this open, get inside the city, and take the treasures we're all here for. I thought we were close to the end! And *now* Priam's princeling prances out here and announces the bitch has *remarried*? You cannot expect me *not* to beat the shit out of him!"

I put myself between Hellenus and my now purple-faced friend. Somehow I'm going to have to get Hellenus down the mountain and into camp without Diomedes knocking him out.

"We need *information* to understand exactly what is happening and what we need to do about it," I say over my shoulder to him. "Control yourself."

Turning back to Hellenus, I add, "I don't understand. Why did Priam allow this? And why would *you* want to marry her? Nothing makes sense."

"My father has been a shell of man since Hector's loss and humiliation," Hellenus says. "He does nothing but stare into space. The queen still has the wherewithal to meet with advisers. She advised casting Helen out but was overruled. Deiphobus was determined to claim her as his prize as he is now heir to Troy. I suspect Helen was the one to put the idea of marriage in his head."

"Well then, why did *you* want to marry the witch?"

"Because if she were mine, I would've thrown her over a mule, marched her down to your camp, dumped her on her royal ass at her husband's tent, and ended this accursed war. Instead, my older brother thinks I covet his new wife and that I am conspiring against him. The fool."

Diomedes makes another feint at Hellenus, and I swing our prisoner out of his way like a dancer. "Agamemnon and Menelaus need to hear this," I tell my companion. "This changes everything. Keep your hands off him for now, and I promise you'll get first beating rights after the interrogation, but not before, got it?"

Hellenus has to know more about his elder brother's plan of attack now that both Achilles and Paris are dead. He's hiding something. With a little persuasion, we might be able to manipulate this princeling's anger at his brother to gain the one piece of information we need to break this open. But not *too* much persuasion. Finesse is what's needed here.

"Come with me, friend," I say to Hellenus, using a calm, warm tone, remembering that I'd rather liked the princeling once. I'd even offered him a place in Ithaca, I recall.

When Diomedes refuses to budge, I reiterate my promise. "You'll get your chance to use your fists later."

Reluctantly, Diomedes nods, and I'm tempted to say "good boy" like I would to my loyal hound at home. I'd named my favorite dog Argos for the golden one's own kingdom, which Diomedes took as a compliment and not at all as a reflection of my true opinion of him. Swallowing a smile, I signal with my head that he should take the lead as we head down the path toward camp, dragging a princeling of Troy with me.

My wariness stays high throughout because, although it appears Hellenus indeed set forth unaccompanied by guards, we can't take the risk that some may be hiding or watching his back on the path. So I make Diomedes, spear in hand, walk before us. If there are attackers, let the fur-cloaked hero handle the lion's share. It would be only fitting.

As we journey down the side of the mountain, I keep the conversation light and easy with Hellenus. There is an art to interrogation. To get the truth, one must gain trust first. So I chatter with our man, ignoring the looks of murder Diomedes throws my way.

"At my wedding, you wished me happiness and many sons. Do you remember? There wasn't time to sire many, as it turned out, but I did manage one. He is nearly ten years old now . . ."

Hellenus remains silent, but I soldier on. "You're still welcome to visit Ithaca, you know. I remember extending the invitation to you all those years ago, and I never go back on my promises."

A ghost of a smile crosses his face. Good. I want him to relax and lower his guard, to remember that we had once talked at my wedding and liked each other. When we reach camp, I'll send Diomedes to confer with the high king while I invite the captive to my tent, where I will undo his bonds and pour wine for us both until his tongue is loosened. Subtlety and good humor will win words faster than force.

But my heroic allies have other plans. As soon as Diomedes announces our arrival in camp, Ajax and Menelaus and gaunt, vicious Agamemnon surround us in a circle of glowering faces.

"If I might take charge of our guest—" I begin, looking meaningfully at High King Agamemnon, but Ajax steps forward and flattens Hellenus with a massive blow. I hear the crunch of a broken nose, and soon the Trojan prince lies curled on the ground, trying to protect his vitals as the heroes of the Achaean army rain their frustration and rage down on him.

I take a couple of punches to my own body as I try to stop them before they do too much damage. "We need *information,* not his death!" I shout again and again, eventually getting through. Agamemnon gives the signal, and the heroes back away, sweating and huffing like mindless beasts.

"Let me question him," I say. "I can get the truth without—"

"Shut up, Odysseus," Menelaus growls. "All you'll do is just get drunk together and go on forever about your wife and the good old days. Well, fuck that."

In a blink, they have dragged Hellenus' bloodied form into Agamemnon's warping wooden quarters. When I step forward, Ajax stops me, hulking in the doorway.

"Not you," he says, putting a hand to my chest. I look at his hand and then up at his bull's neck and face.

"I am part of this council," I say through gritted teeth, shoving his arm off me.

But again he stops me. "Only Menelaus, Agamemnon, and Diomedes allowed. They will report their findings to us lesser kings and princes when they are through."

"I *captured* Prince Hellenus—"

"No, Diomedes did," says the stupid ox.

I will kill Diomedes. Slowly, I swear. And although hot blood pounds in my ears, I gain control of my rage, knowing that I will only make things worse for Hellenus if I push this issue now.

"Just don't kill him!" I yell into the tent before I stomp away. "He is a guest-friend of mine, and Zeus' laws of hospitality forbid it!"

I hope that is enough to save him.

A few hours later, a priest marches through the camp blowing a ram's horn and pronouncing a prophecy proclaiming Achaean victory if only we bring the Palladion—the sacred statue of Athena—out of Troy and into our camp.

Air leaves my body as if I'd been punched in the chest. By the gods, he has to be joking. Stealing the Palladion is *impossible.* It's Troy's most sacred object, tucked safely within the great walls of the city and likely on the citadel's highest point! The impossibility of it staggers me.

And I am not alone. Most of the men exchange disbelieving, despairing glances before slinking back to their tents with heads low and shoulders slumped.

"Ach, it's all bullshit, boys!" I yell out, trying to lift the darkening mood. "Remember when our own fat priest, Calchas, swore on his balls that Troy would fall if we killed Prince Troilus? Well, we dispatched Troilus years ago, and yet here we are. And then there were the bullshit prophecies about Philoctetes and Heracles' bow and Achilles' son? We fulfilled them all, yet Troy still stands. So obviously they mean nothing. And this one holds no power either . . ." I trailed off when all I got from the men were scowls and spitting into sand.

If Hellenus intended to demoralize our armies, then he succeeded, the bastard. How could Agamemnon have let this get out? If we can't storm the city, how in Hades are we supposed to go in and steal their most sacred object right from under their nose? Hellenus played us. A trickster always knows when he's been tricked.

I find Hellenus tied like a dog to a post outside Agamemnon's quarters. It is all I can do to not go inside and give the high king the thrashing he deserves for allowing himself to be manipulated this way.

"Here," I say to Hellenus, bringing him a cup of watered wine. "Drink," I tell him, forcing myself to sound calm and disinterested when what I really want to do is throw the vinegary swill in his face instead. But even I'm not that cruel. His eyes are so swollen he can't even open them, and his skin is cut and bleeding everywhere. He groans with even the smallest movement, but at least he drinks deep.

"What kind of bullshit prophecy did you make up, my friend?" I say, sitting heavily beside him.

"The one that made them stop beating me, of course," he says in a thick, scratchy voice.

Gods help us. This is why I wanted to approach him with subtlety. But no, that would not be manly or heroic enough, so now we are left with this mess.

"Take it back," I tell him. "Admit you made it up."

He snorts and then winces. "Now why would I do that? The prophecy has already spread among all your warriors, and they rightfully despair. The Palladion will always be ours; the most sacred relic our city possesses, other than the vessels that carry Troy's spirit itself. And if you decide to leave in the face of this *insurmountable challenge*, all the better."

"That will never happen," I say. He gives me a mirthless smile. Or maybe it was a grimace. It's hard to tell with all his injuries.

"Prophecy is the string you've been chasing all through this war, *my friend*," Hellenus says, closing his bruised eyes for a moment. "You know how many we've made up over the years and floated over the walls on the wings of rumor just to stymy you. You need the bow of Heracles, you need the bloodline of Achilles, you need the Palladion—sooner or later, you'll break under all the godly disapproval we can make up and finally take your hateful black ships home."

I shake him hard at that. "Tell the high king. *Tell him.*"

"No." Hellenus does not flinch, and his eyes—despite the blood and bruising—shine with a flinty determination. "Let it be my contribution to your defeat, Ithacan."

A new thought strikes me, making my stomach drop. "Is this your sister's prophecy?" His twin, Princess Cassandra, appears to be a true seer, even to a skeptic like me—if she says we must obtain the Palladion, then we are truly and royally fucked.

Suddenly, I'm not so sure Hellenus is playing us. "Did this prophecy come from Cassandra?" I repeat.

But he does not answer. "My sister, the seer, spouts truth and is never believed. Perhaps only lies may be taken as truth these days."

What in Hades' hot breath does *that* mean? But I can get no more out of Hellenus. He has turned his face to the wall and refuses to speak.

As the days go on, the "prophecy" takes such deep root in the minds of all our men even I begin to wonder if some god actually took hold of Hellenus' bitter tongue. Who am I to say that the gods do not or cannot speak truth through liars? Indeed, the gods regularly mock us with such tricks.

Which has always been my defense against the charge that trickery is unheroic, that outwitting an enemy is somehow less worthy of admiration and glory than stabbing him through the heart in combat. After all, the gods play tricks on us regularly and with much relish. So why should it be beneath us men?

It's clear the only thing left to do is figure out how to do the impossible—sneak into the impenetrable city and steal their most prized and sacred possession right from under their noses. To no one's surprise, the council elects me to figure out how. And, as usual, I prepare for them to disparage my strategy, even as they are forced to admit that I'm their only hope for getting the job done.

"*OUR* plan?"

"For stealing the Palladion," he says. "We must act soon, or else the men will lose even more heart."

"First of all," I say, reaching for my goblet of wine, pointedly not offering him any. "It will be *my* plan, not *ours*. And second, I haven't come up with one yet," I lie.

For naturally, *I have an idea*. And it doesn't involve him.

If it were up to our golden hero, he'd try to muscle his way in and end up skewered on the tip of some guardsman's pike. Diomedes, like Ajax, may be strong and noble, but gods bless, he's as sharp as a Myrmidon's perfectly round shield.

Later, as night slides her cool arms around the camp, I lay on my back, staring at the creased seam on the ceiling of my leather tent, floating in the gods' realm between dreaming and wakefulness. Soft footsteps approach, and I reach for my dagger out of habit and instinct. The flap slowly opens. A shrouded figure approaches. The banked campfire light creates a nimbus of pale orange around what appears to be the shape of a graceful young woman.

"Penelope?" I whisper.

And then I realize my dream mistake.

It is another one of Agamemnon's "gifts"—a lithe servant whose beauty evokes my Penelope. I appreciate the sentiment, but I tire of these mute young women. They come to please me, and I take them with no complaint, but this silent coupling with the ghosts of my wife is wearing thin. Afterward, the sense of loss is too great, the loneliness too draining.

And so, when left to my own devices, I choose bedmates that look nothing like my copper-haired, honey-eyed nymph—the strong-jawed, short-haired Nubian, the long-haired, round-limbed Aegyptian, the raven-maned, pale-cheeked Cretan.

It matters not, as long as she doesn't look like my beloved.

This one is young. So young my heart—and my balls—squeeze in memory of our early days together. Of the creamy softness of Penelope's skin, the long copper hair that covered my head and chest like a veil when she leaned over me, her light laugh when we lay in each other's arms. The whispered attempts to outdo each other with lines from obscure songs and tricks of the tongue—both literal and figurative—in games of wit and pleasure.

My brilliant, funny girl. Are you safe? Has someone tried to take you from me?

Penelope's cunning was so subtle most people never even saw

it. I remember distinctly the moment I knew I was hers forever. It was at a feast celebration for—as always—Helen. One of her many admirers once again complimented the so-called daughter of Zeus for her extraordinary beauty.

"You are truly a goddess!" he'd said to the princess.

Even by then, young Helen had grown bored by the constant comment and adoration of her beauty. Distractedly, she asked, "Which goddess?"

"Aphrodite, of course," said the forgotten man.

Helen turned to her cousin—my Penelope—for her reaction.

"Eris the absolute truth!" Penelope agreed quickly, so wide-eyed and innocent, the pun went right past the beautiful Helen and, it seemed, everyone else. They heard, "HERE IS the absolute truth," but my mischievous bride-to-be had most definitely called her beautiful cousin Eris, the goddess of misery and discord. I'd almost spit out my wine. Penelope's wink when Helen huffed at my barbaric laughter is seared onto my heart.

And of course, Penelope was right. Helen is indeed Eris, the goddess of discord. And chaos. And strife. She proved it again with her latest move, marrying another son of Priam before Paris even boarded Charon's boat to cross the Styx.

My attention is brought back to the present when the girl steps out of her robe and slithers naked under the thinning blanket Penelope wove for me so many years ago. Then I lose myself in a different type of memory.

THE others on the council nodded gravely.

I sighed. "Diomedes, the only thing I need from you is your absence."

While that earned a small smile from Menelaus, I was still over-ruled. And once again we fight over my tactics. We meet at dusk between our two camps. I am in slave's rags. He is not.

"What?" he asks, raising his chin at my growl of irritation. "I'm not wearing my lion cloak."

"Diomedes, you can't possibly think to go anywhere near our enemy's city so obviously an Argive warrior."

"Well, I'm not going weaponless."

"Fine, but can you at least put on a *dark* tunic and wear unbuffed armor so that you don't stand out like white Apollo in moonlight?"

He agrees, which only delays us more.

Silently, we circle the plains toward the east side of the city near the grove of figs where the wall is weak. I scoop up black earth and work it into my forearms and neck. I don't bother asking him to do the same. He'd refuse anyway.

He does not refuse, I note, when I tell him to punch me in the face a few times. I can't take the risk that someone inside may recognize me, so a couple of black eyes and a swollen nose and lip should help. In hindsight, however, I should've asked him to mar me *before* telling him he would not be entering the city with me.

He accused me of coming up with a plan that would "steal all the glory and rob him of honor."

No, I came up with a practical strategy that will not bring down all of Troy upon our heads. One that just might work. I have to soothe his bruised honor by reminding him that I need "the best of men" to be ready to attack in my defense if I do not succeed in tricking the guard into allowing me through this entrance. And when I return with our prize, he has the most important job of all because I can then pass the sacred thing to him if I'm being chased. "With your long legs, you'll fly as swiftly as Ares' spear!" I say, loading up on the compliments, and he likes the idea. Especially the image of entering the camp with the Palladion in his own hands, reaping all the resultant glory.

Well, he can *think* he'll be the one carrying Athena's sacred statue into camp all he wants.

I have an idea about that, too.

When we are within sight of the crumbling section of the wall, we hide among the trees. Unsurprisingly, a guard stands before it. Over the years, we'd had countless conversations about charging into the city at this vulnerable point, but even with its clear weakness, its position facing an inner circle of impediments means that a force of any moderate size would immediately be trapped and slaughtered like pigs in a pen.

And I will not be turned into swine for anything or anyone.

Still, I'm surprised to find the area guarded only by one skinny, gray-haired elder.

I pat my hidden wineskin. "Here we go," I whisper, signaling Diomedes to be ready in case I am unable to talk my way through.

I stagger out of the trees toward the guard, and he instantly tenses. "Announce yourself!" he commands.

"Help me," I say in the accent of one of the western mountain villages as I half stagger, half hobble toward him. I'd perfected the local inflection with the help of a girl I'd taken in one of our early raids.

"Let me in! I need to make sure my family is safe."

I am surprised the guard is so old, then I remember how the war has ravaged the population of their young men, too. "Why didn't you come in through the gate you left from?" the man with thin arms asks in a scratchy voice.

"Because we were set upon by Achaean thieves," I cry. "My daughter and the grandchildren were with me when the terrible-smelling Achaeans attacked—"

"Why were you outside the city at all this time of year? Everyone knows travel isn't safe until the sea-wolves hole up in camp for the winter." A snort. "It's not entirely safe even then."

"We were visiting the gravesite of my wife on the mount. We were ambushed on the way back—I tried to fight to give my family time to make it inside the gates," I say, pointing to my bruised face.

"They must think me dead. When I woke, it was past curfew, and you know the guards will never open the gates after the sun sets. My poor girls will be frantic for me. Please . . ." I make my voice croak and quiver, "a favor from one old man to another. This broken wall entrance is my only hope!"

I begin to choke up, pretending panic and confusion. The man sighs, moves aside, and shows me a crumbling vent in the walls—hardly more than a low slit—through which I must crouch.

I mutter my thanks as I pass through, all the while making sure I do not give the signal for Diomedes to attack—a crow's caw. His job is to keep watch and help me through when I have taken my prize.

Once inside, my heart pounds like the hooves of chariot horses on hard ground. *Breathe.*

Although by now it's fully dark, there are still plenty of torches in alleys and watch fires on the walls to light my way through the dense serpentine streets. I stumble along, pretending to be drunk, all the while sorely resisting the temptation to guzzle the contents of my wineskin to calm my nerves. Not only do I need all my wits about me, but this wine is critical to my plan.

To my surprise, I am not alone on the dark streets, as others seem to roam aimlessly. My kingdom is small and quiet—few, if any, of my proud people would be out aimlessly wandering or setting up for sleep in empty doorways. Indeed, there would be no "strangers" among us, yet everyone here seems to barely acknowledge each other.

The streets of Troy are narrow and twisted and filthy. They smell of urine and waste. A starved dog with patchy fur trots past me, stopping to nose piles of rot for something to eat. Babies wail. A woman cries. For a moment, I wonder if I've stepped into Hades' domain, leaving me drowning in yet another wave of the familiar ache for my rocky, shining Ithaca.

My small kingdom on the cliffs. The bracing winds that whip past our craggy edges, washing the air clean with their briny, cooling spray. The calls of seabirds. The tinkling of goat bells from the jagged hills. We may be rustic, but I would never trade all of Ithaca's charms for this . . . this monstrosity of packed humanity, filled with the cold stares of suspicious eyes, the sneers of strangers, and the reek of rotting garbage.

It is clear the people of Troy are suffering. I don't know what these streets would look like in the bright sunshine—only that it appears already resigned to a life in the dark of the underworld, as if their end is inevitable. And it is. I must make it so.

After endless walking, I wonder if I'm traveling in circles for suddenly, all of the dingy alleys seem the same.

In the shadows of one dark passageway, I almost go headlong over something that darts between my feet. In a flash, my dagger is out.

"I . . . I am sorry, Grandfather," says a young child, rubbing his head. A small fire from inside the boy's hovel illuminates the child, a dark-eyed, curly haired boy who looks so much like my dreams of my son I am struck dumb with shock. The child quickly scoops up a wooden soldier, crudely painted in the colors of Hector's honor guards.

Before I can say anything, a young woman rushes out the door and pushes her child behind her. "Go back inside," she orders him. Turning back to me, she adds, "Please, we have nothing. We both go hungry tonight. I . . . I can spare some well water, though . . ."

She thinks me a criminal. Or a beggar. Her voice, while clearly afraid, is light and sweet.

Penelope, are you alone and frightened, too, this night? Protecting our young cub alone because I stand in this accursed place?

"No, no," I rush to assure her. "I seek nothing."

She nods, walking backward into her tiny dwelling, the dirty bottom of a type of tall, stacked series of living spaces that reminds me of a crumbling dovecote. I hadn't even known such structures existed until I came to these lands.

"Wait," I call out, and she freezes. "Can you direct me to the temple of Athena?"

She blinks, her forehead crinkling. Her hair, while darker than Penelope's, is thick and long like hers. *Fool. Had I just given myself away?*

"How do you *not* know where the goddess' temple is?" she asks suspiciously.

"I am a recent refugee from one of the villages on the far mount and am still confused by your streets," I say. "In my dreams, the Palladion goddess came to me and ordered me to pray to her tonight. So you see, I must go to her. I do not wish to bring her anger upon us to any greater degree."

Thankfully, she accepts what I say, nods and points, directing me to my left and to climb onto the ridge just south of the palace.

"I thank you. May the gods keep you safe this and all nights," I say, bowing, and begin walking away. She releases a breath and shuts the door behind her. But I do not keep going. Instead, I move closer to her door and listen.

"Katu, what were you doing? Why were you outside at this time of night?" she scolds in a strained voice.

"I was waiting for Father," the child says.

"But I have explained this to you . . . he is not *ever* coming . . . he cannot . . ."

"He told me to wait for him *right there*," the child says stubbornly. "He hasn't come because you haven't let me wait properly for him. Once he realizes I am on the stoop like I promised him I would be, he *will* come back."

There is a long silence. "Your father is not returning because he serves the great Hector in the underworld," she finally manages wearily, as if she's had this conversation many times before.

"But he will come back for me because he *promised*," the child insists. "He told me so in a dream."

I can take no more and leave, my chest and breath squeezing hard. Was that the voice of my son, also waiting for me in the dark on the other side of the ocean?

By the gods, I *must* find a way to finish this! When Hector died, we thought we could make an end. When Achilles and Paris died, we thought the same. So many hopes, all shattered because we are unable to end this cursed war yet also unable to leave it.

I will find a way. Perhaps not with heroism, but I will find one.

WHEN I finally stand before the temple, all I can do is gape. Our rustic sanctuaries at home are to this gleaming masterpiece as a hare is to a chariot horse. Its pediment appears to scrape the underside of the night sky. Torchlight glimmers off of red-and-gold painted columns and buffed marble steps. A massive statue of Athena holds court in the center. According to a Trojan prisoner I interrogated, the Palladion is inside a small niche to the right of the main statue.

A priestess peels out from the dark like a shadow separating from a wall when I approach the main altar in the courtyard.

"Do you come to honor the goddess?" she asks, clearly blocking my way.

Hunching my back even more, I bow. "I do, priestess. For in my dream, Athena commanded me to come to her in the fullness of night."

The priestess, like the guard, is old and quite thin. Are no youths left in Troy except children? The old woman examines me, taking in my clothing, my bruises, the dirt on my neck. "If you are looking for charity, we have nothing. Everything goes to the soldiers."

"Oh no," I say. "I need no charity. Indeed, I came bearing a special gift I consign to the goddess."

She raises her eyebrows.

I pull out my full wineskin from under my cloak. "The darkest of wines sweetened with honey. From a hidden store in a mountain village."

Despite her years of fierce control over her body and facial expressions, I do not miss the flash of hunger in her eyes. It seems the priests and priestesses, too, are starved for the basics in this dying city.

She puts her thin arms out, and I ceremoniously place the skin in her hands. We are so quiet I can hear the sloshing of the liquid inside the soft leather, still warm from being pressed into my side.

"The goddess thanks you."

"I seek Athena's guidance in dreams," I say, asking permission to spend the night. To my surprise, few people are curled in sleep in the courtyard. I'd expected it to be full of supplicants seeking guidance and help for their suffering. Again the air seems heavy with a sense of despair and weariness.

"You may invoke the immortal lady there," she says, pointing to an inner ring of rush pallets, closest to the temple, clearly reserved for wealthier supplicants. Despite my appearance, my gift has well pleased her.

At the dreaming mat, I move my arms and body as if in prayer and then, drawing my cloak around me like a blanket and my hood over my head, I curl up as if to sleep. Like the desperate few around me, I pretend to wait for the goddess to speak to me in my dreams. Through my hood, though, I bide my time, watching the elder priestess.

She murmurs invocations as she pours a bit of my wine directly onto Athena's sacred altar. Smiling to myself, I can't help but notice she is not very generous with the libation. With the same miserliness, she sprinkles some of the wine into the altar fire and even at the feet of the large statue in the center and the small figure in the niche that is my prize.

From there, she moves to a small stucco dwelling where another servant of the goddess awaits. A man, I think, from the shape of his shadow. She hands the skin to him, reaches out for its return, then drinks deep. Her flickering shadow fairly vibrates with relief and pleasure. Back and forth the skin goes, and I grin under the wool covering my face. I had guessed that good wine was scarce inside the city, so I pulled from Agamemnon's best. The irony, of course, is that "Agamemnon's best" is the strong, biting stuff we've taken from trading ships headed for Troy. I'd just gifted the priestess with her own wine.

Now I wait.

Images of the little boy holding vigil for the father that will never return prick at my heart. When my father left us to fight invaders or go on raids, I remember the excitement and terror, the fear that he would not return, and the overwhelming pride when he did. But I have not yet returned to my boy. What is left for him when he has never seen his exultant father return in victory? Only fear, only shame.

Closing my eyes, pretending sleep, I think of this generation of boys who have known nothing else but war. Achilles' son Neoptolemus is one such. He joined us a matter of days after his father fell, indifferent to the passing of his sire, his eyes cold and dead as a reptile's. A boy-daemon who kills while grinning with pleasure.

Despite all I have seen and done, I shiver at the memory of my last interaction with the boy. There had been little serious fighting between the two armies in the month after Achilles' death—only small sorties—and this angered the newly arrived, glory-seeking child. I thought it good for him to learn patience. He had other ideas.

One day, my chariot driver came to me reporting that the son of Achilles had taken one of our war prisoners against the ruling of Agamemnon.

"Why didn't you stop him?" I asked. "Why didn't any of the other men?"

He shrugged, coloring, and I didn't berate him. There is something daemon-touched in that boy, and unless ordered to, few men desire to tangle with him.

"Where did he take the prisoner?"

"He dragged him to the eastern forest."

There was, of course, no forest left—outside of the small remaining groves of fig and olive trees—in the lands surrounding the city since we had ravaged the hard woods for our weapons, tools, ships, and fires over the years. Still, a long thicket of trees said to be sacred to Apollo stood by the Scamander, and that was where I headed after grabbing my sword.

Finding him was easy. All I needed to do was follow the screams.

He'd tied the naked young Trojan prisoner, standing spread-eagled, ropes on wrists and ankles, between two trees. The man—boy, really—was covered in blood from deep gashes all over his naked body.

"What are you doing?" I thundered. "Agamemnon did not give you leave to torture this prisoner!"

The son of Achilles turned to me. He was still such a youth—fifteen, maybe? He was big for his age and looked to grow even bigger than his father, judging by the size of his feet and lankiness of his bones. Despite myself, I swallowed the irritating awareness that within one summer this dead-eyed boy likely will be a head taller than me.

"I am not torturing him. I am *practicing*," he called disdainfully as I jogged up to him.

His victim had lost awareness, his head lolling, and I wondered for a moment if he was dead. But no, his chest continued to move, albeit shallowly.

Something about the little shit's attitude made me grip my sword hard. But I would not show it.

"If you must practice," I drawled after unclenching my teeth, "there are plenty of experienced fighters who will spar with you."

"I don't want to *spar*," he spit. "I want to learn to cleave a limb with one stroke. Like my father."

That's when I saw the gleaming white of the poor Trojan's shoulder joint. An exposed kneecap. A bludgeoned hip. I pushed the boy away, hard.

"Then apprentice with a butcher," I growled. "And leave this man in peace. There is no honor in attacking an unarmed man."

But Neoptolemus rippled with menace at my laying of hands on him. Hatred lit a fire in his eyes. I didn't care. With one quick stroke, I slit the agonized prisoner's throat in a move of mercy.

Achilles' son roared as if I'd stolen his favorite toy. I could feel Neoptolemus' rage burn hotter than his father's, like a predator's panting breath before it leaps. But I ignored him, cutting through the man's ropes so that he fell like a child's puppet, crumpled to the ground.

"Now," I said in a quiet, casual voice, as if we were talking about the weather or the season of the year. "You will tend to this man's body and give him the rights due a warrior."

"And if I don't?"

Gods, how I wanted to wipe that sullen smirk off that smooth-cheeked face!

"I will punish you for disobeying a king's command." I put a hand up as he puffed up to argue. "You may be big, but I am stronger, and I will not hesitate to take you over my knee. Just try me."

"You cannot! I am the leader of the Myrmidons!"

Who already detest you. "I am your senior, nonetheless. None will fault me for laying a hand on you, I promise you that."

He must have seen something in my eyes, for he took a step back, bottom jaw jutting out like a pouting child.

Reluctantly, he did as he was told, but I prayed never to have another conversation with that young serpent bearing his father's face. At his age, he should have been running races with his mates, learning to hunt game, play-training with wooden swords, rowing a small boat—anything but practicing cleaving limbs from a living prisoner.

Suppressing a shiver as I lay prostrate before Athena outside her very temple, I think again, for all our sakes, *I must find a way to end this war.*

STILL, it is strange to see Athena's shields in the colors and design of the Hittites, her cloak painted in stars instead of the broad brush of deep red—a reminder that I am in enemy territory.

I try to keep my rustling to a minimum as I get up. If any of the others wake, I'll just say I'm going to relieve myself. But they don't. No one even twitches.

The stillness makes me think Athena is helping me. It must be that she, too, wants this tiresome war finished and forgives me trespassing in her sacred house. Or so I tell myself, for surely the goddess would expose me if she were unhappy with my plan.

Soundlessly, I weave past the sleeping priest and priestess inside the small dwelling that also serves as the storeroom for the trinkets, statues, and charms they sell. I release a breath once I've made it to their inner courtyard.

As my vision adjusts to the darkness, it's clear business has not been good lately. The overgrown walkways spill over with unsold clay charms—some in the form of the goddess' shield, others in the shape of her owl—sold for beseeching the goddess in the hopes of her wisdom and guidance. Behind them are lined-up rows of small shrine goddesses and statues of household gods for use in the home. On the ends are large, magnificent marble replicas of the temple's main statue of Athena, likely destined for the gardens of the rich. My teeth clench as I realize I have not seen any fakes of the Palladion. Is it too sacred for them to copy and sell to the faithful? That would complicate everything.

Finally, there, in the very back, I see what I was hoping to find—lines of roughly cast duplicates of the sacred statue. They seem about the right size, though slightly smaller than the original. The colors are different. The goddess' cloak is painted red instead of blue. My hope, though, is that Athena's servants are so accustomed to their ancient statue they won't notice the difference until I'm well away. With any luck, they may not even notice the change at all, for we humans are creatures of habit and see only what we expect to see.

I grab one of the fakes from the farthest back, where I'm sure no one will miss it. The house of priests fairly vibrates with snores as I move past them and out to the temple. Keeping to the shadows, I sidle up the marble steps like a cat, my heart pounding in my ears.

Goddess protect me. This is the moment I dread—entering the sacred sanctuary. No one but the sanctified servants of the god may step inside a temple. But then I remember: I am king of Ithaca, which sanctifies me by rights, but that will not save me if I am caught. Murmuring a prayer, I enter the silent inner chamber. I make a quick obeisance at the large statue, marveling at the beauty of her gleaming shield, then move directly to the niche. Again Athena must be watching over me, for there is not even a wobble when I make the switch and place the fake statue in the Palladion's place.

I wrap my prize in my dirty cloak, begging the goddess' forgiveness for the slight.

As I slink out of the inner sanctuary, every muscle is screaming, *RUN! RUN!* But I dare not lest my quick action awaken anyone. A sense of almost giddy exhilaration moves through me like a wave, and I know it is the goddess laughing along with me.

Yes, and why wouldn't she? She is the goddess of wisdom and warfare. *And* warfare, not *just* warfare. Which means she values cunning just as much as she honors blood victory on the battlefield. When most look upon her image, all they see is her helmet and shield, but I see her canny intelligence. Surely, she must appreciate victory won with brilliance and not just brawn! If she does, if she blesses me and I get out of this alive, I will know then that she is my true patron goddess.

As if Athena herself whispers into my ear, my attention is drawn to the dying altar fire. If any of the supplicants wake to find it this way, they will become alarmed and seek out the priestess, find her drugged, and raise the alarm. The longer no one realizes I've replaced their goddess with a fake, the greater my chances of making it out. So I feed and stoke the fire in its gleaming bronze bowl until it flares and crackles and takes hold for good.

A sleeping supplicant turns over and mumbles as I pass but just as quickly stills. In a square outside the temple complex, I pause to get my bearings. There! The Scaean Gate—just as tall and imposing from inside the city as from outside. My heart pounds at being this close to it, for here—*here*—is the reason we have not succeeded in ending this terrible war. If we could only get past them. This tired, grieving city is more than ripe to be taken.

To my surprise, only two men guard the gate. *Two.* How is that possible? Then I remind myself, Earth-Shaker Poseidon and the Bringer of Light Apollo built the gate. And those high walls. *Just look at them.* It would take a giant to tumble them. Truly, they are a marvel of power and engineering. Two men could lay toe to head along the thickness of the immense doors alone.

Troy only needs two sleepy men at the gate because the gate's construction guards itself.

It must be opened from the inside if we are to take the city. For a wild moment, I think about running straight down to the gate, dispatching the guards, and forcing the vast doors open, screaming for my men to attack.

But of course, none of our warriors await. It would do nothing but ensure my instant death. And yet there has to be a way to get a large force inside quickly, without being seen advancing across the broad plain. But how? *How?*

I become aware of people in the street stirring, the hiss of fires flaring in the dark, hoarse coughing and murmured conversations—the sounds of slaves rising to prepare for the day—and I realize dawn must be approaching. Gods, I've spent too much time staring at the gate.

The sound of tinkling fountains behind courtyard walls lets me know I've exited into a higher class of neighborhood. The streets are cleaner. And wider. And then I understand why—the broader causeway is likely for accommodating royal processions from the palace. I must be near Priam's fortress. Which means I need to get myself to the poorer section of the city as quickly as possible. There are likely to be more guards on this end of the city.

As inconspicuously as possible, I begin hurrying, crouching low over my prize, checking to make sure my cloak covers it completely. The newly lit torches of predawn risers make me unsure of the time. Normally, I can sense how far we are from sunrise by the slight changes in the sky, but the city's many fires confuse me. I peek up, trying to read the stars when I barrel into a wall of flesh and I'm thrown back, landing on my ass on the rough-cobbled pathway.

Thankfully, the statue remains safe in my arms, but without thinking, I curse in the dialect of my people.

A musical voice murmurs, "How interesting. I haven't heard an accent like that in years."

Staring past the royal guard who purposefully knocked me down—while noting that his sword is drawn—I see a veiled woman covered in jewels and shimmering in a cloth of gold hovering behind him. For a moment, I think it's the goddess come to avenge me for the insult of taking her statue, but Penelope's Eris pun flashes into memory, and I know exactly who stands before me.

"Despite the attempt at subterfuge," the woman in gold continues. "I know only one man capable of making up curses about the improper use of long Ithacan rocks," she says blandly.

"Odysseus of Ithaca, if I am not mistaken."

"Helen of Sparta." I look her in the face, my disguise useless. How could this be happening? Of all the people inside this city, it's Eris herself who stops me? I was *so close*! The gods must be laughing at me. But I must stay calm. Think, *think. Do not let her know you are rattled.* But all I can manage is, "How strange to find you outside the palace at this hour."

"It is Helen of Troy now," she says in a low, purring rebuke. "And I visit the temple of Athena in the purple light of predawn so that I can speak to my goddess-aunt undisturbed and unseen."

Choosing not to laugh aloud at her declaration that she is Athena's blood relation—no matter what the stories say or she claims, I have never believed Menelaus' former queen hatched from Zeus' egg—I look around, trying to judge my next move. While I have a dagger, her guard has a very sharp spear. I can't release the Palladion, nor can I let them know exactly what I have in my arms. If she commands her guard to take me, there will be nothing for it—swordless or not, I will fight to the death, for I will under no any circumstance become a prisoner of this woman or of this tired kingdom. The dishonor would be unbearable.

A chuckle escapes me as I straighten and dust myself off, still cradling my covered prize. So it appears my sense of honor has found its demarcation line. This point and no further. I am, then, not so very different than Achilles and Diomedes, after all. Only my line for dishonor is different than theirs. More, shall we say, *practical.*

"Leave us," Helen commands her guard, and I raise an eyebrow.

"But this filthy beggar—" the guard begins.

"Leave us," she repeats, and the ice in her voice could cut through a bronze shield.

The guard stares at her with surprise, but he obeys, stepping away from me and melting into the shadow of the dark alley. He will not go very far—my neck will always be well within reach of his spear, I know—but at least I don't have to see him.

Soundlessly, she glides to the *herm* at the crossroads, signaling me to follow. The shrine provides scant privacy, but it is better than being in the middle of the lane.

"So, King of Ithaca," Helen says, turning to me, trampling on dried flowers long ago left there by those seeking protection from the god of crossroads. Flicking her gaze at the bundle in my arms, her lips quirk. "You have been hunting, I suppose?"

With a cold sinking of my stomach, I realize she is well aware of what I have in my arms. And why. She must have heard of Hellenus' prophecy. Word spreads fast in wartime. But then why has she not called an alarm? "How come you to be sure of my identity?" I ask, pretending casualness. "Surely, my accent isn't *that* distinctive."

Helen stares at me with the impassivity of a goddess. "I saw the boar hunt scar on your leg when you fell," she says. "You bragged on it quite a lot in your youth. And I have an excellent memory for detail."

I bet you do.

Her eyes take in my bruised face and dirtied appearance, but she says nothing. We stare at each other like wrestlers circling on the sand. What game is she playing? One word from her and the guard will take my head. Why does she pause? To discomfit her, I raise an eyebrow and smirk. She breaks first.

"I have a message for you to take to my husband," she says.

"Paris? But he's dead. Oh, you mean Deiphobus—"

"No, Menelaus," she says slowly, closing her eyes for a moment, and it's clear, under the surface calm, she is bone weary. "The husband from whom I was stolen."

Her audacity astounds me.

She does not meet my eyes but busies herself removing a circlet from her arm. Handing it to me, she adds, "Tell him that I did not leave his house willingly."

I stare at the golden bangle carved with the three stripes of the House of Menelaus. Idly, I wonder how she hid its presence from not one but now two Trojan husbands. Gods, she is sly. The bitch is hedging her bets.

Laughing, I shake my head. "You, my dear, will outlast us all."

"Oh, I have no doubt I will outlast all the Achaean 'heroes' who pretend to fight for my honor but really seek to enrich themselves with Trojan gold at my expense. Certainly, I have outlasted those who sought to protect Troy—Paris, Hector, poor Penthesilea . . ." she trails off, giving a brief, bitter glance at some ugly inner vision, but she pulls herself quickly back to the matter at hand.

"You will deliver the message?" she asks.

For a brief moment, I imagine pulling my dagger and slashing her throat. Finish this. Finish her. But her death would do nothing to end this conflict, no more than Hector's did. Or Paris'. Or Achilles'. Not now. One of us—the god-born of Troy or the sea-wolves of the Achaean lands—must fall. And it must not be us Achaeans.

Should I blame her for wanting to survive the coming catastrophe, even if she caused it?

"Yes, I will deliver your message." I turn, then pause, give her my most winning smile, and say, "You know, Helen, I used to wonder if you were an evil, lying, vain, chaos-inducing harpy. But now I know."

"Dear Odysseus, I am but a lowly woman," she says without missing a beat. "And yet I suspect that if you were as devoid of freedom and power as I have been, you wouldn't have lasted *half* as long—nor with half as much wealth and style."

With that, she floats past me as silent, mysterious, and perfumed as a queen's funeral barge.

Swallowing a bark of laughter, I shove her bracelet into the pouch hanging from my belt and set off without another glance. I wind my way down the city's narrow circular alleys as quickly as I can without drawing attention to myself, for even at this hour, people are stumbling about this strange, smelly, overcrowded city. In my sleepy kingdom, only the guards—those watching the sea for invaders—are awake at this hour. Suppressing a shiver, I know in my bones what my future nightmares will look like: me, lost and alone forever in the filthy, stinking labyrinthine streets of Troy.

Just make it out. Go, go, go.

At the sight of a familiar pathway, I pause as if the goddess herself bade me, noticing a small bundle curled up on the doorstep of the lilting stacked house I passed earlier.

Something propels me to move toward the shape in the dark. As if in a dream, all goes quiet save for the sound of my own breathing.

It is the child from before, as I suspected. He has sneaked out again to wait for his beloved father despite his mother's entreaties. My throat grows thick and tight at his sweet determination.

Ah, my son. Are you, too, waiting for me on the other side of the world? Watching the seas for my ships?

The sleeping child stirs, slowly sits up, blinking, as if I'd spoken aloud. Perhaps I had.

"Abba?" He stares at me through dream-filled, unseeing eyes, then grins, wide and sweet. "I told her you'd come for me," he murmurs. "I *told* her."

A chill slithers up my spine. My heart aches for the child, but I am also confused. Under what spell has heavy-eyed Hypnos placed him that he talks yet still sleeps?

This child is younger than my own boy. I know this. Yet in my heart and in my dreams, this is the age in which he comes to me, chubby-cheeked and soft-limbed, plump with milky innocence.

"I am here, my son," I manage.

"Take me with you," the child begs. "I miss you."

Swallowing hard, I breathe out, "I can only visit you in your dreams."

His face crumples in despair, and I fear he may wail, but it almost instantly transforms into an expression of delight. "Did you see how I fixed it?" the child whispers.

I blink, looking around, unsure of what he means.

He reaches behind him and holds out a small toy. A warped little wooden horse on wheels, black paint chipping along the flanks, fading yellow marks and holes outlining the harness and trace of what must have been an accompanying toy chariot.

I don't dare ask what he has "fixed." Maybe in his strange sleep he imagines that the missing doll-sized chariot and warrior are still attached? A worn and dirty gray strip of linen winds around the horse's middle. Maybe the toy had a hole in it. But none of that matters. It is clear he seeks only his father's affirmation. "Yes, well done, my son."

He grins again, eyes closed. A strange warmth and dread fills my chest. Is it possible that the gods have me talking to my own son through this child? That bright-eyed Athena rewards me with this strange, precious moment with my boy across the sea?

"Take it," the child says.

"What?"

"I sacrifice it to you," the boy says with the deep solemnity of a young child, and I remember the sacrifice of a horse that bound the suitors of Helen to support each other in war. So many years ago. So many deaths ago.

Afraid he will awake from the strange spell if I do not obey, I pluck the toy from his small hands.

He leans forward over his knees and whispers, "The treasure is all there."

I look down at it. It is so old. Perhaps it was once his father's. Thrusting it back to the child—I do not want to take his only toy—I see that he has curled up on his side again, a smile of relief and satisfaction twitching on his tiny mouth as he murmurs non-sense words to his dead father in his sleep.

I know then that I must take it. He must feel and see that he has done a son's duty to his father, as he'd promised. If he wakes and finds the toy he sacrificed to his father beside him—that it was all a dream and his father had not returned to the underworld with his gift—he will be crushed.

I turn to leave but cannot. Not knowing why, I feel compelled to add, "Child, you must protect your mother."

Do you hear me, my son across the sea?

"I am the big man now," the child murmurs, as if his mother had said the very thing to him.

"Yes, you are," I whisper. Then, as if Athena herself speaks through me, I add, "Leave the city. Take your mother and go into the hills. Soon. Do you promise?"

More unintelligible mumbling.

Still unsure why I need to, I push. "Do you hear me, Son? Leave the city with your mother. Tell her I have commanded it. Give me your oath. Swear on the soul of your father."

"Yes, *Abba*. I swear."

Air escapes my clogged throat in a slow, tight wheeze. I put my palm gently on the child's crown of curls and whisper the ancient blessing of fathers to sons.

"Good-bye, *Abba*," the child murmurs, releasing a sigh so deep he seems half his size in the expelling.

When I remove my hand, I suddenly come back to myself. What am I doing? How much time has passed? I scurry away, head down, trailing prayers for the safekeeping of that child and his mother, and for my own son and wife.

Hurry.

Just as I reach the crumbling section of wall where I gained entry, a man steps out of a dark doorway in front of me, dagger glinting, "Give me everything you've looted, old man. Now."

For fuck's sake, I don't have time for this. Instantly, I switch the Palladion and the child's toy under one arm and punch the man hard in the throat with the other. He goes down to his knees, dropping his dagger, wheezing, eyes wide at the surprising strength of the "old man" he tried to rob. To keep him quiet, I slam my elbow down on his head, and he drops bonelessly to the worn paving stones.

A woman in a dingy doorway watches us, but she scurries away the moment I look at her. Too many people about. No time to spare. On the other side of the wall, I make a low, soft owl hoot, letting Diomedes know that I have arrived with my prize. I hear a grunt and a thud and know that he has knocked out the old guard so that I can pass. As I rush through, I see that Diomedes has cut the man's throat. I had told him *not* to kill—to only knock him out. Now his replacement guard will call the alarm. Idiot.

When I am through the pass, Diomedes reaches for my prize, but I shake my head, and we sprint for the side of the broad fighting plain, as planned.

"By the gods, how much time you took," Diomedes complains as we run back to our camp. "I was about to go in after you."

Dressed as you are, you wouldn't have lasted a hare's heartbeat, I think. The folk at the citadel's bottom would've torn him apart for his metal clasps and fine sandals alone before a guard or warrior would have even got near. But I say nothing.

The low rumble of men's waking voices and the hiss of torches being lit signal the nearness of our encampment, and we slow. Fatigue makes my limbs heavy and my breath short.

"Let me see the prize," Diomedes says, stopping and turning to me, his eyes overbright in the rosy light.

Without thinking, I extend the child's gift to him. He slaps it away, and it crashes to the ground at my feet. "Not that! The *Palladion.* Let me see the goddess!"

In the crook of my arm, I gently move the cloak off her face, holding my breath like a mother revealing her babe to the world for the first time.

Diomedes stares down into the painted face of the goddess, and his eyes fill. He blinks the tears away, presses his fingertips to his forehead and then his heart in a gesture of obeisance.

I am moved as well, for I had not properly looked upon the face of our goddess-savior. Holding her in my arms, I become exquisitely aware of the power of Hellenus' prophecy, of the pull of Athena's ability to lead us to victory, for I am now as convinced as anyone that this is what we all need—that surge of hope and strength that comes of knowing our future is gods-blessed.

"Let me carry her aloft. The men will see her better and be uplifted if I bear her into camp," he says, reaching out to take the statuette, but I snatch her away.

Rage rumbles up my chest, and I lower my head like a bull over it. Of course he wants all the glory for my hard work, for *my* victory. Once again he will set himself up as the valiant hero and paint me as a lowly trickster.

No. *I* am the one who took all the risks, who found my way through the city's stinking serpentine streets and stole gray-eyed Athena from under their very noses. *I* will bear her aloft into the camp to the praise of all.

But before I can get the words out, he asks, "How did you kill the priests?"

I blink in surprise. "What?"

"Did you cut their throats? Spill their blood on her altar? That's how I would've done it!" His eyes gleam with a warrior's excitement. "Did you have to fight and kill any others, too?"

"No, I—" And then I remember I'd refused to tell him my plan of the poppy-wine because I knew he would hate it. Second only to Achilles in valor, he would demand besting by blood and brawn. In the face of his rules of "honor," how do I begin to explain that I used simple trickery?

How do I explain that I would not dare shed blood—especially the blood of the goddess's servants—lest she curse me and my family for generations for the sacrilege? His approach would only beget an endless cycle of bloodshed. And yet because I shed no blood, I should be ashamed?

My own blood goes thick and cold as I understand exactly how this will play out. Even as I tell *my* tale, he will reshape it to sound more and more heroic to the hooting, excited men who seek blood like thirsty savages. His violent version will be more thrilling, and so that will be the story that is told. And remembered.

My gaze moves to the sand, and I spot the child's now-broken toy at my feet, and I am suddenly too tired to fight the weight of his heroic aspirations. No matter how I explain my careful planning and bloodless victory, my version will look cheap and unworthy in the face of his story of danger and daring. While I'd been studying the Scaean Gate for a way into the city to end this war, he was busy spinning a tale aimed at enhancing his *arete,* his personal glory.

Another wave of heaviness fills my bones as I face the truth: I am but a farmer-king of a rocky, harsh land who only wants to go home to my humble palace and my beloved family. Who am I to think my name will be remembered when I am measured against the glory of godlike Diomedes?

"Take it!" I say, thrusting the statuette at him. "Let all know of *my* victory."

His fine brows crinkle for a minute at my words—because already in his mind it is *his* victory—but then he snatches the goddess and, with one hand, carries her aloft like a torch of victory as he races through the gates and into the camp, bellowing, "Here comes the bearer of the goddess, the fulfiller of the prophecy, the deliverer of triumph."

The air fills with the swishing slap of countless bare feet running toward the hero of the day, accompanied by the whooping and crying of joy that comes with promised victory.

Below me, the boy's toy horse lies forlornly on its side, the stained wrapping tied around its middle partly unraveled.

The treasure is all there, the boy had said.

Treasure.

I'd thought it was the child's dream-talking, but there before me, I see it: he'd tied a tiny toy soldier to the horse with the linen strips. The soldier had fallen head down—in such a way—that it looked like he was being born straight out the horse's belly.

The child's heart and hopes became instantly clear—his father must have loved horses, must have driven a chariot. The little boy wanted to comfort his dead father in the afterworld with his own beloved toy horse.

I swallow hard, staring and staring at this broken child's thing on this foreign soil.

And then, to my own dismay, begin to laugh.

At first it comes out like a bark, but then it rolls off of me like a hard rain coming in off the sea, needle-sharp, strong, and cleansing. My busted lip cracks, my swollen eyes ache, but still the strange joy pours forth.

Borne from a boy's love for his father. *This* is the gift from the goddess, I think, not the statuette. The goddess who does, after all, love me better than Diomedes. The goddess of wisdom who does not spurn cunning, as I have always feared. *She* let me take her statue, and *she* gave me this small boy's horse.

The gift that will ensure I get home.

To Penelope. To my son. To my land.

Scooping up the toy, I saunter back into camp wearing a grin, no longer caring about Diomedes' claims to fame and honor. Let them sing about his shield strength all they want. My song will be more interesting.

For I have an idea.

A most excellent idea.

THE SEVENTH SONG

THE FALL

by SJA Turner

Endure, and save yourselves for a better fate.
Virgil, the *Aeneid*

1—HUBRIS

ROSY-FINGERED dawn is but a dream of a day yet to come, though the darkness has been pushed back by a golden glow the likes of which I have never seen. The wine-dark waters of the strait, usually so turbulent with deep currents flowing in both directions, this night seem to be silent and flat, as though in mourning for a world now lost. And in the glassy depths: dancing flames twisting and writhing like a priestess with her serpents, golden and red, mocking me for my failure to save that which could not be saved. It is an eerie sight, for the world should not glow golden from below, yet I cannot bring myself to turn my head and look upon the source of that fire that dances, reflected upon the waters.

Hubris has brought us to this point—that damning pride in oneself that blinds us to love and justice and even piety. I am prideful, like all men, though perhaps I am less tainted in that I am at least aware of the fact. Hubris is all too often the downfall of men, and since cities and empires are built of such men, so, too, is this all-consuming pride often the downfall of worlds.

I am Aeneas, son of Anchises, who was cousin to King Priam of Troy, and of Ishara in the old tongue, who men of the new world call Aphrodite. I almost spit at the Achaean tongue fouling the name of my divine mother, but it has for many years now been the impious habit of my people to succumb to Achaean fashions even while sneering at them and calling them wolves of the sea. I am Aeneas, prideful prince of Troy. Last prince of Troy. And it is my sad song to sing of the end of a world.

THE prideful idiocy of my fool cousin Prince Paris, stealing away that dreadful woman, Helen from Sparta, and bringing her and the entire Achaean world to our doorstep was the first such disaster. Then the loss of our king's heir, brave Prince Hector, to that deadly Prince Achilles of Phthia, who was the very *embodiment* of hubris. The theft of the Palladion by one of the few Achaeans I might have considered noble—a man at whose wedding I had unexpectedly befriended—Odysseus, king of Ithaca. And countless lesser tragedies, all the way to this night of awful visions: Troy had become a city of nightmares.

But there was no going back to my former home, and I knew that. The palace there was little but a ruin now, deserted for years, overgrown and ravaged by Achaean raiders in their desperation for supplies, like so many other once-thriving Trojan settlements. Attention centers on Troy itself, and people forget that a world of lesser allies and subjects came to help us against the Achaeans only to have their own settlements ruined and looted by the enemy. I myself had brought the men of Dardania to the cause, after all. And as the years of horror wore on, I begged Priam to send to Hattusa for aid in driving the enemy from our shores, though I knew in my heart that the days of Hittite power were past, and they would likely be of little help even if they came. Yet Priam—arrogant, stupid Priam—would not even send to ask, for he was king of proud Troy and would no more bend a knee to Hattusa than he would to Sparta, for all that we owed the troubled Hittites fealty.

Sickening.

I digress.

It began with a bad dream. I thrashed and sweated through images of burning ships and chariots and torn, ragged bodies and of stinking, bloody death, and suddenly found myself sitting alone in a dark place in my dream-world, looking upon a war-ravaged and bloodied figure. My cousin Hector seemed as noble in death as ever he had in life, for all that his ruined form was a thing of nightmare. I was not afraid, though, as this was not the first time I had communed with those long gone. For the god-born and all truly pious men, the gods and lost heroes are never far away, if we but know how to look. Hector's flesh was torn and dusty, and my rage at Achilles' triumph once more surfaced, though I quickly pushed it aside, for such spirits as this one do not visit us lightly.

"Mighty Hector," I greeted him, somehow hoping that he was come to deliver us from the dreadful depredations that so many years of war had heaped upon us. But I could see an expression of saddened acceptance past those rents in his once-handsome face. Hector was urging me to do something, or perhaps warning me of something. His voice was inaudible due to the irreparable damage his throat had suffered as his corpse was dragged behind Achilles' chariot. A warning, I believed, and was suddenly awake, drenched in sweat and shivering at the clinging aura of the other-world that remained from my dream.

I could hear my father, Anchises, snoring in the next room and the sounds of revelry, muted through the walls, filling the houses and high places of Troy. For you see, the war was over. Two days ago, as the weather began to change slightly, heralding the last flourish of our warm Trojan summer, the Achaeans had begun to take down their camp. A near decade of war, some said, had been enough even for the greatest Achaean warriors. We knew that food was becoming ever scarcer for the besiegers, and other essential supplies were just as lacking. In the end, the invading army had returned to their fleet and sailed away, leaving a vast field of debris where their great fortified camp had been. Necessity had forced them to take only that which would fit upon their ships, and so huge piles of detritus remained.

As soon as their sails had disappeared over the horizon, the people of the city had opened the Scaean Gate cautiously, emerging like a man from a long sojourn in a cave, blinking and slow, and had begun to loot the remains of the Achaean camp. Most of what they had left was useless or worthless, but there were weapons in there and expensive oils and even gilded furnishings that the poorer of Troy's citizens would take home as a prize.

And there was the horse.

By some sort of shrine to one of their odd Achaean gods at the heart of their camp, they had constructed a wooden stallion of crude work but impressive dimensions that was adorned with garlands and offerings. Our own nobles and priests had gleefully claimed the Achaean offering-horse as our own and planned to bring it to Troy's highest places—to the temple of the glorious goddess the cursed Achaeans call Athena. I had watched from the walls all that day as our people swarmed across the abandoned camp like ants, ferrying goods back into the city. I had no wish to own what the Achaeans did not want nor, in truth, even what they *did* want, those impious shadows of men. No, I watched from the walls as they looted, and I had been there for some time before I realized that my dark-skinned cousin, the Princess Cassandra, had silently glided to a halt beside me and was watching with a sour face. I had enquired of her the reason for her mood.

"No good will come from taking that monstrous horse into our bosom," she had said, her wild eyes strangely vacant, as if she were wedged tight between this world and that of some dark prophecy. Then she pushed past me and was gone. Priam in earlier years had kept her confined to a cell, but since Hector's death, he no longer cared about the actions of his mad daughter, and she was regularly to be found flitting hither and thither in the city, often gone swiftly with a parting of doom-laden words.

But Troy did claim the massive horse. In the midst of the mass looting, that enormous creature had been brought through the Scaean Gate with great difficulty. It continually stuck on the threshold, and parts of the decorative mane were scraped off by the gate top as it was heaved and forced inside behind the carts of discarded armor and weaponry.

It was then that I saw Cassandra again.

She had stood in the Scaean Square, swaying slightly on unsteady legs, a polished axe in one hand and a burning torch in the other.

Something in her had snapped when the horse passed our city's threshold, and she'd lurched forward, screeching a bloodcurdling scream that would have scattered the shades of our fallen warriors, the axe held aloft.

She'd hacked at the horse, shrieking obscenities that no one could understand. When the crowd surged toward her, she had just snarled like a rabid dog, "Keep away!" shaking the axe and jabbing with the torch. "This horse means our end, you worthless fools!"

I had moved to help her, but it was too late. Before my feet touched the flagstones of the square, they had overpowered her, knocked the axe from her hands, and thrown her to the ground. The torch lay guttering at her side.

"Take the slack-wit away!" one spectator had ordered. "Kill her if you have to keep her from touching the horse again!"

I had been too late to assist Cassandra, but I would die before I let a gleeful mob touch a hair on her head.

"Step away," I'd said in my most commanding voice. "No one touches the daughter of Priam."

At that, the worst of the crowd had fallen away. I'd helped Cassandra rise, and together we left the square, her shaking like a leaf in the face of an impending storm.

"We are doomed, Aeneas," she had whispered. "Troy will soon be nothing more than a funeral dirge for an era long since passed."

The looting went on all day, and for much of that time they tried to take the horse up to the citadel, but the difficulties of maneuvering it through narrow streets and steep slopes proved too much, and in the end the priests and their men gave up, leaving the great offering in the square behind the gate to deal with another time. For as the sun set upon the first day of Troy's freedom, the city had other things on its mind. Wine flowed like never before. Men and women feasted and drank and fornicated and laughed. We had little in the way of supplies, of course. So many years of siege had ruined us, and even though outlying colonies had still managed to slip us food from the hinterlands, the city was starving. No one cared that night. The war was over, and soon food would be plentiful again, so the people gorged on the last of our supplies and sent themselves into a stupor.

I was never a man given to such behavior. My wife, Creusa, was of a similarly sober disposition, though my father was given to nights of affection for the grape. In truth, though, I probably would have indulged in the celebrations had it not been for Cassandra's dour attitude that had passed to me.

I rubbed weary hands through my unruly hair and stretched. The slightly warped bronze mirror by our bed displayed an older man than I remembered. Handsome enough in my way—a gift from my divine mother, clearly, given my father's knobbly features—but now running to gray and care-lined in places. I sighed. My father snored thunderously, sleeping off more wine than he had drunk in years, and Creusa and my strong, proud son were still abed and peaceful, but Hector's shade had woken me for a reason. I crossed to the door of the chamber, throwing on a light kilt for modesty, and swung open the portal, stepping out onto the balcony and shutting the door behind me. The night air was cool after the hot thrashing of my dream, and I could feel the sweat cooling on my back and beneath the rich linen kilt. Many of the upper city's windows glowed golden with welcoming light as the celebrations waged on through the night, but even as I watched, those lights were beginning to go out as the revelers succumbed to weariness and drink. The streets of the lower city were empty and dark. The chill of the night air had driven them all indoors, though on the citadel large communal fires burned in squares, and there would be dancing and music for hours yet. Down below, in the dark . . .

My eyes were drawn automatically to the horse. Our house—given to us by the king when we came to the city so long ago with our small force of Dardanian warriors—was in the lower city, yet high up and close to the walls of the citadel. From my balcony, I could see the horse looming in the square—a great, dark thing of dread like something Lelwani, whom the Achaeans call Hades, might send to the living world.

My eyes roved this way and that across the dark streets and roofs of the lower city. I'd half expected to see drunken youths trying to ride the great horse, but it stood alone and glowering in the dark square. Only one figure was visible down there on a balcony above the square. I couldn't make out details, but I instinctively knew who it was. Sleep had fled me for good now, and there was little point in returning to my bed to stare at the dark ceiling, so I determined to go down to the city and keep that lonely figure company. I briefly considered entering the house once more to collect my sword and my helm with its high plume the color of the sea in spring, so chosen to honor my mother, who had been born from the sea. But no. I had no need of my weapon or my high plumes, and I did not wish to disturb the others in their slumber. Instead, I grasped my cloak from the balcony rail where I had left it earlier and threw it over my back, gently trotting down the steps on bare feet. The narrow alleys of the lower city could be filthy and filled with debris, but for all its glory, the city was not a huge place, and the wider streets were well paved and, in better times, were swept clear of muck daily. I padded along the various flagged ways until I approached the Scaean Square. One street back from the wide space, I climbed a staircase and passed between two now-silent houses to the high balcony where that lone figure stood, keeping vigil by the light of a heavy moon.

Cassandra had not slept. Her face was taut and troubled, her hair wild and feet bare; I wondered whether she had stood at this square all day and through the night. Nothing about my strange cousin would surprise me, though I felt an odd kinship with her that was lacking with most of Priam's selfish brood. Cassandra, like me, felt the closeness of the gods and communed with the lost.

"Everyone calls me names, as if their words might still injure me," she said without even looking around to see who had approached. "Madwoman. Mouth of Evil. Ebony fool. But *they're* the fools. I don't know how, but this cursed horse . . ." she trailed off, shaking her head.

I stepped forward and leaned on the rail beside her, shivering as I looked out across the dark square below, the walls beyond, and in the distance, the wine-dark sea. The memory of Hector's ravaged ghost was still fresh, and his warning glance when added to Cassandra's certainty was enough to make me feel distinctly uncomfortable. "What could a wooden horse do?" I asked, though my mind was already running wild with images of the huge beast trampling warriors to death beneath its great timber hooves.

"We will know soon. Perhaps this night," she said.

I shivered again. Perhaps it had been a step too far to steal an offering to the gods. Had we not condemned the Achaeans for their theft of the Palladion? And now we somehow felt comfortable taking a divine offering from its own sacred place into our home? Hubris was not the only sin in Troy. Hypocrisy was also rife. Something thrilled through me as I watched that horse, and I felt suddenly far too naked for my own good despite the kilt and the cloak.

"I think I shall return home for my sword," I said quietly, but as I turned away, Cassandra's hand shot out and grasped my wrist.

She was strong despite her delicate bones, and I stopped, my brow furrowed as her nails bit into my flesh. She was pointing, and I peered down into the dark square. A figure was moving through the shadows, exiting a narrow stairway between two buildings and scurrying toward the great beast. There was something about the way he moved. I could not say what it was, but he appeared to be neither drunken reveler nor inquisitive local. There was something shady about him. I watched with growing apprehension. A thought struck me, and my eyes slipped back to that stairway, tracing its course behind buildings all the way to the tower above the Scaean Gate. A burgeoning golden glow rose from the parapet. That was no simple torch burning through the darkness like those to be found here and there around the walls. It was a beacon, high and bright. My skin prickled with dread, and I truly wished I'd bothered fetching my sword and sea-colored plumes. What could a beacon do? What could a horse do? What could one peasant do?

My eyes dropped to the square again. The figure disappeared beneath the horse, and just for a moment I wondered whether Cassandra's otherworldly ambiance and dark words were making me fear things that were not there. Perhaps this *was* just a drunken youth climbing up to ride the great horse. But after several heartbeats, he still did not appear atop the beast, and I knew that was not the case. He was hidden from sight somewhere beneath, but there was an odd wooden *clonk*, and suddenly he dropped from its belly back to the stone flags of the square. He was not alone. My eyes widened. Man after man dropped from underneath that horse like excrement fouling our city. I heard Cassandra's sudden intake of breath and nodded, but she was not looking at the men emerging from the great wooden beast. Her eyes were higher, looking out from our lofty viewpoint over the walls at the horizon. I tore my gaze from the men to focus on what she had seen, and my heart pounded.

Ships! A *great number* of ships, spotted across the moonlit sea like a black infection. The Achaean fleet was racing back toward our shores in the darkness, barely noticeable in the night, yet my eyes have always been keener than other men's—another gift from my mother, who sees clearly into the darkest place of all: the hearts of men. I saw with her keenness those dark hulls that were mere specks on a dark sea and cursed because I should have known that the hubris of High King Agamemnon would never allow him to return to his home without finishing what he started. Without avenging the many hundreds he had lost. Without Helen.

My voice rose in cries of warning, and Cassandra's, too, but they were just two voices in a city of drunken revelers. Those who were awake could not hear us over their own din; those asleep were dulled by wine. I tensed and made to rush for the long staircase down into the square, but Cassandra simply held on to my wrist and shook her head with sad, haunted eyes. There were ten men down there now, Achaeans equipped for war. I thought I recognized Odysseus and King Menelaus of Sparta and that vicious runt son of Achilles named Neoptolemus, all with their war gear. Even the grizzled, limping Prince Philoctetes of Meliboea, who came last from the horse, could have taken me down with ease, for I was in a light kilt and entirely unarmed. Facing them now would be futile and would help no one, and Cassandra and I both knew it. While those ten men ran for the gate, preparing to open it to the Achaean flood, my cousin continued to howl her warnings, as unheeded now in our moment of dire peril as she had been in our moments of joy.

"Stop them!" she cried to any Trojan who would listen, tearing at her hair while tears poured down her sunken cheeks. "Save your city, your fools, lest you feed the carrion come dawn!"

She may as well have shouted at the sun not to rise.

I determined to race to the tower and grab a sword—there would be weapons there, surely? Then I could hopefully reach the gate and face the invaders, maybe even stop them letting in their allies while Cassandra raised the alarm. I ran.

Perhaps I slipped and fell in the darkness between high house walls. It was possible since I was barefoot and not every path was dry and clean. Certainly, my world seemed suddenly to spin sickeningly, and everything went black. As I opened my eyes again, Hector stood before me in all his gory splendor, blocking my path. Could a man run through a ghost, I wondered? I had no wish to find out, in truth, and I was floundering on the ground, blinking away the darkness.

"Flee, son of Anchises," Hector said, his mouth opening and closing as his torn throat flapped and rippled. I simply shook my head in disbelief, and when I blinked, Hector had gone. I slumped, dispirited and weary, and blackness overcame me.

Fingers crawled across my skin, grasping at me. I blinked back into the world suddenly, shocked, and almost broke Cassandra's neck before I realized it was her that was shaking me, her face full of concern. I looked about, confused.

"Hector. Where is Hector?"

Any other in Troy would have thought me deranged, but Cassandra knew what I knew, and she accepted it without comment. "What did he tell you?"

"He told me to flee," I said with distaste, choking even on the idea.

She nodded again, her voice strangely calm despite the tear-salt on her cheeks. We had failed to raise the alarm. "Then you must go, Cousin."

Around me, I could hear the sounds of a city embroiled in desperate battle, which shocked me alert. Desperate shouts and the ring of bronze on bronze rose from the square. How long had the darkness claimed me? Oh noble Hector, had you kept me from my doom only to condemn the whole city?

The sounds of reveling had gone, and now there were cries of terror and panic and anger, shrieks of those falling beneath Achaean swords and hopefully a few Trojan ones. I floundered for only a moment before resolution filled me. I could do nothing unarmed. I needed to return home and equip myself. There, eight Dardanian warriors of my household were quartered in the lower rooms, and they would not be drunk. I did not approve of such base pleasures in my house when I myself would not indulge. Nine more blades could be raised in defense of the city if I hurried, and even nine blades can turn the tide in a battle.

"Come with me," I said, expecting that Cassandra would be grateful to do so, but expectations were ever to be cast aside when dealing with my cousin, and instead she shook her head sadly.

"It is not my path, Aeneas. Tyche has no hold on my future—only the Fates, and they have decreed a lonely end for me."

I felt that thrill of closeness to the divine, like artful fire crackling across my flesh, once more at such certainty, but my pride was upon me now, and I could not allow myself to accept such a thing. "Cassandra, come. I can save you. You need not walk into destiny willingly."

I don't know where that came from—it was not a common thread of thought for me.

Cassandra gave a strangled laugh. "I have been anything but willing when it comes to accepting this night's destiny. Now I am only resigned." My cousin's strange smile remained, and she gripped my shoulder for a long moment. "Dearest Aeneas, you cannot save me. You will try, and you will fail, for I have seen the path of my life laid out before me like a banquet table of rotting food. Indeed, you will not be able to save *any* upon whom you set your sights, and those whom you *do* save will come to you unexpected. Do not mourn for me, cousin, for I shall see you once more this night. Watch for the sign, Aeneas . . . a sign from the gods. You will know what to do."

I shivered, but already she had released my shoulder and was walking toward the din of battle. I fought a brief war with myself over whether to follow her, but she paused as if hearing my thoughts and held up her palms to halt me.

Or perhaps in surrender.

Cassandra was ever one to pursue her own destiny, so I cast a sad look after her and then rose and raced by the most direct route back to my house, ignoring the filth of the alleys underfoot, swift, though being careful not to slip again. I could ill afford to spend another moment in the blackness. As I reached the higher places, I looked about. Troy was already aflame, in the lower city, at least. I could see a house of my cousin Prince Deiphobus burning and wondered rather harshly whether Helen, who was now his by marriage after Paris was killed, might be burning inside it for all she had done. But divine justice is never that neat. The house of Priam's closest advisor similarly burned, as did the homes of numerous lesser folk. The Achaean ships were surely all ashore now, and the streets of the lower city were packed with warriors, hungry invaders filled with battle madness and desperate Trojans trying to hold back a tide of the worst of humanity.

My own house was in uproar, though my relief at finding it unassailed was paramount. Creusa stood in the common room in her white skirt, naked from the waist, her expression weighted with worry, our son wide-eyed and wary nearby. My father was already fully dressed and shouting orders to our Dardanian warriors. The eight of them were busy arming, each with a shirt of scales reinforced by bronze shoulder plates. Each bore a spear in hand, a sword at their side, and a moon-shaped shield of ox-hide with metal plates. Their helms were horned and of gleaming bronze.

Ten years of depredation had damaged almost everything, but a true warrior never lets his armor dull.

As I burst in through the door, Creusa ran over, with our son close behind, and threw her arms about me. I embraced her warmly but quickly let her go once more. This was no time for such pleasantry.

"How is it?" one of the warriors asked quietly as my father grunted, "They took the gate?"

I nodded to both. "It is bad. As yet, I think the invaders are caught up in the lower city and the citadel is untouched, but the upper city is unlikely to hold for long unless we do something."

I paused in my account to crouch and lace my bronze greaves, and as I straightened again, I held my arms out to the side while two men fitted my bronze breast and back plates and secured them.

"All we can hope to do now is hold the high city and keep them from the sacred places. We can safely reach the upper walls ahead of the fighting, I think." It was effectively suicide, of course, since I knew we could never hold the Achaean mass for long now that they were in the city, but I did not speak of it in that manner in front of my son.

I reached down for my helm with its proud plumes the color of a summer sea and shook my head sadly at them. Their glorious color seemed to mock me.

"If we go now—"

The door to the house slammed open once more, and we all turned, hands leaping to the hilts of weapons, to see old one-eyed Chryses standing in the doorway, heaving in deep, exhausted breaths. Three figures hovered behind him: his pregnant daughter, Chryseis, also panting, and two boys with their arms full, one with a golden *kithara* lyre, the other a delicate gilded wreath of laurels. Chryses was the priest of Istanu, who the hated Achaeans call Apollo, an advisor to the king and a close friend of my father.

"Aeneas," he said, spotting me in my war ensemble long before old Anchises in the corner. "Troy falls."

I shook my head defiantly—see how even then hubris flooded through me? "Troy will prevail. We go to save the high places."

Chryses stared at me with his one good eye as though I were an idiot. "Aeneas, we must save what we can. I bring the relics from the temple, and we must take them to safety. Would that I could have reached the palace and retrieved the likenesses of the ancestor gods, but at least Apollo's relics can be preserved."

I tried not to look at Creusa, who stood comforting the priest's weeping daughter. I knew her face would urge me to run. She was a proud Trojan, like me, and would never say as much, but I knew that in her heart she wished I would take old Chryses, our young son, and everyone I cared about and usher them away from here, to safety. The memory of awful, ravaged Hector drifted through my mind, urging me to flee. It seemed the world around me and the world beyond both wished me to leave Troy. But how could I? How could I leave good men and women to die under the blades of the Achaeans while I tucked my tail between my legs and ran for the hills?

"The city is at war. The Achaeans are both inside and outside our walls. Our Dardanian palace by the sea is but a shell, as is almost every Trojan tributary. This is the only home we have left. Where would we go?"

It was, I thought, a convincing speech. Hoary Chryses, though, waved his hands about, his face desperate. "They cannot take the sacred relics, Aeneas. We must get them away." He lowered his voice and leaned close in a conspiratorial manner. "Aeneas, you know where the remaining Trojan ships are. The last three vessels from our fleet, the ones that carried that bitch Helen here from Sparta—you hid them for Priam, on his orders. And three vessels can carry a lot of men."

I straightened with a frown. "While there is still a Troy to save, I have to save it," I said with an air of finality. I do not know even now whether it was pride that drove me to turn my back on the notion of flight, or whether it was the call to duty that every warrior feels, for I suffer from both in equal measure. All I *do* know, as I look back on that decision, is that it was made in defiance of the urging of both men and gods, against the weaving of the Fates, and it brought us only more pain.

2—DUTY

I look about me. The oar benches are filled, though not one wooden blade dips in the water. There is little more than a faint breath of wind, yet we let the combination of our limp sail and the upper current carry us from the burning city, for we dare not risk the splash of oars drawing the attention of any scattered Achaeans who might be about. For we are Troy. We twenty-seven men are Troy. Each man sits silent, lost in his own thoughts as he watches the flames reflected in the calm waters. None of us can look back at the city now.

We are all fathers and sons, heroes and cowards, teachers and students, but we are each, above and beyond all else, warriors. No matter how lost a cause might seem, when that cause chooses a warrior, he can do naught but accept his destiny and fight for it. Of course, sometimes the Fates have other futures in mind for us, and when that happens, we find ourselves torn.

SNARLING, I grasped the beautiful plumes and wrenched them from the holders in the helmet, casting them to the floor. I had not realized until I stood, staring at the bald bronze bowl, that all other movement and conversation in the room had halted and everyone was watching me.

"I am god-born, but today I am ashamed," I snapped. My son scurried across the floor and began to gather up the beautiful plumes, but I ignored him. Instead, I grasped an old brush that hung from a hook on the wall, used for sweeping the surfaces in the house. Gritting my teeth, I wrenched the black, filthy bristles from the brush and knotted them carelessly into shape, jamming them into my plume holders. They jutted from my bronze helm higher than the beautiful ones had, stark, filthy, and dark. I tipped the helmet upside down so that the few that were not secure could tip out, then jammed it onto my head.

"Husband—" Creusa began with a concerned look, but I waved her away.

"I wear an ash plume to honor a burning city while I try to save what I can." I noted that Anchises was reaching for a corselet of bronze and I shook my head. "Stay here, Father. Look after the family. I . . . I have been told I will not be able to save those I seek to protect, so their safety must fall to you. Stay here as long as you can, and if the Achaeans come and I do not return, then take the others through the Rhoiteion Gate and north to safety."

My father paused for a moment and finally nodded, putting back the cuirass. He was too old to fight such a battle, and he knew it, though that ever-pervading pride had almost driven him to do it anyway. Pride and duty. Duty and pride. The cause of all wars.

I rushed out into the street, noting with dismay how the lower city had already mostly fallen. More and more houses were burning, and the din of battle had moved up the slopes away from the Scaean Gate toward the citadel walls and the noble houses. Soon the Achaeans would be at my own doorstep, and I prayed that my father would be able to save those I loved. I knew Cassandra and her gift well, and I could not find it in myself to doubt her words. I could not try to save them.

As we descended the stairs to the street, my eight warriors at my heel, five other figures emerged from the alleyway ahead, already marked by battle. We almost charged them, but at the last moment, in the gleaming light of the inferno that was our city, I marked four warriors I knew well who had fought for our cause these past years and, alongside them, Coroebus of Phrygia, come to Troy to woo Cassandra, who had repaid him with less attention than a flittering butterfly. Coroebus, who was like kin, gestured at me. "We came to find Aeneas, son of Anchises, but it seems a raven has taken his armor."

I frowned for a moment but realized he was pointing at my ash plumes. I nodded. "We go to the upper city to save what we can. Where are you bound?"

"To your side, Aeneas," said elderly Iphitus, a man who should be coddling grandchildren and not suited for war.

"Come, then," I roared and led my small band of thirteen warriors into the fray. We had not far to travel to find war. Two streets away, a dozen Achaean warriors were busy beating back a pair of young men with nothing to defend themselves with but two shoddy spears and a single small ox-hide shield. Behind the two youths, an old graybeard lay on the ground, bleeding and groaning as the women of his household tried desperately to help him up and out of danger. We fell upon the Achaeans from behind—there is no nobility in this kind of war. It was not the time of glorious duels, as it had been when Hector and Achilles still lived. We felled them like sacrificial beasts, for they were unaware of our approach until it was too late. I took down one of the largest men, swinging my double-edged blade and digging it deep into his neck, above the corselet of scales and below his boar's tusk helmet. When I wrenched it back out and he fell away, his head lolling at a dreadful angle and blood pumping from the wide rent, I caught another warrior with the edge, opening the large vein of his neck. I ignored him further as I set upon a bear of a man, the neck-wounded warrior staggering around and clutching his neck, trying to contain the violent spray of his crimson life.

We felled all twelve in short order, though one of my Dardanians took a terrible blow to the inner thigh, and his life was flooding out with every heartbeat. I said a prayer for him but moved on with just a fraternal squeeze of the shoulder. We could afford to waste no time. The women and the old man ran from us as though we were the enemy, disappearing inside their house.

Another corner brought us closer to the gate of the inner walls, but as we rounded it, a small party of Achaeans stumbled upon us. We fought like lions then. I was not a young man, even a decade ago when my damned cousin Paris first set eyes on that wretched woman and decided to bring her to Troy, and my sword arm was never the match for Hector's, nor my bow-skill like that of Paris. But I was still god-born, and there was an accuracy and a tenacity to my moves that gifted me a dance-like efficiency that had thwarted many an opponent. I punched my short blade into a man's chest, tearing into the hide shirt he wore as though it were ewe's cheese. I felt it grate between ribs and spear the heart, and the man spluttered bloody spittle at me as I wrenched the blade back out, twisting despite the ribs to free it from the sucking wound.

A second man swung a spear round and thrust at me. Though I ducked to the side, the tip struck my helmet and danced along the bronze bowl with a noise that, from the inside, sounded like the shrieking of harpies. I made him regret the damage to my war gear when I took his spear arm with a simple slice, then dropped and jammed the blade into his nethers, where protection was low and mortality high. He screamed and fell, torrents of red pouring from his groin.

By the time I rose again, the enemy was dispatched, though two more Dardanians lay gasping out their life on the ground. Once more we muttered prayers, looked upon them kindly, and ran on.

Along the street where a councilor's once-grand house was now a skeleton of blackened columns rising to support timber ribs, the whole wreathed in all-consuming fire, we came across another party of Achaeans, led by a man in a curiously tall helmet with a yellow plume that rather stood out in a crowd. I opened my mouth to bellow my men forward, but as I did, the yellow-plumed warrior turned and waved at me.

"We're nearly through the gates!" he yelled with glee. "You were almost late to the party!"

I had no idea for whom this Achaean hero had mistaken me, but I simply grinned, waved in a comradely fashion, and hurried up the street to join him and his dozen or so warriors where they were busy administering the mercy kill to a small band of Trojan defenders. The sight inflamed me, and my knuckles whitened on my sword hilt. Then, in a heartbeat, we were among them, the Achaeans having raised not a weapon to defend themselves, duped as they were by their own leader's mistake. By the time I ripped my blade out and jammed it into Yellow-Plume's armpit beneath his raised, comradely hand, two of the other enemy had already fallen to spear thrusts. My men moved among the Achaeans like starving wolves among sheep, tearing and rending, and in less time than it takes to sing a paean chorus, the Achaeans were dead at our feet. As the others took a moment to catch their breath, I moved to the next corner and looked around it. The street from here to the high gate was filled with gangs of slavering Achaeans, roaring their victory cries. It would be a hard fight pushing on to the inner gate, and I said as much to the others as I returned.

"But they are expecting this yellow-plumed man, yes?" murmured Coroebus with a sly smile. I looked from him to the body on the ground, the blood still slicking from beneath his arm, and I caught that smile and returned it. Not wishing to be caught by random wanderers, we dragged the bodies from the street into a house and stripped them of only their most recognizable gear. To a civilian, there might seem to be no real difference in the way Achaeans and Trojans armor themselves, but a warrior notices things. There are telltale giveaways, even down to the clothes beneath the panoply. We threw on their bloodstained *chitons*, which covered our own tunics, and the blood could just as well be that of men we killed. It *was*, in truth. Coroebus looked the part in the high yellow plume, and we others were all lesser miscellaneous Achaean warriors now. I kept my ash plumes, though. I decided no one would look closely enough at me to worry when I was next to glorious Coroebus.

We emerged from the house and turned the corner. Now the Achaeans were at the citadel's gate, wielding a ram and hammering at the timbers. The defenders were jabbing down with spears, loosing poisoned arrows and throwing rocks, but the tide of invading life at the gate was too strong. Soon they would be inside. I knew at that moment that we were too late to save the upper city. The citadel would fall, and the Achaeans would ravage our sacred places. But then none of us had come this far in the belief that we could win. This was about duty, pure and simple. We were warriors of Troy, and if Troy was to fall, then its warriors would do their duty and shed their blood along with it.

We exchanged looks, all of us, and I could see the acceptance in their eyes. We were all dead men, but we would exact a heavy price in Achaean blood and flesh for every stone of Troy they secured. At the near end of the street, a few bands of stragglers hurried to join the fight, late arriving from the ships, and we moved among them with ease—we were all Achaean brothers now, after all. The opportunity fell to us three times to dispatch small groups of stragglers without drawing the attention of the main force at the gate. It was satisfying, even in the moment of our doom, to bite deep into filthy Achaean flesh with good Trojan bronze. We must have killed two dozen more before we reached the mass of attackers. As we moved among them, pushing and jostling like all the rest, we each took any opportunity to subtly jab into bodies, wounding where we could in the press so that no one could tell it was us.

Our lust for Achaean blood was far from sated when the first defense of the citadel gave with a deafening crack. The gates gave under the repeated blows of the ram, and the great log was dropped immediately, the warriors at the head of the force using axes and brute strength to wrench the ruined wooden gates aside from the hole smashed in the center. Scores of Achaeans perished at those gates, giving up their lives to widen the breach for their fellows. I almost admired them, but I would rather have their necks beneath my sandal and my blade in their throats, so I ground my teeth and pushed on, trying to force my way through the crowd. The others were still mostly with me, though I could now see only two of my Dardanians. It was hard to keep track of them all, disguised as they were.

We burst through the gate like water from a broken dam. The defenders were already away, pushed back by the Achaean tide, and the enemy filled the upper city with every heartbeat, flowing through the walls and charging for all the glorious, bright palaces and temples of our most holy places. Troy was doomed. I could only pray in my desperation that my father had managed to get the others away. Or perhaps the Achaeans had not gone to my house with the lure of the upper city filling their eyes?

Then all thought of heroic deaths, of flight, even of righteous killing, abandoned me, for through the crowd of roaring Achaeans and the pockets of desperate Trojans, I saw her.

Cassandra, her narrow form dark amid these golden foreigners, stood out.

I did not know how she had reached the inner citadel ahead of me—perhaps she knew some hidden temple way known only to the priestesses to whose ranks she had once belonged, or perhaps she had been caught by some Achaean spearman and dragged along as a prize. Now she lay sprawled on the age-worn stones of the temple of high Arynna, whom the Achaeans in their base tongue call Athena, hair like a pool of dark flames on the ground. Cassandra's bloodied lip and her torn kilt that was still askew stood as evidence of the base crime so freshly committed. The ox-like Achaean Prince Ajax readjusted his stained battle-kilt as he spit upon her, and I knew then what my poor cousin had seen in her visions, what nightmare she had always known hunted her.

The hulking warrior bound Cassandra's wrists and held tight to the other end of the leash, yanking hard so that she yelped and lurched to her feet as the leather bit into her wrists. A sizable force of Achaeans surrounded her in the next instant.

I was angered beyond reason, but my ire was as nothing to that of Coroebus, who was once more beside me, his high yellow plumes easily marking him among the press. Coroebus, the prince of Phrygia, who had owed no oath of fealty to Troy at all, who had come from his distant home with his warriors solely in the hope of winning the hand of Princess Cassandra. Coroebus snapped. It was almost as though I heard his soul fracture at the sight of his intended, raped and now being dragged away as chattel by the enemy. With a roar of incandescent rage, my friend launched himself at Ajax's men, and I was instantly caught up in the fire of it. My cousin had said she would see me once more this night, but I would not be able to save her. Maybe *Coroebus* could, if I helped him? We fell among the Achaeans like farmers reaping a field of barley. They were utterly unprepared, shocked at this apparent assault from their own men, and we hewed them in their astonishment. I took arms and legs and heads with my sharp-edged blade, tearing heedless through armor, *chiton*, and flesh. I was sure that we would be able to reach Cassandra. My other companions were with us now as we ravaged Ajax's force. We would win. We would save her, and we could cheat my cousin's prediction, for it would be Coroebus that did it, and not I.

The tide turned on us in a single heartbeat. A band of Trojan warriors appeared as if from nowhere, and I gave it no thought until they began to cut into us. I saw one of my companions disappear beneath a flurry of sword strikes from men who had shared a dinner table with him. We were Achaeans to them. Coroebus was still madly hacking and smashing at the Achaeans, as were four of us, but the others were now protecting our backs from our own people, yelling out at them our true identities. Confusion reigned complete as the Trojans thought we were Achaean, but the Achaeans were now hearing us claim to be Trojans. And *everyone* was attacking us.

I would have upbraided Coroebus for what had, in the end, turned out to be a disastrous idea, but as I rounded on him, his head suddenly exploded like an overripe pomegranate trapped in a bowl. That bronze helm with the yellow plumes had been cleaved so heavily that the axe had cut through it and into the brain, and through the gore and the mess as he slumped, I saw his killer. Before him stood that monster in human form Neoptolemus, son of Achilles. The animal barely registered the death as he turned to his mighty companion.

"Stop messing about with whores, Ajax. Their feeble old king cowers in his palace, waiting to be slain!"

And with that, the bastard was off. I tried not to tread on Coroebus' shuddering corpse, but we were now fighting a last desperate struggle. All but one of my Dardanians were gone, as were most of the companions I had brought from the house. Only two remained with me now.

Somehow the Trojan defenders had finally grasped our identity and had pulled back, but we were just three now to the Achaean's scores. I watched, helpless, as Cassandra was dragged away from the temple, a sea of warriors between us. She gave me a sad last smile and a final nod, and then she was gone, huge Ajax and his men driving her on. Despite the clear futility of it, I made to go after her, but half a dozen Trojan hands grabbed at me and pulled me back. I looked at the temple and the shade of my poor cousin's violation hovering there, but warriors grasped me and turned me.

There would be time to mourn her later, her and so many others.

"The palace. The Achaeans are besieging the palace. The king and the queen, Aeneas!"

I quickly focused on the man before me. I recognized him, though I couldn't put a name to the face. My gaze rose beyond him to the palace, and my heart shuddered. The sea of Achaeans now surrounded the last stronghold of Troy's ruling family. And within that complex stood the temple of the ancestors and their sacred likenesses. All that was left that could be said to be Troy was trapped in that building. Even now more Achaeans were pouring into the upper city, and the men who had pulled me back were suddenly fighting, pushing against an unstoppable tide.

"What do we do, Aeneas?" Iphitus asked.

"We save the king and queen, or we die trying," I answered severely. There is a strange sort of calm acceptance that settles on a man who knows he is about to die, can do nothing to prevent it, and has little wish to live on anyway.

"How do we get past that lot?" breathed Iphitus.

"I know a way. Come on."

I led them away from the open space and the noise of battle into a narrow side alley that ran alongside the temple. Two buildings back, close to the eastern walls of the citadel, there was a heavy door built into a wall of large, rough blocks. It was a vague thing, not hidden, as such, but still barely distinguishable from the surrounding wall unless one was looking for it. I found it and jammed my finger into the narrow hole in the door, yanking it wide open. Inside was a storehouse for the main palace and the various chambers where slaves and servants went about their business, its construction of heavy stone and not the painted, smooth plaster of the palace proper. A subterranean corridor led off down a flight of steps toward the palace, undiscovered as yet by the enemy.

"What is this place?" Iphitus asked.

"A simple back entrance. They are often overlooked. Hector's wife, Andromache, often used this passage to visit his family without having to pass through all the guards and officials. You know what she's like, hates a fuss." I had always quite liked Andromache. She was unassuming and natural, unlike many of Troy's women. The perfect consort for noble Hector. But like so many great men, Hector was now gone, and Andromache would never be queen. And unless we could do something, in the stroke of a night she would go from royal princess to Achaean war prize.

We ran along the corridor and back up the steps into the palace's ground floor. As it entered the main building, we were faced with a choice. Ahead lay the official chambers and the sacred shrine of the ancestors. Up another flight of stairs lay the royal apartments. It was a choice easily made, for the sounds of furious battle reached us from the stairs, and so we ran, taking them two at a time. The noise seemed to be coming from the roof, and we ignored the king's chambers and emerged into the night air once more, though there was little in the way of darkness or coolness now. The burning city had given the entire world a bright golden glow, and the heat emanating from the lower city was as searing as the warmest of summer days. A good warrior knows to check his terrain before he commits, and the moment the three of us arrived on the roof, we moved about, taking in the situation. It was dire. Down below, the palace was surrounded by Achaeans. The main entrance was of a large, ornate, bronze-plated door, but some earlier ruler with a nervous disposition had installed a heavy timber gate that could be closed upon its outer surface to provide extra defense. Even now I could see the Achaeans hammering upon it and trying to split it with axes while others raised ladders, attempting to gain access to upper windows or to the roof. The valiant defenders—a mix of Trojan warriors who had been pushed back from outer defenses, palace guards and servants, and even some of the palace's women—were busy fighting the laddermen off any way they could. The warriors and guards jabbed down with spears or cut away the tops of ladders with axes and swords while the beleaguered women and those without weapons tore up tiles from the roof and cast them down on the attackers, smashing skulls and breaking bones. The slaughter was as great as I had ever seen on a battlefield, and I had fought for our Hittite overlords in their glory days, when armies of thousands crashed into one another on the plains near Hattusa.

There was little we could do, I decided, but join in. Wherever we fought, we would make little difference to the outcome, and wherever we fought, we would kill Achaeans. As my companions busied themselves pushing away ladders, I prised a stone the size of a goat loose from the parapet, bloodying my knuckles, and pushed it outward. The stone hurtled through the air, smashing into a climbing man and sending him falling from his perch, then snapped the ladder as though it were naught but dry reeds before striking a hapless Achaean below. His head disappeared, the helm crushed flat along with the skull, the whole mass driven down into the man's torso where, even there, shoulders and bones shattered and pulped beneath the falling weight. I stared, fascinated and horrified as the squashed man fell to the ground, mush spilling from him as the piece of parapet clunked to a halt.

Iphitus had seen me at the battlements, and he nudged his fellow Dardanian. Moments later, the three of us were repeating the procedure, loosening the old, brittle mortar and heaving the stones out into the air to pulverize the Achaeans below. It was hard work, and grisly, too, but it was having an effect on the morale of the attackers, and for precious moments the tide seemed to draw back from the walls.

Then their tactics changed. Some among their numbers found firebrands and began to hurl them up onto the roof. We tried to move them, kicking them away once more, picking them up by the cooler ends and hurling them back. But their numbers were impressive, and many of the roof tiles had been used as missiles, leaving a great deal of dry timber exposed. Within fifty heartbeats, the roof was aflame, and there was nothing we could do, there being no source of water nearby. Helpless, we tried to peer over the edge, repeatedly ducking back as flaming torches hissed past us to land among the rafters.

Down below, the palace gates were under pressure. Two Achaeans with long bronze shields were covering the lattices, preventing the hidden phalanx from jabbing with their spears, while that monstrous son of Achilles, Neoptolemus, hewed at the gate again and again with a stolen Trojan axe. Even above the roar of the flames and the din of people, we could hear the timbers of the gate beginning to give. Then others joined in; I saw Odysseus and Menelaus among them, each with an axe, hacking at the timbers. Had not dancing flames sent me back away from the edge, I would gleefully have dropped a rock on Neoptolemus or the Spartan king. Perhaps even the noble Ithacan king with whom I had once broken bread.

The palace was on the brink of falling, as the rest of the city had. I had retreated through Troy with the Achaean tide, rising higher and higher into the citadel as it fell, then past the temple and now to this highest point of Troy, and this would be the last. From the roof, across the dancing flames, I could see the Achaean fleet. I fancied that if I strained hard enough, I could see my ruined home on the north coast. I put that from my mind. It was too late for such things now. The roof was no longer safe. Soon the flames would be all consuming. Even the Achaeans had taken away their ladders, giving up on it. With the help of a few warriors, I ushered everyone back to the entrance and down into the staircase, its walls painted with bright reds and whites, murals of processions and ceremonies. For generations, my family had ruled the richest city in the peninsula from this building. Even the dreaded Hittites saw more use in us as allies than as an impediment to their empire. And now it was falling because of a bunch of hairy sea-wolves, a young, lustful prince, and a woman with the mark of monsters upon her heart.

I led everyone back down into the palace and told my companions to take them all back through the slave passage and out of the burning building. Then, if the gods were kind, they might make it to the overlooked eastern walls and flee to impoverished, ruined, desolate safety.

As they all trooped off, I turned away. *My* fate would be different. Hector and Cassandra and the priest, Chryses, had all urged me to run from this city, but duty held me here. Here, in this building, were my father's cousin, King Priam, and his wife, Hecuba, as well, no doubt, and many of their lesser children. My duty was clear. Save the king and queen or die trying. A nagging little voice in the back of my head reminded me of Cassandra's warning: that I would not be able to save anyone I sought to. But it was my duty to try, nonetheless.

I could now hear brutal action at the front of the palace. I needed no line of sight to tell me what was happening, for I heard little but screams, splintering wood, and repeated shouts of the name Neoptolemus. Achilles' daemon son was leading a brutal assault on the palace. I found my way via several lesser rooms to the king's megaron, but it was empty. Then I heard Hecuba's voice from the temple to the ancestors, which lay adjacent. I passed through the door into that room and almost snorted at what met my eye. Hecuba, regal and cold, stood berating her husband with a wagging finger. Priam, old and worn as he was, was busy trying to fasten a bronze corselet around himself, an ill-fitting helmet formed of perfect boar tusks with high feathers of pure white perched on his crown. This was his old panoply, from when he had been a true warrior. As he finally succeeded with the corselet, he angrily tore the helmet from his head, accepting that it would no longer fit, and cast it away. The fine helmet rolled to a halt at my feet and I stooped, collecting it.

"My king."

Priam turned a suffering look upon me, and once more the humor of the situation insisted itself upon me despite everything. Priam had lost a city, almost an empire, this night. His many sons had nearly all met their deaths in the war, and now the enemy burned and invaded his house. And yet the thing that had raised ire in him and had him spitting feathers was a wife who berated him for trying to act like a young man when he so clearly was not.

Priam tilted his head slightly with widening eyes in the age-old gesture that means "help me."

I could not.

"Tell him he cannot fight," Hecuba snorted. "He oozes from his panoply like cheese from a press."

"I will die a Trojan warrior, not a cowering king," snapped Priam, and for a moment there was something of that young hero within him, and my respect for my king was unbreakable. I would fight and die alongside him. But Hecuba had other ideas.

"Aeneas, you are the last, apart from this old fool and our Polites, now the last of Troy's princes. The others are just children and daughters. You are the last true blood of Troy. You must run, while you still can."

I stared. Even my queen? Surely not. How could I run now?

"Andromache has the children in hiding," the queen said with a hint of resignation. "*You* must take the ancestors," she hissed, and I realized then that she was clutching the ancient revered likenesses of the founders, the most sacred relics in all of Troy. She held these symbols of Troy, ancient wooden figurines, as if they were the most precious of newborns. I felt again that faint frisson that spoke of the closeness of gods. Chryses had been right, of course. There was no saving the city now. Troy would burn, and the royal line would be extinguished. But I carried that same blood. I and my father and my son. And while we were the *blood* of Troy, these simple figurines and the prizes that Chryses carried were its *spirit*. Together we still had Troy. The walls may fall and the towers burn, but wherever we went, we could carry Troy with us.

Before I realized what I was doing, Hecuba had thrust the sacred symbols into my arms, and I struggled, clutching them and the king's helmet with its ghostly white feathers. I unfastened my own chinstrap and let the fire-blackened bronze of my helm with its ashen plumes fall away with a clang, pulling Priam's own helmet down over my pate and finding it a surprisingly comfortable fit. The king had been considerably smaller when this was his new panoply.

Hecuba shooed me away with delicate hands. "Go. Save what you can."

I retreated into the deepest shadows at the back of the temple of the ancestors, but before I could leave, my attention was grabbed by a commotion, and I lurked in the shadow of a great pillar and watched the last dreadful scenes of the fall of Troy unfold.

The king's young son Polites burst into the room from the corridor. He was armored for war in an ill-fitting borrowed adult panoply but had lost his weapons and shield. The blood coating him told a tale of courage and violence, and he shouted his father's name as he entered the temple, but another figure appeared silhouetted in the doorway behind. This was a figure of nightmare far more than the shade of Hector who had visited me in my dreams. This leering monster, slippery with gore and with eyes of flame, stepped into the room, a spear held raised in his hand. Neoptolemus bore the martial skill of his father, Achilles, and the gods-given rage, and even some of the looks, but he carried none of the grace and nobility of the Achaeans' greatest hero. He was his father's *shadow* at best, dark and lifeless.

That sickly grin turned to a sneer as he cast his spear, which hit young Polites in the back, bursting through his scale corselet near the breastbone, the spearhead glistening red with the life of the prince. I could hear the gasp of his father from the shadows and wondered how I would feel were that my own son there, collapsing to the floor as gobbets of blood burst from his mouth, unable to lie flat as the spear point held him up like some sort of flesh tent. Neoptolemus strode into the room, grabbed the shaft, and jerked it this way and that, agonizing the dying young man, and I could see Priam shaking.

"Is it not enough that your father killed my Hector? And now you must torture my last children before my eyes?"

"I will see your line extinguished this night, old fool," the son of Achilles barked, leaving the expiring boy and marching over to the king, who struggled in his shock to draw his sword. Now another figure appeared in the doorway, and I recognized the shorter, barrel-chested figure of Odysseus. Not far behind them would be the other Achaean leaders, I realized. I felt myself begin to rise, to run to the assistance of my king in his last desperate moments, but somehow the weight of the sacred objects in my grasp held me down. To fight in the defense of my king was to offer up Troy's most sacred relics to mere chance.

"If you seek to kill," Odysseus shouted at Neoptolemus, advancing angrily on the younger man, "then kill. Quickly and with good grace. A warrior is not a torturer." He turned melancholy eyes to Priam. "Greetings, king of Troy. I am saddened that what might have been resolved by words has come to this."

Priam tried to reply, but Achilles' son was on him like a starving wolf on a lone goat. He grasped the king's hand, yanking it away from his sword, drew that blade, and threw it across the room. As the old king struggled, Neoptolemus, snarling like a feral animal, grasped Priam by his graying hair and dragged him to the altar, now devoid of sacred figures. Priam cried out and tried to fight, but Neoptolemus was strong, his grip unbreakable.

"Quickly," reminded Odysseus, "and with good grace."

Neoptolemus was deaf to his companion as he drew his short stabbing blade and jammed it beneath the lower rim of Priam's bronze cuirass, into the king's gut. Priam hissed in pain, but that only served to excite his attacker. He withdrew the blade and stabbed again and again, ripping it out with sprays of blood. Then, shaking and with an otherworldly grin, the son of Achilles let the agonized king go. Priam clung to the altar, heaving ragged breaths, and then Neoptolemus returned, gripping his axe. I could hardly believe what I was watching, and neither could Odysseus, who shouted at the maniac to stop. But the son of Achilles had the Rage of Ares within him, and the axe rose and fell three times until the cords and tendons in the king's neck gave way and the head came loose.

Once again, as my gorge rose, I made to do so myself, unable to bear witnessing such dreadful vile dishonor. And once again I felt that vague frisson crawl across my flesh, reminding me that what I held were worth more than any man, be he hero or king.

Neoptolemus held aloft the head triumphantly as the kings and captains of the Achaean horde burst into the room. I could see Odysseus' calculating face as his speedy mind sought the best of a terrible moment. Rushing over to the queen, he grasped Hecuba by the arm. They were close to me, in my shadowed corner, and I could see the sympathetic concern in the eyes of the Ithacan king.

"I claim the queen!" he shouted above Neoptolemus' hungry yelping.

Hecuba rounded on her captor, haughty defiance in her expression. "I am not chattel," she snapped. Odysseus lowered his voice to a whisper and leaned close. I barely made out his words, which were the wisest I heard from an Achaean all that day.

"Be quiet, queen of Troy. Would you prefer to be *his*?" he hissed, pointing at Neoptolemus. "Or raped by Ajax, like your dark-skinned daughter?"

I felt another piece of my heart die at his words, verification of what my own eyes had seen.

"No," Odysseus said in a hiss. "I thought not. Now keep quiet so I can keep you safe."

A tear crawling down my cheek, I silently padded backward, deeper into the shadows.

Duty.

I had *done* my duty, and more besides. Now I had a new duty, though. Troy the *city* had fallen. Troy the *world* was in my arms. I reached the megaron and broke into a run, hoping they had not yet found the slave passage.

3—FATE

WE are almost across the strait now, drifting with slow current and sagging sails. The dancing fires in the dark waters are more scattered and fainter. The tense silence has relented a little. Men breathe heavily, sigh, cough. The boys are crying, as much with relief as with sadness. I will not cry, for if I weep over my lost world, I will become a dry husk of a man, such is my grief. But I know now that, despite struggling to do my duty to my king and my city, I was always meant to do this, and I carry Troy with me now. Like a snake shedding its skin, we have left a brittle, hollow shell behind and carried the meat, bone, muscle, and heart of Troy in search of a new place to build a life.

Only those who can claim to truly fear the gods can hope to know the joy and horror of seeing them or of seeing those friends and heroes long gone. I can see them even now, for the dead occupy the empty oar seats between the living. Their spirits will not stay in that place of destruction, for they wish to be part of a new Troy and not part of the cenotaph of the old. I can see them: those I have loved and lost. And while those who live are unaware of the spirits traveling beside them, we all know that we are children of Fate and that the gods set us on this course.

I burst from the palace's ancillary building, my armor dulled with smoke and grime, Priam's brilliant white plumes the only clean part of me, my arms cradling the sacred likenesses of the ancestors, and my sword clattering at my side in its scabbard.

Miraculously, the enemy that had been so busy looting the palace, killing, and raping, had not yet found this plain, nondescript structure, and I emerged into an empty alley. The buildings of the citadel were, through a combination of defense and respect, largely constructed some distance from the walls, and to cross to one of the now undefended and overlooked eastern gates, I would have to rush across a wide space, which was dangerous with victorious Achaeans now running along the wall. I resolved to sneak back past the temple of Arynna, which was by happy accident the closest to the walls, and use that shortest jump to reach safety.

And then as I approached the temple, despite everything I had resolved, my heart lurched at the memory of my poor cousin Cassandra lying there, wounded, abused, ravaged, and desperate. I dithered for a moment. What if vile Ajax had shut her back in there? He had been dragging her on a leash when last I saw her, but the citadel was filled with thrashing, mad warriors butchering one another, after all, and how could he hope to lead her through that carnage untouched, especially if he meant to claim more prizes? In my heightened state of urgency, I resolved to be certain. What harm could one small detour do?

The Achaeans were flooding the main area of the citadel, out by the front of the palace and across at the other grand buildings. I crept along the side of the temple and, biting down on my fear, slipped around the exposed front and to the great temple. Past the serene stone lions, I ducked in the portico with its tall brightly painted columns, blinking to adjust my eyesight to the darkness within. It may have been night outside, but the burning of the city made it disturbingly bright in places, and lights danced in my eyes as I strained at the darkness. The antechamber, its walls painted with images of divine offerings and scenes of the kings of old, was empty. I had half expected a small force of Achaeans to be holding the place. All was silent within. It was eerie after the town outside.

I nodded to the line of carvings of the gods all along the far wall and slipped through the threshold into the main room of the temple. My heart was in my throat. This was dangerous. I had been tasked with saving the most sacred items of the city, and instead I was selfishly trying to find someone I felt I had failed. Would Cassandra be here? Would Ajax?

My eyesight resolved in the even dimmer inner sanctuary, where the goddess the Achaeans had claimed as theirs once rose in great painted glory, twice the height of a man and an almost perfect copy of the Palladion that had been kept in this selfsame temple until wily Odysseus had taken it. The great statue lay defiled upon the temple floor, a sight that saddened me to my very soul. But there was no shape of a ravaged woman lying on the floor and, in a mixture of sadness and relief, I made to turn away when there was a tiny shuffling sound at the back of the room. I stopped and snapped back to the fallen statue. A shadow moved behind it, barely visible in the gloom. Then a face appeared. It took me a moment, in that shadowed place, but I knew that face well. Everyone in Troy knew it. Gods, everyone in the *world* knew that face after this war.

Helen. Bringer of doom. Cause of the downfall of worlds. Helen of Sparta, and then of Troy. Helen of where next, I wondered? My rage got the better of me. I suddenly formed a new plan. I would kill that worm of a woman who had brought so much destruction and death upon us all. I prepared to drop the sacred likenesses and draw my sword, but then another noise drew my attention, this time behind me. Someone else was coming.

Lost in indecision, I was close to being undone, and at the very last moment stepped back into the shadowed corner as a new figure emerged into the room. I wondered for a moment why Helen did not shout his attention and give me up, but the reason came to me clear: she was hiding from *everyone.* After all that had happened, she was as afraid of the Achaeans as she was of me, and with good reason, the treacherous witch.

The big man stepped forward past me, his form illuminated by the light from the doorway. He was a huge figure—an Achaean hero of note, clearly, though the lion pelt that hung from his shoulders was somewhat scratty and had definitely seen better days.

"Ajax?" the man said in a booming voice that echoed irreverently around that sacred place. "Ajax, are you here?"

He was searching for my cousin's ravisher. And he would find instead Helen. And me.

Before I knew what I was doing, I had taken two steps forward and brought one of the ancient sacred idols in my hand down on the back of the big man's head. It was a powerful blow, and the hero crumpled into a heap on the floor, his dirty, threadbare lion pelt coming loose from his neck. I had only moments, I was sure, before more Achaeans came looking. Just enough time for a righteous kill.

I consider myself a pious man, but a fiery rage overcame me so strongly that I pushed aside my reverence for a moment. My people had suffered so much war, and the need to avenge them rose in me, suffusing my blood, and I reached for my sword, dropping the most sacred symbols of the city carelessly to the floor as though they were nothing.

But there had been no sound as the idols fell. How could that be?

Snapped from my rage by fuddlement, I looked down. The ancestors' likenesses had fallen to the lion pelt, which had very likely saved them from damage or destruction. I felt cold as ice suddenly, and my hand slid the sword home in its sheath once more. I had almost thrown away the future of our world for simple revenge. I crouched and was momentarily struck by just how much one of those figurines resembled my own divine mother. She had an imploring face, her mouth formed into an *O*, and I knew that, like Hector and Cassandra and Chryses and Hecuba, even my mother was urging me to flee.

Swiftly, I gathered the figurines in the pelt, folding it and using it as a makeshift bag. I slung the sacred burden across my shoulder and prepared to leave once more. I had come looking for Cassandra and had found instead both rage and resolve. Perhaps it was the will of the Fates that I came here, so that I could draw a shroud over the corpse of the old Troy. As warriors, we try to do our duty, but as humans—even god-born ones—we are always subject to the whim of the Fates.

"May your husband find you and take you home, Helen of Sparta," I said quietly. Her pale face emerged from behind the statue once more, questioning, her beauty now gone, unsure as to my intentions. I simply sighed deeply. "You have ruined my world. Now let your husband take you home to ruin his. May you bring flames and destruction to Sparta in its turn."

The cause of all our ills opened her mouth to speak, her face already creasing in her most calculated expression of manipulation. I turned my back on her, closing my ears to whatever poison she now spat.

As I spun away from that face, I felt a great weight lifted from my shoulders, as though I had been absolved somehow of any part I had played in this tragedy. Hefting the sacred likenesses in their lion-skin bag, I stepped over the prone figure of the Achaean hero, pausing only briefly to kick him viciously in the testicles, and slipped from the temple. Outside, everything was manic in the square, the enemy rushing this way and that excitedly, looting and burning. I spotted Odysseus in the crowd, dragging a chastened Hecuba. He looked my way for a moment, though I was not sure whether it was me or the temple that he saw. Whatever the case, his attention was distracted briefly, and while he looked away, I slipped from the entrance, past the stone lions and into the shadows of the alley, where I passed along the stone wall, hurried across the open space, lifted the heavy bar at the northeastern gate, and slipped from the citadel into the lower city.

Here I was at the far side of Troy from the sea and its Achaean invasion, and there was as yet no fire, only quiet, dark houses, where very likely women and children lurked, terrified, waiting for the return of their menfolk who had died on the citadel or in the streets. There was nothing I could do for them, though it rent my heart to know it. Cassandra had warned me. Fate had decreed that I would save no one by design. Anyone I sought to preserve from these houses I would doom by that simple wish. Instead, I ran back home.

Rounding a corner, I almost bowled over a boy who stood in the street with a look of sad acceptance. I stopped suddenly, looking down at the lad in my way.

"Mother has died," he said. I was lost for words. What *could* I say to such a thing?

"First Father went off to serve Hector in the underworld, and now Mother has left me alone. Take me with you."

"I cannot," I replied, biting down on those bitter words. How could I? If I took him, I would by that very act damn him. He could not be saved by me. With a regretful glance, I ran on, heading for home and my family. I had gone only two streets farther before I realized that the boy was following me.

"Go away, boy. Go hide until it is safe. I cannot save you."

"Then I shall save myself," the boy said defiantly and kept coming. I blinked as I turned and pounded on down the street. Could that be an answer? Could this boy save himself by following me? I shortened my stride slightly to give him a chance, and he was still with me when I bounded up the steps to my house, two at a time. My father was within, dressed in a cloak and with a spear at the ready, defending the house. My son was with him, and Creusa. All the other warriors had gone with me, leaving only old Chryses and his daughter and attendants alongside my family. The boy ran in behind me and staggered to a halt, breathing heavily and looking nervous.

"Who is this?" my father asked quietly.

"I do not know. He followed me home."

"I am Katu, master," the boy replied and respectfully shuffled into place beside the two lads bearing the laurels and the lyre. Frowning, I unslung the lion-pelt bag and undid it, revealing the sacred figurines. Chryses stared with disbelief. "Where did you *get* them?"

"They were delivered into my hands by the queen herself. They must be saved. Would that we had the Palladion that the Achaeans stole. But still, with these and your own relics, we carry the very heart and soul of Troy." I passed the figurines to Chryses, retaining only the one that had for a brief moment been my mother. This I handed to the boy Katu. "Preserve her," I said as I tied the lion pelt around my middle like a scraggy, dangling belt.

"What do we do now?" the old priest said, still peering wide-eyed at the sacred likenesses in his hands.

"Now? Now you leave," I said quietly. "I cannot save you, but Katu has shown me the way. If I do not lead, you can save yourselves, and if the gods are kind, I can save myself alongside you. The Achaeans are atop the walls now and likely out in the surrounding area, but *only* the surrounding area. Priam's remaining ships are at Dardania in the bay below my father's palace—I know, for I supervised their removal myself. They were sunk beneath the waves to keep them from the Achaeans, but they will still be good and seaworthy if they can be raised. Dardania is blessedly free of the ship-rot worm."

This revelation brought a new fire of hope into the eyes of the assembled. I had not the heart to tell them we were too few to raise the ships ourselves without help, but I felt certain the gods would show the way.

"The Achaeans will be looking for groups fleeing the city, and some have bows. You will all be safer alone. There are three gates as yet untouched by the enemy. Split up, take different gates out of the city, and once outside, different paths. You all know the old temple of Telipinu near the sea to the north. It is abandoned, long since fallen into ruin, and the Achaeans are unlikely to be watching it. Meet there, and you should be beyond the Achaean raiders. From there, we can run to the ships openly."

I frowned as I realized that my father, Anchises, was busy collecting his bronze corselet.

"You will move faster unarmored, Father."

"I am not going, Aeneas," he said quietly. "I am too old and slow. I will not make it."

He began to armor himself with difficulty, and I gripped my hands into white fists, losing my temper. I grasped his bronze plates and ripped them from his hands, throwing them down to the stone flags once more. "I have already lost too much this day, old man. You may have only a thousand paces of running left in your life, but you will use them now to reach the old temple."

I turned and gestured out of the open doorway and was surprised as a streak of silver shot across the black canopy of the night high above the burning city, falling to earth far to the north. "See how even the gods tell you where to go? There, where their sign fell, Priam's three ships wait beneath the threshold of your very own palace, Father. Ships enough to take all of us and more."

"Carry him," my wife urged. "You arc strong. He is tired."

"I cannot, Creusa. I can save no one—Cassandra told me as much. It is my fate that those I try to save I cannot. But anyone, it seems, can save themselves."

Mere moments later, I grabbed my old cloak, and we left the house, descending the stairs into the burning city: nine figures, including two old men, two women, and four boys. Just one warrior among us, whose hands had been tied by the Fates. We moved through the dark streets at the eastern edge of the lower city, where the Achaeans had not yet brought their bronze and their flames, for they had concentrated primarily on the rich and the sacred. They were atop the walls, ready to sack the narrow alleys below. As we moved, we separated. My father, my son, and young Katu went one way, Chryses and his daughter and attendants another, Creusa and I a third. Each group made for one of the lesser gates in the eastern walls. My world became that of my wife and I, and I barely looked at the city we were leaving as we passed through it, though more than once I caught Creusa glancing up at the citadel and the blazing buildings therein. Finally, we reached the Gate of the Leaping Horses. The gate was utterly deserted. We waited long moments for three Achaean warriors who passed along the walls above to disappear, and bent to our task. It took little work to slide back the heavy timber bar that secured it, so well designed were the gates of the city. Before we passed through, I wrenched the clean, very visible white plumes from Priam's helmet and dropped them to the dusty ground.

Outside, Creusa turned to me and grasped my arms. I pulled her into an embrace. "All will be well," I told her. "Father will look after our son."

She smiled sadly. "I know, Husband." She turned and craned her neck, looking up at the citadel beyond the walls, wreathed in flame. I followed her gaze and noted the silhouettes of figures here and there on the battlements.

"Would that we had a year, a month, even an hour to spare. I would never let you go." I kissed her and smiled sadly. "But you *have* to go. Now. Take this."

I passed her my dusty brown cloak. It would conceal her as well as anything. She kissed me once, threw the cloak over her head and shoulders, scurried down the slope, across the great chariot-worn road, and disappeared among the gnarled trunks of ancient olive trees. I watched her go, my heart in my mouth as I waited for the guards on the wall to shout, but there came no such warning. I paused long enough to give her a head start and then slunk across the track myself and into the shade of a tree. I had no cloak, but I realized I had the Achaean's lion skin. Lions were rare this close to the city, but their very nature made them more camouflaged than a man in his fine clothes. By the time I emerged from the tree and began to scurry through the dusty landscape, my way lit by the blazing city behind me, I was crouched and enveloped by the skin of a lion. If I was spotted from the walls, I suspected the Achaeans had enough to deal with without bothering to try and bring down an old, lean lion.

It was a strange, brown, flickering, and silent world through which I ran. The roar of flames and the shouts and screams of those still in the city were oddly muted from beyond the walls and merged into some background noise of muffled nightmare. Instead, I concentrated on my path. The abandoned temple of Telipinu, whom the Achaeans claim as Demeter, rose dark and solemn from a coastal promontory six or seven *stades* from the city walls. I fixed on it but made sure to curve my route to the left. We stood the best chance of success if we spread out well.

I reached the flat ground between the rise upon which Troy stands and that of the temple and began to pass through the remains of farms that had been abandoned for nearly a decade due to the proximity of the warlike Achaeans. I rounded the corner of an old building, now tumbled and overgrown, and found myself in an old, open yard only forty paces from a patrol of Achaean warriors. This was what I had feared: not all the enemy was in the city, burning and looting. Some were in the surrounding countryside, presumably looking for those people of Troy who had grabbed their most treasured possessions and run for open ground. They had been successful, too, apparently. Half a dozen Achaean warriors had rounded up a small column of slaves, all roped together, and the last of the patrol carried a bag of impounded loot over his shoulder.

I stopped dead and stared, and the Achaeans turned and spotted me for the briefest of moments. I scurried away, still bent double, even as two of them raised spears to throw.

"Did you see that?" one said to his friend. "A brave beast, that one."

"Looked hungry to me," said another, "and a bit sick. Probably just about starving enough to attack us. We should kill it."

"Let it go," said his friend with a chuckle. "You'll have your fill of death this day."

I crouched in the darkness below a sprawling fig tree and waited, my breath held, as the Achaean patrol passed, laughing and jesting, their string of slaves dejected and faceless, their visages downcast in sadness. I wished I could save them, but even if I was not constrained by fate, I could not hope to best six men myself, armored only with a mangy lion pelt and a plumeless helmet.

Once they were safely gone, I rose again and ran on. I prayed as I pounded through the dust, muttering under my breath invocations to the gods, and it took me by surprise when I looked up to check my distance and realized I had arrived. The dark temple stood silent testimony to the piety of my dying people, its stones painted bright but now peeling and faded, untended for years. I rounded the building's corner and approached the entrance, and my eyes widened. Here were my father and my son. Here were Chryses with the three boys all clutching their sacred burdens—his daughter, too, the lovely young Chryseis, clutching her pregnant belly and refusing to wilt.

But here also were Trojan warriors, each exhausted and wounded, blackened by smoke and crusted with blood. I recognized a few. Acmon, son of Clytius, Misenus of the loud trumpets, Iapyx, favored of the sun. Once-great names who had stood defiantly on the walls of Troy and watched the Achaeans crash like pointless waves against them. Men who had helped burn the enemy's ships, now tired and spent, seeking only freedom and a future. Misenus and his fellow warriors shared a look, and I realized then that they had been privy to the ships' location, for Misenus had been Hector's own herald, and I myself had told my mighty cousin of the three vessels beneath the Dardanian waves.

But my searching eyes found no sign of Creusa. I dashed up to them, pushing warriors aside, looking amid the columns.

"Creusa?"

Urgent panic gripped me. "Creusa, where are you?"

Now Anchises and my son joined me. "She was with you," old Anchises said.

"We split up, like everyone else. She has not arrived?"

"Not yet."

And the realization sent waves of sickness through my heart. I had given her my cloak. I had tried to save her. And in doing so, I had doomed her.

"No!"

I was on my knees a moment later, my father and Misenus crouching, helping me up.

"No. She was with me. The slavers must have taken her. She might not be dead. They will be taking her back to the city."

I made to pull away, but Anchises held tight.

"She is gone, Son."

"She might be *alive*," I said again, wrenching myself from their grasp. "I have to *find* her."

"If you find her, then you doom her all over again," my father reminded me, a voice of reason that I really did not want to hear at that moment. How could I hope to build a new world for my people and a life for my son and yet leave half my heart amid the burning ruins?

"Run for Dardania," I told them. "Father's palace is less than seventy *stades* distant, and once you are five from the walls, you should be free of marauding Achaeans. Even with a slow, careful start, you can be at the ships long before dawn shows you to your enemies. There are enough of you now to drag at least one ship out of the water and empty her, and Anchises knows his ships. And while you are doing that and preparing to leave, I will find Creusa." I could feel their disapproval—their sense of the futility of my plan, and I smiled sadly. "I will be back. I *will* return."

I paused as my son walked solemnly toward me, holding out his hands. In them were the sea-colored plumes I had cast aside at the beginning of this dreadful night.

"We will watch for your colors, born of the sea, Father. We will not leave without them."

And once more I felt pride, though this was not the hubris that had brought our world low, but the righteous pride of a father in his son. I embraced my son, grasped my father by the upper arms, then turned and left without another word.

I could not save Creusa, and I knew it. But I still had to try.

4—LOSS AND DISCOVERY

THE first hints of dawn are now lighting the deep blue above the darkened hills of the peninsula, somehow lessening the flames that still burn as they have all night. Now, as the light begins to grow, the fires of destruction seem to be diminished, but the tall columns of black smoke that, like tomb markers, indicate the passing of a world are beginning to show. We have emerged from the strait now, and the craggy isle of Imbros looms great and black to the northwest. We are not sure for where we are bound, but the matter of initial importance was to escape from Troy, and the proximity of Imbros confirms that we have achieved that goal. Soon the flames of the city will be lost to us altogether, and even the smoke will have faded into the horizon. Once that happens, the city is truly gone for us. Not Troy, though. Troy was more than a city. Just its shell is lost.

It matters not, for we have made our peace and done our part. It is time to finally let go of the past and look to the future, and, oddly, it took an Achaean to make me truly realize that.

I ran through the dusty brown countryside once more, filled with hopeless urgency. I was, I will admit, not entirely in my right mind. I had lived through—endured—the end of my world, the burning of my city, the death of so many friends, including the king and numerous cousins. Yet to have Creusa so cruelly ripped from me was enough to send me grief-mad. I recognize now that I *was* maddened. I was snarling and shouting imprecations against the Achaeans even as I ran through the wilderness despite the danger in which such behavior could place me.

All the way back through the ruined farms, I growled and snarled and shouted, occasionally bursting into fits of calling my wife's name in the hope she might just be lost among the scrub. Between the gnarled olive trunks I hurtled and up the slope to the gate from which we had emerged, still standing ajar as we'd left it. I had no plan. A man in grief-madness cannot plan. Everything that happens is triggered by unhappy accident or momentary fits of mental illumination. It takes something unexpected to snap him out of it.

I ran through the city without knowing where I was going until I rounded the corner and saw my house atop the next rise. Three Achaeans were on the balcony, and smoke was already rising from the roof. I pictured Creusa inside choking and panicking and ripped my sword from my scabbard as I ran. The three men had looted my house, finding, I suspected, little of interest.

I lived a generally ascetic life, after all. Having scoured the rooms of my home, they had brought their flaming brands to it. I cared not. A house is just a shell, and I had already lost the one at Dardania when the Achaeans arrived and we went to Troy. But the very possibility that Creusa could be in there . . .

I bounded up the steps three at a time, sword in hand. My blade was of good Hittite bronze but western design: strong, long, heavy, with a wicked point and two very sharp edges. It was the perfect killing device for almost any circumstance, and I used it well. The Achaeans heard nothing, as they were joking and laughing with one another, and that, added to the spit and crackle of timber-fed flames, drowned out my pounding sandaled feet. My sword took the first invader in the throat, smashing through his teeth, sinking into his brain and grating against the inside of his skull for a jarring moment until I ripped it back out, spun like a dancer, and bit two hand-widths deep into the next man's chest, cleaving lung and heart and shattering ribs. Both men had fallen, spilling out gore, before the third even knew I was on him. He tried to defend himself, but he was too late. I rammed the tip into his gut, wrenching it back out with a twist and leaving him to groan as I ran inside.

The house had begun to burn properly now. I searched every room, leaping aside as blazing beams fell and clouds of sparks engulfed me like dancing fireflies. I shielded my sore eyes from the terrible heat as I searched each chamber, coughing in the roiling black smoke. Creusa was not there. Why had I expected her to be? I was wasting time here. Bursting back out onto the balcony, I spotted the man I had gut-wounded sitting on the floor, clutching his bellyropes in horror. His friends were both past the last river now, cold and still. The madness was still on me, though, and I placed the tip of my sword on the thigh of the seated warrior, just above the knee.

"What did you do with all the slaves?" I snarled at him. "The ones captured as they fled the city!"

He seemed barely aware I was there, such was the horrible fascination he had for his spilled innards. I pressed down on the sword, and it cut through his leg muscles, scarring the bone until it touched the stones below. He screamed. I had his attention now, so I pulled the sword back out and placed the tip very gently in the same place on his other leg.

"Where are the slaves?"

He looked up at me, and I suddenly realized how young he was. He could barely be called a warrior, really—not much older than my own son. Normally, I would abhor such torture. In any ordinary world, I would have beaten a man for doing what I had just done, but I will claim only that grief-madness was driving me. The youth whimpered. "The citadel." He pointed up the hill, and more of his gut-ropes escaped with the movement. He shrieked and grasped them again. I nodded.

I ran on. I did not administer a mercy kill as I should have. Grief-madness, again. Clearly, it *was* madness, for the city crawled with victorious Achaean warriors, and I walked through it as though I were a Titan, not bothering to hide my nationality. Perhaps it was the stolen lion pelt about my shoulders that saw me through. It certainly cannot have been my clearly Trojan arms and attire, or the smoke-darkened, sea-hued plumes rising from my helm. Many of the Achaeans were now leaving the high places. Some were spreading out into the lower city in the same way as the three I had killed, looting and burning whatever was yet untouched. Others were heading back out to their abandoned camp near the shore, carrying their slaves or their loot, or both. None of them gave me more than a passing glance as I moved through the city against the general flow of humanity.

I stalked through their midst, and they often stepped out of my way rather than challenge me. *No one* challenged me. My sword was in my hand and still dripping blood as I stomped on up the steep street to the ruined inner gate for the second time that night. Gradually, as I ascended, the flow of people thinned out. I emerged into the open area of the citadel hardly troubled by other passersby, and took in the scene with a mix of desperate hope and saddened disgust. Heaps of looted goods lay piled around the square, enemy warriors sorting through them, just as our own had been sorting through the spoils from their ravaged camp less than a day ago. And here and there were lines of dejected captives, stripped of all but their essential clothes, their smoke-stained faces cast down hopelessly to the ground. Around them, groups of Achaean warriors moved, gathering, organizing, roping.

I noticed two commanders deep in conversation near the center, seemingly in charge of this process, and I knew them both. Philoctetes of Meliboea, the gray-bearded archer who had cut down that foul coward Paris, and ever-present Odysseus. As I say, the madness was upon me, and I stormed into the heart of that gathering as though I owned the square. I am not sure whether the two Achaean heroes saw me at first as I pushed their warriors out of the way angrily and ran in among the lines of slaves, yelling my wife's name over and over, grasping at shoulders and lifting heads to look into faces, fighting despair and hoping that one of these poor wretches would be her. Again and again I spun amid this tableau of human misery, peering into hollow eyes and pulling aside emaciated and ravaged bodies. And suddenly she was there!

I was staring into Creusa's face. I leaped toward her, but my arms were held. I turned back and struggled, but two Achaean warriors now held me tight, and as I watched Creusa among those sad lines, I realized that what I was seeing was impossible. My wife was so pale as to outshine the moon. So *unbelievably* pale. And the line across her throat was wide and dark and clotted where already all her lifeblood had flowed out, much of it crusted on her neck and chest. She was dead. I was looking into my Creusa's eyes, but she was dead. And she shook her head with an air of finality, as though trying to confirm her demise for me. I heard someone shout my name, and my head snapped round reflexively. I could not see who had called, and when I looked forward once more, Creusa was gone. In her place was a pale woman about her age with a slave-rope around her neck.

"Aeneas, son of Anchises," called that voice again.

I was stunned. Creusa had been there, and dead, but not there at all, and this had been no dream. Slowly, still trying to make sense of it all, I turned my head, and a new feeling began deep in my heart. Rage.

Neoptolemus, son of Achilles, stood in the open space, a long spear in his hands and a cruel grin on his face. The rage burned up like the inferno in my house, searing my chest, scoring my throat, and filling my mind and mouth with burning, blazing fury.

I went for the vicious prick.

All the anger I experienced at what had happened since night fell on my city and brought with it doom, at the treatment of my people by these arrogant invaders, at the Fates for allowing such things, at myself for not being able to do more, at the loss of Creusa . . . it all combined into a shining diamond of hate directed at this boy who embodied all I found most vile in the Achaeans.

My sudden rage was so thorough and unexpected that the two men gripping my arms were taken by surprise, and I ripped free of their grasp. I still had my sword in hand, and before they knew what was happening, I was swinging and lunging, swiping and stabbing at the rancorous son of Achilles. I will give him his due: not only was he not afraid, but he was also quick and skillful.

Given my sudden onslaught, many a warrior would have been dead in a heartbeat, but Neoptolemus raised his spear to block me, which snapped it in two but robbed my first true killing blow of much of its force.

He danced out of the way, using the two halves of his spear as sword and staff, jabbing with the bronze leaf-point as he swung and swiped with the shaft in his other hand, striking low, trying to take my legs out from under me. In actual fact, he hit me there more than once, and had I been in a normal state, I might well have gone down. But I was in grief-*rage* now rather than grief-madness. The Achaeans call it the Rage of Ares—their war god. We Trojans know that it is all the province of man, for the gods do not *have* to gift us madness. We make it for ourselves.

I barely felt the bruising of my legs that almost broke bones. Instead, I tried my hardest to kill the cruel animal. My second true killing blow also failed, for suddenly those two Achaean warriors were on me again, trying to restrain me. Even as I fought them off, Neoptolemus snarled at them to stay out of it, and from the corner of my eye, I saw Odysseus motion for them to step back.

We circled like stags in the rutting season, each watching the other's eyes for a sign of movement. Slowly, as we did so, the son of Achilles threw away one piece of spear, drew his sword, and then cast the other stick aside. Still we circled, and with each cycle, the gods slowly drained my rage and replaced it with determination.

Neoptolemus was good. His eyes betrayed nothing, and I was lucky to see the muscles in his leg ripple as he put his weight into the left. I spun even as he lunged, dropping to the side out of danger. I tried to strike out at him as we passed, but gods, he was quick. We circled again, this time even more warily. Again I watched, and again there was no tell of his plan. He leaped, swinging his sword, and I brought mine up only in the last moment, barely deflecting the blow. My reply almost took his leg off, but that quick, short blade of his dropped ridiculously fast and turned aside my own blow. We danced again.

"I've not seen anyone hold Neoptolemus off so well before," Philoctetes said casually nearby to the captain of the Myrmidons. The man nodded, and Odysseus gave a noncommittal grunt.

The son of Achilles was watching me carefully. I did not think he would be the first to strike next time. I had come close to wounding him badly with that last blow. Now he watched, waiting for me to move. I wondered how arrogant he was. He had surely no more than fifteen years, big and fast as he was, and boys are always cocksure. Breathing steadily, I flicked my glance to his left for just the blink of an eye and then swept to his right. As I predicted, he could not believe I would be sharper than he, and while I leaped, he swung his sword in a block at entirely the wrong side. As he flailed, I slashed at his side and felt the blade tear through his corselet's leather and the bronze scales attached to it. I did not draw blood, but I know that sort of wound, and I had left the sort of bruise that covers half the torso and takes weeks to heal. I likely broke a rib or two as well.

He twisted away, hissing in pain and clutching his side with his free hand, and I almost missed his riposte, which could easily have ended me. I dropped at the last moment, barely seeing the lunge coming, and the blade raked across the top of my shoulder, drawing blood down to white bone and narrowly missing the cord that connects a man's neck.

The gods were protecting me. But then, they were protecting him, too. I was the son of Ishara, but he was the grandson of Thetis, and we could neither of us consider ourselves untouchable. We watched one another like wary wolves around a carcass in a hungry winter. To his credit, and most unexpectedly as far as I was concerned, he did not boast. Perhaps he did not need to. His heritage did his boasting for him.

He came suddenly once more, and I met his blows with my sword again and again, the repeated ring of bronze on bronze like the tolling of a sanctuary offering bell rung by an overeager priest. We hammered at one another now, finesse forgotten, swords smashing and swiping, stabbing and slashing, each time caught by the other. The dance of bronze became frantic, and we twisted and turned, ducked and leaped, each determined to kill with every stroke.

At the climax of this play of skill, we both struck. I was the lucky one. My sword bit into his leg. Most of the force was taken by his bronze greave, but I cut a deep gash in the calf that would leave a lifelong weakness there. *His* blow struck me on my white-plumed helm. Had it been a finger-width lower, I would have been searching for my head. As it was, it struck the short neck guard and the cheek piece, the latter crumpling painfully into my cheek.

I went temporarily deaf with the noise of the bronze helmet taking the strike, but the reverberation caught Neoptolemus, too, by surprise, and even as he stumbled and fell backward from my leg strike, he lost his grip on his sword, which clattered away across the ground, raising a shower of dust. My head ringing with an echoing bronze chime, my brains addled and shaken, still I managed to step forward, raising my sword, ready to end the son of Achilles once and for all.

I could have delivered the killing stroke, even with my brains spinning in their case. But as I stumbled forward, someone tore my helmet from my head and rapped me smartly on the skull, sending me into dark oblivion.

I was not out for long. I knew it because my head was still spinning a little as I woke.

The room was dark, lit only by the orange glow of the ever-present flames through the windows and open doorway. I was seated against a wall, a blanket behind my head and another across my lap. I was still dressed, and, oddly, my dented helmet and sword were close by, the latter cleaned and sheathed by some unknown hand.

"I must apologize, Aeneas, son of Anchises," said a sympathetic and soothing voice. "I know that Achilles' son is an insufferable arse, but he is also the child of our greatest hero, and something of a symbol of victory to the entire army."

My eyes gradually accustomed themselves, and the crouched form of Odysseus swam into focus. Strangely, I remembered how he had crouched to string his bow at the archery contest in Sparta during his wedding, when the two of us had become friends and I had been cheering his victory against vain, strutting Paris. That had been ten years ago, and we had both been younger men—men without lines of grief on our faces and threads of gray in our hair—but somehow that sunlit image seemed closer to me than anything else in the long bloody decade between that moment and this one.

"I couldn't let you kill him there, though I will admit to having wished I'd done just that once or twice over these past days. But it is done now, Aeneas. Killing Neoptolemus would resolve nothing. If anything, it could lead to further atrocities, and now is the time to *end* the killing, not *renew* it."

The Ithacan king, possibly the only man in the entire Achaean army whom I held in esteem, smiled sadly. "I wanted to end it all without such bloodshed. I hope you know that. I may have been instrumental in this horror, but that was never my wish. I wanted to come to a word-wise solution for Menelaus' wife. And even after all those years of war, we might just have done so. When Paris died, she could have been returned. I suspect she never *wanted* to, but it would not be her say. And yet King Priam went and married her off to another of his sons. When he did that, he doomed Troy, and there was nothing else I could do but bend my efforts instead to being the victor."

"I saw Helen," I said, my voice hollow. "On the citadel, hiding from friend and foe alike—the most despised woman in the world. I almost put a sword through her then. Maybe I should have, but it is perhaps more fitting that I leave her for her husband to gut. She has been found, I presume?"

Odysseus snorted, though there was no humor in the sound, and his eyes were flinty cold. "You could say that. One glimpse of her naked and the old goat took her back before she tripped over his tongue."

"She lives?" I said, sitting up straight, astonished.

"As a queen once more. I swear that woman will outlive the gods to the end of the world. Ten years of war started by one woman's shapely form and she leaves your world a smoking ruin as queen of Sparta once more, by that same token. Foul woman."

I wanted to nod, though I worried I might be sick if I did, with the faint ringing still going on in my ears.

"Besides," the sly Ithacan added with an unexpected smirk, "I know you to be a man who appreciates the jokes the gods play on the cruel. Neoptolemus is promised to the daughter of Menelaus on their return to Sparta. The young animal is facing long years with Helen as a mother-in-law."

Despite everything, I could not help but let a smile cross the bars of my teeth at that.

A scream ripped through the night somewhere close by, carrying across the general hum of Achaean victory and the gentle rumble of a dying city. "I would curse Menelaus and his brother for what they have done to my world, though it is in truth more the fault of my own cousin's hubris than either of those monsters.

Regardless, the *gods* will curse the house of Atreus for their many impieties, for the murder of children and the desecration of sacred places. It is not my place to curse, it is theirs."

"Go home, Aeneas—I will not stop you. We are near the east gate. Run back to your pretty little coastal Dardania and live out your life there. Your home can be rebuilt, and now that Troy is fallen, the Achaean kings will care nothing for small tributaries. I will soon return to my own quiet and rural Ithaca. Men like you and I, Aeneas, we are meant for higher things than killing. And these great cities do not suit us. We are country folk."

I smiled again. It was easy to smile at Odysseus. He was that kind of man. He had been my enemy for nearly ten years, and yet I would rather break bread and share wine with him than many of my countrymen.

"Dardania is as lost as Troy," I sighed, the smile sliding away once more. "The whole peninsula now will be a land of ghosts—haunted by the memory of what it was and of the vengeance of the Achaeans. My people are gone. My family is gone. Almost all the line of Ilus is crossing the final river or penned among the slaves of your allies for who knows what fate. Cassandra, my cousin, she . . . Ajax, the mighty Achaean hero, *dishonored* her."

The wily Ithacan's expression darkened for a moment. "But she lives, Aeneas. Cassandra was taken by Agamemnon."

I snarled my anguish at this news, and Odysseus sighed.

"She is *alive*, Aeneas, and she seems resigned to her fate. Others have had it worse. Hellenus and Andromache have been taken by Neoptolemus."

Cassandra was alive, yes, but my strange cousin had foretold her own end to me before the first flames licked at our world. *The Fates have decreed a lonely end for me,* she had said. *I have seen the path of my life laid out before me like a banquet table of rotting food.* No safe life awaited Cassandra in the court of our enemy, and I doubted that even brave Hellenus could protect Andromache from the vicious son of Achilles, though even in my despair, I knew that the Ithacan king was doing his best to spare me the worst. He was a good man.

"You are alone among the Achaeans, Odysseus. An island of sense in a sea of the sick."

Again he flashed me a sad little smile. "Soon I will be home with my wife and my son, and all this will be a bad dream. The world will move on. It does that."

"For some. For others, it remains an empty shell. My wife . . ."

"I know, Aeneas. I am sorry. It happens in war. The innocent are never spared the horror. Just remember that she is beyond pain now. You will always miss her, I know. I have not seen my Penelope for nearly ten years, and never does a day go by but I think of her embrace. You have a son, yes?"

I gave a gentle nod and blessedly did not throw up.

"Then flee for him. Flee *with* him. Go and be safe, Aeneas. Your wife is now the past. Your *son* is the future."

I found standing difficult, but the king of Ithaca helped me and supported me until my legs regained some of their strength. I looked down at Priam's ravaged helmet, sporting my old soot-stained, sea-hued plumes. They were no longer of importance. Sea-colored, white, black, who cared? It was only a color worn to reflect the pride or sorrow of a man. And now, as Odysseus had said, it was time to concentrate not on my own being, but on my son.

And Troy, I thought silently to myself as I picked up the sword and, staggering, emerged onto the dark street with the eternal stench of smoke. This was no longer Troy. It was a shell and nothing more, shed in a dreadful night to allow Troy to grow and change, to perhaps become greater—more noble and less prideful than our fallen home.

I thanked Odysseus and bade him good-bye, wishing him a speedy return to his wife and child. He did the same to me, though he stayed with me until we reached the city gate. There, about to depart, I suddenly realized he had that flea-bitten lion skin over his shoulder, and I frowned, gesturing at it. He laughed raucously. "My friend Diomedes has been kicking stones around angrily all night wondering where this went. I think I shall tell him just to irritate him. Good travels, Aeneas, prince of Troy."

"And to you, Odysseus, king of Ithaca."

It was the last I saw of him or his people, and the last time I passed through the walls of the city. My resolve had been built anew by a man who should have been my enemy. A man who spoke the most sense I have ever heard from god-born lips. I made my way past the ruined farms and olive groves to the old temple, then past that as the moon slid slowly across the sky, and on to my former home—to Dardania, where I did not spare a glance for the ruins of my old home, only for the ships waiting with my son. My father and our friends had raised a swift, small, dark vessel with only minor difficulties and made it ready to leave.

And so we put out to sea, pushing off from the shore into the strait, silently relying on the faint wind and the current to carry us away from the burning city. A huddled band of exiled warriors carrying a hope for a greater future, the small boy Katu hugging himself tight against the pregnant belly of Chryses' daughter, the sacred relics of Troy nestled in our grasp. We would build a new Troy somewhere safe, somewhere green. Somewhere with a high place for a powerful citadel, good land for crops, and far from the shores where prideful Achaeans can beach their ships.

A new Troy.

And so my song has come full cycle.

Rosy-fingered dawn is but a dream of a day yet to come.

But at least now we know there will *be* a day yet to come.

ACKNOWLEDGMENTS

WE would like to thank our friends, families, and beta readers, including Michael Alvear, Stephanie Dray, Annalori Ferrell, Maria Janecek, Kelly Quinn, and Jenny Turney. We'd like to thank our cover designer, Kim Killion; also, our copyeditor, Jennifer Quinlan.

For resources, we owe much to Homer, Virgil, and Euripides. Also, Peter Connolly's *The Ancient Greece of Odysseus*, Barry Strauss' *The Trojan War: A New History*, Silvia Montiglio's *From Villain to Hero: Odysseus in Ancient Thought,* Jeffrey Barnouw's *Odysseus, Hero of Practical Intelligence,* and to Gordon Doherty for various academic works to which he pointed us.

NOTES FROM THE AUTHORS

THE APPLE

THE trouble with writing any novel-in-parts is that whatever historical moment you decide to cover, there is inevitably one "big moment" in the historical narrative—the eruption of Vesuvius in *A Day of Fire* or the defeat of Boudica in *A Year of Ravens*—and only one author in the group gets to cover it. But the Trojan War was different from the start because it's a span of time covering many, many big moments. From the beginning, we were each fascinated with different high points and different personalities in the vast cast of characters that makes up the *Iliad.* More than any other historical epoch we've covered so far, the Trojan War is ideally suited to multiple writers.

The first tale of any novel-in-parts has the challenge of setting the scene and then wrapping up before any real conflict has had a chance to kick off. But from the start, I wanted to tell the story of Helen and Paris' fatal meeting—and the team all agreed that since we weren't showing the Greek gods scheming away on Olympus to kick off events, the most famous elopement of the ancient world needed rougher, more political motivations behind it than simple passion or magic apples. I quite liked Helen as she turned out: tough as well as beautiful, and any ruthless survivor like Helen would have to be because, once Homer's mythic gloss is stripped away, this epoch of Greek history is proved to be a bleak time to be a woman. As the wife of the *Iliad*'s greatest hero was to find out.

Andromache has always been my favorite figure of the Trojan War: the tragic, heroic wife of the tragic, heroic Hector; a woman who sees the entire conflict from start to finish, endures tremendous loss, but survives everything. I have always wished I could write her a happier ending than the one she endures, and here, in a way, I had my chance. Enter Hellenus, a character I adored writing—a humble, lovable Everyman in the middle of all these larger-than-life heroes.

Traditionally, Hellenus is a son of Priam and Hecuba, not the offspring of a concubine as I have changed his tale here. But when Stephanie Thornton decided to write Cassandra, and we realized our narrators were twins, we explored the reasons why Cassandra, as a priestess and a princess, would have been so thoroughly ignored by her family. She was somehow different, we decided, and so was Hellenus. Definitely unwanted. Perhaps other. By making them biracial outsiders to the royal family, we could provide some explanation for Cassandra's tragic exclusion, as well as show the rich cultural mix of the historical geography where Anatolian, Greek, Egyptian, African, Hittite, and many other cultures intermingled. Hollywood loves to whitewash the ancient world, but the reality would have seen many different kinds of faces. We wanted to reflect that.

Hellenus is another survivor of the Trojan War that killed so many of his royal brothers. Andromache, too, survived, though the fate of her infant son is not as certain: according to most myths, he was killed after the sack of Troy (the Greeks were nervous about letting a son of Hector grow up to seek revenge), but some later stories posit his survival thanks to a trick played by Andromache or Odysseus. Either way, Andromache lost her son and became the slave of Neoptolemus, but she was destined to end her long life as the wife of Hellenus. He took Andromache away, some say before and some say after the death of Neoptolemus (Achilles' son did not long survive his marriage to Helen's daughter). Andromache and Hellenus went on to raise more children together in Epirus, which was founded in Troy's name, and Aeneas later visited them in his travels. So Andromache does end her life a queen . . . and I like to think she found some happiness despite her many losses. It was my pleasure to seed the roots of that happiness at the very beginning of Troy's tale, when Helen and Paris have yet to set their fatal elopement in motion, when a young bride has yet to become a tragic heroine, and her silent admirer nurtures a love destined to be fulfilled fifteen years or so down the line.

Ancient Greece is completely new territory for me, so thank the gods for my co-authors. Stephanie Thornton went down the rabbit hole with me over many profane Facebook messages trying to parse through a plot tangle that became known as "that ****ing Trojan fleet problem"; Libbie Hawker and Vicky Alvear Shecter video-chatted with me for an hour trying to figure out why Hellenus got himself captured on Mount Ida; and Si Turney and Russ Whitfield could be counted on to pour the (virtual) whiskey and keep us all laughing across nine time zones with jokes about Agamemnon's midlife-crisis chariot, why the whole project should be subtitled "The Commando Sex Raid," and how The Commando Sex Raiders would be a great name for a rock band. There's no one else I'd rather sack a city with!

—Kate Quinn

THE PROPHECY

THE Trojan War is one of the most oft-told stories from human history, passed down through the ages first by bards, then written into books, and now even performed on screens and stages around the world. Yet most retellings tend to center around a handful of major players: Paris, Helen, Achilles, and Hector, to name a few. When I was asked to contribute to this project, it seemed natural that I do as I'd done in my novels *The Secret History* and *Daughter of the Gods*, to breathe new life into the story of one of history's forgotten women.

When I saw the character list for *Song of War*, there was one woman who grabbed me by the ear and demanded in no uncertain terms that her tale be told.

Cassandra.

There are two long-held views on Priam's doomed seer of a daughter: either she was mad or merely misunderstood. Why, I asked myself, couldn't she be both? There is no arguing that Cassandra's tale is a true tragedy, as she foresaw the destruction of Troy yet was powerless to stop her city's inexorable—and sometimes even gleeful—march toward war. It seemed entirely plausible to me that her knowing such a future and being unable to stop it could drive her to madness.

Knowing that Cassandra's tale gets only more bleak during and after the fall of Troy, I needed to give her some sort of bright spot, if not a lasting legacy. Most ancient sources are fairly quiet about Cassandra until centuries after the Trojan War, which allowed me a fair bit of leverage in regards to her personality and family relations. Thus it's no coincidence that Cassandra's closest connections were with her twin brother, Hellenus, and also the black sheep of Priam's family, Aeneas. Both men managed to escape Troy's smoking ruins and found new civilizations, Hellenus at Epirus and Aeneas in Rome. So even if Cassandra was doomed from the beginning (and likely knew it), I think she'd have found some solace knowing that at least two of her loved ones would survive and eventually prosper.

I was actually relieved to be able to leave Cassandra's ending off these pages as I'd become quite attached to the poor girl. After her rape by Ajax of Locris in the temple of Athena, Cassandra was claimed by Agamemnon and taken back to Mycenae. (As a side note, in a book with an already lengthy cast list, we combined the characters of Ajax of Salamis and Ajax of Locris for reader ease.) Aeschylus' play *Agamemnon* is our best source for Cassandra's life after the Trojan War, as both she and Agamemnon are murdered by his wife, Clytemnestra, and her lover. It was a tragic end for a tragic life.

I'd like to thank my fellow *Song of War* authors for inviting me to take part in this truly epic project. I was nervous at first about joining a group of such high-caliber writers, but I've enjoyed every moment of it, especially bemoaning the cursed ship problem and brainstorming possible band names. (For what it's worth, I'm still partial to Bats of Astyra.) Of course, no book is complete without me thanking my husband and daughter for keeping me sane while I juggled multiple writing projects at once. Thank you, Stephen and Isabella, and keep those slices of midnight chocolate cake coming!

—Stephanie Thornton

THE SACRIFICE

WHEN I was given the task (and I should add, honor) of writing the Agamemnon section for *A Song of War*, I was reminded of a quote from one of my favorite movies:

> ". . . And unto this, Conan, destined to wear the jeweled crown of Aquilonia upon a troubled brow."

Why? Well, because *Conan the Barbarian* is an epic movie, but more to the point, Agamemnon was my *protagonist* and not the villain—a role he plays in most stories written about the Trojan War. To make a character like that someone a reader could sympathize—or at least empathize—with was a challenge, and only you reading this can decide if I in any way succeeded.

For me, being forced (as Agamemnon sees it) to sacrifice his beloved daughter, Iphigenia, on the altar of the war was the moment that broke him—forever. How anyone could recover from such a deed—no matter what the justification—is simply unthinkable to me. In *A Song of War*, Agamemnon certainly never gets over it. It drives him to drink, causes him to sink into a bitter depression wherein he comes to hate everything about the war, down to and including the men that fight and die on the battlefield, and makes him turn away from the gods—after all, it was to appease Artemis that he struck the fatal blow at Aulis.

Imagine, then, that when he finds some semblance of happiness in the arms of the sexy (and utterly self-serving and manipulative) Chryseis, another Olympian pronouncement forces him to give her up. Couple this with the fact that the "oh so perfect" Achilles is constantly berating him about running the army—akin to a Special Forces operative telling a five-star general how to run a war—and Agamemnon is a bitter man.

On top of this, he's the high king—the one that carries the weight of the entire campaign on his shoulders—fail, and history will remember his name above all. To me, it is no wonder that such a person is driven to acts of petty vengeance and cruelty. It is no wonder that, at the end of it all, Agamemnon is nothing but a burned-out husk of a man.

So—if you didn't feel sorry for the guy, I hope that at least Agamemnon's Song gave you a look inside his head and a steer on what makes him tick.

As I wrote in my notes for our last project, *A Year of Ravens* (available from all good online retailers and some rubbish ones, too), if this kind of thing appeals to you: do it. If you want to, for example, write a Persian soldier's eye view of the Spartans' last stand at

Thermopylae, please put your fingers to the keyboard. The Internet age has given all of us an opportunity to get our stories—whatever they may be—out there. It might not make you rich, it might not make you famous, but it will, ultimately, entertain people (though not all of the people, it's fair to say!). If you don't fancy traditional publishing, self-publish your work—get it out there and put a smile on some faces. For me, one of the most rewarding things in writing is when someone takes time to drop me a line to say that they enjoyed something I wrote—there's no feeling quite like it. There's a saying that everyone has a novel in them—and it's a saying I believe wholeheartedly.

I'd like to take this opportunity to thank my colleagues on The H Team for being so awesome and supportive through this process, with a special shout-out for Kate Quinn, who took on the Herculean task of editing this book. More than that, she's our overseer, the one that thinks of *everything,* the one that can throw you a brilliant line when you're struggling with a turn of phrase, the one that encourages you when you're going through the "my story is awful" phase, the one that makes that awful story so much better with a word of advice and a nudge in the right direction. While it's true to say that all of us played our part in writing *A Song of War,* there would be no Songs without Kate. She's an absolute legend.

I need also to shout out to Maria Janecek for test-reading Agamemnon's story and giving me some great pointers. Cheers, Maria—you're a superstar.

And finally, thank you to my wife, Sally, and my daughter, Sam. Sally, for putting up with me for so long, and Sam, for not yet being at the age where she sees me as an embarrassing dad (that day fast approaches, I fear).

And thanks so much to you for reading *A Song of War.*

—Russ Whitfield

THE GAMBIT

WHEN Kate and Steph approached me to add a story to the ones already written, I was honored. Then they informed me my task was to cover most of the events in *The Iliad*.

Rewrite Homer. Sure, that'll go well.

Fear quickly turned to delight, because my research challenged all my misconceptions about *The Iliad*. It had been so long since I read it in full—not since high school, probably—that I mistook a lot of the zeitgeist around the story for the story itself. Like people thinking Rick says, "Play it again, Sam," or that Darth Vader ever uttered the line, "Luke, I am your father," my brain had rewritten some of *The Iliad* based on pop culture (Achilles "sulking" in his tents, and so on).

Revisiting Homer's text, I was astonished by several things. First, I was amazed to find a huge chunk of the story (Book 10 through Book 18) takes place in a single day. A day of close fighting that causes everything to change. It is indeed, as Hector intends, the pivot of the war, the day that starts the dominoes falling. To focus on that, I invented the conceit of Apollo's Day, because I wanted the war's longest day to be both literal and metaphorical.

Second, I was surprised to discover how very anti-war this war story is. Deaths are not pretty, nor are they glorified. Homer's warfare is filled with dire consequences, and rightly so. As someone who firmly believes in not glorifying violence even as I write about it, I was deeply impressed. Achilles, especially, does the unthinkable by questioning the cause for which they fight. Russ wove that beautifully into the Fourth Song, so I just continued to pull on that thread while I addressed the violence itself. After allowing all three leads to exult in their successes, I then reversed their fortunes and turned their exultation to remorse. Whatever the intentions, nothing honorable is achieved in this story. Violence rebounds upon the violent, undoing the dreams of men.

Thirdly, reading Homer's text, I discovered that everything I thought about the death of Patrocles was wrong. Oh, I remembered him dressing in the armor of Achilles, then being killed by Hector. But I had misremembered the disguise as working, causing Hector to believe he had killed Achilles. Reading the text, that is absolutely not the case. Hector knows precisely who he is killing. Moreover, the switching of armor is something that had been happening all through that day. Which brought me to question why the exchange of armor at all? What was the dramatic purpose of it, if not to fool Hector?

Well, just because Hector wasn't fooled, that didn't mean someone else could not fall into that error. Poor Menelaus. He does not deserve the indignity I heap upon him.

I so enjoy flouting audience expectations—why tell a well-known story if you don't bring some new understanding or angle to it? Yet my fear was that readers might feel cheated. After all, most people focus on two events in *The Iliad*—the death of Hector at the hands of Achilles, and Priam sneaking into Achilles' tent to beg for the return of Hector's body. The first is exciting and tragic, the second is tender and heartbreaking. But they are the consequences of this day, the denouement, not the climax.

I am always fascinated by these pivot points. Longtime readers will be unsurprised that I turn to Shakespeare for the best examples. In *Romeo & Juliet*, the climax is the deaths of Mercutio and Tybalt, with the demise of the titular lovers being the inevitable result. The same is true in *Julius Caesar*, with Caesar's death as the climax and Brutus' suicide as the denouement. These are the moments upon which a whole story turns. In *The Iliad*, the climax is the death of Patrocles. That's when order is overthrown, and events speed to a headlong fall, ending in death.

Yet I could not ignore those famous consequences. I shared my concerns with other writers, and it turned out the answer was right before me. Early on I had written Hector having a brief foreboding vision and thinking, "Cassandra, I'm so sorry. I didn't know." When Kate read that, she saw the possibility, and suggested I weave those visions through the rest of the story. Just as in *R&J*, where the characters have misgivings and direful visions before the tragic events, Hector's life is made more tragic by knowing how it will end. In that way, he is like Captain Pike in *Star Trek: Strange New Worlds*. Star-crossed, cursed, ill-fated—however it is phrased, heroes become more heroic if they know they are doomed.

The quote about Tragedy comes from an amazing play by Sean Graney entitled *All Our Tragic*. In this eleven-hour spectacle, a modern festival of Dionysus, Graney combined all thirty-two existing Greek Tragedies into a single narrative. The line about tragedy coming from loving something one should not has haunted me, and with his permission I invoked it here, retooling it for my purposes.

Tragedy is about separation, ending in a metaphorical death, while Comedy is about unity, ending in a metaphorical marriage. While our subject is certainly Tragic, I am honored to have my work married to these other amazing authors. Like the ancient Greek chorus, we are united in our song.

—David Blixt

THE BOW

ALTHOUGH I've written many books set in the ancient world (as I write this author's note, I'm at work on my ninth, tenth, and eleventh novels—a trilogy—with bronze-age settings) this is the first time I've written about ancient Greece or Troy. Ancient Greece is fascinating, of course, and full of the kind of rich, exciting history that makes for great fiction. But I've always been so drawn to Egypt and the Levant that I simply never got around to Greece.

I wasn't originally on the *Song of War* team. I was a late addition, brought into the project when another author had to bow out due to a scheduling conflict. (I think I've become the industry go-to when you need somebody to write ancient historical fiction really fast.) My lack of familiarity with the setting, and with the history behind the *Iliad* and the *Odyssey*, made me a little hesitant to accept. After all, I'd be working alongside authors who are well-known for their work set in classical antiquity. I would definitely be the odd man out. But I do love a challenge, and once I learned that I'd be writing the part of the story where both Paris *and* Achilles are killed, I was excited to begin. I love a good death scene.

The other authors' deep familiarity with the source material and with ancient Greece in general left me feeling a bit intimidated from the start. I had only a cursory knowledge of Homer's works—thank God for Cliffs Notes, or I never would have finished my portion of the story on time.

Eventually, though, I got out of my own way and got to work. I soon realized that I really enjoyed both of the point-of-view characters I'd picked to carry my story. Immersing myself in their struggles helped me skate past my own concerns and do the best work I could, even if I wasn't very familiar with the setting.

As a group, we kicked around several ideas about Achilles' final scenes—how they might play out, what we wanted to accomplish with his character. We determined that we could work with Penthesilea, the Amazon warrior-queen whom Achilles kills and then falls in love with immediately afterward, or we could exclude her altogether.

I chose to keep the Amazon in the story, as her death provided a useful way for the reader to witness Achilles' final unraveling—his rejection of the hyper-masculine, heroic image that was thrust upon him by the expectations of others and the embrace of his emotional (and now broken) self.

Philoctetes was a pure pleasure to write. He struck a chord with me, more than most of my characters do. His older age gave me the chance to explore the cynicism and matter-of-factness that comes from close involvement with a long, drawn-out war. My husband is a veteran of the Iraq War, and some of his feelings about military life and conflict helped me shape Philoctetes' response to the Trojan War. Additionally, Philoctetes' unrequited love for Achilles made him exactly the type of hopelessly tragic personality I always enjoy exploring.

There isn't anything in the source material to indicate that Philoctetes may have been homosexual. But our group decided to paint Paris as a real sleaze, the kind of guy whose face just seems to invite a thorough punching. So I wanted to give Paris' death a lot of weight. I wanted to make payback feel just and deeply satisfying when it came. That meant I needed to give Philoctetes a particularly compelling reason to strike Paris down—something more emotional than "You've got the magic bow of Heracles, so go shoot that Trojan, buddy."

Once I hit on the idea of giving Philoctetes a passionate love for Achilles, I could envision a suitably satisfying death scene for Paris. There was one tidbit of mythology I could use to support a one-sided love affair, too: Achilles sold a captive into slavery on the island of Lemnos, and Lemnos was where Philoctetes was stranded for many years, after suffering a snake bite that wouldn't fully heal. I simply tinkered with the timeline a little and had Achilles visit Lemnos near the beginning of the war instead of near its end.

I welcomed the opportunity to write a central, even heroic, figure who didn't fit the pattern of heroism we've all grown to accept. Gay men are seldom allowed to be heroes in fiction. They are rarely depicted in a serious light, rarely allowed to play important parts in story or in history. All too often they are cast in supporting roles, as the best friends of heterosexual heroines—or as comic relief, where stereotypical affectations are played for a laugh. I was happy to write a character who didn't pander to many contemporary readers' notions of what a gay man "should" be like. Philoctetes is a rough, no-nonsense fighter with long experience of war. He's not squeamish about life's unpleasantries. He is lauded for his considerable skill with the bow, and both his personality and his sexuality are respected by all the other characters save for Paris. No one whispered behind their hands, "But, you know, he likes other men." He was simply himself, a man with many more facets than his sexuality alone.

I don't often write from male points of view. There's a large market for women's historical fiction featuring female characters and focused on issues that typically resonate more with women than men. The majority of my fiction is intended for that market, so naturally the majority of my lead characters are women. But I very much enjoyed the chance to flex my writer's muscles a little and ride around inside the head of a character who is so different from me. After having such a great time with Philoctetes, I fully intend to write more male leads in the future.

All in all, working with these excellent authors on *A Song of War* has been a great experience—one I hope to repeat someday—allowing me to challenge myself as a writer and to learn from some of the best in the field of ancient historical fiction. Will I write more fiction set in ancient Greece? Maybe. We'll see if Egypt releases its hold on me long enough to try it.

—Libbie Hawker

THE HORSE

MY first choice was not to write as Odysseus. I mean, come on—who in their right mind would willingly take on such a bold, iconic, and beloved figure of mythic history? The hubris! But as we all negotiated and worked out our parts, somehow it ended with me on the shore, smiling uneasily at this charming trickster, and asking him for help to tell his version of things.

I've always loved the wily one. As a docent at the Carlos Museum of Antiquities, I stop at any artifact that "might" relate to Odysseus and hold forth about his antics, so maybe it was meant to be. To school children, I talk about Odysseus as a symbol of the Greek ethos moving from celebration of "brawn" (physical prowess as embodied by Achilles) to a respect for "brains" (Odysseus) and use of intelligence to get out of tight spots.

Imagine my surprise to learn that some ancient thinkers reviled Odysseus for exactly this. One even called him "the worst of those who fought at Troy," in opposition to Socrates, who called Odysseus a "wondrous man." (*From Villain to Hero*). Why would anyone think badly of Odysseus, I wondered, when he was the hero of the *Odyssey*?

But then I remembered human nature: changes in ethos are often painful for those living through them. The ancient conservative class, I imagined, probably worried a great deal about a dilution of manly honor and pride if one were to put Odysseus on the same platform as Achilles. Good old-fashioned warrior strength was the pinnacle of heroism, not someone who talked to himself, sometimes ran from armed conflict when necessary, and used trickery to save himself and his men.

My section involved the stealing of the Palladion. Imagine my surprise to reread in the *Iliad* that golden Diomedes—second only to Achilles in bravery and glory—got all the credit for the theft. From there, it became easy to work out the dynamic: Diomedes represented, like Achilles, the pinnacle of male greatness—fearlessness, pride, great strength, manly beauty, and a preoccupation with honor. Odysseus represented the new ethos: think things through carefully and believe that there is no shame in outwitting your opponent and using trickery as long as you get the job done.

I also played with Odysseus' legendary love for his wife and family in the development of his most famous trick to end the seemingly endless war.

As always, I am extremely grateful to be included in this project. I deeply admire the works of every one of the authors in this collection. I'm especially grateful to Kate Quinn, who herded us into completion, and for her wise counsel in the development of Odysseus' narrative. The brilliant Kate, as her fans already well know, is a miracle worker.

—Victoria Shecter

THE FALL

I write Roman novels. I mean, I vary here and there and explore new eras, but my heart and soul are anchored in the Roman world. So when we discussed, at the conclusion of *A Year of Ravens*, the possibility of tackling the Trojan War, it was a natural choice for me to grab the tale of Aeneas. After all, Aeneas is the bridge between Troy and Rome. In Homeric myth, he is a prince of Troy and a noble hero, if something of a peripheral character with little in the way of excitement. But Virgil, in seeking to build on the idea of this last hero of Troy being the progenitor of the Roman world, all to please his emperor, Augustus, created a new tale of this man: the *Aeneid*. And with minimal overlap, the *Aeneid* begins with two chapters on the war and the fall of Troy. Bingo. I had my main source.

It was only after leaping up and down, knocking over my Lego Imperial Shuttle in the process, and shouting, "Ooh, ooh . . . me, me, me . . . I want Aeneas. Please . . . AENEAS!" that I then realized I had kind of accidentally landed myself with the climactic and all-important fall of Troy. You know, the iconic "Greeks pouring out of the wooden horse" and all that. Moreover, being the last of the seven tales, I set myself the task of tying in any scenes or characters that might fit from other stories, in order to improve the connectivity and flow of the whole. Cassandra, Odysseus, and

Diomedes, the young boy with the horse toy, the priest—it's all dragged in on purpose.

Aeneas is, at least in my portrayal, a very different character to the others in the book, both Greek and Trojan. This is deliberate in most ways but probably also partially a symptom of having drawn his tale from the works of a different ancient writer to the others. They have their Homer. I have my Virgil. And having spoken in depth with my friend Gordon Doherty, who is currently researching the Hittite world, and then with Christian Cameron, Kate Quinn, and the other fab folks in this collaboration, it became important to me to portray Troy as something very different. It could not be the Greek-style world that is the natural product of Homer, for Troy was a subject of the Hittite empire, for all its semi-autonomy. It owed fealty to Hattusa and nothing at all to the powers in Achaea, so I sought to find a reason why the other Trojans would refer to Zeus and Athena and Hera, and so on, when that should not be natural in their world. The answer came simply: the Hittite world is now in thorough decline, and with their fading, Greek culture is on the rise in its influence. Thus I had Troy as an old Hittite-style city now succumbing to Greek trends, even while they fight those same trendsetters, and had Aeneas constantly lamenting the Greek-ifying of his world and clinging to ancient names.

This allowed me to make Aeneas old-fashioned, holier-than-thou, anachronistic, and saddened by the inevitable progress of his world into a Greek future. It also gave me a reason for Aeneas to accept that he has a future—a destiny to save the old world—and to try for it rather than simply go down fighting. The strange dichotomies produced by the worlds warring in his soul almost tear him apart and, I think, make him three dimensional rather than A.N.Other Trojan hero.

My basis for Troy is a composite of several reconstructions while my basis for the temple atop the citadel, which does not conform to Greek standards, is the Syro-Hittite temple of Ain Dara in Syria, which owes more to Egyptian culture than to Greek. My arms, armor, and clothing are torn from various references, but most notably the work of Peter Connolly.

As in the previous collaboration, in which I was involved with many of the same writers, I owe a great deal of the finished tale to my co-authors, whose constant bouncing about of ideas set off spark after spark in my imagination, and who solved more than one problem for me. Anyone who kept abreast of the production of this book on social media will probably be aware of the "problem of the damn ships." The nature, location, and fate—even the very existence of such a fleet—was hammered out over many weeks and finally only settled on after the first round of edits. The ship issue is the prime example of how the whole team could come together to solve a problem. A special nod here has to go to Christian Cameron, an early contributor to this book, since lost, for his impressive knowledge of ancient Greek naval detail. The idea of the ships actually being sunk beneath the waves, which initially dumbfounded me, came from him.

Aeneas, then, got to see the end of the tale. Amid seemingly endless death, destruction, and fire, it was important to try and end the collection on a positive note. And that is possible because, of all the survivors of the Trojan war, Aeneas is one of very few (can he be the only?) heroes or heroines who actually come out well in the end. I suppose Odysseus, too, and he deserves it because he is clearly cool as a freezer-box full of cucumbers. And that, of course, is why Odysseus and Aeneas have their closing scene. Aeneas, then, can take the very heart of Troy with his small group of companions, face terrible dangers and ordeals, but can end up on the shores of Italy with a destiny that will produce descendants who died in flames in the first H Team collaboration, and who died by the Celtic sword in the second. Nice to see these things come full circle, eh?

—SJA Turney

ABOUT THE AUTHORS

DAVID BLIXT is a bestselling author, blending history and fiction set everywhere from ancient Rome to Shakespeare's Verona to Nellie Bly's New York. Living in Chicago, David describes himself as "Author, actor, father, husband—in reverse order."

LIBBIE HAWKER, who also writes under the pen names Libbie Grant and Olivia Hawker, is a bestselling author of historical fiction and a finalist for several awards, including the WILLA, the Washington State Book Award, and the Audie for Outstanding Audiobook. She lives in Victoria, British Columbia.

GLYN ILIFFE is the author of nine books about Greek mythology. He studied English and Classics at Reading University, where he developed a passion for Greek mythology. He is married with two daughters and lives in Leicestershire, England.

KATE QUINN is the *New York Times* bestselling author of many historical novels, including *The Alice Network*, *The Rose Code*, and *The Diamond Eye*. A native of southern California, she attended Boston University, where she earned her degrees in classical voice. Kate and her husband now live in San Diego.

ABOUT THE AUTHORS

.ALVEAR is the author of multiple books about the ...rld. She writes as Vicky Alvear Shecter for children and ...a Alvear for adults. Her novels include *Cleopatra's Moon* ...*ses and Smoke: A Novel of Pompeii*. Her biographies include ...*tra Rules!* and *Warrior Queens*.

...EPHANIE THORNTON is a writer, librarian, and history ...acher who has been obsessed with women from history since she ...vas twelve. She is the author of eight novels and lives with her husband and daughter in Alaska, where she enjoys hiking, beekeeping, and being entertained by her three rescue cats.

SJA TURNEY is bestselling author of more than fifty Roman and medieval historical fiction, fantasy, and Roman nonfiction books. He lives with his family in rural North Yorkshire.

RUSS WHITFIELD is the author of the Gladiatrix trilogy, a historical fiction set in Ancient Rome. He lives in South West London, UK.